MW01031421

ANCESTRAL
HUNGERS

TOR BOOKS BY SCOTT BAKER

Ancestral Hungers
Dhampire
Drink the Fire from the Flames
Firedance
Night Child
Symbiote's Crown
Webs

ANCESTRAL HUNGERS

SCOTT BAKER

TOR

A TOM DOHERTY ASSOCIATES BOOK
NEW YORK

ANCESTRAL HUNGERS

Copyright © 1995 by Scott Baker

Material in this book was previously published in substantially different form under the title *Dhampire*.

Edited by David G. Hartwell

A Tor Book
Published by Tom Doherty Associates, Inc.
175 Fifth Avenue
New York, N.Y. 10010

Tor ® is a registered trademark of Tom Doherty Associates, Inc.

LIBRARY OF CONGRESS CATALOGING-IN-PUBLICATION DATA

Baker, Scott.
　　Ancestral hungers / Scott Baker.
　　　　p.　cm.
　　ISBN 0-312-85868-X
　　I. Title.
　　PS3552.A4345A53　1995　　　　　　　　　　　　94-44447
　　813'.54—dc20　　　　　　　　　　　　　　　　　CIP

First Tor edition: April 1995

Printed in the United States of America

0 9 8 7 6 5 4 3 2 1

This book is for my brother John, who endured bats and rattlesnakes to help me research it, and for Suzi, who encouraged me to keep on writing it while at the same time helping me see where it went wrong. I also received invaluable help from Norman Spinrad and Jacques Chambon.

He who would enter the Kingdom of God must first enter with his body into his mother and there die.

—PARACELSUS

ANCESTRAL HUNGERS

Chapter One

W e'd been hoping you could give us a hand with the inspection," the chief customs officer said. He was thick-necked, overmuscular, about thirty-five; he reminded me of a wrestling coach I'd particularly hated at St. George's Academy. His assistant—taller, older, visibly nervous—was standing behind him, as far as possible away from the unopened crates at the other end of the small cold room.

"Excellent," Alexandra said, giving him her Dragon Lady smile. Her features were beginning to take on that blue-gray blurriness, almost as though I were seeing them through a thin mist, that they sometimes had when I'd been too many days without sleep. "If we handle the snakes ourselves there's less chance of an accident. Many of the snakes are too delicate to survive rough handling."

"All the better, then. Do you have everything you need?"

"In this suitcase," I said.

"Good. Then let's get this over with as fast as we can." He picked up a list. "It says here you've got fifteen Colombian rattlesnakes, eleven fer-de-lances, two sea snakes, species unknown—" He glanced up. "Poisonous?"

"Very," Alexandra said. "They're related to cobras."

"Ah. Then an anaconda, seven eyelash vipers, one bushmaster, nine emerald tree boas—"

An unexpected piece of luck. "That should read four emerald tree boas," I said, and he made the correction.

"And three Colombian coral snakes."

Which meant that the time had come to complicate things. I frowned, said, "There should also be a crate with a half-dozen different kinds of small boas and some burrowing snakes in it."

"It didn't arrive with the rest of your shipment."

"You're sure?" Alexandra demanded. "You couldn't have misplaced it or something?"

"I doubt it. People don't lose crates stamped DANGER! POISONOUS SNAKES!! in bright red letters. It's probably been bumped to the next flight. Are the snakes dangerous?"

"No, not at all," Alexandra said, "but the burrowing snakes are very delicate. They can't take rough handling or cold, and if somebody rerouted them to L.A. or San Jose by mistake—David, can you take care of things here without me while I go check with the airline, put a tracer on it or something?"

Fuck. Not again. "I guess, if you're not gone too long. Do you have the ticket stubs?"

"I should. Be back in a few minutes."

I caught the chief inspector staring at her ass as she walked out the door. Which was only to be expected: Alexandra's idea of what the well-dressed lady snake handler wore consisted of cream-colored boots halfway up her thighs, skin-tight French jeans, an equally tight red top setting off her red-gold hair. Part of her Bread and Circuses theory of getting through customs.

"Your wife's got lovely hair," the inspector said as soon as she'd closed the door behind her.

"Very," I agreed. "Where do you want to start?"

"What's in that crate there?"

"Two sea snakes."

"How are they packed?"

"Separate cloth bags inside a larger insulated bag. If you give me a second, I'll open the crate for you."

"Please."

I opened the suitcase, took out my folding fence and set it up: a ring a little over three feet in diameter, two and a half feet high. I screwed the two parts of my snake stick together, took off my suit coat and put on my gray leather vest and long gloves.

"Will that fence hold them in?"

"No. But snakes aren't very smart and if anything goes wrong it should take the smaller ones long enough to escape for the two of you to get out of the room. Put the crate in the ring and give me a pry bar and I'll get started."

I took the boards off one side of the crate, lifted out the insulated bag.

"They're both there?"

"I think so. The bag's still sealed—" I ripped it open, carefully lifted out the two cloth bags, taking care to keep them away from my body. "They're both here."

"Good. Could you hand out the crate and insulated bag?"

He nodded to his assistant, who came up and took them from me, gingerly sorted through the Styrofoam peanuts in the crate.

The chief inspector picked up the insulated bag, examined it.

"What's this foil lining for?"

"That's the insulation. Like space blankets—you know the ones I mean? They sell them for camping. I had to perforate it to keep the snakes from suffocating."

"I've seen them. Can you open the cloth bags and hand them out to Jim? One at a time."

"Sure. Could you give me some of the spare sacks from my suitcase? It's safer if I rebag the snakes as soon as possible."

He examined the sacks, handed them in to me. I loosed the drawstrings on the first bag with the hook on the other end of my stick, waited until the sea snake poked its tiny rounded black and yellow head out, then snared it with a stick. It writhed feebly a bit, hardly protesting as I got it behind the head and dumped it in the other sack. I handed the empty sack to the assistant, who looked at it, shook his head.

"Can you turn up the temperature in here?" I asked. "It's too cold for the snakes."

"I'm sorry but the thermostat's preset. An economy measure."

"Then let's hurry. I don't like the way that sea snake looked."

"What's in that crate?"

"Rattlesnakes."

Only two of the snakes rattled when I lifted their cloth sacks from the insulated envelope and none of them tried to strike at me through the cloth. I had to push the first one with my stick to get it to leave the open bag; two of the others were dead, as was a coral snake in the next crate.

The emerald tree boas were all alive, as were the fer-de-lance, but they were all sluggish. Had any of the snakes been a little more active, I would have hesitated to take the bushmaster out without Alexandra to back me up if something went wrong—it was a magnificent specimen, almost thirteen feet long, with four-and-a-half-inch fangs—but as it was I had no trouble getting it behind the neck and immobilizing it before it could strike at me or damage its delicate neck with its struggles. Bushmasters are slender-bodied and even my thirteen-foot specimen was no heavier than a six-foot eastern diamondback rattlesnake, but I could feel it slowly coming alert as my body heat revived it. I was almost as relieved as the inspectors when I had it safely back in its sack.

Which left only the anaconda. And Alexandra still wasn't back. Which meant that either she'd locked herself in a toilet cubicle in one of the women's bathrooms or she was gone altogether.

"I'm going to need a lot of help with the anaconda," I said. "It's not poisonous but all anacondas are pretty evil-tempered, and this one's nineteen feet long and close to three hundred pounds. We'll need at least four more men to help hold it while you check out the crate."

Alexandra made her entrance while the chief inspector was telephoning. Her face was flushed and excited, even through the blurriness. "They claim they don't have any record of the shipment," she said. "So I called Richard and had him tell them that we were going to sue them for some enormous sum if they didn't produce the snakes alive and in good condition very soon. Are the rest of the snakes OK?"

"We haven't gotten to the anaconda yet," I said. "Two of

the rattlesnakes died, and so did one of the coral snakes, but I think the others are going to make it, at least if we can get them somewhere warm pretty soon."

The anaconda was stout and ugly, a muddy olive green with black splotches. About ten feet behind its relatively small head the goat it had eaten in Bogota had produced a huge bulge, half again as big around as the snake's body. I was holding the head, Alexandra had it by the neck, and the four new customs men were holding its body while the chief inspector and his assistant went through the packing material in the crate.

"Why's it all swollen?" the man holding it just behind the bulge asked.

"It ate a goat a while before we shipped it," Alexandra said. "Snakes can dislocate their jaws to swallow things much bigger around than they are. They have to, since they eat their prey alive and don't have any way to chew them up into smaller pieces. Their teeth aren't made for it."

"Thanks." He didn't seem particularly pleased with the information.

"That's one reason it's so sluggish," I said. "That and the cold. Otherwise it would be giving us a lot more trouble."

"I'm afraid we're going to have to X-ray the anaconda," the chief inspector said when he'd finished going through everything else. "I want to examine that bulge."

"It's a goat," I said. "We've got pictures of the snake eating it, if you want to look at them."

"No thanks. Just put it back in its sack and we'll take it into the next room—"

He stared at the X rays for a long time, finally admitted that the pictures showed the goat's skeleton, still partially intact, inside the anaconda.

"Can you give us some help loading the truck?" I asked. "It's pretty hard to find porters who'll handle crates full of poisonous snakes and some of these crates are pretty big for Alexandra and me to handle, even with our dolly."

"We're not supposed to," he said, "but after the cooperation you've shown us, I don't see why not."

The truck was a lemon-yellow Dodge van with the scarlet head of a cobra flanked by the words BIG SUR SNAKE FARM and SPECIALISTS IN VENOMOUS REPTILES painted on the sides. The little cobra in the glove compartment cage raised its head and spread its hood when I opened the side door.

"All the other cages in back are empty," I said. "Just put the anaconda's crate about halfway up front and the rest of the crates behind it."

Alexandra waited until we were on 101 South, then put on one of her Baroque cassettes—the kind of tinkly harpsichord music that all sounded the same to me though she could tell them apart with no trouble—and slipped on her long protective gloves so she could take the vial of coke out from under the rock in the baby cobra's cage. She held the spoon to my nostrils four times before snorting any herself. The blue-gray vagueness began to dissipate. Another eight spoonfuls and it was gone altogether.

She was smiling—white teeth, long smooth red-blond hair—but behind the smile her jaw was knotted and ugly with the tension that never left her, that ground her teeth together while she slept no matter how many sleeping pills she took, that turned on her and tried to destroy her as soon as she stopped moving, pushing, striking out.

But for the moment she was riding her tension without berating herself or striking out at me and I welcomed the respite, the chance to go inside my head with only the coke for company and play with my thoughts and hopes for a while.

Chapter Two

We made it back to the coast about two-thirty. The sky was black and gray and out over the Pacific you could see ball lightning but it hadn't started raining again. Alexandra got a stack of letters out of the mailbox while I unlocked the gate and drove the truck through.

"There's another letter from your father," she said after I locked the gate again. "Marked 'Reply Urgent.' What do you want me to do with it?"

"Save it till we get back to the cabin, then stick it in the fireplace and forget it. Like all the rest."

I put the truck in low and started up the road. It was little more than an oversized jeep trail and the spring rains had left it in bad condition: I'd had to have special shocks and springs put in to keep all the bouncing and vibration from panicking the snakes I carried.

"What about this?" Her voice was bright, artificial, and I was sorry I'd snapped at her. "Somebody calling themselves CET-VER Laboratories in New Mexico wants five hundred dollars' worth of rattlesnake venom as soon as possible."

"Good, but I don't think we have that much on hand. How long's it been since we last milked the pit vipers?"

"About three and a half months."

"That should be long enough."

"If John hasn't killed them all."

"He said they were all doing fine when we talked to him on the phone last week."

"When *you* talked to him on the phone. And that was last week. Anyway—David? Why don't I milk the rattlesnakes this time while you and John put away the new snakes? OK?"

"You sure? It's my turn, remember?" Alexandra was as

competent with snakes as I was, but she'd never learned to feel comfortable working with them. We both preferred to have me milk them whenever possible.

"Yes, but—a couple of things. First, I'd like to get the venom centrifuged tonight so we can send it off Federal Express tomorrow and you're going to be too busy with the other snakes to have the time."

"What's the second thing?"

"Something felt really wrong at the airport today. As soon as we get home I want you to get all the drugs and paraphernalia out of the house."

"You think we're going to get raided?"

"I'm sure of it. That customs man, the one in charge—it was like he was watching us through a one-way mirror. Studying us all the time, even at the end, when he should have been satisfied. And they wouldn't have helped us load the snakes if they hadn't wanted to check out the truck."

"If you thought there was something wrong, there was something wrong. You don't make that kind of mistake."

"No. Look, why don't you and John go swimming after you get the snakes in their cages? You look tired. I'll join you when I'm done."

Which meant she wanted to make up for having abandoned me at the airport without having to admit anything.

We'd made it up out of the clouds, a gray-black plain stretching away to the western horizon behind us, and onto the ridge: sloping sunlit meadows filled with fuzzy blue lupine and vivid orange California poppies. A few minutes later and we were making out way down through the thick oak and madrona forest on the inland side. The sky directly overhead was cloudless but the trees blocked out most of the sunlight and little brown mushrooms grew in damp clusters by the sides of the road.

John's Toyota was parked just outside our second gate. There was a painting in the backseat, hundreds of tiny black-and-white portraits against a violet, yellow and pink background that made the clustered faces look like the dark centers of pastel flowers. It was a lot better than most of the stuff John had done—and I'd always liked his work—though it had the same uncomfortable amphetamine precision to it. I recognized some of the portraits, Alexandra's and mine among them. Most of the portraits were pretty good—he'd gotten me down perfectly, as far as I could tell—but he'd put Alexandra in the center of the canvas and then completely missed the tension in her expression, turning her into just another of the unmemorably pretty blonde girls in their twenties and thirties who work in health-food stores or as cocktail waitresses all up and down the coast.

Or maybe not. I'd just noticed four more portraits of Alexandra, one in each corner, all of them stark, grim, and exquisitely rendered, when I heard John's voice.

He hugged us both, then unlocked the door and took out the painting. He propped it up against the windshield and steadied it with his right hand.

"Do you like it? I finished it four days ago."

"Very much," Alexandra said.

"Good, because it's for the two of you. A homecoming gift."

John had brought the dolly up from the cabin. We loaded it with the crate of buzzing rattlesnakes and the bushmaster, then started down the path to the herpetarium.

I'd set up my herpetarium in a natural limestone cavern I'd discovered in the cliff behind the cabin soon after I inherited the property from my aunt. The entrance was low and you had to hunch over to enter, but about a yard past the mouth the cave opened up. The ceiling was high and for most of its fifty-foot length the cave was at least thirty feet wide. At the far end it narrowed suddenly, then ended in a wall of purplish red rock. An eight-foot fissure split the red rock from floor to ceiling, but though my flashlight had given me tantalizing glimpses of further caverns the red wall was at least two feet thick and there was no way I could break through it at present, though I had vague thoughts of someday renting a jackhammer or miner's drill.

But for the moment I was well satisfied with what I had. The floor was almost perfectly level, and I had all the space I'd need for a long time to come. I'd installed fluorescent lights and tiers of heated snake cages along the walls, all running off the power generated by our water wheel, windmill and solar panels, while in the center of the chamber I'd placed some of the larger cages, the tank in which I'd originally housed my turtles but that I was planning to use for the sea snakes, and the apparatus for milking the poisonous snakes and preparing their venom for storage and shipment.

This was my domain. Alexandra was the one who was street smart, as good with her network of upwardly mobile urban professional customers in San Francisco and L.A. as she was with the less savory types we got the coke from in the first place. I was good with the snakes, provided her with the steadiness and stability she lacked. We complemented each other well.

The rattlesnakes were happy enough to be out of their bags and into their cages but the bushmaster coiled and struck at the glass whenever I came near. I finally covered its cage with a tarp to keep it from hurting its nose.

John went back to the truck for another crate while I checked the snakes he'd been caring for.

"They all look healthy," I told him when he returned with the sea snakes. "You didn't have any problems?"

"Not really. The green mamba refused to eat the first two months. I was afraid I was going to have to try to force-feed it but I finally got it to take a mouse."

"Excellent. And thanks. I can give you half an ounce now but we'll have to wait until the anaconda finishes digesting the goat to get the rest. You should have seen us trying to shove the goat down the snake's throat. And for that matter it was pretty grim getting the five kilos of coke into the dead goat."

"No problems getting through customs?"

"Nothing overt, but Alexandra thinks they're still suspicious. I'm moving everything off the property as soon as I get the sea snakes in their tank. Do you have anything on you they could bust you for?"

"Nothing I don't have a script for."

The sea snakes were as graceful underwater as they were clumsy on land. John watched them swimming back and forth investigating their tank for a while, then went back for more snakes while I hid the drugs in a hollow log just off the edge of the property. When I got back Alexandra was standing at the milking table holding a squirming five-foot western diamondback and massaging its poison glands to get more venom into the beaker on the table.

"You sure you chilled that snake long enough?" I asked, being careful not to startle her. "It looks pretty active."

"Probably not," she admitted, making a face, "but it's too late to do anything about it now. I'll chill the others a little longer. The thing is, I think we're going to run short. Is it all right if I milk some of the Mexican rattlers?"

"No, the venom's not quite the same. If you want, I can try to catch some new snakes as soon as I'm done unloading. With any luck there'll be a half dozen or so in the woodpile."

"Wait till tomorrow morning. I might be able to get just barely enough."

John and I saved the anaconda's crate for last. Alexandra took a break between snakes to help us get it onto the dolly and down to the herpetarium. It glided listlessly around its new cage for a while, then coiled up in a corner.

"Ugly," John said.

"Mean too. You want to go swimming? I rolled a joint with some freeze-dried spores while I was hiding the rest of the drugs."

"Sure. What with cleaning up my mess and working on the painting and getting your truck to the airport, I might as well still be living in Minneapolis. I haven't gotten any sun all week."

"They're saying sun gives you skin cancer now."

"No they're not. What they're saying is, sun now gives you skin cancer later. If I listened to stuff like that I'd probably have ended up as a plumber like my brother. And then they'd tell me that shit gives you skin cancer too."

Chapter Three

For a while after we smoked the psilocybin everything was gentle luminosity, a succession of drifting silences. Neither John nor I spoke. When the rocks got too hot for me I'd dive in, angling deep, and chase the small trout in the pool through a few zigs and zags before they darted away from me, then come up under the waterfall until my head was just beneath the surface and I was lost in the icy-white dazzle that was the waterfall exploding into foam where it hit the surface of the pool.

It was perfect: peace at last after the months of cocaine and tension. When I felt myself starting to come down I wandered out into the woods to look at the mushrooms and wildflowers and wash the scent of pine sap through my lungs.

John joined me after a while. With his beard and hair he looked like some small woodland animal—a chipmunk or woodchuck, maybe, or some sort of small bear that ate nothing but pine cones and berries. He had some of the same tension in him as Alexandra, but he never let it out, even though that meant living in the woods away from anything that could trigger it off. I'd only seen him lose control once, at Nepenthe, when he'd tried to punch out a drunken developer twice his size who'd sneaked a half-dozen up-market tract houses past the zoning commission, and John had been so ashamed of himself he'd stayed locked up in his cabin for ten days, until Alexandra coaxed him back out again.

"David, why do you like snakes so much?" he asked me after a while. Because he was a friend and he trusted me and I felt bad at the way I'd snapped at Alexandra I made an exception and tried to tell him.

"It's because—it's complicated. Look, one of my ancestors

was a man named Vlad Dracul. His son was the historical Dracula. 'Dracula' means 'Son of Dracul.' OK? Anyway, at home they always told me that 'Dracul' meant 'Devil' in Romanian—my family used to be Romanian—but when I went away to school I learned that it really meant 'Dragon.' Because King Sigismund made Vlad Dracul a member of the Order of the Dragon. And where my family came from people thought dragons were winged snakes and even normal snakes could protect you against evil and—I don't know. I can't explain it any better than that."

Talking about my past had given it the reality I always tried to deny it. I'd grown up in Illinois, in a dark silent house more like a medieval castle than a conventional home. I was told my mother had died when I was two; I'd never known her and my father never mentioned her. He was a cold, closed man, too busy managing his money to have any time for my brother Michael or myself: as soon as we were old enough we were sent away to St. George's Academy (named after the Russian, not the English, St. George).

From the academy Michael had gone first to Yale and then on to Harvard Business School; I, two years later, to Stanford for a year, then Berkeley for a semester, after which I drifted around for a number of years—San Francisco, Boston, Ibiza, and Mexico, where I met Alexandra—before my aunt Judith, the only member of my family I'd ever loved, committed suicide and left me her property in Big Sur.

"Was Dracula really a vampire?" John asked, which was so stupid it ruined what little chance I might have had of getting my head back where I wanted it.

"No. He got a reputation as a bloodthirsty monster because he killed something like a hundred thousand people, mainly by impaling them. Which means killing them by sticking sharpened stakes through them. That's all."

"You don't have to treat me like an idiot, David."

"It was an idiotic question. Forget it." I was tired, too tired; I couldn't feel the psilocybin anymore and there was a dry scraping behind my eyes. My jaw ached. I didn't want to think about the kind of world that could produce people like my ancestors and turn them into folk heroes. I needed Alexandra.

I remembered our first day together here in the woods, grabbing a projecting rock and pulling myself up out of the water, my whole body tingling, feeling newly awakened, newly alive as the warm dry breeze and late-spring sun began to steal the water from my back and shoulders.

Alexandra was lying on her back, her legs spread slightly, tanned body glistening with sweat and coconut oil. Her eyes were closed and she was smiling, almost totally relaxed for the first time since we'd met. She looked very young and innocent, almost gentle, and that was the first time I'd ever seen her look that way.

I stood over her and let the cold water drip from my outstretched hands onto her body. She started and opened her eyes, staring wildly up at me before she recognized me, her eyes wide and deep and intensely black. Then the last tension went out of her and she smiled at me, a relieved, inviting smile.

She spread her legs and I knelt between them on the smooth white stone. I ran my hands up the insides of her oil-covered thighs and over her slippery stomach to her breasts, then down again between her legs. She took my still-cold, still-soft cock in her hands and held it between them, rubbing gently until her warmth passed into it and it grew hard. I rested my elbows on the rocks and she guided me into her.

Later we'd swum for a while, holding each other beneath the waterfall until our lungs were bursting, then returned to the rocks and sun to make love again.

"John? I'm sorry I snapped at you. I think I need to be alone with Alexandra for a while. I haven't slept for a couple of days and it's getting to me. Do you mind just heading back to your car without stopping by to say good-bye to her? You can come by again tomorrow afternoon, maybe around five."

"Sure. No problem. You look like you could use some sleep."

We walked back to the cabin together without saying anything. I shook his hand, thanked him again, then made my way back to the herpetarium.

I bent low to enter the cave, straightened:

Saw Alexandra lying dead or unconscious on the floor, her right arm swollen huge and purple. And on her chest, coiled, its head raised and swaying like a cobra's as it tasted the air with its tongue and vibrated its rough-scaled tail in warning against the bright fabric of her top, the bushmaster.

I grabbed a long snake stick and tried to get it away from her, but it avoided my clumsy attempts with a contemptuous intelligence I had never before seen in a snake, struck at me whenever I got too close. It was guarding Alexandra's body like a jackal with its prey and that was impossible, something no snake would ever do.

And I couldn't get to her, couldn't even get close enough to her to find out if she was still alive. If she was, there was a chance to save her by cutting open the wound and draining the poison while giving her a shot of antivenin, but with every instant the chances grew slimmer.

If she was still alive, if there was any chance at all. And I couldn't get past the bushmaster.

At last I gave up and retreated, hoping somehow that it would attempt to escape like a normal snake. It stayed where it was, head raised, watching me, its tongue flickering in and out of its mouth. Guarding her body.

I couldn't tell if she was still breathing. Her arm had swollen to twice its normal size; she hadn't moved since I'd first seen her. I hung back, watching for any sign of life, trying to think of a way to get the snake away from her.

The fluorescent lights flickered. Alexandra's skin was steaming, misting: she was evaporating, dissolving into a blue-gray fog that thickened and spread, hid her from me. I could see shapes forming in the fog, things moving with horrible liquidity, like rotting flesh melting from disintegrating bone, maggots swarming in the empty eye sockets of dying birds . . .

The cloud was a door opening into red-lit shadow where obscenely mutilated figures danced and capered and coupled around a gigantic man-goat who stood fondling an erect cock like a great legless centipede. I cold smell the faraway sweetness of rotting flesh. The chill shadows reached for me, wrapped themselves around me as the black flames in the man-goat's eyes drew me to him through the thickening dark—

The bushmaster: I could hear its rough scales, impossibly loud, rasping the limestone floor as it glided toward me through the shadows. I wrenched myself free of the goat-man's eyes, turned and stumbled out of the cave.

Just outside two men in gray suits grabbed me

"Federal narcotics agents," the one holding my right arm told me. "You're under arrest. We have a warrant to search your house and grounds, and it's our duty to tell you that you have the right to remain silent and that anything you say may be held against you."

I began to laugh, couldn't make myself stop.

"What's in the cave?" the other agent asked.

"A snake. It just bit my wife and she's dead and it's coiled on top of her guarding her and I can't get her away from it because, because—"

"Because what?"

I started to cough, choked. "She's in there."

The agent holding my right arm nodded and the other one stooped down, started into the cave.

"Watch it, Mark," the one still holding me yelled after him. "There might really be a poisonous snake in there."

Mark came out a few minutes later. "He was telling the truth. There's a dead woman on the floor in back."

"Any sign of the snake?"

"Yeah. It got away through a crack in the wall. It was a fucking monster, sort of pink and black."

"Alexandra's really dead?" I asked him. The agent holding me let go of my arm.

"Yes. I'm sorry. Do you want to take a look at her? The snake's gone."

I nodded and they escorted me back into the cave. But when I looked down at her body, her frozen contorted face and dry staring eyes, I felt nothing.

Nothing at all.

Chapter Four

The agent who'd found Alexandra's body phoned Salinas to report her death, then sat across the kitchen table from me while his partner and the six other agents who'd accompanied them searched the cabin and herpetarium.

There was a leather-bound manuscript, one of the grimoires from my aunt's collection, lying open on the table. Alexandra must have been glancing at it while she waited for John and me to get out of her way so she could start work with the snakes. She'd been after me to sell the collection for a long time.

The agent picked it up and I recognized it—*The Grimoire of Honorius the Great,* considered for centuries the most diabolical of all sorcerers' manuals because it contained a forged papal bull demanding that all Catholic priests add the summoning and control of demons to their sacerdotal functions. I'd read all of Aunt Judith's grimoires after she died, not so much because they interested me in themselves but because they were so important to her and I wanted to understand what had happened, if they could have anything to do with why she'd killed herself. But not being a Catholic priest myself, I hadn't found the book very diabolical or, for that matter, even very interesting.

"Is this in Latin?" the agent asked.

"Yes."

"What is it?"

"A grimoire. Means 'grammar.' Supposedly written by Pope Honorius III."

"Oh. I see." He looked at the other books and manuscripts in the glass-fronted case against the far wall. "You collect books?"

"My aunt did. I inherited them from her."

"I see." He carefully closed the book, put it back on the table. "I'm sorry about your wife."

"It's not your fault." Around us the other members of his team were sifting through bags of flour and cutting open pieces of soap, checking for things taped to the backs of drawers and making sure nothing was hidden in the toilet's float tank. All they found were our prescription drugs, in plain sight on the kitchen counter, and those they left where they found them—proof, I suppose, that they were going out of their way to be no harder on me than minimal performance of their duties required, since the normal procedure would have been to confiscate everything for laboratory analysis.

I watched them without interest, and if through some fluke they'd chanced across the drugs in the hollow log I don't think I'd have been greatly disturbed. I felt nothing, no grief for Alexandra, no curiosity about the blue-gray cloud and the things I'd seen in it, only a thirst that glass after glass of water did nothing to satisfy, that scraped the backs of my eyeballs raw and made my skin itch intolerably.

The agent in charge saw me scratching myself and came to the conclusion that I was going through withdrawal. He checked my arms for tracks, then made me strip naked so he could check the insides of my thighs. Finding nothing, he let me put my clothes back on.

When the coroner's deputy arrived with the men from the mortuary, the agent sitting with me was glad to surrender me to him.

The deputy was delighted with Alexandra. I watched him prodding and pinching her swollen and discolored arm, probing the two large puncture wounds with his fingers.

"You said she was milking your rattlesnakes for their poison when you left to go swimming with your friend?" He couldn't keep his eyes off her.

"Yes."

"And you don't think that was a strange thing to do?"

"No. We always worked like that."

"Ah. But she was killed by that South American snake, that bushmaster. The one that got away. Was she trying to milk it too?"

"No. The venom's too different."

"But the snake couldn't have escaped from its cage and attacked her on its own?"

"No."

"Then either she took it from its cage herself despite the fact there was no reason for her to do so, or somebody else let it out and then closed the cage afterward? Is that right?"

"I guess."

"And you can't think of anything she might have wanted to do with the snake or anyone else who might have opened its cage or any way in which the snake might have escaped on its own?"

"No. I'm sorry."

He questioned me for perhaps another hour, then surrendered me back into the custody of the narcotics agents, who in turn booked me into the Salinas jail on suspicion of possession of narcotics with intention to sell while they waited to search the field and woods.

I filled out the forms I was given (David Bathory, twenty-nine years old, five feet eleven, hair and mustache brown, eyes green, no distinguishing marks or scars, no previous record) and let them fingerprint and photograph me, then fell asleep in the booking cell.

When they awakened me the next morning they told me I was free to go. It didn't seem very important. I hitched a ride to a friend's house in Monterey and he drove me the rest of the way.

There was a note on the door from John, telling me to call him as soon as I got back. I called him.

"How are you doing, David?"

"OK, I guess."

"You don't need any help?"

"I don't think so, but thanks."

"You don't even care, do you? She's dead and you don't even care."

I was suddenly angry. "What are you trying to tell me? That she'd still be alive if I'd cared about her a little bit more? That if she'd been with you instead of me she wouldn't be dead?"

He hung up on me. Over the last few years I'd watched him falling more and more hopelessly in love with Alexandra. But he had a strong sense of honor where his friends were concerned: he'd said nothing to either of us, done his best to keep his feelings concealed. I owed it to him to call back and apologize.

"Just promise me you'll tell me when her funeral is, David? Just promise."

I promised and three days later stood next to him holding him by the arm as they lowered the coffin into the ground and began shoveling dirt on top of it. He was smiling to himself, so loaded on a combination of psychedelics and primate tranquilizers he could barely stand.

"That's not really her," he whispered. "She's not really dead. She'll come back and when she comes back she'll be in love with me. I know she will, David. I know she will."

I dropped him back at his cabin after the funeral. The ceremony had been for him, not for Alexandra or myself. Anything I might have owed him had been paid and I had no desire to ever see him again.

The next day I put the grimoires in storage and put my cabin up for sale. Some of the snakes, the local specimens, I freed; the others I arranged to sell to zoos and private collectors. Finally I called an old friend in Provincetown, on the tip of Cape Cod, and arranged to sell him the coke.

A week later the anaconda finished digesting the goat and excreted the surgical fingers of coke with which I'd stuffed the body, leaving me free to sell the snake. The new Orange County Zoo had ambitions of surpassing the San Diego Zoo's snake house and I was able to unload the anaconda, the sea snakes and a number of other specimens to them at good prices.

From Orange County I left for the East Coast. The cages in the van were filled with snakes for zoos in Boston and Chicago; I'd put the mattress that Alexandra and I'd used when we went snake collecting in the Sonoran desert in the back. Most of the coke was in two false-bottomed cages of South American rattlesnakes but I had a vial with a little over three ounces for the trip hidden inside the glove-compartment cobra cage.

I was in no hurry to get anywhere. Selling off what remained of my former life at a profit seemed like the logical thing to do, but I was just going through the motions: Alexandra had always been the businesswoman, the hustler, the one who set so much store on her status with her upscale clients and lowlife suppliers. I had no plans for the future and no desire to make any, only a vague curiosity about some of the more inhuman geologic formations of the Southwest. Something about them—the bare dry rocks, the hot wind, the empty landscapes—felt as though it would be right for me.

Chapter Five

I was sitting eating at a table in front of a taco stand just off the freeway when I saw a slim, dark-skinned girl with shiny black hair streaming out behind her in the hot desert wind walk up to the freeway on-ramp.

She was wearing dusty but new-looking black jeans and a spotless scoop-necked black T-shirt, carrying a shiny green nylon backpack by one shoulder strap. She leaned the pack up against the freeway entrance sign and stood in front of it with her thumb out. I'd passed dozens of hitchhikers since leaving Big Sur, but something about this girl broke through my deadness, made me notice her. I left the remains of my meal on the table and walked over to her.

Her face was strong but finely drawn, without trace of bluntness or heaviness, and her eyes were large and strange. They were golden—not yellow like a cat's, but a true metallic gold, soft and shining, with strange shimmering depths, alive with an intelligence that made them seem for all their unexpectedness neither freakish nor bizarre.

"Would you like a ride?" I asked. "I'm going east."

"How far are you going?" Her voice was fluid and unhurried, with something odd about the way she pronounced her words.

"The Grand Canyon first, for a few days, then on to Carlsbad Caverns and a few other places like that, finally to Massachusetts by way of Chicago."

"Good. Is it all right if I ride with you all the way?"

"Yes, but—do you see that van over there? The yellow Dodge with the cobra painted on the side. I'm carrying a load of poisonous snakes. It's perfectly safe, they're all in cages, but a lot of people wouldn't want to ride with them."

"I'm not afraid of snakes."

"Are you sure?"

"Yes." She lifted her left arm so I could see a spiral of dull gold in the shape of a nine-headed cobra, an Indian Naga, twisting halfway up her forearm. The Naga's eyes glittered red with what looked like rubies; her skin was smooth, deeply brown, yet almost translucent.

"Is it real?"

"Yes."

"And you feel safe, hitching with something like that?"

"Very safe."

"You're Indian? East Indian?" I picked up her backpack and we began walking back to the truck.

"My mother came from there."

"So did mine, or at least her family did. She died when I was two."

"I'm sorry."

I shrugged. "I was too young. I don't remember anything about her."

I unlocked the passenger's side door and let her in, then went around to put her pack away. When I climbed in on my side I saw she had her face pressed to the glass of the baby cobra's cage. The cobra was just on the other side of the glass, its head raised and its hood spread, absolutely still, seemingly as fascinated by her as she was by it.

She straightened, looked away; the cobra retreated to the flat rock in the rear of its cage. "He's very beautiful, your little cobra."

"Very beautiful," I agreed, somehow uncomfortable. "I'm David."

"I'm Dara."

I started the truck, let it warm up an instant before pulling out onto the on-ramp. "Do you drive, Dara?"

"No. I'm sorry."

"It's not important. I don't mind driving."

"Thank you."

"Is Dara an Indian name?"

"No. My father was American."

We fell silent. Dara was watching the road, seemingly perfectly at ease except for the way she was playing with a strand of her long thick black hair, unconsciously twisting it, rubbing it back and forth between the thumb and forefinger of her left hand. I was intensely aware of her, excited by her in some way that only began with my consciousness of her beauty, her sexual attractiveness, and yet the excitement took me, not exactly away from her, but somehow back into myself. Into the past that had only hours before been so dead and distant.

And yet nothing was the way it had been before. The nine years I'd spent with Alexandra—the years of coke dealing and lovemaking, everything seemed false, empty. A desperate search for something we'd had at the beginning and then lost, yet looking back I could find no beginning, no time when we'd ever truly shared what we'd spent the rest of our time together trying to recapture. The beach in Acapulco where we'd met, the two perfect months together in Yucatan—I remembered the sun and the landscape, the drugs and the sex, but beyond that, behind it, nothing. No one. Only the need to believe in something that had never happened.

And before Alexandra, only my family. The Bathorys. Not so much my aunt and uncles, my father and brother, but our history, our inheritance, the tradition that had shaped and marked them as it had shaped and marked me.

One of my ancestors had been a seven-year-old girl when her denunciation of her mother resulted in the woman being hanged in the Salem witch trials. An earlier ancestor, David Mathewson, had been a Scottish "witch finder" who confessed on the gallows to having fraudulently accused and caused the deaths of some two hundred and twenty women. He'd been paid twenty shillings for each woman he accused. And there'd been crusading priests and ministers, sin and heretic hunters aplenty in our family tree.

But the family's previous history was far grimmer, despite the comic-opera names of many of its Central European protagonists. Some of them—Mihnea the Bad, Peter the Lame,

Radu Mihnea, Vlad the Monk and others—though well enough known in their day, were now almost forgotten, but at least two of my ancestors were still famous: Vlad Tepes—Vlad the Impaler, the historical Dracula—and the Countess Elizabeth Báthory, whose fame came from her practice of luring young peasant girls to her castle on pretext of employment, then torturing and killing them and bathing in their blood, in the belief that it would preserve her youth and legendary beauty. To which end she sacrificed an estimated twenty-five hundred girls before she was arrested and imprisoned.

And they were real to me now, all of them, in a way I had denied for as long as I could remember. Real not in any stupid storybook way but in the fact that their cold crazy cruelty had shaped me as it had shaped the rest of the family, had been one of the elements making me who I was, limiting who I could become, determining who I would never allow myself to be.

It was getting dark. I felt lighter, somehow. Not free, but relieved of some of the strain that my lifelong refusal to recognize myself as who I was, as a Bathory, had put on me.

But relieved or not, I was tired and I wanted to make it a lot farther that night. Which meant cocaine.

I pulled off the road, turned off the motor. I hadn't spoken to Dara since I'd begun driving, respecting her silence, though I'd never lost my awareness of her presence. Now, putting on the long glove and reaching across her to get the coke out of its hiding place inside the cobra's cage, I felt awkward, even apologetic, as I asked her if she'd like some. Yet it never occurred to me that I might be risking anything by letting her know that I had a stash of cocaine in the truck.

"No, thank you. I don't like drugs."

I hesitated, almost returning the coke to its hiding place, then went ahead and snorted six quick spoonfuls.

But back on the highway and driving again I began to feel ashamed of myself, lost, as though the silence that Dara and I had shared before I snorted the coke had been in reality a strange and perfect communion, an intimacy without reservation, that I had violated. I started talking, going faster and faster as I tried to tell her everything, all about Alexandra and coke dealing and my family, but she reached over and brushed my cheek with her fingertips and when I looked at her, saw her eyes golden and shining in her dark serious face, all my shame and desperation were suddenly gone.

When at last we'd driven far enough for the night I pulled into a deserted rest stop and parked.

"I've got a tent and an extra sleeping bag," I said. "Or you can share my bed with me if you like."

"I'd like to share your bed."

We undressed in the darkness of the truck, slept naked but untouching, keeping to the outside edges of the bed. There was no sexual tension to resolve, no need to establish ground rules or make promises: the silence we shared was more precious than any backseat coupling could have been and I would have done nothing to endanger it. Yet when I awoke for a moment in the middle of the night I found we were in each other's arms.

Chapter Six

The sunlight slanting in through the panes of the stained-glass window in the right rear door of the truck—the one window Alexandra had completed during her brief fascination with stained glass—lit Dara's face and shoulders with rich mustards and rust oranges. When she opened her eyes they shone like tiny suns.

I'd awakened huddled in the far corner of the bed, my back pressed against the empty snake cage in which I kept my clothes, as though I'd been trying to escape from Dara in my sleep. Yet as we lay there, I in the shadow and she in the light, I remembered awakening to find her in my arms. I wanted to reach out for her and take her in my arms again, but something restrained me, held me back, as though I had awakened from my dreams to find myself in the midst of a dance as measured and stately as the unfolding of a flower or the slow drifting of clouds across the moon, a dance that could not be hurried in its inexorable progression toward completion.

"Good morning," I said, feeling awkward and not knowing what else to say.

"Good morning," she said, and within her voice, behind her grave smile, I felt again the silence, the intimacy, the communion.

"I'd like to start driving again in about fifteen minutes," I said, relaxing. The banality of what I had to say didn't seem to matter. "I've got enough food in the cooler to last us till lunchtime and we can shower and wash your clothes if they need it when we get to the Grand Canyon. OK?"

She nodded. I put on a pair of jeans and a heavy sweater—the morning was still cold—then slipped into my sandals and pushed past the curtain into the front of the van.

The sun was just breaking free of the horizon. The only other car in the rest area was another van parked at least a hundred yards away. I got out the coke and snorted my breakfast ration.

"David." Dara's voice surprised me. She pushed back the curtain and joined me. She was wearing the same jeans she'd worn the day before, though they no longer looked dusty, and a tight long-sleeved black top that clung to her, emphasizing her breasts, her narrow waist. Her hair fell black and silky down her back.

"What, Dara?"

"If you hadn't taken your cocaine you would have known I was there before I said anything. Like you knew I was going to open my eyes before I opened them this morning."

It was true: I *had* known.

"And I knew you were watching me. But you've cut yourself off from me now."

"With the cocaine."

"Yes." Her eyes were luminous and strange, beautiful.

"And you don't want me to cut myself off from you? It's important to you?"

"Yes."

"Why?"

"Because of who you are, who we are together."

"I don't understand."

She started to say something, decided against it. "I can't explain, David. Not yet."

I shook my head, said, "Please tell me what you're trying to say. What you really mean."

"No. I can't. I'm sorry, David."

"And you just want me to take this—whatever it is—on faith?"

"Until the cocaine wears off again, yes."

"And then you'll tell me?"

"When I can tell you, I will. I promise."

It would have been easy enough to explain away the little she'd said, implied: she was trying to manipulate me or she was another chemical casualty—maybe that even explained her eyes—or a follower of the new messiah in Fresno, perhaps just a young girl driven touchingly schizophrenic by the pressures of parents and society. I could have explained it away, but only by denying what I'd felt behind her words, somehow *recognized*, the way being with her had broken through the deadness since Alexandra's death. I didn't try.

I started the truck, concentrated as best I could on my driving. There were no other cars on the highway. Every few minutes I glanced over at Dara, trying to read her expression, figure out what she wanted from me. In the distance I could see mountains like rain-smoothed heaps of gray slag, on either side rippling scrubland where only scattered bushes grew. Dara was as alien and inaccessible as the statue of some twelve-armed Hindu goddess, with only the nervous way she was playing with her hair to recall her humanity.

The countryside had begun to take on a stark beauty, gray-green scrub giving way to occasional trees and green bushes, while the ground itself was breaking into delicate beiges and red-oranges. I was beginning to come down from the cocaine. As the excitement, the sense of unnaturally extended alertness, faded to a dull headachiness, I found myself becoming more aware of the things I wasn't looking at or paying attention to. Concentrating on the road or looking at Dara, I found the granulated surfaces of the dead mountains and foothills, the sound of the wind whistling in through my half-opened window, the smell of the sun-heated dust the wind brought with it all coming together, becoming part of what I felt and knew. When a trucker honked at me to let me know he wanted to pass, the sound was as much a part of the landscape as the trees and hills, no more intrusive than they were.

And Dara. We sat without speaking, without needing to speak. Without having to watch her I was becoming aware of her slightest movement, beginning to anticipate even the most imperceptible gesture or change in her expression. And with this anticipation came the excitement, the sense of your life opening onto a new and unexpected future, that sometimes accompanies the discovery of another person, yet at the same time it was as though I were remembering things I'd known my whole life, as though I were an old man reunited after a long separation with his wife of seventy years, an old man who finds her every action reawakening long-forgotten familiarity. Yet I did not feel old. I felt young, full of energy, excited.

I was driving deeper and deeper into a dream, into a new reality that obeyed its own strange imperatives and owed nothing to the world that had ended for me with Alexandra's death. A reality in which everything that Dara and I shared—a flock of birds wheeling by overhead, two cacti by the side of the road, the horizon huge around us and a car passing us on a blind curve—had a resonance and a meaning it had never had before. A reality in which I was beginning to feel the hope and fear behind Dara's silence, share in them without understanding them or needing to understand the reasons behind them.

I remembered the way Dara and the baby cobra had stared at each other, sharing something I'd been unable to perceive. The way the bushmaster had stood guard over Alexandra's body until it was too late to save her. I wanted to ask Dara about the blue cloud, the satanic man-goat and his dancing worshippers.

Instead I said, "You were waiting for me there, by that freeway entrance."

There was no need for her to say anything: the answer was there in her silence, in her eyes. I didn't understand the necessity or the fear driving her, but I recognized them, knew them, shared them.

And I trusted her. There was no way I could have not trusted her.

We made it to Grand Canyon village by eleven. We did our wash, showered and ate, then arranged for hiking permits and campground space, finally repacked our packs for tomorrow's hike.

The rest of the day we spent studying the canyon.

It was not just a piece of landscape, a pretty view, a monument to blind erosion. It had spoken to me in Big Sur, drawn me to it despite my paralysis. And now, looking out on its immensity, down on its malachite green domes, purple temples, colored spires, to the dirty ribbon of rushing water a mile below that was the Colorado River, I knew that the canyon was alive, an entity, a potent force, and I respected it.

Something was going to happen to us in the canyon, the reason Dara had been waiting for me by the side of the road. I could feel her longing, her terrified anticipation.

Dara's hand was dry in mine as we watched the sun setting over the canyon. We were lost in the canyon and each other, paying no attention to the gawking tourists around us, but just before the sun vanished completely and the tourists began to drift away I heard a woman exclaim:

"Ron! Look at her eyes!"

"Don't stare, Mary. Probably just contact lenses."

We stayed staring out over the canyon long after the last trace of the sunset was gone. There was a half moon and in its light the canyon was shadowed and strange, blue and mysterious. Yet its nighttime visage was less terrifying, less threatening, than its daytime grandeur, and for all Dara's fears I felt that it was not only alive and powerful beyond imagining but something I could trust.

We returned late to the campground, undressed in silence in the darkness of the truck. We reached out for each other, tentatively explored each other's body, yet even as we touched we knew that the time had not yet come for fuller union. The desire was there but we sidestepped it; yet as I stroked her hair and held her breasts cupped in my hands, as she pressed against me and I kissed her gently on the lips, I knew the time would come when our lovemaking would be complete, and I knew that that time was coming soon.

Chapter Seven

I awakened knowing that somehow in my sleep I had grown gigantic, so gigantic that I contained worlds, whole stellar systems, yet I contained nothing, it was I who was contained, supported, cherished. Dara sleeping in my arms contained me as I contained her, both of us grown immeasurably vast there in the back of the truck, between the clean sheets.

I must have dozed off again because the next thing I remember was Dara shaking me awake.

"Get up, David. It's late."

We dressed and ate some fruit from the cooler, then drove to the rim. I locked the truck. We shouldered our packs and started down the trail, Dara leading. She was wearing another pair of jeans and one of my T-shirts, plus a pair of tennis shoes we'd picked up for her in a supermarket the day before; I was shirtless.

There were only a few clouds in the sky, and as we worked our way down the morning temperatures climbed rapidly through the nineties. But it felt good to sweat, good to be walking down the trail with a pack on my back, good to be with Dara. The only problem was avoiding the puddles of mule piss and piles of mule dung, but even with my sandals it was not a problem to be taken seriously. Occasionally we had to flatten ourselves against the wall to let a mule train pass.

We walked slowly, letting the other hikers pass on. There was an unhurried, dreamlike quality to our descent that the weight of my pack, the tourists and mules somehow only intensified.

It was well past noon and immensely hot—I heard one of the people passing us say the temperature had already hit a hundred and thirteen—when the day began to cloud over. We'd worked our way down through the layers of yellow limestone and pale pinkish sandstone into the brick-red hermit shale and below that to the slightly paler red of the Supai formation. Thick clouds were sweeping out of the northwest to cover the sky and the hot canyon air was growing thick and muggy.

And suddenly I was an ant dangling precariously over the abyss: I could feel the trail shifting beneath me, the rock splintering and cracking, crumbling away from beneath my feet, and I knew that I was going to fall, that nothing could save me from the abyss. Dara was somewhere immeasurably distant; I could see her only a few feet away but I knew I was alone, unsupported, beginning to fall—

But Dara turned, reached back and brushed my forehead with her fingertips, and the trail was solid beneath my feet again. We continued on, switchbacking deeper and deeper into the canyon.

It was almost dusk by the time we reached Indian Gardens, which we'd planned as our halfway point. It didn't seem to matter that we'd never reach the river or Bright Angel Campground by nightfall, but there was no question of staying at Indian Gardens. People were everywhere; mules were tied to all the hitching posts and brightly colored sleeping bags littered the ground; there were long lines for the drinking fountain. What we had come for was elsewhere.

We were a long way past Indian Gardens and it was getting dark before it started to rain. Though the air had begun to cool it must still have been in the eighties and the first raindrops felt good on our sweat-soaked bodies. But as the temperature dropped and the rain increased to a cold torrent we began to shiver. We were soaked though, and since the weather report had been for three days of clear skies I hadn't thought to bring any rain gear—we had no tent, no jackets, not even a ground sheet to put under our sleeping bags, nothing with which to warm or protect ourselves.

We continued on in the twilight and then in the darkness,

using my flashlight. The storm showed no sign of letting up, was if anything getting worse; water ran in little rivulets across and down the trail. We hugged the wall, afraid of losing our balance on the slippery rocks.

Lightning flashed two, three times. By its light I could make out what looked like a small cave some ways off to the left.

It might provide us with shelter for the night. I took the flashlight from Dara and scrambled off across the loose, slippery rocks and up to the entrance.

At first I thought it was too shallow to use, but when I shone the light into it I detected an oval hole big enough to crawl through in the back. I knelt down and aimed the light through the hole.

Inside it was unexpectedly beautiful. Delicate crystalline formations grew from walls, ceiling, and floor, like an intricate three-dimensional lattice of glass lace. The formations were totally unlike anything in the guidebooks: instead of the crushed and flattened roots of long-buried mountains I'd found fairyland. The floor near the entrance was not only level and free of crystals but dry. We could sleep there.

"It's not only perfect, it's beautiful," I told Dara when I returned for our packs.

She lit my way back to the cave with the flashlight but stopped just inside the outer entrance, refused to go any further.

"No," she said. "It isn't safe."

"Why?" For some reason the fear I could hear in her voice, see on her face, was suddenly irritating, contemptible. "Do you want to stay outside and get wetter?"

"No, but—David, we *can't* go in until we're sure. They're stronger in caves."

"Who are?" She wouldn't answer me. "There's no reason not to sleep in there, nothing to be afraid of."

"Nothing? David, can't you *feel* it?"

There was only the noise of the storm, the tattoo of the rain on the rocks outside, the cold wet wind cutting into my back and neck. And yet—

I reached in through the opening, felt something like a greasy membrane resist my hand. Before I could pull it back the membrane gave way, stretched without breaking to clasp my hand like a tight glove of flabby lung tissue.

And suddenly I was afraid. Afraid of the dark, afraid of the closed confines of the cave, of the millions of tons of rock overhead. Afraid of the unknown. Afraid even of Grand Canyon rattlesnakes, the pale pinkish rattlers found nowhere else in the world. This cave would be perfect for them.

And then Alexandra lay newly dead on the floor of the cave, hundreds of flesh-pink rattlesnakes squirming over her body like maggots or the boneless fingers of dead children.

I yanked my hand back. The membrane clung to it for an instant, reluctant to release me, and then I was free and Alexandra was gone.

The cave was empty. All my fears seemed absurd. I had far deadlier snakes in my truck. But the membrane, that had been real, that was something to fear—and Alexandra had been killed in a cave.

"There's something stretched across the hole," I told Dara. "Like a flabby membrane. When I touched it it made me afraid, and I saw my wife lying dead—"

But she was smiling, shaking her head. "No, it's all right. I hadn't dared hope they'd still be so weak. I was afraid—" She caught herself, said "Here!" as she stepped forward and reached past me to thrust the arm with the Naga coiled around it into the hole. There was a brief flash of light, like a spider web burning, then nothing.

"Let me go first, just in case." She climbed in through the hole, sweeping the air in front of her with her Naga-wrapped arm. After a few seconds she smiled and gestured me in after her.

I put the flashlight down on a rock and handed the packs in to her, then picked it up again and followed them in. It was warm inside the cave, much warmer than outside.

"Dara—"

"I still can't answer your questions, David. Not yet."

"When, then?"

"Soon. I promise. Very soon."

We spread the sleeping bags out, undressed and crawled in between them. And then, without warning, the sense that the time was not yet right that had kept us apart for so long was gone and I was reaching for her, pulling her to me, and she was holding tight to me, kissing me. And as I touched, tasted her, felt her hesitant fingers exploring my stiffening cock, I was diving into a sea of light, into the center of some unknown sun, yet at the same time I was being caught up in a gossamer web, encased in sheath after sheath of darkness.

"Please, David. Make love to me." With Alexandra lovemaking had been all prowess and technique, all pride and control; with Dara I regained a simplicity I'd never known I'd lost.

Her flesh against mine, the taste of her mouth, her skin, the curve of her thigh beneath my hand, all were new to me, new and exciting in a way that Alexandra's expertise had never been.

When I entered her there was a momentary resistance—she was a virgin, I realized—and then we were moving together, joined in a rhythm at first gentle, almost languid, but swelling, accelerating, beating faster and more powerfully until finally I exploded into total synesthesia, into an orgasm that blasted my eyes with color and my ears with sound, a total experience like nothing I had ever known before, claiming all of me, destroying me and re-creating me out of nothingness.

And then it was over and we lay together in the still darkness of the cave, our arms around each other, my limp cock still in her, still joining us as we kissed.

Her face was wet. I put my hand to her cheek. She was crying.

I kissed her softly beneath her eyes, held her until her breathing changed and I knew she was asleep, watched over her until I too fell asleep.

Chapter Eight

That morning we passed from sleep into wakefulness and from wakefulness into lovemaking so naturally that there was no sense of transition: we were asleep, and then we were making love. We were gentle, tender, almost shy with each other; there were no pyrotechnics like the night before, and yet for all our shyness we met and merged and were changed.

When it was over we lay side by side in the cool darkness. I was at peace, content for the moment to lie on my back and feel the warm sage-scented breeze from the entrance blow across my body, yet I felt alert, awake, full of energy, with none of the torpor or dullness that so often follows sex.

I slowly became aware that though the only light in the cave was a dim glow filtering through the entrance hole, I could see the ceiling above me, its delicate crystal stalactites glowing with a ghostly silver light, the dark stones from which they hung shimmering faintly, as though coated with moonlit spider webs.

But what I was doing was not seeing, or not just seeing, for I had become aware of the roof in the same way you feel the heat starting to go out of the air just before the day begins cooling off. And now, looking up at the ceiling, I could *feel* it in much the same way as, blindfolded, you can *feel* the pressure of a wall you're groping for against your fingers just before you touch it.

"David." I rolled over on my side to face Dara. Her skin shone with the palest of silver glows but her eyes were still golden, small suns in this place of the moon.

"David, you just realized that you can see in the dark now." I nodded. "And you want to know why."

"Yes."

"Because making love with me has changed you, just as making love with you has changed me. You are no longer the same person you were yesterday. Nor am I."

Her voice was very tired, very sad. I didn't understand. I put my arms around her, felt her shoulder muscles knotted tight with tension. I tried to work the tension out of them, felt her relax slightly.

"Who are you, Dara? Why are you here, with me?"

"I don't know anymore. I—agreed not to know and I let them take my memories away from me so I could be here with you now and we could make love, but—"

She shook her head, forced herself to go on. "David, all this was planned for us. By someone else, for his own purposes. I was put by that highway to wait for you. Everything was arranged in advance."

"Everything . . ." I remembered feeling suddenly hungry, looking for an exit, deciding I had a better chance of finding something without meat in it at the taco stand than at the hamburger stand across the road. Everything.

"Alexandra?"

"Yes." A whisper. "I'm sorry, David."

"Why?"

"To get you here, with me. Because we are—not like other people. You can see in the dark now, and there are other things that you—that both of us—will be able to do later.

"Because of this we are necessary to the man who—arranged all this. Who killed your wife. He took me away from my grandparents when I was very young and brought me to live with him in a huge cave underground, but he couldn't prevent them from giving me this—"

She held up her left arm so I could see the nine-headed cobra twisted around it. It shone with a subtle, almost imperceptible blue radiance, paler by far than the silver cave-glow, while its eyes—red by day—shone golden as Dara's own.

"He brought us here so he could make use of us. But, David, the . . . what we are together, we really are. The way you feel about me, the way I feel about you—none of that was forced on us. It could not be forced on us. This is vital and you must understand it, you must believe it. Our love, our lovemaking was planned, yes, but only because he knew it to be inevitable if we were brought together. He did not create it or force it on us; he only makes use of it."

"But why do you let him—use you?"

"Because I had no other choice and because he is—I don't *remember* him, David, not who he is. They took that away from me. All I remember is what I thought about him, what I believed and what I knew was true, but not . . . why I believed it or how I knew it was true. But he isn't, I remember that he isn't, altogether evil and he—owns my death. Controls it. Not how I'm going to die, or where, or when, but what will happen to me afterward."

"You don't remember what that is?"

"No, but—I used to know and it frightens me, David. It terrifies me."

"Do you remember, not who he is but *what* he is, if he's even a human being, or— I saw something when Alexandra was killed, like a blue cloud with demons and . . . things inside it—"

"He's human. But what you saw were his enemies, and not all of them are human. Though the ones you saw might have been human and keeping their true forms hidden. But they're our enemies now, because he wants to use us to defeat them and they know it."

"Use us how? For what?"

"I don't know how, but I know that—once he's safe from them and he no longer has to worry about them or be afraid they'll use us against him, then I'll get my memories back and he'll free both of us. But if they defeat him my death will pass from his hands into theirs and they . . . hate me, David, and they're evil, what they want to do is evil. That's why I let him take my memories away, so his enemies can't use me against him, because he's the only chance I have. That either of us has. But if he succeeds in defeating them we'll be safe."

"If what he's told you and what you remember are true. If he can do everything you say he can, then he could plant false memories, like brainwashing, so none of it's true whether or not you believe it."

"I don't know. There's no way I can know."

"Dara, do you remember—when you got into the truck for the first time, the way you and the baby cobra stared at each other?"

"You're asking if he used me to make the bushmaster kill her."

"Yes."

"I don't know. I was there, I remember . . . watching him, but not—I don't remember what he did."

"Or what you did."

"No, but—I don't think he forced me to help him, David."

"Good, I guess, but—but he's still set it up right now so you don't know enough to do anything except what he wants you to do. No matter what that is. And if I believe any of what you've told me, I have to, maybe not believe all of it, but act as if I do, as if the only hope for either of us is to help him get what he wants—"

"And you believe me."

"You. Not him, not what he made you believe. But—Dara? Why *me*? Is it because of my family?" I was afraid of the answer, didn't want her to say that I'd fallen into the world of vampirism and eternal damnation that all the books I'd sought out, all the historians who spoke of Elizabeth Báthory as pathologically insane, Vlad Tepes as a cunning Renaissance prince and technician of terror, had enabled me to deny.

"Because of who we are and what we are together. That's all I know, David. I'm sorry."

I put my arms around her and held her, not questioning her, letting her know as best I could that I believed her, that I loved and trusted her. Not her hidden master, not his plans for us, but her, Dara, the girl I was holding.

"His enemies," I said a while later. "Why did I see them there if he was the one who killed Alexandra?"

"Your wife was involved with them, maybe she was one of them. What you saw was their attempt at protecting her."

"They failed." She was only two weeks dead but I could summon up no bitterness, no sense of loss.

"Because they're still weaker than he is. But his power is waning and they're growing stronger. Soon they'll be more powerful than he is and then they'll try to destroy us or gain control of us. The attack they made on you on the way down, the membrane—those were just to test us, find out how strong we were. But as long as we keep them from separating us or turning us against each other, our powers will keep increasing. We should be strong enough to protect ourselves soon."

"If what he told you—what you remember him telling you—was true."

"Yes."

"What am I suposed to do?"

"Just continue visiting the places you planned on while our powers grow and we wait for his summons."

His summons. Right out of *Robin Hood* or *Le Morte d'Arthur*: "*And the King summoned his courtiers and bespake them, saying—*"

The shocking thing was how easy it was to accept.

"I don't have any choice, do I?"

"No." She kissed me gently. "Neither of us has a choice."

We dressed and repacked the sleeping bags, then climbed out into the light.

"Are we supposed to do anything else here?" I asked.

She shook her head. "Just spend the night together in the cave."

The sky was clear and the day already hot, though the rocks were still glistening with the previous night's rain. We made our way to the path, started up it.

Climbing out of the Grand Canyon is like climbing a mile-high mountain. But though we stopped to rest from time to time, we were never as tired as my experience told me we should have been.

"Why were you so afraid when we found the membrane?" I asked while we were resting and eating some fruit we'd packed in.

"Because they'd attacked you on the path down and because both the canyon and the cave are places of power. Where power is concentrated like that his enemies can use it against us.

"Look." She pointed to a spot far below us on the canyon wall, where even in the bright morning sunlight I could see a faint cool shimmer totally unlike a heat mirage. "That's the cave. Even from here you can feel its power."

We soon began meeting hikers on their way down from Indian Gardens. Many seemed to be staring at us with unusual curiosity, but I didn't pay any attention to them until a heavyset man of about fifty in a too-tight red nylon bathing suit stopped me and asked, "Excuse me, but is that the latest thing?"

"The latest thing?" I repeated stupidly.

"You know. Your eyes." He gestured to include Dara. "Gold and silver."

So my eyes were now silver? "Contact lenses," I told him confidently.

"But what about the dark pupil?"

"One-way glass, to make them look natural."

"Ah. Thank you. I must say the effect is startling."

I waited until he disappeared around a bend in the trail, said, "Dara?"

"I'm sorry, David. I've always been able to see the silver there, in your eyes and under your skin. I didn't realize there'd been a change in your eyes people like that could see. I just thought I could see the power in them better now. But you handled him well."

"My years of experience as a part-time dope dealer," I said, then realized how smug and stupid I sounded. "Are there any other signs of, of my transformation?"

"Not that someone like that can see, no."

"But that you can see?"

"I can see the power in you more clearly, as though it's closer to the surface of your skin than it was before or shining a little more brightly, but that's all."

We reached the rim by midafternoon, spent the rest of the day looking out on the canyon while we explored Dara's fragmentary memories together, looking for something that would be of use to us but finding nothing.

Watching the sunset over the canyon through the window of the restaurant in which we were eating dinner, I found myself wondering again about the matter-of-factness with which I'd accepted the new terms of my life. How could I be sitting in a restaurant with all the tourists, knowing what I now knew?

As if to emphasize the changes taking place in me, the gathering darkness revealed that almost every rock formation in the canyon shimmered with its own spectral light.

"A place of power," Dara said again. And that was that.

It seemed the most natural thing in the world to follow my original plans and spend the next day at the Petrified Forest and Painted Desert. Dara and I behaved like typical tourists. I even bought her a piece of petrified wood.

We spent the night at a campground just past the New Mexico border and arrived at Carlsbad Caverns late in the afternoon, after driving all day through the most monotonous country I had ever seen. We took our places in the small stone amphitheater facing the caverns' entrance, watched as the bats, ten thousand of them a minute, came spiraling up out of the ground, their thousands of beating wings creating a wind rank with the smell of bat guano as they angled off to the southwest in a cloud that stretched from us to the horizon.

The entrance to the caverns blazed like a door opening onto a cold subterranean sun and I could feel the power of the place twisting and burning in my spine.

Chapter Nine

T he caverns had closed to the public at three and would not reopen until eight in the morning. We stayed a while longer, trying to find our way to the feeling of personal contact with a living entity we had had at the canyon, but the forces twisting at us were unbearable and we had to leave.

We rented a room in the town of Carlsbad, some miles away. Even there the caverns were a rasping agony that was all the worse because it was almost pleasurable.

We tried to make love but as soon as we touched each other the caverns would reach out to us through our interface, try to draw us to them. We had to stop and lie side by side without touching on the bed.

And then something interposed itself, shielded us from the caverns' energies.

"They're outside the window," Dara said. I got to my feet, threw back the curtain.

Hundreds of tiny albino bats were clinging to the window's screen and shutters, naked wings wrapped tight around them, blind red eyes glinting in the light from the room. Hundreds more were darting around in the air outside like a cloud of impossibly quick moths. Their dirty white fur shimmered, gleamed with power.

"They won't hurt us," Dara said in a taut, overcontrolled voice. "Not while they're still his to command. They've been sent to help us."

His to command. Not Vlad the Impaler, Renaissance prince inhuman only in his cruelty, but Count Dracula. Bram Stoker's invention. Bela Lugosi in his black cape and feelthy foreigner accent, the rubber bat with the strings you could almost see.

"Are they vampire bats?" Keeping my voice as calm as I could.

"I don't know, David. They might be." Dara's voice was impossibly distant, as if she were reading a grocery list to me over the phone. "He won't let me remember."

The bats clinging to the screen never moved. At last we closed the curtains on them and went to bed. Eventually we slept.

When dawn came we were sitting waiting in the stone amphitheater. At first there was just a low buzzing, the sound of thousands of paper-thin wing membranes, but with the first light we could see the bats as they flew high over the entrance, folded their wings and dived straight down into the caverns.

There were no silver-shimmering albinos among them, nothing to indicate that any of them were anything more than the useful, harmless insectivores they were supposed to be.

When the caverns opened for the day we had to walk back up to the Visitor's Center, pay our fees, and be fitted with the radio receivers that served as tour guides. They dangled from our necks like bulky toy telephones.

A man in a ranger's uniform examined our fee receipt, waved us on.

Once past the stench of the bat cave we began to see the giant stalagmites and stalactites, the limestone formations that resembled fossilized squids or Portuguese men-of-war, the helictites like the roots of impossible trees pushing their way sideways out of the rock, twisting and gnarled and interwoven, the cave coral like clusters of stone barnacles, the drapery stalactites like folds of hanging fabric, the pits, pools, columns and chasms—but for us the sculptured rock was only context for the living energies of the caverns. Columns shone with the light of silver suns; networks of flaming lines the color of burning aluminum ran across the roof, walls, floors; blinding lights shone through the solid rock as through murky glass, burning at us through the asphalt of the path.

We tried to maintain a normal pace, never taking our radio

receivers from our ears. Our eyes were almost always drawn to blank walls, unimpressive columns, small boulders. Only rarely did we find ourselves looking at the same formations as the other visitors, and then we might stare for long moments at something no one else gave a second glance.

We made it as far as the Green Lake Room before attracting anyone's attention. We were standing half blocking the path, lost in a thousand-petaled flower of silver-blue flame pulsing just beneath the surface of the asphalt, when the guard stationed in the chamber noticed us. When we finally realized he was watching us, we—I don't know how to describe it exactly, but we turned his attention away from us so that he ceased to be aware of us.

It was as natural and effortless as blinking your eyes to get rid of a cinder; in the confusion of forces and powers through which we were moving such a feeble manifestation of personal power seemed so totally insignificant that it was not until much later that I realized it was in any way unusual or out of the ordinary.

At last we moved on to the next chamber, the so-called Queen's Chamber. And found the source, the center, the heart.

Within and between and around the interlocking helictites projecting from every side, powers complex and alive flowed and changed, sang through shifting spectrums. And from a hole in the wall hidden high behind fluted drapery stalactites like the fossilized mantle of a giant jellyfish, a waterfall of suns burst, fell soft and shining through air and stone.

We wrapped ourselves in concealment, climbed the rough cave coral to the hole, wriggled through it into a long, low tunnel, the energies singing through us growing ever subtler, ever purer as their intensity increased, as we crawled deeper and deeper into the radiance.

At last we came to a large chamber, its far end covered by a pool of water. Bubbles rose from the bottom of the pool, burst with a soft plopping sound. And here, at the center, there was only clarity, only silence.

A slab of rock by the edge of the pool drew us to it, pulled us down onto its rough surface to make love, merge ourselves with the vast grid of living energies that coexisted with the caverns, sent tendrils of itself out to every part of the living earth.

We were lost to ourselves, making love with bodies forgotten, when a sudden glaciality, an invading tension, froze us into our separate selves and I saw, superposed on the scene before me, a hand mounted on a wooden rod, bone fused to wood, jutting from a basin of thick yellow liquid into which nerves and tendons, arteries and veins, dangled like roots. The fingers curled slightly inward, the skin was weathered and rough, and to the tip of each finger an eyeball glistening with moisture had been sewn. The eyeballs gazed inward, down at the palm, each burning with a different color flame—green, orange-red, pink, blue—and in the center of the palm a sigil the color of a livid bruise had been drawn or stamped, and I was there, trapped within the lines of the sigil.

Then the hand melted, was gone, leaving me poised above Dara, trapped in her sucking mucous membranes by the impersonal lusts of my body, feeling my substance draining out of me and into her. And yet even as she leeched my essence from me I was one with her, sharing her violation, feeling my cock penetrating and rending her, but though I knew she was as aware of what was happening to me as I was of what was happening to her, though we tried to break through the horror that had been imposed on our bodies' mindless mechanical coupling, somehow return to the lovemaking it had supplanted, our mirrored awarenesses of what had been done to us, what we were being made to do to each other, did not cancel each other out but only reinforced each other, resonated and grew stronger as I felt myself building toward a dark orgasm that I could not stop but which I could not survive, as I felt myself losing control, dying—

I was crawling naked through blue-white tunnels, dragging myself over ridges and spines of knife-edged ice, leaving behind me a trail of frozen blood. Light shone through the tunnel walls. Ahead of me fat hairy ice spiders spun their brittle webs, but I always managed to break through the half-completed webs before the spiders could fasten themselves to my body. I kept on crawling, crawling toward the cleansing fire that waited for me at the end of the tunnel, the fire I knew I would never reach . . .

He was me and he was not me and though I knew him they had hidden his name from me. Four men in black held him down on the long blue-white table while the fifth severed his head from his body. The head was wrapped in dark cloth; the blood was saved.

There was a garden beneath the earth where giant fungi grew in moist white rows. The men in black planted his head at the end of the last row as I watched, terrified, unable to move, unable to turn my head away to protect my staring eyes from the dirt raining down on them.

They watered the ground over his buried head with the blood they had saved.

Something was growing, pushing its way up through the sticky black earth—

And I was lying naked on the cold rock and Dara was gone.

Chapter Ten

I tried to get to my feet, could not, lay sprawled and helpless in the caverns' pulsing heart.

Dara had been taken from me, summoned back to her mysterious master or taken prisoner by his enemies, and without her I was only a crippled fragment of myself, voiceless and blind, my thoughts and feelings as meaningless as the pain an amputee feels in his missing limbs.

I could hear the distant voices of the tourists in the Queen's Chamber. I reached for my clothes, could not force my fingers to close on them.

And pulsing through me the energies of the caverns, lulling me and soothing me, making it almost impossible to hold on to my thoughts, drive myself on.

The visions of the ice tunnels and the man who was me and not-me were losing definition, fading into each other, like dreams that slip away before you're completely awake.

But I hadn't been asleep, I'd been forced into unconsciousness. My visions could have been spun around me to keep me distracted and helpless while Dara was being stolen from me—or while she was being compelled to surrender herself to whoever had used the hand against us.

Whoever had used the hand against us. If what I'd seen had been real, some sort of clairvoyant vision made possible by my new powers or the caverns' energies, then Dara's master was dead and Dara was in the hands of his enemies. *If* it had been Dara's master I'd seen killed. *If* the vision hadn't been designed to trick me into thinking he'd been killed when in fact he had not.

But the hand—I had *seen* it: there was no way it could have been a hallucination or an illusion. It reminded me of the hands of glory described in my aunt's grimoires: the hands of hanged men, specially prepared and dried, the fingers set aflame when the sorcerer who had created the hands wanted to use them to render someone unconscious. But I had at one time or another read every grimoire in my aunt's collection—and her collection was reputed to be one of the best existent—and none of them mentioned the yellow fluid, the sigil on the palm, the eyeballs sewn to the fingers. And this hand had done far more than just render us unconscious. How much more I could only guess.

Dara had been taken prisoner. Either forced back to a master she had believed meant her no harm but who had used me to violate and torture her just as he had used her to violate and torture me, or in the hands of the man-goat and his dancing worshippers: *Dara chained naked to the altar, two of the mutilated dancers holding her open to the man-goat, his huge segmented cock a hungry bronze centipede, the other dancers watching and waiting, skillful knives cradled in playful hands—*

And after she was dead, when they finally let her die, they'd do to her whatever she'd been so terrified of. And I didn't know what it was they could do to her, how to find them, recognize them if I did find them. Didn't know how to rescue her from them if I found her.

But I was beginning to feel stronger. I tried to stand, had to grab a stalagmite to keep from falling. I got my pants on, had to sit down for my shirt and sandals, finally hung the radio receiver around my neck and crawled back through the tunnel to the Queen's Chamber.

And maybe she hadn't been captured yet, maybe she was hiding from me somewhere in the caverns or out in the desert, still gripped by the horror of me the hand had forced on her. Somewhere I could find her, let her know I still loved her, make her believe that I wouldn't hurt her.

Find her before they found her. Before she fled the area altogether in any of the hundreds of cars leaving for almost anywhere.

Even if she was a prisoner they might have to keep her here so they could use the caverns' energies on her or force her to use the energies for them.

The drapery stalactites blocked my vision of the Queen's Chamber but I could hear people talking off to my left. Half remembering the means Dara and I had used to make ourselves unnoticeable, I tried to shroud myself in concealment again before making the ten-foot drop to the floor.

I must have succeeded because dozens of tourists passed within a few yards of the spot where I lay stunned without seeing me.

When at last I felt strong enough I staggered onto the path and took my place among the tourists. All I'd been able to think of was to make a thorough search of the caverns and the desert around them. The whole area was honeycombed with caves.

And if she fled from me again, if I couldn't find a way through the fear and horror to the part of her that still knew I loved her?

They could have taken her away, taken her anywhere.

She wasn't in the Papoose Room or the Boneyard or the Lunch Room or the Big Room, she wasn't back at the truck, on the nature trail, sitting in the amphitheater, in the Visitor's Center, the main corridor, the bat cave, Devil's Den, the Green Lake Room, or the Queen's Palace. I crawled for hours through side tunnels closed to the public. Nothing.

She could have broken free, be looking for me, not finding me because we were both moving around. I sat in the Lunch Room, an untouched cup of coffee in front of me, waiting until long after the lights had been turned out and the caverns closed for the night, then made a final search and returned to the surface.

People were beginning to fill the amphitheater. I sat down, let myself fade into noticeability.

The caverns were blazing with ever-increasing brilliance and their energies soothed me, pulsed through me and carried away my weakness and confusion. I accepted the strength they gave me as I had accepted the power to conceal myself, without questioning it.

The bats came swirling up out of the caves in counterclockwise spirals, flew away. The tourists left. In the gathering darkness I could see the landscape burning with thousands of silver fires.

I wrapped myself in my unnoticeability, returned to my truck for a length of rope and a flashlight. After a second's thought I discarded the flashlight—with my altered sense of vision I could see without it and its beam might give me away to anyone able to penetrate my concealment—and got my knife out of my tool kit.

As a weapon it was a joke—a Boy Scout–type jackknife with a two-inch blade, corkscrew, can opener, nail file, and screwdriver—but it was all I had. Maybe the screwdriver would come in useful.

Most of the caves I found were insignificant guano-stinking holes or ended in sheer drops. I explored every cave I could, the silver powerflame with which they burned giving me all the light I needed. I used my rope, sometimes jumped crevasses or worked my way around deep pits when what I could see beyond them looked like it might conceal something.

It was almost dawn before I found a cave with a different feel to it. The powerflame with which it burned looked no different, but something about it twisted at me, rasped me, yet with none of that undercurrent of almost pleasurable attraction that had made the main caverns so unbearable at first.

The entrance was free of brush, the ceiling high enough so I could make my way in without stopping. The cave slanted down for about twenty yards, then angled sharply off to the left, ended a few yards farther on in a long vaulted chamber.

Just inside the entrance to the chamber a young couple—both park rangers by the evidence of their discarded uniforms—lay dead, their bloodless bodies covered with hundreds of small dry wounds. There was dried blood on their clothing, on the khaki blanket on which they must have been lying when they were attacked; blind cave insects swarmed over their bodies as they would have swarmed over baby bats fallen from the roof, crawled in through the small wounds to feed on what remained of the muscles and internal organs.

Ignored by the insects, nine albino bats lay dead and crumpled on the cave floor, dirty white bodies still shimmering with a faint residue of the power that had been theirs in life. They'd only been able to kill nine of the tiny bats before they died. Nine, out of the hundreds we'd seen outside our motel room window.

There were two sets of footprints in the thin layer of guano covering the cave floor. Small shod footprints skirting the bodies, leading back to a shallow depression where someone might have lain on the guano for a while, then the prints of one shod and one bare foot leading out again.

And by that shallow depression, Dara's left shoe.

I searched the rest of the cave, found nothing, no other footprints. Dara had been alone, then, under compulsion—the fear of me the hand had aroused could never have driven her to hide herself here, lying in the rank guano next to the dead lovers' desiccated bodies—and now she was gone, could be anywhere.

Back at the truck I searched her backpack for something that would tell me more about her, where she came from, who she was. Everything was new, unused; her sleeping bag had never been slept in. I could have duplicated it all in twenty minutes in any of a thousand stores.

When tourists began arriving for the morning bat watch, I asked them all if they'd seen a black-haired girl with golden eyes and a missing shoe. No one had.

I searched the caverns again, drew strength and confidence from their vast heartbeat but learned nothing, gained no new powers or abilities.

At the Grand Canyon Dara had told me that I was supposed to continue with my trip exactly as I'd planned it while waiting for her unseen master's summons. He'd killed Alexandra, killed the couple in the cave, and if he wasn't dead he'd been the one who'd used the hand of glory to turn our lovemaking into something altogether evil. But I couldn't think of anything else to do.

Chapter Eleven

The other geological wonders proved to be just wind- and erosion-sculptured stone, dead and meaningless, totally without power. I conscientiously looked at the first few, hoping for I don't know what—a message I alone could read on the surface of some boulder, a fat man in a checked suit with a collection of dirty postcards he'd insist I examine, a rabbit with a pocket watch who'd tell me to follow him down his hole. Even Dara, somehow free and waiting for me. But there was no one, nothing, and I soon gave up on my list.

I drove straight through the rest of the way to Chicago. I felt no need for sleep or rest, didn't even bother to get out to stretch at gas stations.

A quick stop to deliver some snakes to Loren Beldon, a herpetologist known for his work with African cobras and mambas with whom I'd kept up an occasional correspondence over the last few years, then on to Boston to drop off the other snakes, and from there to Provincetown, the end of the line, where Larry was waiting to buy my coke. And if no one summoned me, no one contacted me—

I'd have to track them down, work my way past the neurotics and the sadists and the showmen to the real black-magic underground, if there was one. Maybe join the Church of Satan in San Francisco to show people I was interested, then let them know who my ancestors had been and hope someone would try to recruit me for something.

Try to work my way through my family's self-indulgent and pretentious morbidity to whatever reality must have at one time preceded it. There'd be nothing to be learned from my brother Michael, a social Darwinist whose imagination was limited to schemes for getting his while the getting was good, and even less to be learned from my father, but there might be something in the house itself—some of the old privately printed books in the library, maybe diaries or records hidden away in a trunk in the attic, something like that.

Aunt Judith would have known what I needed to know if anyone in the family did, but she was dead, a suicide. Maybe I could find a way to parlay her collection of grimoires into contacts of some sort.

Uncle Peter had spent a year in a Catholic seminary before retreating to his Pennsylvania hermitage; from what little I could remember of him he was slow and stupid, pathologically timid, but perhaps his shyness and stupidity were only pretexts for his solitude, masks behind which he hid something more sinister.

As for my uncle Stephen—he was an exhibitionist, a publicity-seeking poet of very minor talents who would have traded his obsessive treatments of decadence and decay for rhapsodies to spring and eulogies of the honored war dead in an instant if he'd thought it would bring him more public attention, but perhaps he'd learned something real while researching his image. If not, there might be some way I could put his morbid reputation to use.

I could go to Romania, waste months checking out Snagov's Monastery, Castle Bran, Visegard, the palace at Tirgoviste. A sentimental pilgrimage.

And if none of that got me anywhere, back to zero. Research, card catalogs, and cross-references while they had Dara, could be torturing or mutilating her. With about as much chance of finding her as a graduate student researching his thesis had of being taken on as apprentice to a black magician.

I didn't get to the zoo where Loren worked until long after it had closed for the night, but I'd called ahead and he was waiting for me outside the gates.

We shook hands and introduced ourselves. He didn't notice my new eyes. I'd experimented with my ability to turn people's attention away from me whenever I stopped for gas, found I didn't need the caverns' energies to make it work and that I could fine-tune the ability, keep people from noticing my silver eyes or, say, that I was holding my hand up in front of their faces while carrying on an otherwise normal conversation.

It could only have been this ability to make ourselves unnoticeable, veil ourselves from others' attention, that Dara's protector had wanted us for. So whoever his enemies were, it would work against them too, if only I could find them. When I found them.

The gatekeeper unlocked the gate and we drove the van up onto the sidewalk in front of the snake house, then worked together bagging the snakes and transferring them to their new cages. Without the theatrics for the customs inspectors it was dull routine, work I'd done a thousand times before, and I wasn't paying much attention to what I was doing.

Loren had just gone inside with the emerald tree boas and I was reaching into a cage for a Sonoran coral snake when I realized that Dara was there in the truck with me. I couldn't see or hear her but I could feel her presence, sense a change not in my surroundings but in who I was, no longer just the David Bathory I'd been reduced to but David-Dara again. There was nothing like telepathy involved; I couldn't read her thoughts, but she was alive and she healed and completed me, made me once again that which I should never have ceased to be.

"Dara?" I asked aloud. Then the coral snake struck. It had slithered up onto my glove while I was distracted and now it held onto the flesh of my inner arm with its short fangs, its delicate red, yellow and black banded body balanced precariously on the end of my glove while it worked its jaws back and forth to get as much poison as possible into my flesh from its stubby grooved fangs.

Dara was a dead weight in my mind, smothering me, paralyzing me and keeping me from calling out for help. I stood there, unable to move, looking down at the coral snake, feeling the wound burning, the flesh whitening, a great welt beginning to form—

At last I broke free of her, refused her, thrust her from me. I yelled to Loren to get the antivenin out of the drawer in back, lost his reply as the dizziness and confusion hit me. The coral snake had lost its perch on my glove but was clinging to me with its teeth, dangling unsupported in the air like a short length of bright-banded clothesline. I grabbed it with my other gloved hand, ripped it from my arm and dropped it back into its cage, managed to close the lid before I fell.

My vision was going, everything fading into an unfocused blur, and I couldn't breathe. The first cramps had begun in my muscles and abdomen, and my backache was getting worse and worse.

And I was in a ruined temple. Great blocks of rough stone, the roof open to the sky, grass and weeds growing in the cracks of the floor. A bare-breasted priestess with smooth dark skin listening to the whispered words of a green-eyed serpent that coiled itself around her, merged with her as she became a green tree and then a golden Queen with the head of a cobra on a throne of ivory in a palace of burning diamonds.

The Queen looked down on me as I lay there in my agony, reached out to touch my wounded arm with a long golden finger that spread its hood and struck—

And I was lying on the floor of the truck, Loren bending over me still holding the syringe with which he'd injected the antivenin.

There was no pain, no dizziness. I tried to sit up, found I could.

"I'm OK now," I said, certain it was true.

"You shouldn't be." He put down the syringe. "Lie down."

"No, I'm fine. I've gotten bitten before and I've built up an immunity."

"If you had any real immunity it wouldn't have hit you like that. You're lucky you're not dead."

"No, really, I'm OK. Look." I held out my arm so he could see that the welt was going away, stood up and balanced on one foot to prove that I could. "I think the whole thing was psychosomatic. Hysterical. I just panicked."

"I saw the way it was hanging on to your arm—what happened, exactly?"

"I don't know. I got distracted for a second and the next thing I knew it'd slithered up onto my glove and was attacking me."

"Coral snakes don't do that. Mambas maybe, but not coral snakes. There's got to be some other explanation."

I considered telling him about Alexandra, decided against it. "I know. I let myself get distracted and I must have missed something. I'm glad I'm getting out of the business. I've just got a few more snakes to drop off in Boston and then I won't have to worry about any more mistakes."

"Do you have a place to stay tonight?" he asked. "We've got a spare bedroom now that Glenn's off to college and you shouldn't overexert yourself."

"Thanks, but I've already made arrangements to stay with some friends. They'll be expecting me soon."

"Look, why don't you come inside and drink some coffee with me for a while, then I'll drive you over to their house and drop you off. I'll put your van in the back parking lot and pick you up on my way in to work tomorrow if you feel up to driving. If not you can leave the van in the lot until you need it again."

"Thanks, Loren, but—why don't we finish with the snakes, then I'll sit with you for an hour or so and then if I still feel up to driving you can follow me back to my friends' house and make sure I get there all right. Otherwise I'll do it your way. OK?"

"OK, but I don't want you taking any more risks tonight. I'll take care of the rest of the snakes for you."

I agreed, watched as he bagged and transferred the Gabon viper and the two Australian tiger snakes as well as the now-docile coral snake.

While we were sitting in his office waiting for the coffee to get hot I asked him if he'd ever been bitten by any of his poisonous snakes. He said yes, twice, once by a green mamba and once by one of his asps. Which gave me an opportunity to go from there to a discussion of the exaggerated fear most people have of snakes, and from there on to talking about the various kinds of myths surrounding snakes. He didn't seem interested in the subject but he was willing enough to talk about it, probably because he wanted to keep me sitting there where he could watch me and make sure I was all right as long as possible.

When I finally worked up to asking him if he'd ever heard of a goddess with the head of a cobra, he shook his head.

"Not that I can remember. There used to be, let's see, an Egyptian goddess named something like Ua Zit who was portrayed as a cobra with a woman's head. There's a statue of her in one of the museums here. And you've got all sorts of seven- and nine-headed cobras in India, but I don't know anything about them. Except that in the pictures I've seen they've got the heads all wrong and made the teeth look more like sharks' teeth than anything you'd find in a real reptile. Check with the public library here tomorrow if you're really interested."

We talked and drank coffee for another hour and a half. I told him I'd call him early the next morning to let him know how I was doing, then drove out to one of the nearby suburbs and parked in front of a random house until he waved and drove away.

As soon as I was sure he was gone I took the vial of cocaine out of the baby cobra's cage and snorted four spoonfuls. I didn't like the way the drug made me feel—it seemed to dull my perceptions rather than heightening them and there was no exhilaration or freedom in its excitement, only increased anxiety—but I knew it was cutting me off from Dara, building me a wall behind which I was safe from her.

// 72

Or rather, safe from those who were using her against me.
I found an all-night gas station, refilled the tank, and left for Boston. Whenever I started to feel a little calmer I snorted more coke.

Chapter Twelve

Sometime during the night's drive I realized that unless there was some sort of magical or ritual benefit to be derived from killing me, whoever had tried to use Dara to murder me must still think I was at least a potential threat. So either they thought I knew more about them than I did, or they knew some way I could get at them, maybe some way to use my new abilities against them that hadn't occurred to me yet. And even if they were trying to kill me because they thought I knew something I didn't, I might be able to learn what I needed to know from their attempts against me.

Unless, of course, they succeeded in killing me.

And as long as they thought there was a chance they could get to me through Dara they'd have a reason to keep her alive.

If my resistance to their first attack hadn't already convinced them they couldn't use her successfully against me.

If killing me was more important than whatever else they had planned for her.

And *if* she wouldn't be more useful to them dead than alive.

Dara's slim hand mounted on a wooden rod that merges with the bones of her raggedly severed wrist, the rod jutting from a bath of yellow liquid into which her nerves and tendons, arteries and veins, dangle. On the dark smooth skin of her palm a sigil has been branded and I am trapped within it, staring up at the two naked eyeballs that have been sewn to the tips of her long tapering fingers, Dara's golden eyes, and I can see her there, trapped inside the gold, staring helplessly out at me—

I called Loren from a gas station a little before seven to thank him for having saved my life and for the offer of his spare bedroom, then told him I was feeling fully recovered and was already on the road to Boston but would try to arrange to have dinner with him and his wife the next time I was in Chicago. I made sure I was totally coked while transferring the snakes to the zoo in Boston. I kept only the baby cobra, the South American rattlesnakes whose cages concealed the coke, and a small shy rainbow boa of which I'd become somewhat fond over the years.

The reptile-house keeper had originally been trained as a marine biologist and was far more interested in aquatic salamanders and in trying to get breeding populations of at least some of the species of amphibians that were being wiped out by acid rain in their breeding pools than in the snakes in his collection. As far as he was concerned, any religious or devotional interest in serpents could be more than adequately explained in Freudian terms.

Back on the road again, I remembered the way Dara and the baby cobra had stared in silent fascination at each other, the subtle blue radiance the golden Naga she wore had taken on in the cave where we'd first made love. I remembered the golden Queen whose finger had become a striking cobra whose bite had neutralized the coral snake's venom instantly in a way no antivenin could have done, even if I'd had the immunity I'd claimed.

When I couldn't take my thoughts any more I tried the radio, but all I could get was big band music or endless discussions of local politics, and Alexandra's harpsichord cassettes weren't any better. I left one of them on anyway, turning it over again whenever it came to the end of a side.

I made it to Provincetown about three in the morning and parked my van in a lot just inside the city limits, where it wasn't likely to attract too much attention, then walked the rest of the way in. The bars were closed and Commercial Street, which in the daytime would have been packed almost solid with gays, tourists, college students, runaways, and street vendors, plus the occasional Portuguese fisherman or high-school girl, was almost deserted. The only people I saw were a few middle-age gays still hanging out around the benches in front of city hall—the Meatrack—and a young kid passed out on some sort of oversized Japanese motorcycle.

I passed Larry's two junk stores, his boutique, and Second Skin, the leather store with which he'd started, on the way to the bookstore over which he had his apartment.

We'd gotten to know each other at Stanford, where he'd been the graduate student in charge of my floor in the dorms, kept up our friendship when I transferred to Berkeley and he dropped out. He'd tried his hand first at painting and then, more successfully, at leatherworking and handbag design, finally ended up working fourteen hours a day, seven days a week, keeping his shops together during the five-month season, then traveling and playing around with electronic sculpture the rest of the year.

Larry was my oldest and undoubtedly best friend, but I veiled the change in my eyes before taking the key to his back door out of the concealed zipper pocket in the doormat and letting myself in.

Both his Danes remembered me; I scratched them a bit behind the ears and under the neck before going upstairs.

He was in the front room, sitting on the floor in front of a tangled mass of game consoles, wires and joysticks and playing some sort of game against three color TV sets simultaneously.

"Hi, Larry." He looked like a tired satyr, very Greek and bearded; he'd gotten a lot older in the three years since I'd last seen him.

"Hello, David." He stood up, hugged me. He was a lot taller than me. "I'm sorry about Alexandra."

Which had a lot to do with why I liked him: he and Alexandra had hated each other within minutes and yet he really *was* sorry.

"It's OK. I don't think about it much now." Which was an evasion but not an outright lie.

"Sit down." He flicked off the consoles. "Do you want

something to drink or smoke or snort, maybe even something to eat if there's anything around? Or we can go out to a place."

"No thanks. Not yet, anyway. Larry, has anybody come around looking for me or trying to get in touch with me?"

"No. Was somebody supposed to?"

"Not exactly, but—sort of. Nothing to do with the coke."

"About the coke. I'm not going to be able to buy it from you after all. A pound, maybe, but that's it. We're going to have a really bad season this year."

"You're sure?"

"Completely sure. Sales are already dragging way behind last year and the tourists we're getting don't even buy snow cones for their kids. A lot of people in town are going to go under by Labor Day."

"Are you one of them?"

"No. My junk shops'll keep me alive, but you can only sell so many rubber chickens. At least and keep your self-respect. Which is getting harder and harder to do around here anyway. But I've lined somebody up to take the rest of the coke off your hands."

Which meant that there was at least one more chance that somebody was waiting here to contact me. "Anybody I know?"

"No. A friend of a friend, but he comes highly recommended and he's not supposed to be into any sort of heavy-duty violence. Plus he'll be able to give you a lot better price than I could've."

"But you still want a pound for yourself?"

"If you still want to sell it to me. You can get more money for it from him."

"I'll give it to you. Free. No charge."

"You're kidding."

"No."

"How come?"

"I'm getting out of dealing just like I got out of snakes and you're having a bad year. A favor for a friend."

"You're sure? I mean, thanks, but I can't just accept—"

"I'm sure and yes you can. Drop me off at my truck and then we can meet up at that little lake just off Route Six to make the transfer."

There was a police car parked alongside the van, its right door open. One of the cops was shining a flashlight in through the van's side window while the other was radioing in his report.

"Fuck," Larry said, taking in the cobra's head and lettering on the side of the truck. "You might at least have warned me."

"Sorry. Most of the time it just makes people want to leave me alone. Anyway, I've got the coke hidden where they'll never find it. In with the rattlesnakes."

"That's OK, then, but you still should have warned me. Though I don't think we'll have any real trouble. They're local and since I'm a property owner and year-round resident now, they'll probably give me better treatment than you'd get. This is still a small town in a lot of ways. Let me talk to them."

We got out of the car, moving slowly and keeping our hands in plain sight and away from our bodies until they recognized Larry. He said hello to them, shook their hands and introduced me to them, then said that I was his guest and would be staying with him, not sleeping in my van or doing anything similarly illegal.

Which turned out to be insufficient. They'd examined the truck's interior with their flashlights, seen the baby cobra and the rows of cages, heard the rattlesnakes rattling. And ever since a little girl had lost an eye and part of her face to a pit bull the previous summer it was very, very against the law to bring any sort of dangerous animal into Provincetown.

Their report had already been radioed in and was undoubtedly on file not only in the local office but with all the other police stations and law-enforcement agencies they'd have contacted to get information on me and my truck. And while my ability to make myself unnoticeable would have gotten me out of the immediate situation, and would have made the fact that there'd be a report on file about me no more than a minor, if continuing, annoyance, Larry had no such abilities. Any real trouble with the local police, even a minor investigation, and he'd be through in Provincetown. So I had to find a way to convince the cops that no crime of any sort had been committed, that the report they'd radioed in had been mistaken, and convince them in such a way as to make sure the new information would go on file with their original report.

But it turned out to be easy, ridiculously easy, one of those problems whose solution comes to you as soon as you realize exactly what you need to get done. I told them that, yes, I was a dealer in poisonous snakes and that I had been carrying a load of poisonous snakes in the van, but that they'd all been delivered to a zoo in Boston and that what few snakes I still had were perfectly harmless. I told them they'd been mistaken in thinking the cobra was a cobra, that it was just a perfectly harmless hog-nosed snake of a kind that likes to rear up and pretend it's dangerous to scare its enemies away, and I invited them to inspect the glove compartment cage while I turned their attention away from all memory of having seen a cobra, away from the cobra plainly visible before their eyes, while I kept them from considering the possibility that what I was telling them might in any way conflict with what they thought and perceived and believed and remembered.

They radioed in their amended report, apologized for having inconvenienced us, and drove away.

"David," Larry said very slowly, his voice gone neutral in a way I'd never heard before, "you told me you were getting out of dealing like you were getting out of snakes. All right. But what are you getting into?"

I started to turn his attention away, make him forget, keep him from being afraid of me. But I couldn't do it. He was the last real friend I had.

"Magic," I said. "I think. Or something like magic."

"You mean real magic. Sorcery and witchcraft, things like that?"

"Real magic."

He nodded very slowly, waited a moment, then asked, "Black magic?"

"Not me. But other people."

He let out the breath he'd been holding, nodded again. "All right. I believe you. I wouldn't have, but—you couldn't see your eyes while you were telling them the cobra was just a hog-nosed snake, David. That and the way they just drove off—could you do that to me? Just tell me anything and make me believe it?"

"I don't know. That was the first time I ever tried it. But I think so."

"It's scary, David."

"I'm scared too, Larry. Very scared. But I'm as much your friend as I ever was, and you can still trust me as much as you ever could. Let's get the coke out of the truck and back to the apartment and I'll tell you about it. I need to talk about it with somebody, and you're the only one I can trust."

I started telling him about Dara while I weighed out his pound and he shaved down a rock on a piece of black glass so we could snort a few lines. I was still talking when the phone rang.

It was six A.M. He reached for the phone, picked it up, listened a second then handed it to me.

"Hello?"

"Hello, David." It was my brother's voice.

"Hello, Michael. What do you want?"

"Father's dead. You're needed here at home."

"I've got some business to take care of."

"Drop it and get here as fast as you can. If our sister means anything to you."

Our sister? We didn't have a sister.

Unless—

Dara.

Chapter Thirteen

T he family holding was a rough square of land four miles on a side. Like the surrounding countryside, most of it was flat prairie, but its center was a geologically unique deformation of the landscape resembling a lunar meteor crater. This was the heart of the estate. The rest of the land, despite its enormous potential value as farmland, had been left undeveloped and served only to ensure the family its privacy.

Sometimes when a large meteor strikes the surface of the moon a crater with three distinct features is created. Circumscribing the crater is a ringwall, a circular wall of mountains splashed up by the meteor's impact. Inside this is the crater itself, and at the center of the crater is a single central mountain. At one time I must have been told why lunar meteor craters often had this central mountain and earthly ones never did, but if so I have forgotten the explanation. What impressed me as a child was how like a lunar crater my home was.

But if it was a crater, it was a fairytale crater. There was a great circular hole perhaps three hundred feet deep and a mile in diameter, surrounded by steep hills. The crater floor was thickly forested with maple and oak, elm and birch, but its walls were sheer rocky cliffs except in one place where the cliff wall had crumbled to form a gentle slope.

A steep central hill, a tiny mountain blunted by gravity, rose from the forest almost to the level of the surrounding plains. It was moist down on the crater floor, green with the scent of growing things, but as you climbed the central hill the trees and topsoil grew thinner until you found yourself climbing barren rock.

And it was there, on the bare rock, that my ancestors had chosen to build their home—or rather, their chateau, for though built almost entirely of native materials it was a European chateau in design and execution. Almost all its furnishings and fixtures had been brought from Europe, presumably traveling cross-country in covered wagons.

When the first other people of European descent arrived in the area more than one hundred and seventy-five years ago, they found my family already established, their massive mansion complete and fully furnished, their life more that of cultured Europeans in Byronic seclusion than of American pioneers. The first settler to happen upon the house had been met at the door by a servant, entertained, and then sent back to his sod hut.

Or so, at least, my father had told me, and the story was consistent with what I knew of our family's subsequent behavior. We had never mixed with the farmers who settled near us. Occasionally a Bathory would be seen in one of the small towns that grew up in the vicinity, occasionally some local official would visit the house on business. But such visits were rare, and discouraged.

I was a member of the seventh generation of Bathorys to be born in that house. My ancestors were buried in the graveyard at the base of the hill, under stone markers so set among the trees that it was hard to tell where the cemetery ended and the forest began. On each grave a shade-loving wild rose of a type I had never seen elsewhere, with tiny roses mottled pink and white, had been planted and the bushes had thrived and spread, adding to the confusion of cemetery and forest.

It was very beautiful there, the kind of picturesque landscape so many people dream of, and for the first half of my life my greatest dream had been to escape from it forever, to know that I would never have to see it again.

And now I was returning.

"I've got to leave," I told Larry as I put the phone down. "Can you sell the coke for me, take care of everything? I'll phone you and tell you how to get the money to me as soon as I've got things straightened out."

"Sure, if you want me to, but do you have enough gas to make it to Hyannis? The station here won't be open for another half-hour, and I'd like you to sit and talk a little longer before you get going. If you can. Just until the gas station opens."

I looked at him, saw that for him this was the last time, that he expected me to return, if I ever returned, as someone completely different, someone he didn't know and could never know.

"All right. Until the gas station's open."

"What happened? Was that the call you were waiting for?"

"I think so. That was my brother Michael calling to tell me my father's dead and that I've got to come home immediately if my sister means anything to me."

He started to say something, closed his mouth, finally said, "Dara's your sister?"

"Yes."

"You're sure?"

"I think so. Yes."

"David, you said she was nineteen or twenty years old. Right?"

I nodded, knowing what was coming.

"But you're twenty-nine and your mother died when you were two. We're old friends, David; I know all about you. So she can't be your sister unless she's a lot older than you said or unless she's a half sister of some sort—"

"I don't know, Larry. But she said her mother was Indian, and so was my mother. Maybe she didn't die when Father said she did."

"But it doesn't make any difference to you that she's your sister? You're in love with her anyway? I mean, romantic love? Incest?"

"Yes. It doesn't make any difference."

A slow nod. "All right. Then where's your father come into this? Your brother told you he was dead?"

"Yes." I told him about my visions of the ice tunnels and the man who was me and not-me and how he'd been killed.

"So you think that was your father—"

"Maybe my father."

"And then that would mean your father was . . . a black magician who used you and Dara to wage some sort of war against another group of black magicians? Even though you never knew anything about it before. You believe that?"

I hesitated, finally nodded. "Yes. You don't have any idea what it was like in our family, how distant he was. I never knew anything real about what he did, just what he said."

"What about your brother? Was he helping your father, or is he part of the other group?"

"I don't know. If Dara's my sister, then Michael's got to be involved too—but then I don't really know who he is either. I mean, I thought he was just, you know, just a hypocrite, all smiling and friendly and honest outside but sort of small and greedy and trivial inside, just empty, but—"

"But now you don't know."

"No. What time is it, Larry?"

"Just before seven. You better get going."

"I'll be back as soon as I can, Larry. With Dara."

"All right, David. As soon as you can."

It was after midnight by the time I reached the family estate. The surrounding prairie was lit with no more than the faint silver phosphorescence I had come to expect in everything I saw, but when I reached the top of the hill over which the road leading to the house passed I had to brake, stare.

The crater pulsed with silver fires, and now that I was at the top of the hill, no longer shielded by it, I could feel the power pulling at me, shaking me, caressing me. How could I have grown up in the center of all that without feeling it?

But perhaps I *had* felt it, felt it without understanding what it was I was feeling, without knowing what it was that was making me so unhappy, had forced me to leave.

The road, freshly blacktopped, led down into the crater

and through the forest. Every tree, every bush, gleamed with its own silver light. Fallen logs, night-flying birds, creepers and outcroppings of rock—everything shone. The power flowed around and through me, gentle, insistent, irresistible. Even the gravestones in the family cemetery gleamed soft and silvery. The wild rose bushes burned like white-hot wire.

It took an effort of will to remember how I had always hated it there. But no, I had never hated the forest for itself; it had been my one refuge from the house. But the house, the house I remembered as so cold and dark, even the house pulsed and shimmered like something out of a lunar fairy tale.

And it had been this, it had to have been this, that whoever had tried to kill me had been so afraid I'd find.

Chapter Fourteen

I climbed the steps—native black marble, quarried in the crater itself—to the house and rang the bell. There was a cross of wild rose nailed to the door and it burned with white light. Even the door, a solid slab of European black oak, shimmered in the darkness.

Everything I had ever known, believed about my family was false. Worse than false.

Had Michael been the one who'd tried to kill me?

Nicolae, a servant I remembered from my childhood, answered the door. He was brittle and slow-moving; he had been old when I moved away twelve years ago. A rare smile lit his face.

"Ah, Mr. Bathory, come in! Come in. Your brother was just telling your uncle Stephen that he'd been totally unable to locate you. They've been searching for you for five days now, ever since your father passed away."

Five days ago the hand of glory had appeared and Dara had been taken from me. But—totally unable to locate me? He had known I was at Larry's, had called me and summoned me home—

Without admitting to Stephen that he'd known how to locate me. Why?

"Father's dead?" I asked, trying to sound startled.

"Why yes. His funeral's tomorrow. You didn't know, sir?"

"No. I just thought—I don't know why—that since I was in Chicago I should come by. . . ."

"Why don't you wait in the library while I fetch your brother? He'll be able to tell you what happened."

"Of course. Thank you, Nicolae." He hurried off.

The library was more of a reading room and museum than

anything else; most of the family's books were kept in a basement annex while the medieval manuscripts were housed in a
special room of their own. The library itself only housed two
kinds of books: those written by members of the family, usually privately printed and bound in leather, and rare first edi-
tions, also bound, for the most part, in leather. The librarian's
main task was to keep the books well oiled so they wouldn't
dry out and crack.

I'd never taken much interest in either literature or book
collecting, but the family seemed to produce at least one no-
table collector in every generation. In my father's time it had
been my aunt and now it was my brother, if he was still collecting his medieval French anti-Semitic pamphlets.

The books covered three walls. The fourth wall was domi-
nated by a huge black marble fireplace tall enough to stand in
flanked by two uncataloged Goya paintings that had been in
the family since the artist painted them. The one on the right
depicted a witches' Sabbat; the one of the left was a portrait
of one of my ecclesiastic ancestors, a priest who had visited
Spain around 1800.

I sat down in front of the fire, feeling the power of the
house and land weave itself into the remembered bleakness of
the life I had lived there. My blood was dancing in my veins.
I awaited my brother.

I heard his heavy footsteps on the carpet—unmistakable,
even after twelve years—and rose to meet him.

"Michael."

"David."

We shook hands formally, sat down in facing leather armchairs.

"Would you like a drink?"

"Please."

"Whisky?"

"That would be fine." He rang for a servant, ordered two
whiskies.

Michael was about my height, perhaps twenty pounds
heavier, and immaculate. He wore a dark-blue suit, a blue

and gold necktie, a white shirt, and conservative shoes. Dark blue socks. His brown hair was cut short, barely long enough to comb. He had no facial hair and he looked out at you from soft brown Dale Carnegie eyes.

He looked exactly as I would have expected him to look, wore the same mask with which he'd fooled me all my life. But the indoor pallor of his skin was overlaid with the silver phosphorescence of power. His skin glimmered, gleamed, flamed. And his eyes—they were still brown but brown with moving pinpricks of light appearing and disappearing in their depths.

I tried to turn his attention away from my suspicions, to reduce the me he could see to the David Bathory who thought his brother's facade hid only the same petty greeds I'd assumed it hid when I'd last seen him twelve years before. I couldn't tell whether or not I was succeeding.

"I hear Father's dead," I said.

"That's right. We've been trying to get in touch with you since his death. The funeral's tomorrow. It was certainly a stroke of luck, you stopping in when you did after all these years—?"

Which meant what? That I wasn't supposed to tell anyone about his call telling me to come home?

"I was just driving through, not too far away, and I suddenly thought, I don't know, that I should stop by, that you were my family even if we'd never been close or anything and it had been too many years and I shouldn't have burned all my bridges behind me, cut myself off so completely. So I came home."

"I've been trying to find you for the last five days. All anybody could tell me was that you weren't at your place in Big Sur."

"I left right after my wife's funeral."

"I heard about her death. I'm sorry I never got to meet her."

I studied his face. There was a faint air of suppressed triumph around him. For the first time I realized I was very, very afraid of him.

"How did Father die?"

"Suicide. To be exact, he shot himself in the head."

"Why?"

He shrugged. "Who knows? I've lived here thirty years and I never understood him."

"But you must have some idea." Was he afraid somebody else was listening to us? "Business problems? Debts? A woman?"

"As far as I know he had no interest in women, at least after Mother died. Debts? His lawyer told me the estate is worth at least forty-five million. And business problems—do you know what business he was in?"

He was watching me closely, as if hoping for a reaction.

"No."

"Neither do I."

"But after all these years you must have some idea—"

"None. Perhaps I'll be able to find out now that he's dead. You know he was never willing to share anything with us." There was a depth of feeling in his voice that surprised me.

"What business are *you* in now, Michael?"

"Investments. Small-time stuff, mainly real estate. Shopping centers, a small chain of do-it-yourself and hobby franchise stores, things like that. Father advanced me some money to get started with and I've done pretty well with it."

I drank some more of my whisky. "You don't have any idea at all why he killed himself? Nothing different about him—"

"Oh, he changed all right. No question about that. Here, I'll show you."

He stood up abruptly, led me into the manuscript room. There was a new door in the far wall.

"What's that lead to?" I asked.

"A room he added on to the house. Over the years we've always followed the original plans when it's been necessary to enlarge the house. Always. This is the first thing ever built in defiance of them." His voice was thick with remembered anger.

I had never even heard of the plans he was talking about.

He opened the door, waved me through it into a large room. "As soon as I've got legal possession of the house I'm going to have this torn down."

The room was filled with Orientalia. Tibetan scroll paintings depicting the life of Buddha, Indian miniatures, books and manuscripts printed in what might have been Chinese characters, books in English, French and German dealing with Oriental philosophy and religion. A small gilt statue of Kali dancing stood on the mantel. Facing it from across the room was a seven-foot statue of Shiva. There were shelves of statuettes, prayer rugs on the floor, tapestries, a display case full of scarlet cords. The windows were open but the smell of some sort of incense still lingered.

"That's not like Father," I said, startled despite myself. He'd always been the strictest of Catholics, a man so deeply rooted in the European tradition it was far easier to picture him as a black magician than as a dabbler in yoga or Zen.

"Not like he was when you knew him, no. But he got strange near the end."

"I saw a lot of cars outside," I said, changing the subject. "Who's here for the funeral?"

"Stephen and Peter, of course. Then Cousin Charles—I don't think you ever met him. He's a priest. And a Mr. and Mrs. Takshaka. Mother's parents. Why they should show up now, after all these years—"

Mother's parents. My grandparents, which meant Dara's grandparents, who'd given her her golden Naga before she was taken from them by my father with his room full of Oriental religious curios.

"I don't know anything about them," I said, trying to keep from betraying anything beyond a mild curiosity. "Who are they?"

"Indians. Not American Indians, India Indians. But they're

Aryan at least, even if they're almost black. You must have inherited your complexion from their side of the family."

"Are they here now?"

"Not at the moment, no. They'll be back for the funeral." His eyes flicked away to focus on something beyond me. I turned. Uncle Stephen stood in the doorway. He was dressed, as always, in his almost clerical black, and his skin shone with the universal silver sheen.

"Ah, David!" he said. "I'm so glad you could make it home for the funeral. We see you so rarely here." He smiled a patently false smile.

As soon as he spoke I recognized the voice that had summoned me home, though it no longer resembled Michael's in any way. But why? And why had he pretended to be my brother?

I shook his hand and told him it was good to be home.

Chapter Fifteen

What are you doing up, Stephen?" Michael asked with a barely perceptible edge in his voice.

"I couldn't sleep so I came down to look at poor Gregory. Then I heard David and decided to say hello to him instead."

"I was just showing him Father's collection."

"Disgusting stuff, isn't it?" Stephen said to me. "All those cheap prints with their bright colors and those ridiculous statues. . . . I'll be thankful when Michael gets rid of it all.

"David," he said, as if the thought had just struck him, "whatever happened to Judith's collection of grimoires?"

"They're in storage," I said.

"Now that you're home you should send for them. They're part of the family collection and they'll just rot in storage. They should be here where we can care for them properly."

"I don't know how long I'll be staying, but I'll find out about having them sent for."

"Good." He smiled again.

"When's Father's funeral?" I asked Michael.

"Tomorrow evening, around seven-thirty."

"Just before dark. Isn't that a little unusual?

"Quite unusual," Stephen agreed, "but that's how Gregory wanted it and Charles agreed to respect his wishes. It's not contrary to any church rule and we've even been granted a dispensation for a Latin Mass."

"After the ceremony we're burying him next to Grandfather," Michael said. "We had the grave dug today and the headstone's ready, but we could use your help as a pallbearer."

"Of course," I said.

"Good. With you, me, Stephen and Peter that makes four, so I guess we'll have to use two of the servants. William and Alexandru, probably."

"Where's Uncle Peter?" I asked.

"Upstairs asleep, I suppose. You know it's almost three?"

"Really?" Michael said. "Then I better get to bed. There are still a lot of details I have to take care of tomorrow."

"Where do I sleep?" I asked, though I had no intention of sleeping.

"Your old room. Nicolae had your bed made up as soon as you arrived."

"Good night, David," my uncle said. "I just wanted to say hello to you before you turned in for the night. We can do some real talking tomorrow. It's been a long time. Too long."

"Stephen," Michael said as he turned to leave. Stephen turned back to face him. "I just thought of something. Can I talk to you privately for a few moments?"

"Of course, Michael."

"Excuse us, David," Michael said. "Good night."

"One thing first," I said. "Is Father's body in the chapel?"

"Yes. They did an excellent job of embalming him. You can hardly see the bullet hole."

The chapel was lit by twelve long tapering candles in silver candelabra. Father's coffin was on a low table in front of the altar. The top half of the black coffin was open. Michael had been right: the bullet hole in his head was almost invisible. He must have used a small-caliber gun.

His features were composed and there was a faint smile on his lips. I wondered how the mortician had achieved such a peaceful effect, for Father had never looked peaceful in life.

But the longer I stared the less peaceful he looked. It was nothing that would have been visible in a photograph, but I could sense worms of silver light crawling around just beneath the surface of his skin. And he looked stronger, as if death had changed his fat to muscle. He also resembled Michael much more than I'd remembered; there was something about the set of his features, some ingrained nuance of expression that not even death had been able to eradicate and that I'd never noticed before that reminded me of my brother.

I leaned forward, touched a finger to his face. The flesh was soft and faintly moist. I thought about spongy fungi growing in moist white rows, loosened the collar of his shirt to examine his neck. It was unmarked.

Why had Michael and Stephen been up and fully dressed at three in the morning?

They'd gone into the library. I hesitated a moment, looking down at Father, then wrapped myself in unnoticeability. I didn't know if it would really hide me from Michael and Stephen, but it was the only weapon against them I had. I made my way as silently as I could to the manuscript room, through whose thin walls I had occasionally overheard scraps of conversation from the library as a child.

". . . wasn't me." Michael's voice. He sounded angry. I sat down in one of the armchairs against the connecting wall, started to pick up one of the manuscripts laid out for display so I could pretend to be studying it if someone discovered me, put it back again: if Michael or Stephen penetrated my unnoticeability, they'd know I'd been trying to hide from them.

"And only your word that you didn't get him to come back," Stephen said. "Why don't we just ask him and see what he says?" He sounded amused.

"I did. He said he was just passing through."

"You've forgotten the Nagas." An unfamiliar voice, cold, grim, precise.

The Nagas: Mr. and Mrs. Takshaka. My maternal grandparents.

"But why would they want him here?" Stephen asked. "*We* want him here."

"It's not important what they want," the grim voice said. "What's important is that they're dangerous to us and that we cannot tolerate them here. You should kill them now, before they can harm us."

"How?" Stephen asked. "We don't understand them and we don't want to understand them. Look what happened to Gregory. Unless you, Michael, perhaps you could tell us—"

"I repudiate Mother and her race and everything they stand for. As you know well, Stephen."

"But how can we trust you," the grim voice asked, "with your mother's blood flowing in your veins?"

"You need not trust me. You need only obey me. I am a Bathory and a dhampire. I am your master."

"Not yet. Not until you master Gregory."

"I am your master *now*, Grandfather. I can force you to obey me."

Michael's grandfather, our father's father, had died before I was born. Was dead and buried.

Dead and buried and in the library talking to Michael and Stephen. A vampire.

"For the moment," Stephen agreed. "Until you confront Gregory. But Michael, I too am a Bathory and a dhampire and I remember what your mother made of my brother. Why should *I* accept your dominion?"

"Because Father was a fool and a coward, for all his untainted blood. I had to learn to deny him and to deny my mother's blood in me, and that denial forced me to develop the strength he never had."

"Perhaps. He may have been stronger than you think, Michael. But why would the Nagas want David here, if they were the ones who brought him? To help rescue Dara?"

"No," Michael said. "If they'd wanted to rescue her they could have done so themselves, before I had a chance to gain any power from her."

"Unless they wanted you to gain power from her," Stephen said.

"They're here to prevent Gregory's transformation," the grim voice—my grandfather's voice—said. "And they have power over fire: they could burn him in his coffin before he's ready."

"Then they could have burned him earlier," Stephen said.

"But why now?" Michael asked. "Why are they here, if not to prevent his transformation?"

"The three of you are here again now. Their own kind."

"I am not *of* their kind, Stephen. And you would do well to remember it."

"Dara, then. Or David."

"We cannot tolerate them any longer," the third voice said. "You must destroy them or force them to leave us. Tonight."

"How, Grandfather?" Michael asked.

"You could kill them. They can die. Your mother died."

"The first time," Stephen said. "Not the second."

"Gregory will bring her back to us."

"If he survives his forty days," Michael said. "If they don't destroy him first. If Satan accepts her."

"You don't have the strength to master my son alone," my grandfather said. "Should either Dara or David join us before you gain dominion—"

"Then you will have all of us before our time," Michael said. "Perhaps. But they will do what I demand of them, as will you, Grandfather, even now, before my dominion is complete. And as you will as well, Stephen. Only I can protect you from Father."

"Protect me, Michael? Do you really think I fear my fate? I am only sorry that my responsibilities to this family prevent me from embracing it earlier."

"Then join us now," my grandfather said. "Living as you do—as you all do—you only thwart us. When you join us you will see how wrong you've been."

"When I join your communion I'm sure I will, Father," Stephen said. "But until then I have duties I must fulfill."

"It's almost dawn," my grandfather said. "I must sleep. Will you nullify the guardians for me?"

"Yes," Michael said. I heard footsteps, then silence. The door hadn't opened or closed.

"Do you have everything prepared?" Stephen asked a moment later.

"Almost everything. Unless there's a way we can use her to master Father without freeing her for tomorrow, now that the Nagas are here—"

"There isn't any way. If they try to interfere we'll have to stop them. No matter what the cost to the family."

"Agreed. But if David and Dara escape I'll know whom to blame, Stephen. I'm still not completely convinced you didn't bring David here."

"To what purpose? His blood is as tainted as yours, and he is even less fit to rule than you are. But we must finish readying her for tomorrow."

"I'll be studying everything you do," Michael said. "I'll know if you're trying to deceive me."

"There would be no point. As you said, with you gone, who would protect me from Gregory?"

Once again footsteps, then silence. They hadn't opened the door or gone into the hall. I waited a moment longer to make sure, then let myself become noticeable again and opened the door to the Oriental room and went inside, turned the light on so as not to reveal that I could see in the dark if somebody found me. I searched the shelves for something that would tell me about Nagas. The likeliest candidate was a two-volume encyclopedia of Indian folklore. I took it up to my room, snorted some coke for psychic self-defense, and flipped through a lot of cosmological nonsense—as far as I could tell the Indian universe was a mountain resting on the back of four elephants or turtles—and tried to make sense of the article on Nagas. But other than the fact that they were usually associated with water and immortality, were probably the origin of the Chinese belief in dragons—my grandfather had said they had power over fire—and had their home in the underground land of Patala, the article said nothing of interest.

I snorted more coke, then lay on my bed pretending to be asleep while trying to make sense out of what I'd heard.

Both Michael and Uncle Stephen were dhampires, and a dhampire was someone who ruled his undead ancestors. His undead ancestors who were vampires who were my undead ancestors. Michael had been the one who'd taken control of Dara and me in the caverns and taken her away from me—and who'd tried to kill me in Chicago?—but he was planning to free her tomorrow so he could use her to gain control of Father.

Unless I could find out how to take her away from him.

Michael was half Naga, as I was half Naga and Dara was half Naga. Michael suspected Stephen of plotting against him—and Stephen *was* plotting against him, was lying to him and must be planning to use me against him in some way. Because Stephen hated him for his Naga blood, which was the same as Dara's and my Naga blood.

My father was dead now but would be alive again soon, and a vampire. As his father, my grandfather, was a vampire, as Stephen and Michael would become vampires.

As Dara and I would become vampires unless our Naga blood saved us.

Our Naga blood. My long-dead mother was not dead, or not exactly dead, and she was a Naga, perhaps even the cobra-headed Queen on the throne of ivory who'd saved me from the coral snake's attack—and her parents, my other grandparents, would be here tomorrow when Dara was freed.

When we would have what would perhaps be our only chance to escape.

But it was strange that there'd been no mention of God or Christ, Satan's traditional adversaries. Only the Nagas.

Chapter Sixteen

At seven that morning I decided I'd stayed in bed long enough to simulate a night's sleep. I showered and dressed, then went downstairs to examine the rest of the books in Father's new room.

And realized how stupid I'd been in not studying them more thoroughly the night before, because about a third of the books were missing. I glanced through the others, found nothing that would have been out of place in the inspirational section of any West Coast bookshop.

I'd been letting the seeming familiarity of my surroundings lull me into a sense of false security. For all I knew, they'd been aware of me listening to them the whole time and had just waited until I went upstairs to hide everything that could be any use to me.

I went looking for the Takshakas, was told by Nicolae that they weren't expected back until the funeral. I checked out the house again anyway.

". . . sounds a bit like the Manichean Heresy, your idea that Satan is as powerful as God and is the absolute ruler of this world while God rules only in heaven," I heard as I walked into the dining room. Two men were sitting at the end of the long table with their backs to me, talking in low earnest voices. One of the new servants was refilling their coffee cups; I caught his attention and ordered breakfast.

"But if a man commits a sin, hates himself for doing it, yet knows that he has had no other choice and that he will sin again in the same way, how can he beg God for forgiveness? What choice does he have but despair—?" The speaker broke off when he caught sight of me. He was a big man, well over six feet tall but stooped. His long gray hair and full beard looked as though he'd made an unsuccessful attempt at re-moving years of tangles with one brushing. Uncle Peter.

I seated myself across the table from the man to whom he'd been speaking, no doubt Father Charles Bathory. He was a strikingly handsome man, still young, with a smug unthinking look on his face and something to the way his robes fitted him that suggested they'd been discreetly tailored.

"Good morning," I said.

"Good morning," the priest replied. His voice was over-hearty, with a public speaker's sincerity. Peter mumbled something.

"Don't let me interrupt your conversation," I told them as a servant I didn't recognize brought me the omelet I'd or-dered.

"We were just finishing," Peter said with an effort. He was gaunt and colorless, with a fish-belly pallor that made his black eyes seem sunken, and he looked like a man who'd been afraid to go to sleep for most of his life. His skin was splotched with silver and he wore a too-large but expensively cut suit.

"You must be Uncle Peter," I said. "I'm David. And you"—turning to the priest—"must be Father Bathory."

"Call me Charles," he said. Peter mumbled a greeting without meeting my eyes.

"We can continue our conversation later if you'd like, Peter," the priest said, dismissing him. Cousin Charles's skin was so lightly tinged with silver that I was sure he could have little part in what was happening here, but he monopolized the conversation, to my uncle's evident relief. I was treated to an endless monologue about the good father's church in what had once been an upper-class neighborhood in Chicago but was now well on its way to becoming a slum. The loss of many of his well-to-do parishioners had hurt the church fi-nancially, it seemed, but the black and Hispanic children sang so beautifully that some of the richest members of the church had continued to take an active part, even though they'd moved out of the neighborhood, and that, combined with the gas station and butcher shop that two other parishioners had left them . . .

While Charles was speaking, Peter ate his breakfast steak with careful speed. He finished and got up, obviously relieved at the chance to escape.

"Uncle Peter," I called after him, interrupting Cousin Charles. Peter froze like a little boy caught stealing money from his mother's purse, turned unwillingly back to face me.

"Excuse me, Charles," I said, "but I haven't seen Peter for fifteen or twenty years and there are a lot of things I want to talk to him about. I'm sure we'll get another chance to talk later."

"It's been a pleasure meeting you," he said genially. I pushed back my chair and joined Peter, escorted him out into the hallway.

"Where would you like to talk?" I asked. "The library?"

"No," he said quickly. "I don't like the library."

"Good. Neither do I. How about outside? Down in the forest. Of course, if you're afraid of getting your suit dirty—"

"Outside. I feel better outside. And it's a beautiful day," he added as if the thought had just occurred to him.

We walked down the drive. It was sunny out, with only a few cumulus and cirrus clouds in the sky. Birds sang and hopped and flew in the trees and gray squirrels were everywhere. Father had always called them tree rats.

Peter tensed, shrinking into himself, when the first gravestone came into view on our left. He only began to breathe normally again after we were well past the cemetery.

Farther on I found an oak tree fallen by the side of the road. We sat on it and talked.

Or rather, I talked. It was hard getting any information out of him. He volunteered nothing and after the first few minutes I quit trying to keep up the fiction that what had become an interrogation was really a friendly conversation.

He grudgingly admitted he lived in a cave hollowed out of the side of a hill in Pennsylvania. I already knew that. He told me some things about the forest where his cave was, though not how to find it, but he wouldn't tell me why he had chosen to live there as a hermit. He did his best, in fact, to tell me nothing at all, yet he seemed mortally afraid of lying to me or offending me in any way.

He gave each question I asked him careful consideration, like a squirrel turning a nut over and over in its paws trying to decide just where to bite into it, then answered with a flood of inconsequential or trivial details. And after each such trivial disclosure—after revealing that he'd been born two years before my father or that he'd last seen me when I was thirteen—he'd go rigid, sitting with a look of pure terror on his face and refusing to say anything further.

At first I pitied him and did my best to make things easy on him, but as the time passed I lost patience. I bent the power of the forest to my will, used my ability to focus his attention where I wanted it to don a mantle of spurious charisma, but though he cringed away from me he still refused to answer my questions.

Finally I asked, "What do you know about vampires?"

"Nothing!" he stammered, face contorting and twisting. "Just what I read in Bram Stoker's book. I can't read in my cave, the light's too poor. I haven't read a book in years. I don't even remember *Dracula*."

He stared at me a moment longer, then fled back up the hill, leaving me alone on the fallen tree.

Dracula? I hadn't read it since I was nine. Aunt Judith had taught me it was just a malicious fantasy, but it was clear she'd been protecting me from knowledge she thought was too dangerous. Perhaps there was something in *Dracula* I'd forgotten.

I walked back up the drive to my house, asked if my grandparents had by any chance returned early. They hadn't.

The librarian was anxious to help me, but I told him I just wanted to browse in peace while I waited for Father's funeral. He said he understood and left me alone.

I found only two listings under "Vampires" in the English-language section of the card catalog, *Dracula* and something called *The Vampire: His Kith and Kin* by Montague Summers, plus a number of cross-references to the Russian, Romanian, German, and French collections—all languages that I should have known as a graduate of St. George's Academy, none of which I could actually read, though I could get by in spoken Romanian, which they'd drilled into us unmercifully.

Dracula gave me a wealth of information about vampires, but I had no idea whether any of it was trustworthy, though the preface said that Stoker had been a member of the Order of the Golden Dawn, which it described as a society of serious students of the occult that had flourished at the end of the nineteenth century and had included such people as Aleister Crowley.

Montague Summers's book was an irritating pseudoscholarly compilation of legends, superstitions, rumors and errors—he misquoted one of the grimoires I remembered from my aunt's collection—all of which the author seemed to take as literal truth. Some of what he said corroborated Stoker's tale and some was patently ridiculous, like the claim that you had only to scatter mustard seeds on your roof and threshold to keep yourself safe from vampires, since any vampire intent on doing you harm would be forced to spend the time until dawn compelled him to return to his coffin counting the seeds.

But despite its absurdities the book contained some information that clarified what I had overheard, including the statements that a suicide will often become a vampire and that forty days must pass before a vampire can rise from its grave. The book also claimed that vampires could not abide wild roses and though the reason it gave, that the vampires were afraid of being caught in the brambles, was another of Summers's idiocies, there was the evidence of the wild rose bushes planted on my ancestors' graves to lend credence to some sort of connection. But Summers's book made no mention of dhampires.

I'd just skimmed through the books, slowing down and

paying more attention only when something that looked relevant caught my eye, but even so my reading had consumed most of the day. I had unconsciously wrapped myself in unnoticeability while I read, as I realized when, emerging from the library, I was almost knocked down by Nicolae, who failed to see me until he ran into me.

"Mr. Bathory!" he said with the same fussy, disapproving air I remembered from my childhood, when he'd catch me trying to sneak in without washing after playing in the forest. "Dinner's ready and we've been looking everywhere for you so we can proceed."

"I'll be right there," I assured him.

"Excuse me for mentioning it, sir"—he looked pointedly at my faded jeans and plaid wool shirt—"but shouldn't you dress for dinner? The funeral's directly afterward."

I felt like laughing for the first time since my return. "I'm afraid I don't have any proper clothing," I told him. "I've been living in a cabin in the woods, you know."

"Your black suit is hanging in your closet, sir, and Robert shined your shoes for you this morning, while you were out walking with your uncle. If you'll permit me, I'll inform the rest of the family that you'll be down in a few minutes."

I dressed, snorted so much coke for psychic self-defense that my head was spinning and I felt a little queasy, went down to the dining room.

There were five people I didn't know at the table: three undistinguished-looking persons with only a minimal silver sheen to their skins—no doubt the other cousins—and a diminutive couple with dark skin and wavy black hair who could only be my maternal grandparents.

They were small, neither over five four, and very slender, with fine delicate bones. Their faces were smooth and unwrinkled, their movements swift and graceful, but they seemed to wear their age like a second skin, a cloak of wisdom and experience.

Their eyes were the startling blue of a Siamese cat's and their features were veiled by barely perceptible auras of transparent turquoise flame that sometimes suggested the heads of giant cobras with spread hoods, sometimes multitudes of smaller cobra heads, each with its own life and intelligence. Yet they alone, of everything I had seen since Dara and I had first made love, manifested none of the silver phosphorescence I had come to expect.

No. Dara's bracelet, the golden Naga she wore twisted around her left forearm, had the same blue aura. And these two little dark-skinned people, my grandparents, were Nagas, as I was half Naga.

A place had been saved for me between Uncle Peter and one of the cousins, too far away from the Takshakas for me to be able to talk to them during the meal. Everybody was standing behind their chairs. I took my place and Michael, who was sitting at the head of the table, asked Peter to say the grace. Charles looked offended, no doubt because as a priest he considered it his right and duty to say the blessing.

"Bless us O Lord and these Thy gifts which we are about to receive from Thy bounty . . ." Peter said haltingly while Stephen watched him with a malicious smile. Peter stopped, obviously at a loss for words, and Charles finished triumphantly: ". . . through Christ our Lord. Amen." Everyone sat down. Servants brought soup.

I studied the Nagas covertly while I ate. Stephen and Michael were watching them as well, while Peter tried to avoid looking at them, all of us trying to pretend that we were having an otherwise normal formal dinner. The food lay heavy in my stomach, an indigestible nauseating lump, but I forced myself to keep on eating, smiling gravely and making polite conversation in keeping with the solemnity of the occasion.

I felt a momentary urge to shout something, cut through all the lies and hypocrisy to what was really going on, but bit it back. The only thing I had that might give me some sort of advantage was that I was a little less ignorant than they thought I was.

After a while I realized that the Nagas had been watching me while I studied them. As soon as I caught on they grinned at me, then resumed their conversations with their neighbors. Though their teeth were sharp and inhuman, like dog's teeth, neither Charles nor the other cousins seemed to take any notice. But I had no chance to speak with them before the funeral and though Peter sitting next to me drank an immense amount of wine, the more he drank the more tight-lipped he became.

The funeral began with Mass in the chapel. I sat with the other pallbearers in the front pews. Though I hadn't confessed, I took Communion with the others, since it seemed to be expected of me. Fifteen years had passed since I'd last knelt at the rail and the wafer Charles put in my mouth was so unexpectedly bitter that I almost gagged on it.

Before the service ended I'd begun to feel chills and a growing nausea. Helping roll the bier out of the chapel to the waiting hearse, I felt a giant hand clench and start twisting in my stomach. Weak and dizzy, alternately sweating and shivering, it was all I could do to help lift the coffin into the hearse and make my way to the car Michael gestured me to.

Nicolae drove the rented hearse down the hill. I was in the second car; behind us came other cars with more family and the household servants.

The sun had set by the time we reached the cemetery, but there was still a little light in the sky. I staggered out of the car. Around me servants were lighting kerosene lanterns. No one seemed to notice my distress.

I couldn't understand what was happening. I knew I was supposed to carry Father's coffin, but I couldn't connect that knowledge with the black box being unloaded from the hearse.

"Hurry up, David. Give us a hand," Michael called, and I ambled over to the hearse and helped lift the coffin from it, imitating my brother's actions without understanding them. We carried the coffin into the silver-shining woods.

My physical discomfort was going away but my confusion was increasing. Things caught my eye—a glowing leaf, my brother's back, a gravestone with its inscription weathered to illegibility—and held my fascinated, uncomprehending attention.

We lowered the coffin into the ground. Charles sprinkled it with holy water and began the final part of the funeral service. People threw springs of wild rose into the hole. Two servants shoveled dirt down on the coffin.

I was standing by the hole, watching the servants shovel the silver dirt, when I sensed Dara in the woods behind me.

No one tried to stop me as I turned from the grave and hurried into the woods. I saw Dara. She was wearing a long black dress and walking slowly, as if sleepwalking.

I ran up to her and caught hold of her arm. She awakened instantly.

"David!" She looked around. "Where are we?"

I could only stand dumb, clutching at her arm.

"What's wrong?" she demanded. "What have they done to you?"

I nodded and smiled, happy to have found her. The forest was beautiful.

The wind brought Cousin Charles's solemn voice to us.

"We can't stay here. Come on!" She began to run. I followed, happy to be running.

Finally she stopped. "Can you understand me at all?" she asked.

Her words were meaningless. I smiled at her.

"Here." She twisted the Naga off her arm and forced it onto mine. There was a moment's sharp pain, then my head began to clear. "Can you understand me now?"

I nodded, not trusting myself to speak.

"What did they do to you?"

I thought about it for a long time. "Dinner," I said finally, trying to tell her about Michael and Stephen and the Nagas.

"They gave you some kind of drug. Do you understand me?"

"Yes." The words were beginning to come. "Not like anything I ever—" I lost my train of thought again.

"Can you remember what I tell you?"

"Yes." My mind was slowly growing clearer. "Go slow," I added.

"I am your sister. Our brother Michael is our enemy. Do you understand what I'm saying?"

I nodded.

"Uncle Stephen is our ally. Not our friend, never our friend, but he is Michael's enemy too. He freed me from Michael and gave me this ointment."

She took a small metal box out of her dress and showed it to me, then put it in my pants pocket.

"If we get separated, lie down in a safe place with your head to the north and rub the ointment on your forehead. Follow the Naga. It will lead you to me. Can you remember that?"

"Yes."

"Good. How do you feel?"

"Wonderful."

She frowned. "Can you remember more?"

"Yes."

"We are dhampires. That means our grandparents and now our father as well are vampires. Michael is a dhampire too. So are our uncles. Dhampires have power over vampires.

"We will not gain our full powers until Father has been dead forty days. But when we make love our powers grow. Whenever two dhampires have sex together, power is generated.

"Michael has been forcing me to have sex with him. There is power in rape, though not as much as in lovemaking. He has been draining me of my power. Do you understand what I've been telling you?"

"Yes."

"You're sure? Don't try to think, just remember."

"Yes."

"Good. Now we must make love. I no longer have enough power to keep us veiled without your help. We need to hide ourselves and overcome the drug they fed you. Take off your clothes. Hurry!''

I began to take off my clothes. There was something I knew I should remember but I didn't know what it was.

Chapter Seventeen

The woods were silver. A three-quarter moon gleamed through the branches. Dara lifted her dress over her head and drew me down beside her onto the damp oak leaves and pine needles.

Part of me seemed to be watching us from the tannic-acid smell of the rotting oak leaves, yet as we held on to each other, as I fumbled with her breasts and tried to stroke her skin, my cock swelled and stiffened with a need for her so desperate and painful that it pushed the last of the floating confusion out of me.

"I can feel them here in the woods, all around us. I can't keep us hidden much longer. Hurry, David!" Dara said as she pulled me over on top of her.

I pushed myself into her, tried to make love to her. But I could not match myself to her rhythms or find one of my own, could not shrug off the clumsy weight of my body and lose myself in our lovemaking, and as I grew more frustrated, more desperate, I tried to substitute force for the sensitivity I had lost, as though by slamming my cock into her with greater and greater violence I could somehow break through to the missing rightness.

The power swirled through us, burned in us, but only in the instant when it leaped the gap between us did we share it, did it unite us. When I held it, the woods around us were transparent crystal and it was easy to sense the vampires searching for us, easy to wrap ourselves in a shining obscurity they could not penetrate. And when the power passed from me to Dara, it was as easy for her to wield as it had been for me. But the facility with which I could use it, the ecstasy as it exploded in me, only made our separation all the more frustrating, all the more agonizing.

But even as the crystal wind was burning in me, I was sinking into the rotting darkness that had once been my father. The power that had been his in life was leaving him, a dark sluggish tide flowing from him to us and enabling us to tap the luminous energies of the living earth, but he and his power were one, and as his strengths became ours we were trapped with him in his dead unresponding flesh.

He could feel himself rotting and disintegrating, feel parts of himself slipping away no matter how hard he tried to hold on to them, new things springing to life within him, dark cancerous growths feeding off the man he had once been. A terrible emptiness was opening within him, a void that could only be filled with stolen life, stolen blood.

He remembered all those he loved—Saraparajni, his Naga wife, his brothers Peter and Stephen, his children Michael, Dara and even myself—with a strange cold petrified love, but while what little remained of his former self still hoped for our deliverance, that hope was now the channel through which his new hungers flowed, so that it was we above all others whom he desired to drink and empty, we from whose bodies and beings he needed to gouge empty replicas of himself, hollow vessels to contain the void within.

And at the center of that void, Satan, around whom the vampires danced a beautiful, terrible dance that moved in my father with ever-increasing strength as Satan molded and pruned and shaped him. A dance my father could no longer fight, that was claiming him for its own and would soon bring him life and blood and love—

As he was flooding into us, a river of hungry shadows, we were making clumsy violent love, feeling the power building in us, coming closer, ever closer, to the fusion we were unable to achieve.

And then there was a sudden twisting, a wrenching and a falling, and I was no longer in control. I felt, I participated in my body's actions, but they were animated by another's will.

My brother's will.

Dara knew the change that came over me for what it was

and tried to escape, struggling in silence so as not to attract the vampires still searching the woods around us. Michael held her down and thrust my cock which was his cock—a blunt fist gripping a heavy wooden stake a knife-edged shard of broken glass into her again and again. And though I hated him and fought him and would have killed him if I could, yet he was almost me, was the me I had always rejected and refused and thrust from me, and sometimes I found that I was the one grinding myself into Dara, I was the one glorying in her pain and sharing in my brother's laughter. And then Michael had spanned the interface between us, encompassed us both, so that it was me, helpless, being raped by my brother in Dara's and my interlocked bodies.

And all the time he was bleeding us of the power we generated, taking it for himself.

And then I had pulled myself out of Dara, had turned her over and pulled her to her knees, was gripping her throat tight in my right hand while I alternated strokes between her ass and vagina. Her sphincter muscles were tight and tensed, and she cried out with pain each time I thrust myself deep into her ass, yet the strokes in between had become smooth, desperately gentle, futile attempts at transforming what was being done to us, what I was being allowed to do, into lovemaking. And all the power in our love and pain was being drained from us by my brother.

Finally Michael took complete control, pushed me aside to watch from the tannic-acid smell of the oak leaves, to watch and see and know at last what it truly meant to be a Bathory and a dhampire.

Then Dara and I were united again but Michael was reaching through us, through our pain and despair into the fetid darkness that had once been our father. He took Father's burgeoning hungers and needs and passions for his own, mastered them and broke them to his human will, so that only through him could Father feed the void opening within him, so that Father could do nothing but what Michael willed him to do. It was cold, brutal, abstract as some sort of chesslike game played with surgical knives in the body of a patient not expected to survive.

Triumphant and tried, Michael began to withdraw from our minds, was suddenly gone. I lay on Dara, exhausted, my softening cock retreating on its own from between her buttocks. We were both too drained to move. Dara was crying softly.

Uncle Stephen stepped out of the forest shadows, holding two flaming mummified hands in front of him like twin torches. He stuck them upright in the damp ground and traced a circle around us with his finger. The circle glowed a sullen red. I tried to get to my feet and stop him, but I was paralyzed, no longer even able to follow his movements with my eyes.

He squatted down in front of the flaming hands and sprinkled something from a vial of shiny black glass onto the hand on the right. The flames crackled and sputtered. He turned to face us. I felt my cock begin to stiffen.

"Dried semen from a hanged man's final ejaculation," he told us, genial and smiling as a furniture salesman approving your taste in upholstery.

"I'm sorry to do this to you," he said with what sounded like genuine regret, and I remembered Dara had said he was our ally, "but I am fighting for all our lives. When your brother reawakens he will regain control of Dara and the power I gain from you now will be your only hope. I still need Michael's protection—Gregory would kill me if he could and my time has not yet come—but with your help we will soon be free of Michael. And since you will not grant it to me freely, I must compel you."

While talking he'd been taking off his clothes, so that he now stood naked before us, skeletally thin, his skin shining a pale silver. He took a human finger bone from the pocket of his neatly folded wool trousers and dipped it in green liquid from a second vial, then carefully traced complex patterns on our foreheads.

He poured the remnants of the vial's contents on the other

flaming hand and withdrew, circling around behind us. I could hear his heavy, excited breathing as we found ourselves repeating everything we had done and felt before. There was no third presence in our minds but we were helpless to alter a single action, a single emotion. I hated and fought against a Michael who was no longer there, felt him bleeding us of the power that was building up and up in us, filling us without being taken from us.

I was moving in the same violent rhythms that my brother had forced on me when he had taken control of Father, Dara was crying out again with the pain of her abused sphincter muscles, when I felt Stephen's hands on me, a sudden tearing pain in my own ass as he thrust himself into me, joined in our agonized rhythm and took the power we had generated for his own, then directed it back through us against my father who, already defeated, was unable to resist him.

Stephen pulled himself out of me. I lay sprawled once more atop Dara, so exhausted I was unable to see the forest glowing in front of my eyes.

"Sorry again," I heard Stephen's cheerful voice say as I drifted slowly down into unconsciousness, "but I can't afford to let Michael learn about this. You'll have to forget about my part in this business for the moment."

He reached out to me through the channels connecting me to Father, and then I felt myself reaching back out to him, unable to stop myself from cloaking him in unnoticeability until there was only the veil, the knowledge that something had been taken from me, and then that too faded and was gone.

There was a hissing sound and I was coughing on thick, rancid smoke. I lost consciousness.

When I awakened Dara was gone. My aunt Judith, not middle-aged as she'd been when she'd killed herself but young and beautiful, with great pale eyes and long dark hair, was kneeling over me, her lips pressed to my throat. I could feel the terrible suction as she drained me of blood, was glad somehow, in a childlike way, to see her again after so many years. I tried to reach out and take her hand but didn't have the strength.

I slept.

Chapter Eighteen

My father's shadow tides lapped weakly at my mind, cold like the ground beneath me. My heart was beating, I could feel myself breathing, but I could see nothing, hear nothing, smell nothing, and my body would not obey me.

I remembered Aunt Judith leaning over me, her eyes dead sapphires, the way she'd held my hand so tenderly in hers as she fed.

I tried to touch my hand to my neck, explore the place where she'd bitten me, but my arm was too heavy and I couldn't move it.

Strength was flowing back into me from my father, but too little, too slowly. I tried to climb the dark tide to him and take what I needed, but I couldn't get to him, couldn't force my way through the spongy darknesses separating us. I would have to wait, as I had had to wait at Carlsbad.

I tried to reach through the darkness to Dara, found only emptiness where she should have been.

Aunt Judith's eyes so cold, so empty. So hungry, where they had once been loving. And they were going to do that to Dara, make us both like that. I hadn't been strong enough to protect us, too stupid to suspect the Communion wafer Cousin Charles had put in my mouth—

No. I had *participated* in what Michael had done to Dara, could not have been used as I had been used had I not been as much a dhampire as Michael, had I not had within me the potential to become what he was.

What if the only way to defeat him was to fight fire with fire, make myself over in his image and become everything that I had long ago, without knowing what decision I was making, refused to become?

But there was still the Naga, the tight spiral clasping my left forearm. Dara had said to follow the Naga to her.

My vision was beginning to return: I could just make out a faint silvery glow, like a cloud of afterimages. And I was beginning to smell the oak leaves again, hear the branches overhead moving in the wind.

I tried to move my hand again, managed to inch it to my throat. The skin around my jugular was bruised but unbroken.

I groped for my pants, jerked them closer. The metal box was still in my pocket. I had to find a safe place, lie down with my head to the north and rub the ointment on my forehead, then follow the Naga to Dara.

A safe place. My truck? No, the baby cobra made it too dangerous. Where, then?

The silver glow was getting steadily brighter.

Maybe I was asking the wrong question. What could I do to make someplace safe?

I thought about Cousin Charles's priestly paraphernalia—his holy water, crucifixes, whatever I could find—but I couldn't trust them after the Communion wafer. He might not even be a real priest.

Stephen would know what to do, but I couldn't trust him, not after what I'd overheard in the library, not knowing that he'd been the one who'd set Dara and me up to be violated by Michael. Peter was too terrified of everyone—even me—to be trusted. And my Naga grandparents had done nothing to help us. Perhaps I had to follow Dara's instructions before they could do anything.

The woods around me were coming into focus. I tried to sit up, was suddenly very sick. I would have to wait a little longer.

I had to hope that garlic and wild roses would be enough to protect me until dawn. My bedroom had a door that could be bolted from the inside; it was as likely—or as unlikely—to be safe as any other room in the house.

I levered myself up to a sitting position, managed to maintain it despite the vertigo. The moon had set but I could see the forest all around me, the trees like silver-spiderwebbed volcanic glass, the forest floor a dark lake lit from beneath by a trapped moon. And in the distance, but closer, clearer somehow than the forest separating me from it, the house blazed bright as burning metal.

I got my clothes on, half crawled, half staggered up the hill to the house, stopping only long enough to rip some bright-burning branches off a wild rose bush on the way.

The house was deserted. Everyone was gone or asleep. I got what I needed from the kitchen and workroom, then made my way slowly up the stairs to my room.

I shot the bolt on the door, nailed a cross of wild rose and a clove of garlic to the solid oak. I hung a second cross and another clove of garlic on the window, rubbed garlic around the crack between the door and door frame, then did the same for the one between the window and window frame. I strung all but one of the remaining cloves on a piece of twine that I tied tight around my neck, then ate the final clove.

The bed was a massive four-poster, but I finally got it shifted around so I could lie with my head to the north. I put the two carving knives I'd taken on a chair by the bed where I hoped I could grab them in time if I needed them, then lay down and rubbed some of the ointment from the metal box onto my skin. It felt cool on my temples but warm in the center of my forehead.

Within minutes my dizziness and nausea were gone and my sense of urgency had given way to a relaxed alertness. I began to feel a sort of not-unpleasant electrical vibration in my body accompanied by a hissing sound. The vibrations spread to my body, began moving up and down it. My body felt increasingly rigid but the rigidity was comforting, even soothing, as though my previous suppleness had been maintained only through some tremendous unconscious effort. The vibrations gradually increased in frequency.

After what might have been another ten minutes they died away. I lay quietly a while longer, waiting for whatever was going to happen next, then sat up. As I did I felt something give and then break, like the membrane in the cave, and twisted back to see what it was.

And found myself staring into my own face. I was still lying there, mouth slightly open, my eyes closed as if in sleep.

I reached back to touch the sleeping face with some half-formed idea of finding out if it was real—

Only I no longer had the hand I was trying to use. My left arm terminated above the wrist in the nine flaring necks of a Naga.

The Naga was a cool, luminous green, like liquefied jade. Its nine heads were more like those of sculptured Chinese dragons than like those of actual snakes, with high, almost bulging foreheads, eyes like disks of burning crystal, and flaring nostrils over long sinuous mouths. It regarded me a moment out of its eighteen eyes, then twisted away and wove itself forward into the air, pulling me the rest of the way out of my body. Except that it didn't feel as though I was being pulled along; it was more as though I was using the Naga like the hand it had replaced to swim through the air, the way you do in dreams.

As soon as I was completely out of my body my sense of vision changed. The silver fires and phosphorescences my powersight had revealed were gone, as was the darkness underlying them. The Naga was still its luminous green, but everything else, even my sleeping self, was bathed in a sourceless radiance that showed things with an impossible neutral precision, as though I were moving through an infinitely detailed three-dimensional drawing.

I had only an instant to stare down at my body, the bracelet still clasping its forearm, and then the Naga was pulling me smoothly through the air. There was a barely perceptible sense of resistance as we passed through the solid oak door and then we were gliding down the hall toward the staircase, flying at what would have been shoulder height had I not been streaming along behind the Naga like some immaterial pennant.

At the bottom of the stairs the Naga twisted left through a wall into the manuscript room, then through the closed door in its far wall and into my father's Oriental room.

The statue of Shiva burned with close-cropped green and white fires. We flew in tight circles around it, circumnavigating it eighty-four times before plunging through the walls into the library.

A black sun burned in the fireplace, leeching the radiance from the neutral air and filling the room with flickering shadow. We dived into the flames and for an instant I was lost in endless darkness, a sea of thirsty shadows, and then we were plunging through the rear wall of the fireplace and gliding down a hidden stairway, following its meanders deeper and deeper into the earth as it twisted and curved, doubling back on itself without apparent logic. Torches burned with colorless flames in brackets on either side. At intervals skulls with burning shadows in their eye sockets stared from niches.

At last the stairs debouched onto a tiny landing high on the curve of a huge hemispherical cavern. A thick pillar of red-flickering darkness, like a column of burning blood, leapt from the black waters of the small lake in the center of the cavern floor to the vault's apex; four slender columns of black flame rose to the roof from dark pools ringing the central lake. The cavern was thick with drifting red and black shadows.

We followed the steps spiraling down to the floor. Below us I could see a forest of stunted pines clustered around the base of the stairs. A river divided it from the rest of the cavern. As we got lower I could see two concentric circles of dark objects surrounding the central lake.

There was a photographic negative of a man descending the stairs ahead of us. We glided up to him, slowed, floated just behind him. I could hear his hard-soled shoes on the stone steps.

It was my brother Michael.

He turned right at the bottom of the stairs, following a path that took him through the woods to a clearing where a stone altar stood surrounded by stone tables bearing all sorts of Catholic paraphernalia: holy water, vestments, sacramental wine, Communion wafers, crosses, and crucifixes. All the weapons that were supposed to protect faithful Christians against Satan and his creatures.

Michael studied the assortment a moment, then took a single Communion wafer and sealed it in a plastic sandwich bag, put the bag in his pocket and proceeded on.

A stone bridge spanned the river. The cave floor on the other side was a tangled mass of ground-hugging black plants, fleshy bulbous shadows, creepers and fungi, all glistening with moisture. Some of the creepers sported flowers, dark drooping flaccid blooms. No plant grew more than two feet from the ground and there were no woody plants or briars.

The path cut through the growth. Beside it, perhaps a hundred yards beyond the bridge, its base concealed by a thick mass of flowering creepers, stood a great statue of Satan as a satyrlike man-goat clutching the traditional pitchfork in his right hand. The statue burned with smoldering red and black flames.

On the other side of the path, where it must have faced Satan, was the shattered ruin of what had been a statue of Shiva. Though most of the chest was gone and the right arm was missing, the left hand still gripped its trident. The three-eyed head lay on a pile of rubble at the statue's feet. Body, head and broken stone all burned with green and white fires.

In front of the statue of Satan lay my father's open coffin. Its exterior was coated with glossy resin, as though to waterproof it, and a small squarish electrical device with a large two-pole switch protruding from it had been attached to the right side.

And next to him, in an identical coffin, lay Alexandra, her skin smooth and uncorrupted as Aunt Judith's had been. I felt no surprise at seeing her there, only a sense of completion as the final facts about the life I had tried to build for myself fell into place.

This had to have been where they had taken Dara, where she'd been growing up while I read about Vlad the Impaler's tactical genius in the house above.

I could see her there suddenly, the picture so vivid it was more a vision or an impossible memory than anything I could have imagined, see the frightened, uncomprehending little girl whose loving grandparents had taken her from a sunlit world and abandoned her here in the burning darkness, clutching my father's hand as all around her the vampires crowd in, as close as my father's power lets them approach, hungering for her.

And inside that circle, standing next to a sixteen-year-old Michael, Alexandra, her provocative awareness of her own sexuality already as pronounced as it had been later when I had met her. She steps forward, grabs Dara's chin and forces her to stare up into eyes as cold and rapacious as those of any of the vampires surrounding them.

My loving wife. Who would soon be returning from the dead, cold and soulless and seductive as Aunt Judith had become.

Michael touched Father lightly on the forehead with one black finger and continued on.

Closed coffins had been arranged in two concentric circles around the central pool. The resin with which they were coated seemed to drink the red-burning shadows. Every coffin had one of the electrical devices attached.

Michael walked around the outer circle until he came to a gap in the arrangement. Leaving the path—I could hear the black vegetation squelching under his feet, sickeningly loud—he walked up to the last coffin on the right-hand side of the gap and threw back its lid. The interior was as glossy with resin as the outside. Michael took the Communion wafer out of his pocket and placed it, still sealed in its plastic sandwich bag, on the floor of the coffin. Then he sat down to wait, a satisfied smile on his face.

Vampires began to appear, men and women with Bathory faces returning to shut themselves into their coffins for the day. Some of them came walking up the path or across the black vegetation, others dropped from above as huge bats or swirling mists and assumed human form after alighting. They came in perfect silence, without communicating among themselves or with Michael before they closed themselves into their coffins.

A dirty gray bat with a three-foot wingspread landed in front of Michael. It shifted and changed, became a woman in white standing in a half crouch. She straightened and I could see she was my aunt Judith, her face puffy and swollen, without trace of the stark beauty that had been hers earlier in the night.

"Did you feed well tonight?" Michael asked.

"Well enough," she said, dismissing him. She took a step toward her coffin, saw the holy wafer in its plastic bag, spun with inhuman speed back to face Michael.

"You know why," Michael said. "Not while I still need him."

"Then keep him. But let me return to my coffin. I can feel the dawn."

"No. You disobeyed me."

She took three quick steps toward him, but he held up an empty hand and she jerked to a halt.

"I have the power of three dhampires in me now," he said. "You cannot hope to defy me."

"You'd kill me, one of your own, your destiny?"

"*I* determine our destiny, not you, Aunt," he said. "And I no longer need you."

She stared at him a moment, her swollen face expressionless, then said, "Let me return to my coffin and sleep. Let me be dancing with Satan in my dreams when I die. You owe that at least to the blood we share."

Michael was silent a moment, then nodded. "Very well." He lifted the Communion wafer out of the coffin and put it back in his pocket. Aunt Judith lay down in her coffin and he pulled the lid shut over her.

Michael waited a few moments longer, then threw the

switch attached to the coffin and retreated a few yards. The coffin exploded into white-hot flame. In less than a minute all that remained was a small pile of ashes and slag.

When the last sparks had died away and the vegetation had stopped smoldering, Michael turned his back on the coffins and took a path leading away from the river toward one of the columns of black flame.

We floated after him, followed him to Dara.

A circle within a five-pointed star had been cut into the bare rock, and at the center of the circle Dara lay naked and unconscious. She was on her back, her head to her side, as if asleep. Her skin was smooth and unbruised and I could hear her breathing, slowly but regularly. At each of the circle's five points a hand of glory stood upright. Four of the hands were lit and flaming: the hand I had seen at Carlsbad, each eyeball-tipped finger burning a different color; a black hand clutching a thick black candle that burned with a smoky blue flame; a six-fingered hand burning a sulfurous yellow; and the thumbless hand of an infant or a monkey burning a dull orange. The light from the hands flickered over Dara, pooled on her belly and thighs, in the hollow between her breasts.

One hand of glory was unlit. The palm and thumb were normal, but all four of the fingers had been replaced by leathery gray upright cocks.

We were floating just outside the star, perhaps two yards above the stone floor. I tried to swim myself, drag myself down to Dara, but I was anchored to the unmoving Naga like a balloon tacked to a wall.

Michael stripped off his clothes and dived into a pool of water to the right of the pentagram. His back and chest were covered with lines of long-healed scars. He emerged and dried himself carefully, then dived in again. After seven repetitions he rubbed his body with oil from a bottle on a stone table, then dressed himself in a skintight black garment that left his crotch exposed.

He gestured at the pentagram. All the hands of glory except the one with the eyeballs sewn to its fingertips went out.

He gestured again and the hand with the leathery cocks for fingers burst into rose-pink flame.

And suddenly the Naga was pulling me back the way we'd come. I tried to resist it but there was no way to drag my floating feet, nothing to catch at with immaterial hands. My body was sleeping peacefully. The Naga slipped into my left arm like a hand into a glove and the sourceless clarity was gone. I twisted around and lay down, feeling that slightest of resistances as I reentered my body and merged with it again.

I jumped up, grabbed the knives and yanked the bolt on the door. I got the door open but had to hang on to the door frame to keep from falling.

I made my way down the stairs to the library.

Chapter Nineteen

There was a fire in the great fireplace, stacked logs still burning fiercely from the night before. And hanging unsupported within and above the orange-yellow flames, partially obscured by them, was a ball of pale silver powerflame.

Confronted by the two fires, I realized I had no idea how to get through the hidden door that had to lead through the back of the fireplace. The mantelpiece was a smooth heavy slab of unornamented black marble and though three grinning wolves' heads were carved in high relief on either side of the fireplace, I had pushed and pulled and twisted them often enough as a child to be sure that nothing I could do to them would produce any obvious result.

But maybe the only way to open the door was from within the fireplace itself. In any case, I'd have to get to the door before I could use it, and I couldn't get to it so long as the logs were still burning in front of it.

I tried to drag the heavy iron grate with its load of burning logs out onto the hearth with a pair of brass fire tongs, but I was still too weak. I ended up dousing the fire with buckets of water from the laundry room so I could wrestle the logs out of the grate individually.

When they stopped spitting and hissing and the smoke and steam had cleared, I could see that the ball of powerflame was not the pure lunar silver I had thought but veined with scraggly lines of reddish fire like a bloodshot eyeball. Veins would rise to the surface from somewhere inside the fireball, drift languidly around like stands of bleeding seaweed, then sink back into the interior, only to be replaced by new ones.

There was something purposeful about the way the veins drifted and clumped, as though the configurations they formed reflected an awareness of my presence and movements. I put my hand in the fireplace, moved it slowly closer to the fireball. The veins drifted in toward the point where my hand would have struck the surface.

I pulled my hand away and knelt down to wrestle the still-smoldering logs out onto the hearth, carefully avoiding contact with the fireball. I had to catch my breath after each log and I almost passed out when I finally dragged the grate itself out.

Squirming in under the fireball, I groped through wet ashes in search of a hidden catch, then used my hands to explore as much of the sides and rear wall as I could reach while keeping clear of the fireball, finally crawled back out. I got a tall thin leather-bound book off one of the shelves, pushed it up and down against the rear wall behind the fireball.

Nothing. I wriggled back out again and searched the rest of the room. I ripped up the carpet and checked the floor underneath for loose boards or tiny key holes, pulled the paintings from the walls and the books from their shelves. I checked the mantelpiece for pressure-sensitive areas, the light switches, desk lamps and electric sockets for hidden circuits. I pushed, pulled, prodded, twisted and banged on the wolves' heads in every way I could think of, then crawled back into the fireplace and examined it again, all without finding anything.

I gave up, left the books and paintings heaped on the floor and sat down with the two carving knives in my lap to wait for Michael. But I was so weak from loss of blood and the aftereffects of the drugs they'd given me that despite everything I could do to keep myself awake I kept drifting off.

"David." I started, opened my eyes. The knives were gone. Michael was sitting watching me from another armchair. I could feel the power in him like the sun on my skin; he blazed with silver and his eyes were cold stars, intolerably brilliant.

Wet footprints led from the fireplace to his chair, but there was nothing to tell me how he'd gotten through the fireplace or what he'd done with the knives.

"Where's Dara?" I demanded, trying to summon up the spurious charisma I'd used on the two cops in Provincetown and turn his attention away from the fear I couldn't keep out of my voice. But I was too weak, too sick.

"Below. As you obviously know. Do you want to tell me how you knew she was there?"

I gave him the biggest, fakest Jack Nicholson grin I could manage despite my exhaustion. "I would have thought you'd be able to figure that out for yourself."

He nodded once, tightly, before going on. "The way you've torn the room apart proves that's about all you know. And what you don't know can be very dangerous here. In the bosom of your loving family. So to save us both a lot of pointless problems I'm going to tell you some things you need to know if you want to stay alive and safe."

He paused an instant, waiting for my response. I told him to go ahead.

"First of all, there's no way you or anyone else can force your way down to the caverns. None. Even if you could get past this door and its guardians, you'd find the stairs beyond blocked by other guardians you could never pass.

"But you might succeed in getting yourself killed, and that's the last thing I want to see happen to you. Do you remember your encounter with Judith last night?"

I nodded.

"Because of what she did to you—and because she disobeyed me in doing it—I was forced to kill her this morning. As I could kill you, David. Or Dara. As all your undead ancestors will try to kill you the moment I withdraw my protection from you. But so long as the two of you stay useful to me, I'll keep you safe. I may even allow you to live together with relatively little interference once I'm convinced you've accepted the fact that your lives are mine, and mine alone, to control."

"It's good to see you showing so much family feeling, Mike. But what happens when you no longer need us?"

"I no longer need you *now*, David. Either of you. I have a use for you, which is different. And I'll continue to be able to use you as long as I can make you obey me, but I'll never *need* you again."

"Then why not let Dara go? If we can't hurt you and we can't get away from you—"

"No. Other than the fact that I find it convenient to have Dara right where I've got her, you *could* hurt me, David. You could even kill me: it's the traditional thing for a Bathory in your position to try, and you're not as different from the rest of us as you like to think. What you can't do is hurt me in any way that won't end up being a lot worse for you than it is for me, but until you realize that I'd be a fool to let you think you had a chance to defy me.

"If you try to kill me and fail, you and Dara will be punished—and there, too, the family tradition is long and rich. And if you succeeded in killing me—remember, as a dhampire you can only control the vampires of your parents' generation, and through them the preceding generations. You're helpless against a vampire of your own or succeeding generations. Which means that by killing me you'd be creating a vampire over whom you'd have no control and whose greatest desire would be to add you and Dara to the long list of Bathory vampires."

"What happens if I kill myself, like Aunt Judith? We do have a lot in common."

I'd surprised him. He was silent a moment, thinking. "It's true, you're a lot like her, but it wouldn't do you any more good than it did her. There are ways of dealing with the death of a nonreigning dhampire. Besides, Judith didn't have anyone she wanted to protect, but your first victim would be Dara, not me. Which means that as long as you know I'm keeping her alive, I don't have to be afraid you'll try to get at me by killing yourself."

"Unless what you're doing to her is worse than being a vampire."

"Perhaps—but by the time you're ready to make that decision you'll have learned you're no different from the rest of us, David. You won't hate us any less, but you won't do anything to hurt the family, either."

He paused, waiting to see if I was going to say anything else, then asked, "Do you have any other questions? I don't expect you to trust the information I give you but I'd hate to see you do something damaging to yourself or Dara out of simple ignorance. Or because someone else was misinforming you."

"I don't have any questions at the moment, no, Michael."

"When you do, feel free to ask me."

The librarian found me asleep in the library, where I'd passed out while making a last attempt to find my way through the hidden door. I had him bring me breakfast, then locked myself in my bedroom and went back to sleep.

I was awakened by a loud knocking.

"Who is it?"

"Nicolae, sir.

I looked out the window. It was still a few hours before dusk. Besides, I had Michael's promise of protection, for whatever it was worth.

"Just a second." I unlocked the door, returned to my bed. "Come in."

"Sorry to disturb you, sir, but if you're feeling a bit better now your father's lawyer, a Mr. Abernathy, has been waiting to see you since noon, and since he has to be back in Chicago tonight—"

I was feeling much better but I was still weak. And very, very hungry.

"Send him in," I said. "And as soon as he leaves have supper brought up to me. A sixteen-ounce steak, rare."

Abernathy was a tall, prudent-looking portly man with a rather florid face, a slightly receding chin, and blond hair running to gray. We shook hands and he took a seat, moving his chair up to the bed so we could talk more easily.

"I'm here to discuss your father's will, Mr. Bathory. I've already spoken with the other members of the family. But if you're feeling too sick today I could come back next Monday."

"Thank you, but I don't think that'll be necessary. I've been skimping on food and sleep for a few days and it caught up with me this morning, but I'm better now."

"Good. In that case, Mr. Bathory, here's a copy of your father's will. Would you like to read it yourself before I go over it or would you prefer to have it read to you?"

"Just summarize it, please." I took the heavy manila envelope he'd handed me and put it unopened on the chair. "I'll get in touch with you if I've got any questions."

"Well, the will states that you are to receive the sum of two hundred fifty thousand dollars immediately, plus a lifetime income of four thousand dollars a month and two thousand dollars every year on your birthday. In other words, fifty thousand dollars a year. In addition, you have co-tenancy of this house, which was left to your brother Michael.

"Your uncles, Peter and Stephen Bathory, are to receive five hundred thousand dollars apiece, and there are various minor provisions for members of your father's household staff. Your brother Michael is to get everything not specifically provided for otherwise.

"However, your father also left seven million dollars for the construction and maintenance of a temple to the Hindu god Shiva in downtown Chicago. Upon your death whatever money remains in the trust fund set up for you also goes to the temple, as does the total inheritance of anyone attempting to contest this will in court."

"How did the rest of the family react to the last provision?" I asked.

"I couldn't tell what your uncle Peter's reaction was but both your uncle Stephen and your brother were quite upset.

Nonetheless, as you'll see when you examine the will for yourself, there's nothing either of them can do about it. I drew the will up myself and it's airtight."

"How much was Father's estate worth?"

"The cash and securities amounted to some twenty-one million dollars and the house and grounds are worth at least that, though they've yet to be completely appraised. I have the exact figures for the cash and securities here, if you'd like to look at them."

I said I'd look at them later and thanked him. He rose to go.

When he opened the door, Uncle Stephen was waiting outside holding a silver tray with my steak on it. He looked poised, deferential, like an English character actor playing the perfect waiter.

He greeted Abernathy, waited politely while the lawyer made his ponderous way downstairs, then put the tray on the bedside table and sat down in the chair next to it.

"What do you want, Stephen?"

He took a thick sealed letter out of the breast pocket of his coat, held it out to me.

"I'm here to give you the rest of your inheritance, David. The important part."

Chapter Twenty

I took the envelope from him, opened it.

Dear David,
By the time you read this I will be dead, a suicide, and
you and your sister Dara will be in great danger . . .

I looked up at Stephen, who was watching me with undisguised fascination. Dara had said he was an ally. Not a friend, but an ally. And the ointment he had given me had worked.

"Where did you get this?"

"From your father."

"He gave it to you to give to me, is that what you're saying?"

"Not exactly. He was already dead."

"Ah. So, you found it, read it—"

"And decided it would be more in my interest to give it to you than to destroy it or give it to your brother."

I went back to reading, watching him out of the corner of my eye as I skimmed.

. . . I will not pretend you owe me anything for having been
your father, nor that the hatred you have felt for me for so
many years is in any way unjustified, but I ask you to set
aside your feelings until you have read this letter and veri-
fied the truth of what I have to say with Dara.
For many years you and Dara have been under my pro-
tection, but now that I am gone you will have to learn to
protect yourselves. You are in danger because you are Ba-
thorys. To survive you will have to understand what it
means to be a Bathory. What I tell you here I have learned

for myself and I know it to be true, though it contradicts much that the family has always believed.

The Bathorys have for centuries been a family of vampires and dhampires. Dhampires are the living children and grandchildren of vampires; under certain conditions they can command their undead ancestors. All of my ancestors are now vampires, and so I am now a full dhampire. When I too have become a vampire you will be a full dhampire, as will Michael and Dara.

A vampire is a life-thief, a parasite preying on the living. But he is also a dead man, and nothing can alter that fact: the life he steals can never replace that which he has lost. Yet he is incapable of comprehending this: he thinks that the answer is to steal more, always more life, and it is part of his condition that he can never free himself of this delusion. It is a delusion that the living Bathorys have shared with their undead ancestors since the sixteenth century.

The vampire is no less intelligent than in life, but that intelligence is limited by his total inability to imagine anything beyond his present night's hunger. He is incapable of drawing conclusions from his previous failures, equally incapable of imagining the final consequences of his actions. Since his hunger is insatiable, there is no point at which he can stop himself, and without a living dhampire to restrain him, he will always overreach himself and betray himself.

Vampire and dhampire form one being, a being both living and dead. The life that the vampire takes from his victims goes to the dhampire, for only the living dhampire can truly assimilate the life the vampire has stolen. The vampire has at most a brief taste of that stolen life before it drains from him into the dhampire.

The vampire hates the dhampire, since the dhampire takes from the vampire the life that the vampire has stolen for his own needs. The vampire believes that if he could drain the dhampire of life and blood, he would regain that which he needs and which is his and his alone. But the dhampire is the vampire's only true extension into the *world of the living. How can the vampire, who so lusts after life, not love that part of his greater self which is truly alive? So the vampire loves as well as hates the dhampire. But the vampire is empty; he has nothing to give; he can only take and his love is no different from his hunger.*

Since it is the dhampire who benefits from the life that the vampire steals, it is in the dhampire's interest that the vampire not be stopped or destroyed. The dhampire can command the vampire, and he uses his power of command to limit the insatiable vampire for their mutual good—and for this too the vampire hates the dhampire.

Though the dhampire knows that the vampire hungers for his life and blood above all else, he also knows that whatever vitality the vampire possesses the vampire is in the process of losing to him, so that in a contest between them the vampire can only win by stealth or surprise. And to destroy the vampire would be to destroy the source of his own powers. So the dhampire is torn between greed and fear, as the vampire he fears had been caught before him, and superior though his strengths are, he has the limitations of his living flesh, while the vampire has the strength of his eternal hunger.

A Bathory who is aware that he is a dhampire knows that someday he will become a vampire, so that what is in the best interests of the vampires he rules is also in his best interests. But seduced by the stolen vitality he derives from his ancestors, he is as incapable as they are of comprehending the insatiable futility of their hunger. If he does realize it, he either resigns himself to it, accepting it as the necessary price of his powers and pleasures, or, perversely, he embraces it.

I looked over at Stephen, studying him closely for a moment as he was studying me, then went back to reading.

Yet in our family—and we are the only surviving vampires and dhampires in the world today, as the result of a process of extermination and intermarriage that has occupied us for hundreds of years—there are two further motives which animate living and dead alike: a sense of destiny and lust for power. For centuries the family has believed that it is its destiny to rule all mankind as, briefly, it once ruled Wallachia. As deluded as the vampires they ruled, often eagerly awaiting the moment they could rejoin their ancestors, the Bathory dhampires have worked to complete the extermination of their rivals as a prelude to their own eventual dominion.

In each generation there is a single dhampire who commands his undead ancestors. I was the reigning dhampire in my generation. To become a reigning dhampire you must first defeat your undead parents in a contest of will. Then, working through them, you must gain dominion over those vampires formerly controlled by your father, for each reigning dhampire becomes a focus for the wills of his ancestors when he dies.

A dhampire can only control those vampires in his parents' and preceding generations; he has no power over a vampire of his own generation. But there is a period of forty days between a vampire's death and his resurrection as a vampire, and this period can be prolonged indefinitely. For years after Judith's suicide I kept her in this state, but Michael has released her, and though I can protect myself from any physical attack, yet through her the massed wills of my ancestors are driving me to suicide.

They are driving me to suicide not only because of their hatred for me as a dhampire, but because I have become their enemy. I have been using my knowledge and authority over them to destroy them. With your help I can still defeat them.

But if you reject my aid, you will be the one defeated and destroyed. Because you will be fighting not only your family but the power behind that family, and it is from Satan that the vampire derives the strength with which he seeks to satisfy his hunger.

But I am no longer the willing and devoted servant of Satan that I once was. I have pledged myself to Shiva and His consort Kali—or rather, to the reality that lies behind Them.

Satan and His other half, His puppet Trinity, are only one possible manifestation of the Godhead and an incomplete, fragmented manifestation in which Christ and the Christian Heaven exist only as bait, as lures that Satan uses to trap men. It is vital that you understand that all gods are creations of the human mind, forms imposed on . . .

I looked at Stephen again. He gave me a wide, patently false smile that must have looked almost exactly like the one I'd given Michael.

"Why are you showing me this?"

"What if I told you that I too have found true fulfillment in—"

"Bullshit."

"True. As, parenthetically, is much of what Gregory says in the letter. Let us just say that it is in my interest to have you ranged with me against your brother, and for you to be useful you need to know certain facts. All I care about is that you realize that, from your point of view, I am the lesser, and Michael the greater, of two evils. I wouldn't have had much chance to win your wholehearted allegiance no matter how I presented myself; this way at least you know I'm being relatively honest with you. And you *do* need the information to protect yourself. As your brother said, it wouldn't do for you to get yourself killed unnecessarily out of ignorance."

"You were listening."

"I'm always listening, David. In this house someone is always listening."

"Does that mean Michael is listening to us now?"

"Of course. But what he's hearing is not exactly what we're saying."

I went back to reading.

. . . the reality of the Godhead, but Satanism/Christianity is a particularly flawed and unbalanced creation, unable to encompass the reality of the world in the way that the worship of Shiva, who is both creator and destroyer, makes possible. The vampire is the ultimate manifestation of Satanism/Christianity.

Only by making a pact with Satan does a vampire gain the powers with which to try to satisfy the hunger for life and blood opened in him by the combined wills of the already existent vampires during the forty days of his transformation. Though I have as yet made no pact with Satan, I know that during those forty days I will lose whatever strength I have to resist Him. Once I submit to him I will become your worst enemy.

You and Dara could, perhaps, protect yourselves against me for what remains of your lifetimes. It is fairly easy to keep vampires away: garlic and wild roses of the type that grow here will do, as will holy water, crucifixes, and any number of other religious objects that it has pleased Satan to make efficacious. It is somewhat harder to resist vampires when they have the help of human agents such as Michael and Stephen, harder still when they have the help of such persons as your late wife, who was your brother's lover long before she was yours—

And that was so perfectly like him to just drop that in like that, proof that he was still the man I had hated all my life despite his deathbed conversion.

—but it is nonetheless conceivable that you and Dara could preserve yourselves from me while you live.

And it is not necessarily true that as a dhampire you, David, will become a vampire when you die. Certain conditions, such as death by suicide, a prior pact with Satan, or having been the victim of a vampire, must first be fulfilled. But the conditions of Dara's birth mean that so long as there are vampires to infect her with their hunger, there is no way she can escape becoming a vampire.

Your mother, Saraparajni, was a Naga, one of a race of serpent people who live in an underground realm where they worship Shiva in the form of Shesha, Lord of Serpents. It was from your mother that I finally learned to free myself from my hereditary delusions.

But when Saraparajni left the Naga realm she became mortal. Soon after you were born she contracted a form of plague from the rats that live in the caverns beneath this house. When I realized her sickness would kill her, I arranged for her to die in such a way as to ensure her rebirth as a vampire.

Vampires, like gods, are creations of the human imagination, and the laws that govern them were determined by the traditions and beliefs of the tiny principalities of what are now Hungary and Romania, in which vampirism first appeared. Due in part to the hatred of foreigners that their people felt even before they found themselves the West's shield against the invading Turks, a vampire confined to his coffin for seven years without ever tasting blood will regain his humanity for five years if he can emerge from his coffin onto the soil of a different country in which a different language is spoken.

After Saraparajni's transformation was complete and she had emerged from her coffin as a vampire, she allowed me to seal her back into her coffin for the requisite seven years. She accepted her confinement without protest, without having made any attempt to satisfy her hunger for life and blood: though the fact that she was a Naga did not prevent her from becoming a vampire, it gave her the strength to resist her vampire's hungers in a way that would have been impossible for a human.

During Saraparajni's five years of renewed human life, Dara was conceived and born. Then Saraparajni returned to the Naga realm and so escaped the death that would

*have been inevitable at the end of her five years of renewed
life had she been human, though at the cost of eternal exile
from all human realms—*

The cobra-headed queen on the golden throne. "My
mother's still alive?" I asked Stephen.
"So he claims. All we know is that she disappeared."

*But because Saraparajni had been a vampire before
Dara was born, Dara will become a vampire when she
dies. That is, she will become a vampire if there are other
vampires in the world to infect her with their hunger.*

*If there were no vampires to force the transformation on
her she would be safe, but it would be fatal to try to save her
by killing the vampires who threaten her. A vampire whose
body has been destroyed by fire or who has had a stake
driven through his heart is neither dead nor free, but only
forced to reincarnate in a new body. By destroying the bodies of your undead ancestors you would not save Dara, but
only succeed in thrusting your enemies beyond your reach
and hiding them where you could never find them to defeat
them. While the reincarnated vampires' new bodies lived
they would be plague vectors, spreading disease and pesti-
lence; when they died, they would again become vampires.*

*Vampires can neither be killed nor destroyed, but they
can be transformed so they are no longer vampires. If you
can make your undead ancestors understand that they
have been duped by Satan, that the pact they have made
with Him in which He promised to satisfy their hungers in
return for their submission is void because their hungers are
incapable of satisfaction, then they can be freed from their
condition. And once they have been freed, you and Dara
will be free as well.*

*The first thing you must do is to perform a certain act of
sex magic with Dara that will give you control over me and
through me over the rest of your ancestors. The rite is neces-*

sary because Michael, not you, was my designated heir, and you must wrest his dominion from him.

For four days before the rite you must abstain from all contact with each other. You must neither see, hear, nor touch each other. During this time you must wear only new clothing, either entirely black or entirely white, and which you must change completely every day. You must bathe seven times a day in water to which an ounce of salt has been added. On the fourth day you must abstain from all food; on the day of the rite you must abstain from both food and water.

The day before the rite take a cord eighteen feet in length and soaked in a mixture of two parts potassium perchlorate, one part bone charcoal, and two parts oil of garlic and lay it on the ground in as nearly perfect a circle as you can obtain with a single attempt, starting in the east and continuing around clockwise. Then tie the ends of the cord together.

On the morning of the rite you should both rise before dawn and bathe in fresh water, then put on fresh clothing. You, David, should approach the circle from the west; Dara should approach it from the east. You must not speak to each other. When you reach the circle remove your clothes and stand facing each other.

As the first rays of the sun touch the circle you must ignite it and step inside it before the fire dies. When the cord has stopped smoking you should begin having sex, lying face to face with your heads to the north.

As the power builds in you you will begin to sense me in my coffin. When you become aware of my thoughts, reach out and use the power to create a sort of vacuum in yourself into which I will be drawn. You will feel what I feel; my urges and cravings will be as much yours as mine. I cannot tell you how to master them; for each of us it is a different process. But once you do, you will have obtained dominion over me and thus over all the Bathory vampires.

Having gained mastery of me, seal me in my coffin for the seven-year period. The coffin must be placed in a silver box filled with garlic and wild roses and hidden in a place where there is neither too much power nor any danger of my discovery by the ignorant.

I have prepared everything; you will be able to force all the information from me when you master me. But I will fight you with all my strength; I am no Naga to willingly accept such a fate. I will try to summon our ancestors against you whenever you relax your control over me or become distracted, and you will have to overcome me again and again. Your brother will try to steal mastery of me from you and use me against you; you must prevent him from doing so.

As soon as my coffin is safely sealed in its silver box, there is a further rite that must be performed. The preparations and initial stages of this second rite are the same as those of the first, but as soon as you find yourself becoming aware of my thoughts you must visualize me collapsing on myself until I am a small white ball clinging to the wall of Dara's womb. The ball will wait quiescent until nine months before I am to be freed from my coffin, then begin to develop into a child—

I had to put the letter down for an instant, too angry to go on. After everything he'd done, all the ways he'd claimed he had changed, it all still boiled down to him trying to use us, for his own purposes.

Stephen was grinning at me from his chair.

The child will be born at the same instant that I am re-born into the world of men. We will share one mind, though not one soul. If I am unable to complete my work before my five-year span is over, the child can carry on for me. Unlike me, he will never have been defiled by direct contract with Satan, yet he will have all my knowledge of such contact. Even if I fail he will succeed.

But to perform the rites in safety, you must be able to protect yourself against the other members of the family. Your brother is a traditional Bathory and your enemy. My brother Peter is not a bad man, but he is weak: he should have been the reigning dhampire of my generation, but he abdicated the position to me. He will be of little use. Stephen is another traditional Bathory. You may be able to turn his hatred of Michael to your own use, but you will never be able to trust him.

Saraparajni cannot leave the Naga realm. Your maternal grandparents are Nagas and share the indifference of Shesha to the fates and desires of individuals: you cannot count on them for aid. You and Dara are half Naga, as is Michael, but I cannot tell you what, if any, value your mixed heritage will be to you.

Beneath this house lies the cavern in which your ancestors sleep by day. The entrance is through the fireplace in the library. A ball of fire is always burning in the fireplace, but there must be a wood fire in the grate as well before entry is possible. On the palm of your left hand inscribe this sigil:

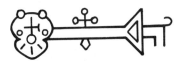

And on the palm of your right hand inscribe this sigil:

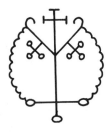

Stand before the fireplace with your left hand open, palm facing the fireplace. Visualize a unicorn and say, "In the name of Amduscias, Duke of Hell, I command you to let me pass." The door to the passageway will open.

Clench your left hand and show the sigil on your right palm to the flames. Visualize a leopard. Say, "Under the protection of Flauros, Duke of Hell, I pass these flames unharmed." You will feel great pain as you pass through the flames but you will not be harmed.

There are skulls set in niches in the walls of the stairway leading down to the caverns. To each you must show the sigil on your right hand and say, "In the name of Flauros, Duke of Hell, I command you to let me pass." Otherwise they will destroy you.

Show this letter to Dara as soon as possible. When she reads it the memories she has forgotten will return, and she will be able to confirm everything I have told you. Then carry out my instructions immediately. Both rites must be performed as soon as possible. I ask you this not for my sake, but for your own, and for the sake of all those whom your actions can free.

Gregory Mihnea Bathory

"Finished?" Stephen asked. I nodded. He stood up, walked over to the door, pivoted theatrically back to face me. "Then I'll be leaving. But before I go I'd like to point out that for all his talk of having reformed, seen the light and so forth, what Gregory *really* wants you and Dara to do is risk both of your lives and immortal souls to save him from his just reward. Not to mention saddling Dara with an unwanted pregnancy and an undoubtedly fairly difficult-to-care-for child, if only because Michael will be doing his best to kill him."

It was uncomfortably close to what I'd been thinking. Did that mean it was true or just that Stephen could read my reaction and was using it for his own purposes?

"That takes care of the three of us. What about you?"

"I'll be doing my best to keep Gregory alive, of course. With Judith gone and Gregory back in the land of the living, but pure as the driven snow, I'll be the reigning Bathory dhampire."

"So why are you trying to discourage me?"

"I'm not. If you go along with Gregory's plans you'll be fulfilling all my childhood dreams. But either way, Gregory is dead now and he's going to be dead at least seven years. And so long as he's dead I need an ally in your generation."

"Against Michael."

"Of course against Michael. And the nice thing about it is, you need me too badly to refuse."

He shut the door softly behind him.

I didn't even know if my father had really written the letter, but Stephen was right. I needed help too badly to refuse it no matter who was offering it.

Chapter Twenty-one

It was just before seven. Soon my ancestors would be rising to greet the night, but I didn't dare wait until they returned to their coffins to get Dara out of the cavern. I had to act now, while there was still a chance Michael thought I was too ignorant to be dangerous.

I drew the two sigils on the palms of my hands with a black ball-point pen. Amduscias's sigil was easy enough, but the best I could do at drawing Flauros's sigil with my left hand was a crude approximation. I could only hope it was good enough.

I went over the formulas again, then folded the letter and put it in my pocket.

Sometime in my attempts to get through the fireplace I'd lost the garlic hanging from my neck, but there were more cloves in the room and I had plenty of twine. Still, a garlic necklace seemed little enough protection against the fifty or more vampires whose coffins ringed the lake and I wasn't sure how effective my brother's promised protection would be if he wasn't there to enforce it.

Stephen I trusted not at all.

There were crucifixes and Communion wafers on the stone tables in the forest at the foot of the stairs. But could I use them effectively? I was no Christian—and I had no proof that what my father had said about the relationship between Christianity and Satanism was anything but more of his special pleading.

There had been something in the preface of my aunt's second book on the Church's persecution of witches. . . . I had it. She'd been talking about the Waldensians or Albigensians, sects against whom the Catholic church had first levied the charges they'd later used against those accused of being witches and sorcerers: the slaughter of infants, mass orgies and the like. But the Waldensians (or Albigensians) had believed that the Church's sacraments were useless unless administered in a state of grace, to which the Church had responded with the dogma that the sacraments were holy in themselves, not by virtue of the men administering them. So if I accepted the Church's authority on the matter, crucifixes and wafers should serve me as well as they'd serve a Christian priest.

In any case, the Communion wafer had worked for Michael, and I would have been surprised if he had been in anything resembling a state of grace.

I put the garlic around my neck, went out to the truck and hid the letter under the rock in the baby cobra's cage, then went back to the library.

The two fires were burning; the librarian was somewhere out of the room, perhaps working in the annex. I stood in front of the fireplace with my right hand clenched to hide its sigil and showed my left palm to the flames.

When I tried to visualize a unicorn I got a vivid picture of a slate-gray beast with white disease splotches, like patches of slime mold, distributed unevenly over its skin. The horn on its forehead had been broken off a few inches from the base.

Speaking slowly and carefully I said, "In the name of Amduscias, Duke of Hell, I command you to let me pass."

I could sense something dry and spiteful, like a malevolent old woman, protesting my command. I repeated the words. A slab of marble behind the flames swung back and away, revealing the passageway beyond.

I clenched the hand with Amduscias's sigil on it and all sense of the spirit's presence vanished. Showing my right palm to the fire, I visualized a leopard.

The leopard's image was somehow wrong, disturbing in a way I could not put a name to. I said, "Under the protection of Flauros, Duke of Hell, I pass these flames unharmed."

The fire in the grate flared up and I had an impression of

childish laughter. I walked slowly forward, feeling the unnatural heat increase with every step. By the time I was standing on the hearth it was almost unbearable, like the heat of a blast furnace.

The letter had said that even though the flames would be painful they would not harm me. But what if the sigil I'd drawn was too imperfect to make the charm work?

There was only one way I could think of to find out. I thrust my right hand, the one with Flauros's sigil on it, into the flames.

It caught fire. My skin shriveled, went black, split open to reveal the muscles, ligaments, nerves burning like gasoline-soaked rags, beginning to fall from the blackening bone even before I could stop the forward motion of my arm.

I yanked it from the flames and the pain stopped. The charred stump was my hand again, whole and unharmed.

Without letting myself think about what I was doing, I showed my open palm to the flames again, then repeated the formula and ran forward.

I slipped on a shifting log and fell sprawling. My flesh ignited, my eyeballs caught fire and burned, were gone, and I knew with a certainty that was worse than the pain that it was hopeless, pointless, to ever try to escape, that I would spend the rest of eternity there, burning. But while I was surrendering to the pain my body's reflex action was bringing me blindly to my feet, carrying me staggering out of the flames through the door at the back of the fireplace. I heard the laughter in my head again as the stone slab swung shut behind me.

I leaned against the cool stone a moment, forced myself on. The steps were slippery, uneven; the air was heavy and hard to breathe, as though it had had to pass through the diseased lungs of some huge animal to get to me. There were long stretches of darkness between the torches burning in their iron holders, but the stone pulsed with power and I could see without difficulty.

At intervals skulls with eye sockets glowing the dull red of an almost extinguished fire were set in niches in the walls: seven on the left, six on the right. When I saw the eye sockets of a skull glowing red ahead of me I'd stop, show the skull the palm of my right hand and visualize the leopard while repeating "In the name of Flauros, Duke of Hell, I command you to let me pass." The fires would die away until after I was past, then flare up again, momentarily bright enough to turn the dark stone of the opposite wall a flickering orange-red.

I had no way of estimating how long it took me to reach the landing overlooking the cavern. The pillar of flame leaping from the central lake was still red, but everything else below was a burning silver, the images from my powersight so overwhelming my normal vision that the forest at the base of the stairs looked like nothing so much as a forest of incandescent aluminum Christmas trees.

There were only two other spots of color in the dazzling landscape. The statue of Satan glowed a dark red; the statue of Shiva, a soft blue.

I turned to continue my descent, found my way blocked by a seventeen-headed golden king cobra with ruby-red eyes. A Naga. Though it was coiled, I estimated its length as between twenty and twenty-five feet.

I held my left arm out to it, showing it the golden Naga on my wrist, but it just hissed at me, its seventeen hoods flaring.

"Let me pass," I told it.

"No," it said. "You may not pass." Its voice was a sibilant whisper, the sounds of the different vowels and consonants coming out of separate mouths yet somehow orchestrated into coherent speech.

"Why?" I asked.

"The task your father set you is impossible and would end in your destruction. Your father could never escape his hunger for personal immortality, and his cravings contaminated his understanding."

"Who are you? Are you one of my grandparents?"

"I speak for them."

"Then will you help me?"

"No. I have done what I can by telling you to return to the surface."

I made a move forward but the cobra's hoods flared. "Be warned," it hissed at me. "I will kill you before I let you pass."

I started to turn away, then turned back and asked, "My ability to make myself unnoticeable. Is that because I'm a dhampire or because I'm half Naga?"

The Naga tasted the air with its forked tongues, remained silent.

I climbed the stairs past the thirteen guardians and came at last to the door at the back of the fireplace. It opened at my command and I was again faced by the roaring flames.

I displayed Flauros's sigil and repeated the formula, then retreated, repeated the formula again, took a running start and leaped through the ball of powerflame onto the burning logs. I had only to step off them onto the hearth. This time there was no malicious laughter as the door swung shut behind me.

The librarian was oiling his books, though it was long after dark. I used my power to direct his attention to make him believe me when I told him I hadn't been there and he hadn't seen me, but I had no way of eradicating his actual memories and no guarantee Michael couldn't direct his attention back to what he'd seen as easily as I'd directed it away.

I found Nicolae in the hallway and asked him who was staying at the house.

"No one, sir. Your brother will be back very late the day after tomorrow, after midnight, I believe he said, and your uncle Stephen will be back the next morning. But you're the only one here at the moment."

"You're sure?"

"Positive, sir."

I searched the house, found no one. If Michael didn't already know that I'd found a way through the fireplace, he'd probably know soon after he got back. My only hope against him was Stephen.

But I wasn't ready to deal with Stephen yet. I was still too ignorant, to easy to lie to. I needed more information.

Perhaps I could get it from Uncle Peter.

I got directions to his forest retreat from Nicolae. It seemed that despite my uncle's reluctance to reveal where he lived, everyone in the house knew how to get there. Nicolae even showed me the best route on a map.

I suppressed Nicolae's awareness of having told me how to go to Peter's, loaded the truck with branches of wild rose from the cemetery and left for Pennsylvania. On the way I stopped at a supermarket and cleaned them out of all the garlic they had.

Chapter Twenty-two

Uncle Peter lived in the Laurel Mountains south of Pittsburgh, in an area that had so far escaped development. The last of the dirt roads Nicolae had indicated ended in a locked metal gate with a big TRESPASSERS WILL BE SHOT sign on it. Peter's property.

I climbed the chain-link fence and followed the road a few hundred yards farther into the woods, to an unlocked garage containing a rusted white station wagon with four flat tires that looked like it hadn't been driven in twenty years. But there was no sign of any path, no matter how overgrown or disguised, leading away from the garage, and after a half hour or so wasted looking for something better I began following deer trails.

I was still following random game trails when night came. The moon was almost full and wherever the moonlight fell it blotted out the earth's feeble phosphorescence. Any hopes I'd had of locating Uncle Peter's cave by its powerlight soon died: these woods were almost completely devoid of power.

The sun was noon-high again before I saw the smoke of his fire. I made myself unnoticeable, descended the hill I was on to his clearing. He was squatting over a fire pit, roasting meat on a spit. He was barefoot and shirtless, wearing a mud-stained pair of overalls. His gray hair and beard were matted with grease. I could see some blue smudges on his chest, part of a faded tattoo, most of which was hidden by his overalls. He looked far older than he was, and when he moved it was with a hesitant jerkiness.

Maintaining my unnoticeability, I crossed the clearing to the cave. His attention never left the piece of meat he was roasting. Inside, the cave had a wood floor on which three dirty red wool blankets had been spread as a bed. An ivory and gold crucifix had been wired to the rock over the blankets. There was a fireplace of cemented natural stone, the chimney leading up through the roof, and, facing it, an ordinary pine dresser with an unlit kerosene lantern on it. The gun rack leaning against one wall contained only three of the four rifles it had been designed to hold. Where the fourth should have been was a silver scourge, the short, thick ornately carved silver handle tapering slightly, the five lashes braided with silver wire.

I took the cartridges out of the rifles and put them in my pocket, then went back outside. Uncle Peter had finished cooking his meat and was sitting on a log gnawing at it. He was facing half away from me; what I could see of his back was completely covered with puckered scar tissue.

I walked up to him and allowed myself to become noticeable. He didn't notice me. I waved my hands in front of his eyes. Still no response.

"Uncle Peter—" I began. He started violently and dropped his meat but he still didn't see me: I could sense his attention swinging through me, past me and back again, never connecting with me. I picked the meat up out of the dirt and pressed it into his hand. He clutched at it.

"Michael? Michael, is that you?" His voice was higher than I'd remembered, thinner.

"It's David," I said. "What happened to you? Why can't you see me?"

"Did Michael send you?"

I considered saying that he had, decided against it. "No. I came on my own. Because I wanted to talk to you. What happened to your eyes?"

"I can't see now. It happens to me— Go away, David. Please go away. If Michael finds out you're here he'll hurt me."

"Why?"

"I can't tell you why."

"I won't tell Michael anything," I said, reaching out for his awareness, turning it away from his memories, his fears, away from everything he could have used to test the truth of what I was telling him, everything that could have made him doubt me. "You can talk to me. I won't do anything to hurt you and I'll keep you safe."

He hunched forward some more, arms tight to his sides, refusing. "No. He'll know you're here. He has things that watch me all the time, just like Gregory did. He's always watching me."

It was possible: I remembered the albino bats outside our window in Carlsbad, the insects crawling over the bodies, in through the dry puckered wounds, of the dead couple on the floor of the cave where I'd found Dara's shoe.

But though Michael might possibly have been able to penetrate my unnoticeability himself, I felt sure I could conceal Peter and myself from anything he could have set here as a spy: Dara and I had had no trouble hiding from the vampires searching for us the night of Father's funeral. But I didn't dare conceal us until I was sure I could suppress Peter's memories of what I'd done.

I concentrated on his awareness again, focusing it on my words, away from his fears, bringing it back to what I was saying as I told him again and again that he could trust me, that he was safe with me, that I wanted to help him and protect him.

He finally began nodding, slowly seemed to relax. I wrapped us both in concealment.

He felt it. "What did you do?" he demanded, tensing.

"I made us both invisible," I said. "To protect you, so we could talk together safely."

He straightened a little. "You can do that, can't you. I'd forgotten—"

"You can't make yourself invisible?" I asked.

"No, not like that, but your mother, I remember, she could . . . just disappear when she wanted to and you wouldn't even realize she was gone."

"Can Michael make himself invisible too?"

It was the wrong question. I had to soothe him again, detach him from his fears and convince him he could trust me all over again, but this time it was easier and he seemed more relaxed than before when I'd finished.

"Can Michael make himself invisible?" I repeated, testing him.

He ignored the question. "What do you want from me, then? Sex?"

I stared at him. He was gaunt and filthy, trembling, an ugly splotchy-skinned turkey-necked old man with a half-gnawed piece of meat in his hand who looked seventy years old.

"What do you mean, sex?"

"That's what they all wanted. Gregory, Stephen, Michael, even Judith one time, when I was already old. They came to me when they needed power."

"I'm not here for sex," I said, amplifying and repeating it until I was sure he believed me. "I'm just here because I need to know more about the family."

"My memory's bad," he said. "It started to go thirty years ago, when Gregory took the family away from me." He was speaking more easily, as if finally beginning to trust me. "Father taught me a lot about the family but it's gone now and Gregory and Stephen never shared their secrets with me."

"Tell me what you can, anyway," I said.

"Only if you promise to do something for me in return. I'll help you if you'll help me."

"What kind of help?" I asked cautiously.

"Nothing evil," he assured me quickly. "Some farmers who live near here just had a baby daughter and I want you to protect her tonight."

"Protect her from what?"

"From me. It's not that—" He shook his head, continued unwillingly, "I don't want to hurt her, but I'm a—a virolac. A werewolf. That's why I'm blind now. I'm always blind the day before I change."

He *was* blind, and he'd been perfectly able to see the day of the funeral, but— "I'll help her if I can," I said. "If you tell me the truth. But I'll need to know more about you to protect her from you. To begin with, what's a virolac?"

"A werewolf, I guess, but . . . Look." He undid the brass buttons at the top of his overalls, pulled the denim away so I could see the sigil tattooed on his chest.

"You see?" he asked. The skin around the tattoo was red, inflamed, as if from some sort of allergic reaction.

"I don't understand," I said. "I can see that that's a sigil, but—explain what it means."

"Marachosias. He's a—a Marquis in Hell. A demon. But when Father summoned him, he came as a wolf with long black wings. You see, I was two years older than Gregory and Father had trained me to replace him as the reigning dhampire when he died but I wanted to be a priest and when Judith—"

"Wait, Uncle Peter," I said. "Start over again, you're going too fast for me. You're a werewolf because your father summoned Marachosias?"

"No, a virolac, because the vampires can take me and make me a vampire when I die even if I don't commit suicide or make a pact with Satan."

"Why?"

"Because Father knew I didn't want to be a vampire. So just before he died he summoned Marachosias and made a pact with him to bind me to the family. Because, you see, I wanted to be a priest, I didn't want to serve Satan, even though I always knew that Satan can do nothing that doesn't serve God's ultimate purposes.

"I was older than Gregory and when Father died I was supposed to use Judith to build up my powers and take control, but Judith refused me and I couldn't force her, so Gregory took her and used her to take the family away from me. It was horrible, I never wanted to be a dhampire, I just wanted to dedicate myself to God's service so I could go to Heaven, but when Gregory took Father away from me it was like dying.

"But then I thought that maybe that was enough, that I was free and I could go away to the seminary and learn to be a priest, but they came and got me one night, Gregory and Stephen, and they made me go to this . . . tattoo parlor; it was late at night and there was no one else there but they seemed to know the man and he . . . put this on my chest with his needles and then they invoked Marachosias and made it so that once a month he comes for me and possesses me and makes me into a wolf. . . ."

"You could get the tattoo removed. They can do that now."

"No, what they do is tattoo over it with a different color ink and that, don't you see, that would mean I'd done it to myself all over again. This way I can't lie to myself and pretend it isn't there; I can see it and fight it. Because that's why it's there; you see? God's testing me. He's giving me a chance to save my soul. That's why He gave me to Gregory and Stephen and Michael, to see if my faith is strong enough to endure the pain and the temptations. I always knew that Gregory and Stephen were using the power they got from me to do evil, but that was the temptation, don't you see, to hate them for that and pretend that the evil wasn't in me too just like it was in them, to not be meek and forgive them for having used me to do evil, but I knew that if I could resist the temptation and the pain, let them use me without hating them or ever honoring or worshipping Satan, then God would free me and save me. . . ."

Moonrise. Uncle Peter knelt naked on the wooden floor, silver chains wrapped loosely around his wrists and ankles, praying.

I stood beside him, veiled from him, gripping the heavy silver handle of the scourge, ready to use it as a club if I needed to defend myself. He'd explained that chains or manacles around his human wrists and ankles were too loose to hold him after his transformation, but that it took him some time to gain control of his altered body after the change, and that during that time I could wrap the chains tight around his new legs and lock them tight.

He jerked and fell forward, began rolling around making snuffling noises. I stayed with him, ready to lock the chains into place as soon as he began his transformation. He got up on his hands and knees, lurched against the wall and snapped at empty air with his stubby yellow teeth, then collapsed, unconscious.

I knelt by him, chains ready, but nothing happened. There was no transformation.

Uncle Peter wasn't a werewolf. He was only insane.

Chapter Twenty-three

It was almost dawn. I'd spent the night watching over Peter, waiting for him to awaken so I could turn him away from all memory of having seen and spoken with me. As soon as I'd realized he wasn't going to turn into a wolf, that he wasn't a werewolf or a virolac and that the sins for which he'd been punishing himself for thirty years had never been committed, were only delusions, I'd tried to pull him out of his trance and back to a reality in which he didn't have to be afraid of killing innocent children. But his awareness was knotted tight to itself in some private region too deep within him for me to reach.

While I waited I tried to piece together what I learned, sifting and rejecting, making connections even where Peter had been unwilling, or unable, to connect things himself.

My father's marriage to my mother had been arranged by his father but had been planned generations before, as part of the same plan that had made the Bathorys the only surviving dhampires and vampires in the world. The Bathorys had survived because they'd taken those dhampires they could into the family through marriage while destroying the others, and they had hoped to extend their dominion in much the same way to the non-Christian world, where there were powers like the Nagas that could oppose them. These powers, Peter explained, were in some way ultimately not real because they owed allegiance to neither Christ nor Satan, but ultimately real or not, they had to be dealt with, and the Bathorys had planned to assimilate those non-Christian powers whose strengths and influences they thought they could turn to their benefit.

So Father had married Saraparajni, to make of her a willing servant of Satan, only to be himself converted to the worship of Shiva. Why the family had expected her to give up her previous beliefs and allegiances was unclear: Peter, with true missionary zeal, seemed to think that simple exposure to Satanism—and, presumably, Christianity as well—should have been enough to make its superiority self-evident.

Michael had been six when Saraparajni died and became a vampire, then allowed my father to seal her into her coffin. Father had been training him as a traditional dhampire, keeping whatever reservations he had had about the family and its destiny to himself while preparing Michael as his successor, and he continued the training during the seven years Saraparajni remained in her coffin. But after her rebirth he began turning farther and farther away from the paths he had trained Michael to follow. Abandoned, but unwilling to give up the destiny for which he'd been prepared, Michael had gone in secret to Stephen to obtain the knowledge that had finally enabled him to force Father to commit suicide.

Stephen was a black magician, a necromancer and an expert in summoning demons whom Peter blamed for making him a werewolf. He was also an accomplished sadist, if I could trust the detailed descriptions Peter gave me of the things he had been forced to submit to whenever Stephen came to him for power.

And Peter himself— While waiting for him to awaken I'd been forced to think about who he was and what the family had made of him, about, finally, the way I'd been planning to use him myself—and that, perhaps, was as important as anything else I'd learned.

Because Peter was too much like me. Like me he'd retreated to the woods, tried to live free from all involvement with, all responsibility for the family, its actions and its victims. With the result that for thirty years the family had been able to use him at its convenience while the responsibility he had tried to refuse but never succeeded in escaping had driven him insane.

And it could not have been coincidence alone that had driven Aunt Judith to her isolated cabin in the Big Sur woods, nor just another coincidence that had put me there in her place after she killed herself. Uncle Peter had had his fantasy life as a werewolf; I had had Alexandra. We'd been stored away until needed, like clothes in mothballs. Or meat in a meat locker.

Even now—I'd been trying to get Dara to some vaguely imagined place of safety, some secluded retreat where we'd have the leisure to study my father's plans for us at length before trying to put them into effect. Like Aunt Judith, studying her grimoires in the Big Sur woods until the time came when the only option left her was suicide.

Peter turned over in his sleep, threw off the blankets I'd put over him. I covered him again, went outside.

Dawn was breaking. I had to leave soon. I'd learned more reasons to be afraid of Stephen and that there were limits to my ability to direct and control other people's attention, but nothing that would have enabled me to deal with him from a position of strength or avoid the need to deal with him at all. He was still the only person who could help me against Michael.

I went back inside. Peter was awake, pulling on his overalls. He smiled when he saw me.

"I didn't kill her! She wasn't there!"

"Tell me about it," I suggested. We walked outside, sat down by the fire pit. "Everything that happened."

"As soon as I began to change, I sensed danger from you and the silver you were carrying. It seemed to take a long time to get control of my body, but it must not have really been very long at all because while I was struggling for control you seemed to be moving in slow motion. Before you could pull the chains tight enough I got enough control to slash you in the arm."

There was a half-proud look on his face. "Go on," I said.

"You dropped the scourge and backed away. I managed to get free of the chains before you got the courage to pick it up again. You threatened me with it and tried to corner me in the cave, but I was too fast for you and I ran around you out into the woods. I ran until I came to my neighbors' farm. They weren't home, but I was filled with bloodlust and I killed two of their sheep. I might have killed more, but their dog tried to stop me. He was bigger than I was and a lot heavier, but he was slow and I tore his throat out.

"As soon as I'd killed him I realized there was a bitch in heat locked up inside the house. I could smell her. I broke in through a window. She was afraid of me but I snarled at her and she let me mount her. Afterward I killed her like I killed the other dog."

Regret and remembered pleasure fought for control of his voice. Regret finally won. "I'll send them some money," he decided. "I'll find out their names somehow."

"You don't know their names?"

"No. The only times I ever see them is when I go there as a wolf. I can't make it that far as a human being."

So they might not even exist. And it was obvious that, hate himself for it as he might, my uncle still lived for these once-a-month nights of fantasy. But I still had to try to tell him the truth. I owed it to him. Not because he'd trusted me—I'd forced that trust on him—but because having forced him to believe that I wouldn't hurt him and wanted to help him, I owed it to him to do what I could to alleviate his pain. Otherwise I was no better than Michael or Stephen.

I didn't expect him to believe me and I was going to have to turn away any memories he might have retained of what I told him, but the information would still be there hidden somewhere in his memory. Perhaps someday he'd be able to face it and make use of it.

"Listen," I said. "Let me tell you what I saw last night.

"First you fell over and shook for a while. Then you got up on your hands and knees and started acting like a wolf. You weren't a wolf, you were just acting like you thought you were a wolf—"

I told him what I'd seen and what I hadn't, that for thirty

years the family had been fostering his delusions to keep him in a position where he wouldn't dare resist the use they made of him. I showed him my arm, reminded him of how he remembered slashing it.

"That's your Naga blood. You heal faster."

I told him he could go back and live among people again, that he could even return to the seminary if he wanted to, and I focused his attention so that he had no choice but to listen to me, hear what I was saying.

Even so, he didn't believe me. I'd known he wouldn't. But at least for the first time in thirty years somebody had told him the truth, and it would be there waiting for him if he ever really wanted or needed it.

He guided me back to the gate and unlocked it. We sat by the road for an hour while I veiled everything that could have been dangerous to either one of us to have him remember, but I told him that he would remember what I'd said if his guilt over the crimes he committed as a wolf ever became unbearable, then left him there and drove back to Illinois.

As soon as I walked in the door Robert told me there was a phone call for me.

"Ah, David." Stephen's voice. "I've just rented a house nearby and I was hoping you could drop by and we could have a little talk."

"I'd like to talk," I said. "But not at your place. Could I meet you at, say, the Howard Johnson's about three miles from here? In the dining room, in about forty-five minutes?"

He was dressed in his usual black and carrying a black attaché case. The fluid way he moved made him look almost as much younger than he was as Peter looked older: he could have passed for a man in his late thirties.

And there was something else I recognized as he made his way across the room. People looked up at him, stared an instant, then looked away, dismissing him. He looked cruel, capable, dangerous, but it was all a little too exaggerated, just barely campy, as if he were mimicking everything, and so the final impression he left was that of an unpleasant poseur, a mere grotesque.

He sat down across from me and ordered coffee.

"What do you want to discuss?" I asked him.

"I've got an offer to make you. But before I do I think you should know that I'm aware that you succeeded in passing the guardians and reaching the landing above the cavern before you turned back."

"What makes you think that?"

"The whole house is bugged. Microphones, cameras, video-tape, all the latest equipment. Installed by Michael at my suggestion."

"Does Michael know yet?"

"Not yet. He won't know until he gets back tonight. At which time, I might add, he will also become aware of your successful attempt at hypnotizing two of his servants and of the fact that you've just returned from a visit to Peter."

He sat smiling, waiting, sipping his coffee, until I said, "You said you had an offer to make me."

"Yes. Because Michael hates me and will be giving me to Gregory as soon as he thinks he's exhausted my usefulness. With you I hope to do better."

"You still haven't told me what you want. Nor what you're offering in return."

"First of all, David, I'm offering to destroy all record of your trip downstairs and of your hypnosis of Nicolae and Thomas. Plus any other records that it becomes necessary to keep from Michael, such as the record of the phone conversation that brought you here. More generally, I'm offering to do every-thing in my power to help you rescue Dara and then make sure you succeed in displacing Michael as the head of the family."

"In return for what?"

"I want you to transfer a share of your power over Gregory to me."

"Transfer it how?"

"Sexually, of course. I thought you knew."

Chapter Twenty-four

Uncle Stephen sat slender and elegant in his tight-fitting black, watching me. Waiting for my response. His eyes alert and ironic, a cool pale green, his dark hair cut close to his head, the hand gripping the white hand of his coffee cup deeply tanned, long-fingered, immaculate. Smiling. A Renaissance fencing master in clerical disguise. He terrified me. I had no exaggerated fear of homosexuality—the early experiments at the academy that had convinced me my interests lay elsewhere had also taught me that homosexuality as such was nothing to be feared—but the thought of having sex with Stephen, of being touched, penetrated, forced to submit to him, threatened me in a way that no physical pain or momentary humiliation could have. Perhaps because of the stories Peter had told of his own pain and degradation, of the murdered children he claimed never to have seen but whose existence he'd known to be an essential part of some of the rites in which he'd been forced to participate. Perhaps because I remembered the way Michael had used me to rape Dara, rape both of us, and because of the way I'd recognized the self I had refused to be in him as he used me.

"I'm interested," I said, keeping my clenched hands under the table where he couldn't see them. "Maybe. But you're going to have to give me a lot more information, and a lot more reason to trust you, before I agree to anything. For example, I've only got your word that these tapes exist."

"That's easy enough to prove. He put the attaché case on the table, flipped open the catches to reveal a small Grundig cassette recorder. "Here, listen . . ."

My voice asking Nicolae how to find Uncle Peter. Stephen turned the machine off.

"Satisfied?"

"That at least some of the house is bugged, yes."

A slight inclination of his head. "You don't have much time before Michael gets back, David. And once he learns what you've done, it'll be too late for me to do anything for you. Besides—I don't suppose Michael has told you that Alexandra is down in the cavern with Gregory?"

"He didn't mention it, no."

"She's not a Bathory. When her forty days are up and she comes out of her coffin she'll come looking for you—vampires always go for their nearest and dearest first."

"Wouldn't that be Michael, then?"

"Michael too, of course," he agreed. "And she'll be completely out of either of your control."

"But not out of yours?"

"No."

I shook my head, managed to smile at him. "If hurrying is so important, then have the records destroyed now, before we discuss your offer. As a guarantee of your good faith, and to prove you really can do what you claim."

He seemed pleased. "And what guarantee are you offering me of your own good faith, David?"

"The fact that I need your help as much as you need mine."

"More than I need your help, David. But, fair enough. If you'll excuse me—" He stood, made his way with stiff, almost military grace between the tight-packed tables, where families of six and eight were bolting all the perch they could eat for the special Wednesday-night price.

I wrapped myself in unnoticeability, followed him to the pay phone in its half-shell.

He dialed an unfamiliar number. I moved in closer, so I was only inches away from the phone. I could feel his breath on my face.

A voice I didn't recognize answered. "Yes?"

"Replace David's tapes."

He hung up. I preceded him back to the table, sat down, let him notice I was there.

The waitress came by and refilled my cup of coffee.

"All right, David," Stephen said when she left again. "You've got your proof of good faith."

"Because you made a phone call?"

"Because you were right there listening to what I said."

"Meaning what?"

"Meaning that I've spent years with all of you—your mother, you and Dara and especially Michael. I've learned how to get around your Naga invisibility."

"What I heard you say was to replace my tapes, not to destroy them."

"Of course I didn't destroy them. They may still come in useful some time."

"If you decide you're better off with Michael than with me."

"Among other possibilities, yes."

"But for the moment you're supposed to be my ally. So tell me more about Michael."

"What do you want to know?"

"Can he make himself invisible?"

"Not like you just did, no. But he . . . fades when he doesn't want you to know what he's doing."

"Can he see me when I'm invisible?"

"I have no idea. But if all Dara had to do was go invisible to escape him, it wouldn't be necessary to rescue her."

"How are you going to do that?"

"I'm not. You are."

"Then what are you offering to do?"

"First of all, show you a way into the cavern that Michael doesn't know about and won't have guarded. Second, I'll make sure he's somewhere else when you go after her. And finally, I'll provide you with the supernatural aid you'll need to get past the back way's guardians and escape with her."

"What do you mean, supernatural aid?"

"A familiar spirit. Which is to say, a low-ranking demon or imp that's taken the form of a small animal, like a witch's black cat or—"

"I know what a familiar is. And that you have to make a pact with Satan to get one."

"Rather, you have to make a pact with any one of a number of demons. But there, you see, is where I come in: I make the pact, pledge whatever needs to be pledged, and you get the benefit of the familiar's services."

"I can't just walk around with a black cat on my shoulder."

"Use your Naga invisibility."

I thought about that for a while.

"I don't have to make any sort of pact, explicit or implicit, with any of the demons you'll be dealing with, including the familiar itself?"

"No. The only explicit or implicit pact you'll be required to make is the one we're working out right now."

"How do I get rid of it?"

"I tell it to leave you."

"What assurance will I have that you'll live up to your part of the agreement?"

"What good would a share in your dominion over Gregory be if you had none?"

"That's not good enough. You know how Michael used Dara and me. What's to prevent you from doing the same thing?"

"Because I couldn't, even if I wanted to, now that Gregory is dead. The struggle for dominion is between the members of your generation. What I'm offering is your only chance to undo what your brother did to you."

"But the familiar will obey you, not me."

"True. But you'll be present at the ceremony in which SUSTUGRIEL grants it to me, and you'll be there when I instruct it to obey you in all things not contrary to our agreement."

"What if something goes wrong while I'm going after Dara?"

"If you fail to follow the familiar's instructions, you could wind up killing yourself in all sorts of unpleasant ways. But you won't have to do anything too difficult."

"What kinds of things is it going to ask me to do, exactly?"

"Turn right instead of left, duck, close your eyes, that sort of thing. Nothing that could jeopardize your immortal soul."

I took a sip of coffee, put the cup down. "Do you know why I stopped at the landing, instead of continuing the rest of the way down to the floor of the cavern?"

He was suddenly very still. "No. Why, David?"

"There was a Naga at the head of the stairs. It wouldn't let me past."

"Ah." His face lost all expression for an instant, as though he'd gone somewhere else to think. "The Naga was able to stop you because you were wearing its token. That thing on your arm. Once you remove it, the Naga will lose all power over you. You'll have to remove it anyway, at least until you and Dara make it back to the surface. The spirits we'll be dealing with have a deadly hatred for Nagas. Michael wouldn't have been able to drive your father to suicide if the spirits Gregory should have been able to call up hadn't been reluctant to obey him."

It was plausible, and Stephen had been the one who'd supplied Dara with the ointment that had enabled me to summon the Naga, but it was too quick, too glib. The Naga on my arm might represent the one chance Dara and I would ever have to break free of Stephen.

"Michael and I are both half Naga. So is Dara."

"It doesn't matter. In dealing with spirits, the symbol is often more important than the reality behind it. That's why removing the armlet will destroy the Naga's power over you."

"What happens when we make it back to the surface?"

"I'll teach you how to take control of Gregory away from Michael, thus fulfilling my half of the bargain."

"And that will involve what? Another rite?"

"Yes, but one involving no demons or other spirits. A way

of focusing and directing your personal power, nothing more."

"And in return you want what?"

"In return I want your participation—yours alone, David, not Dara's—in an act of sex magic that will join my power to yours in such a way that neither of us can command Gregory without the other. So that to command him you'll have to pass through me, and I through you. Like a telephone system where each of us acts as operator for the other but with no other contact between us. That way you'll never be able to use your influence over Gregory to act against me, and I'll be able to share in the power that you, as a member of the generation succeeding ours, have to command him. . . ."

"What, exactly, does this sex magic involve?"

"Ritual sex—which is to say, anal intercourse, with you as the passive partner." Again the avuncular smile, the white teeth behind narrow lips. "Plus a ceremonial mingling of our blood and a certain amount of mutual anger, hatred, fear and physical pain. The last as a result of a scourging, both for purificatory purposes and to obtain the blood we'll need."

"And that's it?"

"Essentially. No murdered babies or sacrificed virgins, no castrations or mutilations or surprise appearances by the Devil. You don't even have to jump up and down on a crucifix and swear to deny Christ forever. Just a lot of formal preparations and ritual acts and words—drawing circles, ritual purification, chanting the praises of God. That sort of thing."

I couldn't trust anything he told me, even when it seemed to confirm what I already knew. Stephen could be telling me just enough of the truth to mislead me about what it really meant. But I couldn't think of anything I could demand of him that would guarantee his good faith or force him to carry out his end of the bargain. I finally decided to go along with him a step at a time: rescue Dara first, then, if she agreed, let him help me take control of father away from Michael, and then see. Maybe Dara would know what to do next, whether to help Stephen, carry out my father's plans, or just try to flee somewhere, use our Naga unnoticeability to slip away from the familiar, hide.

Except that Stephen had already demonstrated he could penetrate my unnoticeability once and Michael was half Naga himself. Except that running away and hiding would be just another repetition of what Uncle Peter and Aunt Judith had done, and probably no more successful.

All I knew was that Michael was my enemy and Dara's enemy, and that Stephen was *his* enemy. I had no one else to turn to, no choice but to go along with Stephen's plans.

As he had known all along.

But perhaps the golden Naga could give me the edge I needed, if the spirits Stephen commanded abhorred it as much as he said.

I still had the ointment that Dara had given me—that *Stephen* had given her—hidden under the baby cobra's cage, and the back of the truck was filled with wild rose bushes. After Stephen showed me the house where I was to meet him the next day, I drove for four hours, parked in a deserted down-state tollway rest area completely devoid of any sort of power, wrapped myself and the van in unnoticeability and rubbed some of the ointment on my temples and forehead.

Once again my tension gave way to a feeling of relaxed alertness. The electrical vibration began in my head, started moving up and down my rigid body. My spine felt as though it were weaving back and forth in slow, heavy curves like low-amplitude sine waves on an oscilloscope.

But soon the sensation died away and when I sat up, trying to duplicate the process that had freed me from my body to follow the Naga the last time, I just found myself sitting up normally.

Maybe you had to be in a place of power. Or else Dara had done something to get the Naga to guide me and the oint-ment had just loosened my ties to my body so the Naga could pull me free.

Perhaps the Nagas had done everything they had any inten-tion of doing for us and had abandoned us to our own devices.

I buried the golden Naga with my father's letter in a field just out of sight of Stephen's house, close enough so I could get to it on foot in a few minutes if I had to. I didn't dare risk returning to the family estate, so I spent the rest of the night driving slowly up and down back roads, trying to think of something else I could try that Stephen wouldn't have been able to predict and plan for.

Unsuccessfully.

Chapter Twenty-five

The house was set back from the road, at the end of a long looping potholed gravel driveway, half hidden by a stand of maples. It was an old two-story wooden farmhouse with yellowing paint peeling from its narrow-boarded sides.

Stephen was waiting for me at the door, wearing a long loose white linen robe and skullcap. The robe and cap should have made him look silly, but the effect was just the opposite: By stripping away the theatrically exaggerated menace of his normal persona, the costume revealed his true grimness. He motioned me to follow him to a room on the second floor.

The room smelled of paint. The ceiling and floor were shiny Chinese red, the walls white. The room contained a straight-backed wooden chair and a table on which a robe and cap like Stephen's lay neatly folded. Next to them was a thick book bound in red leather: Stephen's grimoire, or rather a copy of it, since he alone could use the original. The pages alternated red, black, white; the book lay open to one of the red pages. An open door in the far wall led to a bathroom, also painted a spotless white, with a huge sunken bathtub already filled with warm perfumed water.

Stephen closed and locked the door behind me. I heard the key turn, but tested the door anyway: he would have loved to keep me in a room that I merely thought was locked.

For the next three days and nights I remained alone in the room, studying the grimoire. I neither ate nor drank and abstained as best I could from what the grimoire described as "all sin in thought and deed" while concentrating on my aims: freeing Dara and taking control of the family away from Michael, dealing with Stephen without being deceived, corrupted, enslaved or destroyed.

Much of the material seemed familiar from Aunt Judith's grimoire, but my memory wasn't good enough to tell me how closely the formulas, procedures and diagrams I thought I recognized really corresponded, or whether the operations had been altered or misdescribed to conceal the fact that their ends were other than stated.

I also spent a lot of time getting angry at myself for the way I'd spent my whole life surrounded by the information I needed without paying any attention to it.

Stephen came for me shortly before noon on the fourth day, wearing a robe, cap and slippers of white silk on which a multitude of sigils had been embroidered in red. Around his waist he wore a wide belt of what the grimoire stated to be lionskin and he had a lionskin bag slung over his right shoulder. A white thread was tied to the little finger of his left hand.

A twelve- or thirteen-year-old girl followed him into the room, dressed as I was in white linen, but in place of my cap she had a paper crown encircled by sigils like those on Stephen's robe. It took me a moment to figure out why she looked so familiar and then I realized: except for the fact that her hair was a nondescript brown instead of red, she looked exactly the way Alexandra must have looked at her age. She handed me a fresh linen robe and cap and a pair of white sandals. The clothing smelled of aloes' wood and musk, burnt amber and incense: sweet scents, to help protect me.

Could she be Alexandra's daughter? Alexandra had been three years older than I. . . . Or even—Alexandra and Michael's daughter?

"Now," Stephen said, "repeat after me: 'Through the symbolism of this garment—' "

"Through the symbolism of this garment—" I repeated.

" 'I take on the protection of safety—

" 'In the power of the All-Highest, ANOOR, AMACOR, THEODONIAS, ANITOR.

" 'O, ADONAI, cause that my desire shall be accomplished, by virtue of thy power.' "

If the girl was Michael and Alexandra's daughter, then she was a Bathory dhampire from a generation younger than my own. But why was Stephen showing her to me?

"From here on," Uncle Stephen said in an abruptly conversational voice as I was putting on the robe, "your life will depend on doing exactly what I say and nothing but what I say. Now, follow me."

A narrow strip of white carpet had been laid from the door down the hall and staircase, on through the kitchen and then down a second set of stairs into what must once have been a typical basement recreation room, complete with acoustical tile ceiling, fluorescent lights, knotty pine walls and parquet floor. There were no windows and the fluorescents were unlit: what light there was came from the coals glowing red in two braziers, one in the far right corner, the other in front of the black-draped altar against the far wall.

On the altar were the instruments of Uncle Stephen's art, burning silver in the semidarkness: a sheet of parchment, a quill pen and an inkhorn, small bottles of stone and glass, folded pieces of heavy canvas, batons of blond hazelwood with squiggly characters running their lengths, an asperger and knives ranging from small letter openers to broadswords, some straight-bladed, some sickle-shaped, one with a blade of corroded bronze and another with both blade and handle of polished wood.

Uncle Stephen chanted some words I couldn't make out over one of the stone bottles. He handed it to the girl, who began feeding the powder from it to first one, then the other of the braziers. The braziers began giving off a thick sweet resinous smoke with something astringent to it. The grimoire had specified a mixture of mastic, frankincense, cinquefoil, achates and the dried and powdered brains of a fox.

Was the girl there to show me that I could be replaced if I didn't go along with Stephen's plans for me? Or just to keep me off-balance? Unless there was something more sinister involved: if I let myself get carried away by anger, hatred or fear my emotions could give the demons he was summoning entry to my spirit.

Stephen took the folded pieces of canvas from the altar and laid them out flat on the floor: the pentacles in which we were to stand while the demon was invoked. They were round, each rimmed with a thick red circle with a second circle inside. Between the concentric circles were painted four six-pointed stars embellished with more squiggly characters and the letters A, L and G surrounded by four smaller five-pointed stars. The pentacles all looked identical.

Stephen motioned me into the pentacle to the left of the altar while the girl took her place in the one on the far right, from which she continued to feed the brazier.

As soon as I was inside the inner circle, Stephen knelt and carefully cut the outline of the outer circle into the floor with a small sickle-shaped knife. He walked back to the pentacle in front of the altar and put the knife down in its center.

Taking the asperger from the altar, he carefully sprinkled me and the pentacle in which I was standing. If the water contained the mint, marjoram and rosemary the grimoire specified and if everything had been correctly prepared beforehand, and assuming that the grimoire itself could be trusted, I would be safe as long as I remained calm and inside the pentacle.

Stephen used the sickle-shaped knife to cut a circle around the girl's pentacle, then a second circle around the brazier she had been feeding, connecting them with a straight line, before asperging her in turn.

Carefully setting the asperger and knife down in the center of his pentacle, he turned to the altar and, taking up the lancet, slashed his little finger with the thread tied to it so the blood spurted freely. He caught the blood in an inkhorn, spilling none of it. When the inkhorn was full his finger abruptly ceased bleeding. He dipped the quill into the blood and began writing on the parchment.

The instant the quill touched the parchment the room was

full of shouts and cries that grew louder as he continued drawing, were joined by what might have been bizarrely distorted military marches.

I could see that he was drawing as well as writing, but from where I was standing could make out little beyond the fact that the diamond-shaped main design had words and characters in each corner and that there was a lens-shaped form in the center.

Still following the ritual laid out in the grimoire, he pinned the finished design to the left side of his robe. Taking up two hazelwood batons and a small stone bottle, he stepped into his pentacle and put them down on the cloth beside him, then cut the outline of his circle into the floor. He asperged himself and his circle.

The girl was grinning wildly as she fed more powder to the brazier in the corner, the same crazy grin Alexandra used to get whenever we were about to pass customs or get stopped by the police. Moving so that only the neck of the bottle protruded beyond the circle he'd cut into the wood, Stephen poured its contents into his own brazier. Thick smoke, cloying like rotting meat, poured from it, hid the room. When it thinned I saw Stephen tracing patterns in the air with one of his batons while he chanted Latin Psalms in a high, sweet falsetto.

Finally he held the baton steady while he half sang the invocation to Scrilin, the messenger who would carry his summons to the demon he was invoking: *"Helon-tal-varf-pan-heon - mon - onoreum - slemailh - sergeath - clemialth - Agla - Tetra-grammator-Casolay!"*

The voices and music were gone, replaced by a silent presence. The fluorescent lights flickered on, burning a violet red. Between Stephen and the altar an iron ring five feet across had appeared.

Stephen tossed the first baton into the ring and holding the second baton straight out in front of him chanted: *"Osumry-delmusan - atalsy - lum - lamintho - colehon—madoin - merly-*

// 177

domedo - eploym - ibasil - cisolay - baneil - vermias - slevor - neolma-dorsamot-ilhalva-omorgrangam-beldom-dragin. VENITE, VE-NITE, SUSTUGRIEL!"

Nothing happened. Taking a thick seal of white wax from his sash, Stephen jabbed the pointed end of his baton through it, held it high over the brazier and shouted, "I invoke and command three, O SUSTUGRIEL, by the resplendent and potent names of your Masters Satanicia and Satanachia, and by the Name of their Master Lucifer and by the Great and Unparalleled Name of JEHOVAM SABAOTH, our Lord, to come here to this place instanter. Come, from whichever place in the world thou art and give me that which I desire. Come, then, in visible form and speak to me pleasantly and without deception.

"I have thy Name and thy Seal, SUSTUGRIEL, and I hold them posed on this wand on which are written the Most Holy and Efficacious Names ADONAI, SABAOTH and AMI-ORAM, and this wand I hold over this Fire with which I will destroy thy Name and thy Seal and curse thee to the lowest depths of the Bottomless Pit, to the Circle of Everlasting Burning, unless thou appear to me immediately and in friendship, obedient to my every demand!

"Come, SUSTUGRIEL, through the virtue of the Most Holy and Efficacious Names ADONAI, SABAOTH, AMI-ORAM, come and appear to me in this Circle! Come, I invoke and conjure thee in the name of ADONAI!"

He flicked the baton with the wax seal spitted on its tip through the fire and the room screamed, long and horrible.

A headless angel with black, velvet-tipped golden wings was standing in the iron ring. Blood and lymph dripped from its severed neck to stain its white robe, pool on the floor below.

"What do you want from me, Magician?" The figure's voice was sweet and throaty and seemed to come from where its head should have been.

"I demand a familiar spirit to do my bidding, SUSTU-GRIEL. I bind thee to my services by thy Name and by the

power of the All-Living God, ADONAI, TETRAGRAMMA-
TON, PRIMATON, ANNEXHETON."

"What do you offer me for my service, Stephen Bathory?"
From the bag slung over his shoulder Stephen took out a
small brown puppy that could have been only a few days
from its mother's womb. Its eyes were not yet open and it
whimpered sleepily.

Stephen threw it to SUSTUGRIEL. The demon twisted
around and caught it on its severed neck like a circus seal
catching a ball on its nose. The puppy sank slowly into the red
and yellow wetness. I could still hear it screaming after the
flesh closed over it.

"You may have your spirit." SUSTUGRIEL held out its
right palm. There was a swelling in the smooth ivory of the
palm and something like a segmented gray worm encased in a
flabby pink gelatinous membrane burst forth, inched its way
out of the sheltering flesh. It lay on the demon's white palm
six inches long, glistening, the pink jelly quivering. I could
smell it, like a tiny gangrened limb.

SUSTUGRIEL dropped it to the floor, where it twisted
and curled helplessly within its sack.

"Do I have your leave to depart, Magician?" the demon
asked in its sweet voice.

Stephen made a circle in the air with his baton. "Go in
peace, SUSTUGRIEL, without harm to man or beast. Leave,
now, I adjure you, and be at my disposal whenever I shall call
thee again! May there be peace between thee and me forever.
Amen."

The demon was gone, and with it the iron ring. The parchment pinned to Stephen's robe caught fire and burned without singeing the white silk.

"You can leave the circle, David," Stephen said. "The danger is over."

The girl was already climbing the stairs. "You!" I shouted
after her. "Wait a second!" She stopped and looked back at
me, wide-eyed and innocent as Alexandra when she was
lying.

"Who are you?"

"Lydia." Her voice was a smug teenager's voice, nothing like Alexandra's.

"Your wife's youngest sister," Stephen said. He sounded half dead with fatigue, too exhausted to play his little tricks with his voice, and I knew he was lying. The girl had to be Alexandra's daughter, or maybe her niece, but not her sister. Someone from a generation younger than Alexandra whom Stephen could use to control her when she completed her transformation.

"Stephen?" she asked.

"Go home now, Lydia. You can talk to David some other time." She nodded and continued up the stairs out of the basement.

"Why did you have her here?" I demanded.

"She's my assistant, David."

"And what else?"

"I wanted you to meet her. But don't you have more important things to worry about right now? Such as Dara?"

I hesitated, then walked over to where the demon had been, stooped down to examine the familiar.

The worm inside the quivering jelly looked hard and dry, more like some kind of root than an animal. At each end it had a tiny cruel half-human, half-reptilian face, the features blurred by the membrane and the never-still jelly, but still clear enough for me to see that the thing's heads were caricatured Nagas.

The stench was unbearable. I stood up, backed away. The thing lay there quivering.

"Keep away from it for the moment," Stephen said. "I'll have to bind it to me before you can make use of it."

He stepped forward, stumbled, caught himself, took a deep breath and said loudly, "Spirit! In the Name of SUSTU-GRIEL thy Master and by the power of the Compact he made with me, I demand of thee thy Name!"

An impossibly deep bass rumbling came from the thing, became speech. "I am Monteleur."

"Monteleur, by the power invested in me by SUSTU-GRIEL and by the power of thy Name I bind thee to my service and command thee to obey me at all times and to do no harm to me or mine, either through action or through inaction. I further command thee to cause no harm or unnecessary suffering to David Bathory, he who stands here before thee, or to Dara Bathory, his sister. You are to obey his commands except when they conflict with mine. Do thee bind thyself to honor and obey this compact, Monteleur?"

"I bind myself, Master."

"Pick it up, David," Uncle Stephen said. "It won't hurt you now. Hold it against your belly, just above your navel. Disregard the pain. It will be over in a moment."

"Inside me?"

"Of course. I have one myself, if you'd like to see it." Without waiting for an answer, he pulled open his robe to reveal his belly. The flesh began to roil angrily and then a tiny gray head like Monteleur's burst forth. A trickle of blood ran down Stephen's belly to become a spreading stain in his white robe.

"There was nothing in our agreement about this."

"No. There wasn't. I wasn't sure you'd go through with it if I told you in advance what kind of familiars SUSTUGRIEL grants. But this is the only chance you get. Take it or leave it."

Stephen had followed the rituals in the grimoire to the letter; the instructions given the familiar had been those we'd agreed upon. I picked it up, held it against my flesh, gritted my teeth to keep from crying out as it burrowed into me. Soon there was only a fading red mark on my skin to betray the worm's presence within.

But I knew it was there. The pain had ceased when the flesh closed back over the wound, but I could feel it moving around inside me and I felt defiled.

Chapter Twenty-six

We were both dressed in black: heavy blunt-toed black boots, black denim jeans, thick black wool sweaters, though the day was already hot. A two-seated sports car, dark purple and Italian-looking though no make I recognized, had been left in the driveway the night before. I followed Stephen out to it, trying to ignore the worm squirming in my belly while he climbed in, reached over and unlocked the other door for me.

There was a wooden box the size and shape of a large shoe box on the passenger's seat. Stephen handed it to me to hold while he drove.

"What's in this?" It smelled of cinnamon and cloves, with a mustiness that the stronger odors of the spices almost masked.

"A hand of glory, the only one of its kind in the world. It'll put Michael to sleep for as long as you'll need to rescue Dara."

"What's so special about it?"

"I made it from the hand of one of the last vampires we hunted down in Wallachia. Do you want to take a look at it?"

I hesitated a moment, suspicious.

"Don't worry, it's harmless until lighted."

I opened the box. The hand was shriveled gray skin stretched tight over bone and tendon, a wrinkled talon on a white velvet cushion.

"How long will it keep him asleep?"

"About twenty-four hours. Which gives you far more time than you'll really need."

"How do you know he won't be able to protect himself from it?"

"I arranged to leave several crucial gaps in his education. He has no idea that any such thing could exist."

"What about Dara?"

"Monteleur will protect her the same way he'll be protecting you."

It took half an hour to get to the estate. Stephen left me sitting on one of the gravestones at the edge of the cemetery while he drove the rest of the way up to the house to plant the hand where it would be the most effective.

He was back about fifteen minutes later. "Michael's below but he's unconscious. You won't have any trouble with him."

"You said you'd make sure he wasn't in the cavern."

"That was before I decided to use the hand, when there was still some possibility he could be a danger to you."

"You keep changing things. I don't like it."

"You don't have to like it. Just remember, I'm the only one who can get Dara back for you. That doesn't change."

"Tell me about Lydia."

"Why I used her as my assistant instead of someone, say, more neutral?"

"To begin with."

"To keep you off balance, dear boy. Let you know how little you really know and how badly you need me."

"What else?"

"Nothing else, until I see some point in telling you. Let's get started."

He took an orange nylon backpack from the trunk and strapped it on, then led the way into the woods, following what seemed to be just another of the many deer trails criss-crossing the forest floor. I hung back, staying as far behind as I could while still keeping him in sight.

The trail dead-ended at a gnarled and tangled wall of inter-twined rose bushes at least ten feet tall. Stephen waited until I'd caught up with him, then pushed his way through the bushes. I followed him to a large grassy clearing completely cut off from the surrounding forest by the wall of rose bushes encircling it. I'd never seen it before, though at one time I'd thought I knew everything there was to know about the forest.

At the far end of the clearing, about five yards away, was a single weathered gravestone marked RADU BATHORY.

Stephen took some cloth-wrapped packages from his pack and set them down carefully in the center of the clearing. Then he took a length of black cord and laid out a circle, placing incense braziers from the pack just inside it, one at each of the four points of the compass. He lit the braziers and, stepping back out of the circle, applied the flame from his lighter to the cord. A ring of fire sprang into existence, burning a few inches above the cord without seeming to touch it. The braziers were giving off thick clouds of sour-smelling smoke, almost none of which escaped the confines of the circle despite the faint breeze filtering through the encircling wall of bushes.

Stephen took two withered brown things—roots, perhaps—from an envelope and held them out to me. They looked identical. I took one, waited until he'd chewed and swallowed his before taking mine. It was fibrous but unexpectedly sweet.

"Take off your clothes." He began to undress. He had neither body nor pubic hair, and when he'd finished removing his clothes he startled me by peeling off first his eyebrows and then the close-cropped wig I'd always thought was his natural hair. He was deeply and evenly tanned, scalp as well as body, so thin I could distinguish the individual muscles and tendons. He looked like a man who'd been skinned and then dipped in walnut-brown dye.

He stepped over the ring of fire, looked back and gestured me after him. I told myself that nothing he could do could be as bad as having the worm in me and took off the rest of my clothes, stepped in after him. The smoke was a greasy fog, hot and rancid. The drug was making me dizzy. I could no longer tell the difference between Monteleur's thrashing and the churning and twisting of my own bowels.

Stephen began chanting, long strings of precisely enunciated nonsense syllables. His shape was shifting, melting, becoming unrecognizable.

He handed me the scourge. I took it, whipped him across the chest and genitals until the blood flowed. It was mechanical; he wasn't real; I felt nothing.

He held up his hand and said, "Enough." I stopped. He was Stephen again as he took the scourge from me and told me to turn my back to him.

I screamed as the braided leather cut into me again and again, every repetition as totally unexpected as the first pain.

He put the scourge aside and unwrapped a vial full of some heavy aromatic oil. He shook the bottle vigorously before applying it to my back, buttocks and anus, then rubbed himself with it.

"Lie on your stomach with your legs apart. Concentrate on the pain, on your sense of being violated, on the fact that you don't know whether or not I'm going to live up to my half of our agreement after I'm finished with you. You don't want me to fuck you, you hate it, the very touch of me puts you in a rage, makes you so angry you could vomit or kill me right now—"

And then he'd grabbed me, opened me, and I could feel my sphincter muscles tearing as he thrust himself into me. I tried to struggle, throw him off, but I was too weak, too dizzy, was back in that other clearing on the night of father's funeral was Dara being raped by Michael in my body while Stephen thrust the cock that Michael had stolen from me into my ass as I vomited and he held my face down smeared it in the vomit so I couldn't breathe and there was a lead pipe in my hands I was bringing it down on his head in an ecstasy of hatred and loathing, and his broken head was falling away in shards of brittle wet plastic to reveal the severed neck of an angel with black, velvet-tipped wings singing with a sweet throaty voice that had a screaming inside—

Monteleur's laughter spasmed through me as the familiar sucked the power out of me, bloated itself on the pain and the ecstasy and the loathing.

It was over.

Stephen pulled himself out of me, left me lying there with the worm twitching contentedly in my guts as he walked over to the orange backpack and got two white pills out of a bottle.

"Here." He took one, handed me the other. "This'll counteract the drug I gave you earlier and put you back in shape to go after Dara."

He stood smiling at me while I dressed.

Chapter Twenty-seven

It's been two hours," Uncle Stephen said, handing me the long straight knife in its jeweled silver sheath. "You should be ready by now."

I nodded, glad to have an excuse to look away from him while I attached the sheath to my belt. My back and buttocks still hurt from the scourging and my sphincter muscles felt bruised and torn but the dizziness was gone. I felt strong enough to function.

"Good. Monteleur will have taken care of the rest of the pain before you reach the cavern. Remember, don't touch each other or speak to each other except through Monteleur." He'd explained that if Dara and I touched or spoke to each other before the final rite we'd need three more days of ritual preparation before starting over, and that during those three days Michael would be able to destroy us. "And don't do anything to harm the sexual hand. We'll need it for Michael later."

His voice was once again full of its cloyingly rich self-mockery, the archnesses and ironies that hid the greater falsehoods. He was going to need the hand for something involving Michael, Dara, and me. The avuncular smile, the clean white teeth, his eyes their cold startling green in the tanned face. I nodded again, unwilling to let my voice betray me.

The entrance was under Radu's tombstone. The stone was far heavier than it looked, and it took all our combined strength to push it aside: the entrance was rarely used, and then only when it was necessary to take something human-sized below without passing through the house. Stephen pointed out the holes, little bigger around than pencils, in the surrounding ground that the vampires themselves used.

Just beyond the entrance was a straight drop of about fifteen feet. Stephen lowered me on a knotted rope. From there
the passage continued level for a while, then angled sharply
downward, twisting and coiling like some subterranean intes-
tinal tract. The silver-burning rock was slippery with slime
molds, chill to the touch; the air hung heavy and fetid.

"Left." Monteleur's voice was a mocking bass rumble that
I felt as much as heard, as though my heat and lungs, stomach, liver and intestines had become sounding boards for the
familiar's voice.

"Now right. Left. Left again and then down." The passageway had become a labyrinth of twisting tunnels, some so narrow and low that I could barely crawl through them. There
were deep pits, crevices where spiders as big as my head
lurked. There were foot-long scorpions and nests of giant
ants, pockets of poisonous gases, more pits, false tunnels,
deadfalls. Once the way opened out onto a vast cavern
heaped with human and animal bones, bright-eyed rats staring at me from their nests among the silver-shining skeletons.
But with Monteleur to guide and protect me it was easy, too
easy, and I passed the traps and guardians with no more trouble than if I had been playing miniature golf.

Even the cavern was too bright, too clean. The pillar of
burning blood at the center, the four pillars of black flame
ringing it, the drifting clots of shadow—everything burned a
brilliant silver, chrome and antiseptic.

Monteleur guided me along a path that skirted the center,
avoided the statues of Shiva and Satan, the vampires in their
concentric circles and my father and Alexandra in their open
coffins.

"To your right." I turned, saw Dara lying naked in the center of a pentacle cut into the rock. A pool of water, a huge
rectangular fishpond, behind her. Her legs spread, one
twisted partially under her, and Michael, wearing his black
costume with the crotch cut away, lying sprawled on her, his
cock still buried in her. They were both unconscious, their
breathing slow and regular.

Only two of the hands of glory were burning; Monteleur had taken care of the other three on our way down. The master hand with the eyeballs sewn to the tips of its fingers, each finger burning with a different flame, controlling Dara in a different way, the forearm with its trailing veins and nerves rising from a bath of acrid-smelling yellow liquid. And the sexual hand, burning rose red, the leathery-looking cocks rising from the edge of the upright palm like the long necks of those huge clams you find along the beaches in northern Washington.

I laid out the six cloth pentacles Stephen had given me, forced myself to pause, take a few deep breaths and then check again to make sure I had them in the right order. I put the white leather glove on my left hand, carefully drew the knife from its sheath with my right. The blade was a shimmery silvery alloy, incredibly sharp, inlaid with hundreds of tiny gold sigils that caught the light and seemed to float just above the blade's white brilliance.

The master hand, with the eyeballs sewn to its fingers focused on Dara. The little finger was slightly bent, the skin stained and wrinkled, burning green: Dara's heartbeat, her other involuntary life functions. I held the hand steady, severed the little finger from it with a single blow of the silvery blade, caught it as it fell, its flame extinguished, and put it in the smallest pentacle.

The next finger, burning orange-red: Dara's voluntary muscles. The third finger, the index finger, the flames rose-pink with darker eddies: her perception of her body and of the world around her. The final finger, a brilliant cobalt blue: her physically based emotions, her anger, fear, pleasure and pain. I severed them all, caught them in my gloved left hand, put them in their pentacles. The eyes on the tips swiveled to watch me as I attacked what remained of the hand.

There was a livid design made up of three large circles and a number of crosses, arrows, lines and smaller circles burned onto the palm: the sigil of FORNEUS. The thin yellow fluid leaking from the severed joints was eating its way through my glove, burning the hand with which I held the mutilated hand of glory steady as I carved first a circle around the sigil and then around that a pentacle, the flesh falling away from the blade like overcooked stew meat. The sigil blurred and shifted and something part fish, part reptile, part human looked out at me, tried to reach me before I could complete the design, but Monteleur kept me safe until I finally cut the last line of the pentangle into the palm and the spirit vanished.

I put the hand in the pentacle Stephen had provided for it. I realized I was holding my breath again, forced myself to exhale.

And suddenly I was seeing Michael and Dara lying there in front of me for the first time, Dara's hips grinding beneath his sprawled unconsciousness as his erect cock writhed and wriggled deeper and deeper into her, a thick purple worm feeding, and yet I could see that they were neither of them moving, that it was I who was moving as the swelling waves of my need beat through me, as I let the knife fall and grabbed Michael by the arm, the black rubber or plastic of his sleeve a confusion of chromed reflections, taut and slippery as raw liver in my hand as I yanked him off and out of her—

An explosion of fire and agony in my groin and the lust was gone. In its place only shame and an anger beyond all reason as I straightened and my hand found the knife, hacked the flaming cocks from their hand of glory and I ground them under my boot heel into the rough stone floor of the cave, smearing the gray pulpy flesh across the darker gray of the floor.

This time the burning went on and on.

"You have violated your compact," Monteleur said when the pain ceased. "My master wanted that hand."

"I lost control." I tried to stand, found I could. I seemed to be undamaged. Dara was still sprawled limp and unmoving in the center of the pentacle. A few feet way Michael lay curled around himself in a tight fetal ball.

"What's wrong? Why isn't she conscious yet?"

"I have to awaken her. Stand behind her, where she can't see you until I warn her not to speak to you. Mouth the words you want me to repeat to her."

I moved around behind her, stood waiting.

"Now," Monteleur said.

"Dara. Don't say anything." Monteleur's voice rumbling from my belly. Dara opened her eyes and tried to sit up, saw me. "Don't try to talk. I'm speaking to you through Monteleur, a familiar spirit, but we can't touch each other or talk directly. Nod if you understand."

She nodded.

"Before we leave we have to immerse ourselves seven times each in the pool behind me. Do you feel strong enough?"

She nodded again. I started taking off my clothes. When I pulled my sweater off it ripped the scabs on my back open again. Dara sat the rest of the way up, stood shakily. Michael lay curled at her feet. She looked down at him an instant, then stepped over him and made her way carefully to the pool. The leg that had been twisted under her was badly bruised and she was limping slightly. She hesitated at the water's edge, her back to me, the silver fires of the place glowing on her rich dark shoulders, smooth tight buttocks and legs, shining from the hair falling black and thick to her waist.

She shook her head as if to clear it, looked back at me, then took a deep breath and dived in. The pool was not quite the size of a backyard swimming pool, but very deep: I waited until I was sure she'd be able to make it back to the edge and climb out again. When she dived in again I followed her, keeping far enough away that there'd be no danger of us brushing against each other by mistake.

When we finished Monteleur led us back through the branching tunnels to where Stephen was waiting for us. He lowered the knotted rope. I gestured to Dara and she climbed it first, so weak and trembling I wasn't sure she could make it to the top, then followed her.

"The ritual is simple," Stephen said when Dara had her breath back. "You are to rub yourselves with these aromatic oils and enter the circle from opposite directions. David must enter from the west, Dara from the east. You must find each other within the circle without speaking and remain silent until the rite has been completed and David has established dominion over Gregory. Once you find each other you must lie together with your heads to the north and begin having sex, with David as the dominant partner on top."

I looked at Dara, trying to read her reaction in her face, but could see nothing beyond her exhaustion, her tension and fear.

"As the power builds in you"—he was speaking to me alone now, ignoring Dara—"your father's soul will be drawn to yours. You will become aware of his thoughts, begin to share his transformation, and then you must reach into him and take from him his lusts and hungers, his needs and the strengths with which he intends to satisfy them, and you must make them your own: you must take the vampire within him and make it a part of yourself before you can command it and, through it, him.

"Remember, you will be facing your brother as well as your father. You will have to defeat both of them to establish your dominion. But so long as the hand I've placed in the house continues to burn Michael will remain asleep, so that it will be only the productions of his will, and not that will itself, that you will have to overcome."

Stephen rubbed first Dara and then me with the proper oils and led us to our places. The smoke was so thick I couldn't see Dara, though she was only a few yards away.

At a signal from Stephen I stepped over the flames and into the circle. The smoke was a dense, impenetrable cloud of aloes and musk, amber and incense, violets and vanilla and cinnamon, complex and exciting, so thick it was almost liquid, yet cool against my skin and eyes.

But I was blinded by it nonetheless. Dara and I found each

other by touch, stood awkwardly afraid an instant before risking our first embrace.

Holding her at last, feeling her warm oil-slicked flesh against mine, I knew that she was all and everything I had ever wanted, that I could ever want, and yet I held myself back, still certain that Stephen had no intention of honoring our agreement and that I had to find a way to break free before it was too late, still afraid of the worm inside me.

But maybe I could learn how to rid myself of the worm from Father. Hope and desire overcame my fear and we sank down onto the grass within the circle and began to make love.

Chapter Twenty-eight

I n Dara's embrace I forgot all else, forgot the worm in my belly, forgot that I was engaged in a sexual rite for magical purposes. The spice-scented smoke coiled itself around us, sheltered and hid us as we rediscovered the smoothnesses and softnesses, the unexpected angularities of each other's bodies. At first I was tentative, careful, afraid of hurting her, but as we touched and tasted and held each other, long before I knelt between her legs and she guided me into her, our fears and needs sloughed from us like the clouded skin an emerald tree boa sheds to reveal the glittering beauty of the new scales underneath. We were there, making love; there was no need of anything else.

The power built in us, was us, united us with the living earth and the forest around us. We shared in the jiggling dance of the smoke molecules in the air above; we drew water up from the roots of the grass on which we lay to satisfy the thirst of its blades; we quivered in the wind with the trees, drifted gently to earth with a falling leaf. And as our union evolved toward ultimate consummation, ultimate stillness, we wove more and more of ourselves into the forest and the earth, into the smoke and the wind and the sun.

Monteleur—no longer a worm, but a strange configuration of twisting darknesses—wove itself into the pattern we were creating, becoming, never part of it, yet always somehow in harmonious counterpoint to it.

Below, far below us, we could sense the jeweled palace of the sun where the Queen sat in glory on her ivory throne, and as we sank our roots ever deeper into the living earth we felt its warmth coursing through us, melting the frozen diamonds that covered our eyes and blinded us, opening us to the solar wind—

And we were trapped in the congealed wax of my father's corpse, lying dull and heavy and dead in his coffin as his cravings erupted like a sudden cancer in our lovemaking and we died, broke apart into a David and a Dara struggling to keep themselves from fragmenting even further as they fought against their newborn lust for each other's blood, and then we were Gregory Mihnea Bathory, falling through the insatiable dark his hunger had opened within him, through the endless frozen void and the icy wind that scoured the flesh from his body, gouged it particle by frozen particle from him and whirled it away into the hungry darkness. Soon the naked bone would jut from the crystalline tatters of his flesh and then the bone itself would be gone, eaten by the wind.

Above me, lost in the dark, was the tiny spot of reddish light that meant rebirth. There, if Satan accepted my submission, I would find the blood to warm my frozen soul, reanimate the life-starved flesh lying limp and heavy in my coffin.

There was no transition. I had been him, had shared his hunger and pain; now I was there with him, falling alongside him through the knife-edged wind and the dark.

Or rather, we were there with him, for I shared the body I inhabited with Dara. The right side was male, the left female, with two sets of genitals crowded side by side between the unmatched legs and one full breast on the left side of the chest. A hermaphrodite. Yet though we shared a single body we were no longer a single being: we no longer shared each other's thoughts, knew each other's feelings.

Then, suddenly, we were fighting my father as he tried to use our body as a stepping-stone toward the almost invisible light overhead. Struggling, a tangled mass of arms and legs, we fell through the wind, the cold that was not the absence of heat and motion I had learned about in physics, which stops with absolute zero and the cessation of all motion and change. This was a force sufficient unto itself, an elemental will, enemy to heat and warmth and life and not merely its absence. But my father was three weeks dead and I was in a body not my own: it could do me no real damage.

A glowing pot-bellied imp, like something from a comic book drawn by a man with little imagination but a truly malicious sense of humor, suddenly appeared in front of me.

"Would you like some help?" it asked in Monteleur's voice.

"Of course," Dara said. It was strange to feel my tongue and mouth moving in response to another's will.

"Will you agree to bind yourselves to my service in return?"

"No." This time it was I who answered. The imp vanished.

Father was standing on our shoulders, stretching futilely toward the vanished light. I was supposed to vanquish him in a contest of will of some sort, but he seemed to be in the same situation I was and he was the one making the terrified attempt to climb over us to safety.

"Do you understand what's happening?" I asked Dara, shaping the words and then letting my mouth go lax as I waited for her reply.

"I think so. We're trapped on one level of Father's mind. This is a stage all the undead go through during their transformation."

"What do we do?"

"I don't know."

"Do you have your memory back?"

"No. Some things came back to me when I saw Michael, Stephen, Father's body. But the rest—it's like there's a veil in my mind only I can't even see the veil, just sense it's there somehow.

"Father left a letter—I buried it with the Naga. When you see it you're supposed to remember everything. But I think—he couldn't take your memories away. You had to do it to yourself, the same way we make ourselves unnoticeable. Maybe you can get them back."

I let my mouth go slack.

"I can't, David. If I could just see the veil clearly, then I could get through it to what it's hiding, remember everything, I know I could, but I can't see it."

I tried to reach out to her then, turn her attention to her missing memories, but I couldn't sense her, feel the focus of her attention and redirect it the way I'd learned. We shared a body, but the separation between us was an impenetrable wall, mocking us. I took control of our voice.

"If we're trapped in Father's mind, maybe we can escape by willing ourselves back in our bodies. Try to project yourself back."

I summoned up all my own powers of concentration and tried to visualize myself back in the smoke-filled circle.

"Give up?" This time Monteleur was a great purple parrot with a huge yellow cock covered with warts and spines.

"No," I said. "I thought you were supposed to be helping me."

"I don't seem to be much help, do I?"

"Monteleur, I command you to help me."

"Not unless you bind yourself to my service."

"Why? Is this darkness your work or something Stephen planned for us?"

"No. It's a trap laid for you by your brother. And unless you find your way out of it by yourselves before he reawakens, he'll keep you trapped here forever."

"Go away," I said. The familiar vanished again.

We continued to fall.

Father shifted his weight on our shoulders again. I reached up and hauled him down by the ankle, held him so he couldn't break free.

"What do you want?" His voice was hollow, yet still as arrogant as when he'd been alive.

"What are you trying to climb to?"

"Satan. So He will know I'm doing everything in my power to reach Him." His face was only inches from mine, but I couldn't feel his breath on my face when he spoke.

Dara was trying to use our mouth. I surrendered it to her.

"You've pledged yourself to Satan?"

"I have offered myself to Him but He has not yet accepted me."

"Do you believe him?" I asked Dara.

"I don't know."

"What's in store for you if Satan accepts you?" I asked.

"Blood," my father said. "Satan will send a river of flaming blood streaming down to me." I could feel the hunger behind his words.

"Why would you want that?"

"It would bring me back to life."

"You'd still be here, wouldn't you?"

"No. This is death, the space between lives."

"Then we're dead too?"

"No. You're just here with me."

"What if we drink your blood?"

"Mine?" he asked. "I have no blood."

"And if we drink our own?" Dara asked.

"It wouldn't do any good. You're both already alive. I'm the one who's dead."

"So why are we here?" I asked.

"You came searching for me. You found me dead and now you're trapped here with me."

I waited to see if Dara wanted to use our voice, then said, "What you're telling us is that we'll be here until your resurrection."

"Yes."

"What if you drink our blood?"

"Then I would be alive and you would both be returned to yourselves."

"He's lying, David."

"Why haven't you tried, then?" I demanded, letting his hunger wash over me, through me, until it was as much mine as his.

He didn't answer. I groped for him, grabbed his head, forced it back. "Forgive me if I'm doing you an injustice, Father," I said. Then I bit him. It took awhile to rip his throat open, but when I did the blood he'd denied having began to ooze forth, thick, cold and bitter yet burning a somber red in the darkness of the void.

At first I had to force myself to swallow it. But it was warm inside me, heady and exciting, and as its warmth spread through me the taste changed, became shot through with sweetnesses, like bitter honey.

I drained him, hurled the empty husk away from me to float dead and dry forever in the cold and the wind.

And the forest was dark and chill around me, and I was lost. The wind cut through my thin cloak and the thick branches overhead hid the moon from me, blocked its light as they had blocked the light of the sun during the days I had stumbled, ever hungrier, ever thirstier, in search of the way I had lost. Ahead of me was a clearing with something bright shining in it. A fountain. I ran toward it, tripped over a gnarled root and picked myself up.

There was only a mirror, tall and narrow, standing upright in the moonlight. I could see myself in it, a child of ten, eyes swollen from crying, my cloak ripped where I'd caught it on a branch the night before. Behind me the shadowed forest, the trees' leafless branches like claws, reaching down to rend and tear me.

But the image in the mirror shimmered, rippled, and the dark forest was gone from it, had become a child's bedroom, its walls hung with embroidered silk and lit by the silver candelabra my mirror self held in one hand as he smiled at me and beckoned me in through the mirror.

I felt myself shimmer and ripple as I stepped through into the warmth and the mirror-me was no longer me but was my twin, my identical twin, and yet she was a girl, pale and delicate and lovely with soft shiny red-gold hair. She lay sleeping on her bed and I stood over her, gazing down on her and smelling the sweet freshness of her skin and hair.

I bent over her, kissed her gently on the lips so as not to waken her, straightened again. She smiled in her sleep, raised her hand to touch her fingertips to her lips, smiled again. And as her hand fell away the ring she wore on it, bright silver and razor-petaled onyx, brushed against the paleness of her throat and opened a soft rose, a bright wet flower, in her skin. I stared at the welling blood, the thick fat trickle creeping down her neck to stain her pale hair and the silken pillow under her with brightness as she opened eyes like pale sapphires and laughed up at me, arching her neck in invitation to drink from the flower she had opened for me and me alone.

And yet I recoiled from her, confused, the welling richness of her blood burning in my nostrils, in the cracked dryness of my throat, and yet I took another step back, and another, looked away from her and turned to leave.

"David." My father's voice, grave and resonant, with none of the hollowness it had had in the void. I turned back, saw a woman like my Aunt Judith step from the bed onto the floor, become my father.

"You're strong, David, as strong as ever I was in life, as strong as a son of mine should be. But Michael too was strong. So there is one more confrontation you must win to gain dominion over me."

"What?"

"We must be joined, body to body, heart to heart, so that the same blood flows through both our bodies."

"And the contest?"

"Only one of us can control our heart. That one gains dominion over the other."

"And neither Michael nor Stephen has ever confronted this test?"

"No. It is an ancient thing, rarely used."

"Then why are you telling me about it, Father?"

"Because if I defeat you Michael loses his dominion over me." He grinned, showing gleaming fangs. "I hunger for him and for Stephen even more than I hunger for you, David."

We removed our shirts. He took a golden knife with a serrated edge from beneath the blood-soaked pillow and cut through the muscles and ribs of his chest, lifted them away to expose his naked heart. It did not beat.

He handed me the knife and I did the same thing to myself. The pain was distant, real but unimportant. When my naked pulsating heart was exposed, Father moved closer and pressed his heart to mine so that the two organs fused.

"I can feel your blood," he said. "The warm blood of a living man in my veins."

And I could feel his, thick and sluggish, seeping through me, slowly sucking the life from me as we fought for control of the eight-chambered heart we shared. His dead muscles resisted my efforts to spark them into life; yet I kept my part of the heart beating on despite his efforts to stop it. His thick, unoxygenated blood dulled my brain, but I kept on fighting for control, until the heart we shared shuddered, spasmed into life, sent my living blood streaming through him.

At last he conceded defeat. "You have my heart and my life," he told me. I allowed the eight-chambered heart to fission, making sure I retained control over both halves even after they were separated. We put our ribs and severed muscles back into place and waited the instants it took for them to knit.

And it had all been too quick, too easy, no real contest at all.

"Is that all?" I asked.

"Yes."

He was a too-heavy shadow trapping me in the long narrow corridor in which I was free, where I was the master, the rough-cut stone walls of the corridor also doors, hundreds upon hundreds of locked doors to which I was the key, and I was free to range the corridor, to open any and all of the doors, to close them and keep them closed—

"I have complete dominion over you and all my ancestors now?"

"Yes. Michael and Stephen can still command me so long as their commands do not conflict with yours, but you have final and complete dominion."

The walls were doors leading to the souls and selves of my ancestors, but it was not yet night and they slept there behind the walls. There, in their coffins in the cavern beneath the house.

"Stephen? How can he command you if he's a member of your generation?"

"Through you, David. Through you," he said and suddenly he smiled. "Why not look inside me and learn the answers to all your questions for yourself?"

I looked into him and I saw. And as my memory returned to me and I knew where and how and why Stephen had lied to me, how he'd used me and what he'd done to me, I found myself back in the circle, building to an orgasm it was too late to avoid. But even as I climaxed in an explosion of synesthetic ecstasy I could feel Monteleur twisting and squirming in my belly.

Chapter Twenty-nine

I tried to wrench us out of noticeability but the worm was there, pinning us to the world. I said, "Dara—" but the worm was in my voice and there was no way I could wrap my words with silence and warn her against Stephen without letting him know what I had learned, no way to tell her anything he wouldn't hear.

I had to tell her to go unnoticeable and escape, find a way to warn her that he couldn't tap so she could get away before he realized what she was doing. Until then I'd have to stall him. Hope that the joy he took in cat-and-mouse games would give me the chance I needed.

I reached through and beyond my father to the dark corridor, tried to find the door that would take me to Dara, but Stephen was there in the corridor with me now, a watchful shadow, inescapable as the worm even now roiling through the secret darknesses of my body, and though the corridor was mine my body was the worm's and the worm was Stephen.

I helped Dara to her feet. She sagged against me, trembling and shivering, too weak to stand.

Too weak to escape. Unless I could stall long enough to let her recover.

Her hands found my forearms in the darkness. "The Naga," she whispered in the same sibilant whisper the Naga on the landing had used, then had to pause for breath. I remembered that Stephen's instruments hadn't picked up what the Naga had told me. "Where is it?"

I couldn't answer her without letting Stephen know I'd seen through his deception and bogus ritual. I subvocalized to Monteleur, "Tell her the Naga is hidden. Somewhere safe. I had to take it off to come after her. But she needs to rest. We can talk about things later, when she's feeling better."

Monteleur repeated my message as I led her through the spice-scented darkness over the ring of fire and out into the late-afternoon light.

Stephen grabbed her arm, spun her away from me, and before I could react I was paralyzed, falling, every muscle locked and straining with a pain that went on and on in my belly as he slapped something against her skin, just below her navel, and I smelled again the intolerable stench from that basement floor where Monteleur had lain twisting and coiling on the parquet floor.

And then Stephen let go of her and she was falling, crumpling, but the worm was still in his other hand, gray like a segmented root in its glistening envelope of yellow-quivering jelly.

The pain in my belly died away. I could move again. I got back to my feet.

"Go help your sister, David." Stephen's voice was dry, slightly amused, as though nothing had happened. The worm still reeking in his cupped left hand. "Get dressed, both of you, so we can pay a visit to Michael."

I got her jeans and shirt out of the backpack, helped her on with them. She had to sit down again to put on her shoes.

"And Dara—don't try to go invisible and escape. Because even though Bathomar refused to enter you I was able to persuade Monteleur, an in every way similar spirit, to overcome his repugnance to David and take up residence in him. Which means that if you in any way disobey me David will suffer for it. And should I die, Monteleur has been instructed to kill David in the slowest, most agonizing way he can devise. Do you understand me, niece?"

"I understand you." Her voice was weak but level, unfrightened, though she was still trembling and unable to stand without my help.

"Good. Understand this, then. I have never been overfond of women and I share Bathomar's distaste for Nagas. I tolerate you only because I can make use of you—and that toleration will cease the moment your usefulness ends.

"And as for you, David"—turning back to me—"should it by any chance occur to you that the heroic and noble thing to do now would be to sacrifice yourself in some way so as to allow your sister to escape, let me remind you that, one, not only do you have as yet no idea of the nature or extent of the punishment you'd be bringing down on yourself, and on your sister if I recapture her, but, two, that with Bathomar to ensure Michael's cooperation I *will* be able to recapture her without your help. And I have no need of Monteleur's eons of experience and malicious imagination to devise a very slow and very painful death for her. Do *you* understand me, nephew?"

"Perfectly."

"Then we've laid the basis for what I expect will be a long and successful relationship."

He had us wait in the library while he went below to fit Michael with the familiar. Dara sat with her chair turned away from the fireplace so she wouldn't have to look at the bloodshot ball of powerflame hanging in it. I pulled my chair up next to hers.

"How are you feeling?"

"Better. Not good—never good, here—but a little stronger. I'll be all right soon." And then, without moving her lips, in that sibilant whisper: "David. Don't let your familiar know you can hear me. It can't hear me, no one without Naga blood could, but while it's in you there's no way you can reply without being overheard. So just sit back and look away from me.

"David, Father was afraid Stephen would try to fit me with a familiar. When it touched me my memories came back. All of them.

"As long as you have the familiar inside, there's no way you can escape. It can't read your thoughts but it's aware of everything that goes on in your body, any tension or fear or words you say to yourself. So it's almost impossible to surprise.

"It's not very intelligent but it will report everything back to Stephen. So you can't count on its stupidity, or on fooling it by saying things with double meanings. But if you can get it to leave you, even for an instant, you can veil yourself and escape."

But Stephen had known what I was doing when I'd made myself unnoticeable at Howard Johnson's.

"The golden Naga might force it out of you, if you can get it back on your arm. It comes from the Naga Realm. I think the other familiar refused to enter me because I've worn it all my life. But unless you've hidden it here in the house I can't get to it. In a moment I'm going to ask you a question in my normal voice. Answer yes if the Naga's somewhere nearby, no if it's out of reach."

She was silent a moment, giving me time to think, then asked, "Has it been very long yet, David? Do we have much longer before they get back?"

I shook my head. "No. They just left. We've got a while."

"Good." And whispering again: "When Stephen gets back, ask him about the things you need to know. Not so he'll answer but to tell me what you need to know. But be careful. Neither Michael nor Stephen is at all stupid."

"There's something you need to know. There's no way either one of us can escape."

In her normal voice: "What do you mean?" And, somehow at the same time, whispering: "Don't tell me anything that you aren't absolutely sure Stephen already knows."

"Stephen didn't say anything about it, but he can sense us even when we're invisible." I told her about what happened at Howard Johnson's.

Whispering: "Was he aware of you while you were veiled from him, or only afterward?"

"Afterward, he told me it was because of being around Michael. That he'd learned how to get around our Naga invisibility."

"Then maybe he has some way to check to see if there are any holes in his memory. He probably told himself to watch you the whole time, then when he couldn't remember what you'd been doing it would have been easy to guess. If you'd veiled the fact that he couldn't remember it might have worked."

It was almost dark before Stephen and Michael emerged from the fireplace.

Stephen motioned Michael to a chair. He sat, staring impassively at Stephen, ignoring us completely. But though he managed to keep his face expressionless, his body was rigid and I could see his hands were trembling.

"David, Dara, I want you both to watch Michael very carefully tonight," Stephen said. "I've instructed Bathomar to keep him in some sort of minor pain all the time—a toothache, backache, cramps, that sort of thing. But for twelve minutes every four hours Bathomar is to put him into as close an approximation to absolute agony as he can without doing any lasting physical damage. I'll give you a demonstration in a moment. And low-ranking as Bathomar may be, he is still a demon."

"Why?" I asked.

"Because it amuses me. And because I have a score to settle with him. But also to show you what will happen to you if you refuse to cooperate."

"Cooperate in doing what?"

"Spreading vampirism as widely beyond this family as possible. Because, David, unlike your brother I am an idealist. A Satanist, working for my master's eventual triumph.

"For centuries our family has considered vampirism our private property, a way of attaining personal immortality granted us and us alone. We have taken Satan, our proper master, for someone we can use. I like to think of vampirism as a disease and of all of us, dhampires as well as vampires, as plague carriers, yet what have we Bathorys done over the last few hundred years? We have hunted down and destroyed all the other vampires in the world, then quarantined ourselves and begun our own self-destruction. Gregory would have destroyed us all if he'd been permitted to, as you and Dara would now if I give you the chance. While Michael cares for nothing but his personal immortality and has already, ostensibly as a demonstration of his legitimate authority, destroyed my sister Judith, attempted to kill you, and planned to kill me."

He beamed at the three of us in turn, all avuncular kindness.

"I intend to end all that. To see that vampirism is spread as an end in itself, and not merely as a means of prolonging the existences of a few self-selected individuals. And the three of you are going to help me."

"Help you destroy everything we've worked for over the centuries," Michael said.

"It's a risk I'm willing to take. Which is one reason why I, and not you, Michael, am now head of this family."

"They'll give themselves away as soon as we lose control," Michael said. "They'll keep their fangs long, leave marks on their victim's throats instead of sucking the blood through unbroken skin. And then people will know us for what we are and destroy us. That was the price we paid for getting Stoker to write *Dracula* for us and it's too late to change it."

"Too late for you, Michael. Not for me."

"The family had Stoker write *Dracula*?" I asked. "Why?"

"For the publicity," Stephen said. "Because we derive power from mankind's fear of us. Before *Dracula* was published, nobody outside Central Europe knew anything about vampires. Their lack of belief kept us weak. But with Stoker's book we were able to capture the imagination of the Christian and non-Christian world alike—and that without giving people the information they'd need to hunt as down."

"As long as you keep the vampires from giving themselves away," Michael said. "As long as you keep them under control."

"And what about the Nagas?" I asked. "If we're all such a threat because we're half Naga, what do you intend to do about the *real* Nagas?"

"Ah, but you see, they're like all the other gods and demons. All the powers derive their strength from their worshippers' faith, and that faith is dying, or being replaced with Islamic fanaticism. The various political ideologies that have replaced the traditional religions of the Far East leave their followers without any sort of supernatural protectors, and the fad for Oriental religions in the West has already given way to forms of fanatical Christianity that can only help us. With luck we can hope for new witch hunts or a second Inquisition by the end of the century. Judaism and Islam we can live with; their demonologies and infernal hierarchies are compatible with our own. And with atomic weapons we'll be able to wipe out whole populations of believers should any sort of revival of the faiths opposing us render it necessary."

"But what about Christianity?" I asked. "If Christ still has all those worshippers—"

"Very few of them actually believe in Christ. What they *really* believe in is something very different: that the world and any afterlife that might exist would be too terrible to be endured without the protection and intervention of someone like Christ. And it's that terror, their fear of death and pain and evil—of Satan—that's real and important. Not their futile attempts to convince themselves they're not afraid, or that there's nothing to fear."

I thought about that a moment, said, "What do you expect to get out of this?"

"For myself, nothing. For Satan, everything. And what He intends is nothing less than the total destruction of all life in the universe. The gods and other supernatural beings, then men and all lesser forms of life, and finally Himself. When He too is gone, the universe will have been swept free of all taint and filth, it will be clean and pure and empty and perfect."

"But Satan won't be there to enjoy its perfection."

"No. So why does He want to destroy Himself? Because His only joy is destruction. When all else is gone, what will remain for Him but to destroy Himself?"

"But you yourself will have been destroyed. So, why?"

"For the same reasons. To see it all die, and myself and my master with it."

I suddenly remembered something. "Where does that girl come into this?" I asked Stephen. "The one you said was Alexandra's sister."

Stephen frowned. Michael gaped at me, startled, before he remembered himself and tried to put his mask back in place. But it was too late.

"Alexandra's *daughter*, Michael," Stephen said, beaming at me. "You remember how she had to go away for most of a year when you were, what, nineteen?"

Michael glared at him.

"Does that mean she's Michael's daughter too?" I asked.

Stephen smiled fondly at me, the loving uncle rewarding the clever nephew one more time, only this time there was a sudden agony in the pit of my stomach, gone again before my body had time to react to it. "I'm sure Michael would like to know that too, David. Whether or not Lydia'll be able to control the three of you after you're dead. Wouldn't you, Michael?"

He turned abruptly back to me. "David, you won't be eating here with us tonight. I want you and Dara to take your truck back to your cabin in Big Sur. I arranged to have it taken off the market just after you left—I'm afraid I gave the real-estate people the impression that I was you when I discussed the matter with them over the phone—and you'll find that I've changed things around a bit."

"Why? I asked.

"I'm preparing to hold the Grand Sabbat there this year. On Lammas Day, August first. And getting you and Monteleur ready for the Sabbat happens to be part of the preparations. Which is why I want you and Dara to stop and *fuck*"—drawing out and stressing the word contemptuously—"at Carlsbad and the Grand Canyon, like you did on your way here."

"You can leave in about fifteen minutes, as soon as you've had a chance to appreciate Michael's first real experience of Bathomar's talents."

He turned to Michael. "I think an audience always makes things more interesting, don't you? It's so much harder to tell yourself you're bearing up nobly when there are witnesses around to hear you begging and screaming."

Chapter Thirty

It was long past midnight and we were halfway across Iowa before I realized that Monteleur was manipulating my emotions.

Whenever I happened to glance at the baby cobra in its glove-compartment cage I felt a muted repulsion, a feeling compounded of fear and disgust and even hatred, but so far back in my mind, so attenuated, that had I not been monitoring myself constantly to make sure I did nothing to let Monteleur know Dara was whispering things to me it couldn't hear, I would never have realized my feelings were being influenced.

If I visualized the cobra without looking at it I felt nothing, if I remembered the bushmaster that had killed Alexandra or the coral snake that had almost killed me I felt nothing, yet as soon as my gaze fell on the cobra the repulsion was there, and with it a fear that snakes had never inspired in me.

The next time we stopped for gas I visualized myself feeding the cobra. No reaction: I'd fed it innumerable times before and the thought of doing so again roused no special feelings. But when I turned to Dara and said, "I think the cobra needs to be fed," sudden panic blossomed within me. Monteleur had given itself away.

Dara leaned forward and put her face to the cage's glass front. After an instant the baby cobra slipped out from under its rock and raised its head, stared back at her, tasting the air with its tongue.

"I don't think so," Dara said, straightening and looking over at me. "He won't really be hungry for another week and he's very nervous from the drive. It might be better to wait until California."

I waited for her to ask me what I'd meant, but she seemed to have taken my statement at face value. I said I'd trust her judgment and my panic subsided. I paid the station attendant and got back on the highway.

Monteleur was trying to keep me away from my snakes, and trying to keep me from realizing that I was being kept from them. Which might mean it was afraid of them. Both familiars had struck me as caricatures of Nagas. And Bathomar had refused to possess Dara because she was too Naga. So perhaps their fear of Nagas—if it *was* fear—extended to their earthly relatives like the cobras.

Dara had said that to free myself from Monteleur I'd have to force it out of my body, but maybe I could kill it while it was still inside me. If it could *be* killed. If I got the cobra to bite me, then maybe the venom in my bloodstream would destroy the familiar before it killed me.

Dying, the worm might rip me apart in its death throes; dead, its alien body might poison me. And though I had no proof it was vulnerable to the cobra's venom, I knew the snake could kill *me:* only the cobra-headed Queen had saved me from the coral snake, and coral snakes and cobras had the same venom. Even if it had been my Naga blood that had brought the Queen to my aid, that blood still hadn't given me any immunity to the venom and I didn't know why the Queen had helped me or whether she'd ever do so again. And I'd have to wait until I was certain the familiar was dead before injecting the antivenin, though for all I knew the cobra would kill me first.

Forcing Monteleur out of my body looked more promising. If it really was afraid of the cobra, I could get the snake to look like it was threatening to bite me, hope the fear of being poisoned would be enough to frighten Monteleur out of me. If that didn't work, I'd have to let myself be bitten and hope Monteleur fled me soon enough to save myself.

If it refused to leave me, I could always hope the venom would kill it or that the Queen would once more come to my rescue, even destroy Monteleur for me.

"I'm feeling really depressed," I told Dara. "Or not depressed, exactly, but scared and . . . I don't know. Scared. I can't talk about it."

"You want to tell me something but you can't talk with Monteleur listening?" Dara whispered.

"Could you get the coke from under the rock in the cobra's cage and give me some?" I asked. "I need to cheer myself up, not feel the way I do. Be someone else for a while. There are gloves under the seat, so you don't have to worry about the cobra biting you."

"You want to tell me something about the cobra? About being scared of the cobra?" She got the coke out and held the spoon to my nostrils. I thanked her and she put it away again.

We continued on for a few more miles, identical fields of faintly shimmering corn stretching away into the darkness on both sides of the road, before the exhilaration I was planning to use to mask my reactions hit. When I started to shiver a little I had Dara give me another six spoonfuls, then let my eyes come to rest, as if by accident, on the baby cobra. I looked away as soon as I felt the first stirrings of fear and disgust.

"I know what it is," I said, forcing myself to look back at the cobra, then quickly away again. "What I'm scared of. My snakes. All of them, but especially the cobra. I never used to be afraid of them, and I even got bitten a lot of times without anything really bad happening, but when I think about what happened in Chicago, when that snake tried to kill me just like the other one killed Alexandra, I get scared. Really scared. The way it climbed up on my glove to get at me—"

The more I babbled on about my fear the stronger it became: Monteleur must have decided I was ready to accept the feelings it had been fostering as my own. I snorted enormous amounts of coke, talking about everything and anything but returning again and again to the new fears my snakes, and especially the baby cobra, inspired in me. It took a long time to get what I wanted across to Dara—the coke cut us off from each other at the same time that it masked my true feelings from Monteleur—but she finally understood.

"I'm tired," she announced, "and I need to use a bathroom. Can we stop at the next rest area?"

I said yes.

The sun had just broken free of the horizon when we found a rest stop. Any truckers who'd been there for the night were already gone and there was only one other car in the lot, a tan station wagon with curtains drawn across its windows. I took a space at the far end of the lot, snorted four more spoons of coke, then used the men's room.

Dara was already back in the truck when I came out. I got in, closed the door, locked it behind me.

"David?" I turned, jumped back: the cobra was there in her hands, inches from my face, staring at me while it flicked its forked tongue in my direction, deciding what to do about me.

The fear Monteleur had fostered in me, the jangle from the coke, fed each other, merged into terror. I pulled my arms in tight to my body, tried to shield my face and neck as I huddled back against the locked door, screaming at Dara to take the snake away, not hurt me with it, too terrified to reach up and unlock the door, push it open, run.

"Keep your voice down, David," she said, bringing the snake just a little closer. It was coiled on her cupped hands now, shiny black, just beginning to raise its head and expose its satiny throat. "There's no reason to be afraid of him, David. You're a Naga and he's one of your relatives. Just like you. Nothing to be afraid of."

Her voice was soft, almost crooning, as she stroked the back of the snake's head with her finger, inched it slowly closer to me. I tried to yell at her to get it away from me but the fear had reached my throat and I couldn't speak. Then Monteleur had taken my mouth and lips from me and I heard my voice croaking "No! No! Put it back or I'll hurt you!"

"Nonsense." She was smiling, the cobra rearing, spreading

its head, swaying back and forth. Its lidless eyes stared at me from its shiny black head, the hood extended to its fullest extent, the tongue flicking in and out, in and out.

Monteleur heaved through me, ripping me. My screams caught in my throat, forcing my jaws wider and wider as they tried to push their way out of me. Monteleur bellowed in my guts, pleading, threatening.

Then the cobra struck. My neck burned where it had bitten me, but the pain of its bite was nothing compared to the tearing in my belly, where Monteleur thrashed and screamed and ripped.

Yet there was no dizziness or confusion, no muscle cramps or backache, and the burning in my neck soon went away. In my belly Monteleur quieted. The pain began to fade.

The Queen had not come.

"Nothing of this world can harm me," Monteleur boasted. "Nothing. Your snake hurt me, David, but only a little. Not nearly as much as I can hurt you—"

A white-hot spike between my eyes, up through my bowels, skewering me. When I stopped screaming Monteleur had me start driving again.

Every few hours it had me pull off to the side of the road.

It was a long way to Carlsbad.

Chapter Thirty-one

T hings were a little better in Carlsbad. Monteleur was still amusing itself with me—a flash of agony like a knitting needle through my knee, a sudden explosion of molten metal behind my eyes—but now that we'd reached the caverns, I found I could take their energies, use them if not to resist the pain then at least to endure it.

We switchbacked down through the singing and the radiance, working our way ever closer to the source, the center, the pulsing heart.

A ranger in park-service brown was standing talking with two grandmotherly women in faded dresses just in front of the fluted drapery stalactites that hid the hole from which the waterfall of suns burst to fall alive and glorious through air and stone, ranger and old ladies alike. But he was too close; we would have had to push him aside to climb the cave coral to the hidden entrance. And Stephen had forbidden us to use our "Naga invisibility."

We pretended to examine another set of drapery stalactites while we waited for the ranger to finish his talk and move on to another chamber, but by the time the old ladies were ready to leave they'd been replaced by a middle-aged couple to whom the ranger was already pointing out rock formations with the beam of his flashlight.

"He's not going to leave," I whispered to Monteleur under my breath. "Get him out of here. We can't obey Stephen's orders with anyone here."

I was suddenly assaulted by an unbearably powerful sulfurous stench, a hot hissing sound like lava fountaining from the rock, flowing toward me; all around I could hear the rock grinding and splitting, men and women screaming in pain and terror. Yet the rock was unmoving beneath my feet.

The ranger yelled, "Earthquake! Make for the entrance!" and sprinted into the next chamber after the old ladies. The couple turned and ran back past us and out through the King's Palace.

We were alone.

I followed Dara up the rough cave coral to the entrance hole, wriggled after her through the long, low tunnel leading to the caverns' living heart.

The chamber was as I had remembered it: large, vaulted, its far end a pool of chill water from whose depths bubbles rose to burst with a soft plopping sound.

I could hear the echoing voices of the rangers investigating the Queen's Chamber, but where we were there was only stillness, only radiance.

And Monteleur, a dark maggot squirming through the crystal transparency of my flesh.

I took off my sweater and shirt, had removed one sandal and was unbuckling the other when a white-hot needle jabbed itself up through the roof of my mouth, pierced my brain. I kept myself from crying out, undid my other sandal.

"No more, Monteleur," Dara said. "Not while we're carrying out Stephen's orders."

"Not now," Monteleur agreed. "Later."

The stone was cold beneath us, damp, but the pain was gone and I was free for the instant to forget Monteleur, to forget everything but Dara and the fires singing through us. Not even the knowledge that Stephen would soon drain us of the power our lovemaking was generating could destroy the joy we found in each other, the excitement and purity of our union. We made love as slowly, as teasingly and gently as we could, trying to prolong our freedom and our communion as long as possible, spending hours in caresses that barely brushed each other's skin, in kissing and tasting each other, building with infinite slowness toward union.

The earth's flaming life flowed through us and even as we held ourselves back we were one with it, lifted out of and beyond ourselves on its tides. But all too soon our lovemaking had passed from restraint to union, and our union had impelled us beyond ourselves into the symbolic landscapes of my father's mind.

The cold wind bit into us—we were one body now, though androgynous and complete instead of clumsily hermaphroditic—but we commanded the void to release us and it was gone. My temptation took on reality around us but we willed the bedroom and bleeding girl gone and they disappeared. My father cut open his chest, exposed his gray unbeating heart, but I took the power surging through us, tried to push us deeper into him, somewhere beyond this trial that only I had undergone, somewhere Stephen and Monteleur could not follow us.

We were standing knee deep in the salmon-pink mud of an endless swamp plain. Tuberous liver-gray plants floated just below the surface of the scummy pools.

We were settling slowly deeper into the mud. Sinking. Dara gave me control. I dragged first one leg, then the other, free. As soon as I quit struggling we began to sink again.

There was no sun. Above us an oversized moon pulsed through changes of phase as though its waxing and waning were the beating of some sickly heart. The air and mud were unbearably hot and a pall of steam hung over everything.

In the distance a single green hill thrust itself up out of the pink swamp. I waded toward it, dragging myself slowly through the sucking mud, skirting the scummy pools.

On the crest of the hill a great gray-green plant like a tendrilled melon rested on a tangled mass of interwoven roots like gnarled gray worms digging their way into the grassy hillside. From somewhere within the tangle four twisting rivulets of blood-red liquid made their way down the hill's steep slopes to the shallow lake encircling it like a carmine moat.

Most of the tendrils drooped listlessly down the hillside, but at seemingly random intervals some of them would leap into the sky and attach themselves to invisible things passing overhead. The tendrils would stretch to two or three times their flaccid lengths, then snap back to their original size and collapse back onto the hill.

We were perhaps five hundred yards from the lake. I stopped, shifting from one leg to the other to keep from sinking too deeply.

"Dara, before we get any closer, do you know what that thing is? Or what it's doing?"

"No. I never heard of this . . . level. This reality."

"Can Monteleur follow us here? Or Stephen?"

"I don't know. I can't sense them here. . . . I can still feel Monteleur back in your body and Stephen is—is not *with* Monteleur but connected to it somehow—"

"Can they overhear us?"

"We're still inside Father's mind. Maybe they can learn what we say to each other from him."

"You're not sure?"

"No. But they wouldn't have let us come here if they thought we could escape them."

"Maybe they don't know about it. All Stephen is worried about is using us to gain power."

"Maybe." She didn't sound convinced.

"We have to risk it. Can you teach me how to—do the things you can do? Like how you knew Monteleur and Stephen weren't here. And anything else, any—"

"Like this?" A whisper, sibilant and silent, that had not been formed by the mouth we shared. "I can't, David. I don't know how."

"Can't you just, I don't know, *show* me or—"

"I *can't*, David." Still whispering. "I'm half Naga, David, and so are you, but that doesn't mean that we're . . . halfway human and halfway Naga, all mixed up together. What it means is that we've each got two souls, a Naga soul and a human soul. And before my grandparents gave me to Father I lived in the Naga Realm, Patala, that's where I learned, where my Naga soul learned, to do—the things you can't do. And I was only a child, five years old. All I know, all my grandparents let me remember when I left Patala, was how to reach my Naga soul and draw on some of its powers."

"Wait. You mean, there's something else inside me and it isn't me at all? Like Monteleur, only it's a Naga instead?"

"No. It's you, but a completely different you."

"Like a twin?" She shook her head. "Then some sort of split personality, the three faces of Eve, that sort of thing?"

"David, I can't explain. When I left Patala, it's not like they took my memories away from me, but certain things are veiled, they can't be anything *but* veiled anywhere else but Patala."

"So you can't even tell me how to . . . contact my Naga soul?"

"No. I just do it, I don't know how or how to teach you."

"But if it's inside me, does that mean it's listening to what we're saying, it knows what's going on? It could contact *me* if it wanted to?"

"I don't know."

"Ask your Naga soul."

She was silent an instant, then: "Only in Patala. Otherwise the contact would destroy you."

"When I first got back to the house I heard Michael and Stephen talking. They said Nagas have the power of fire. Could you use your Naga soul to *burn* Monteleur out of me?"

"Nagas can control fire because they *are* fire, fire is one of their aspects. If I summoned up that aspect it would mean that I, the human me, would be destroyed."

"Except in Patala. That's our only hope anyway, right, there isn't anywhere else we'd be safe?"

"No."

"Then where is it?"

"It's within the earth, under it, and beneath the ocean but—it isn't anywhere, exactly, not any one place. When I lived there we could, I remember, look out and see the world, see everything that ever happened, but now— When they took me to live with Father, we just walked out through the gates and then a little longer, it felt like five minutes, through some sunny fields and then we walked into the shadow of a tree and down beneath its roots into the cavern beneath the house. But after they went away and left me I tried to find the way back and I never could, not even when they came to visit him and I'd try to follow them . . ."

"But it's someplace real, not just something like here?"

"Yes."

"Can your Naga soul help us get there?"

She was silent for a long time.

"If Michael came with us, if all three of us went together, they'd let us go back there now. But your familiars would destroy both of you before you could enter."

"So if I can get rid of Monteleur—"

"And Bathomar."

"Why does it have to be all three of us?"

"Because . . ." She fell silent again. "There's a reason Saraparajni came into this world, married Father, and that's . . . part of it, we're all involved."

"Meaning what?"

"I don't know, David. Just that none of us can enter Patala unless we all do."

"And that's all your Naga soul will tell you?"

"It's not like asking somebody else, another person. What I do is, it's like putting on a Naga mask and then I know things, I can do some of the things a Naga can do."

When we reached the lake I bent down, lifted some of the red fluid to our mouth, tasted it. I had half expected it to be blood, but though it had a faintly meatlike odor the liquid itself was thin and almost intolerably sweet, like the nectar of some overripe tropical flower.

As soon as it touched our lips the sky was full of naked men and women. They floated slowly through the air above us, eyes closed, following intricate intertwining trajectories from which they never deviated. When one of the sleepers came too close to the hill a tendril would dart to him, attach itself, and slowly drain him of his substance, leaving his shriveled and emptied body to continue as before along its predeter-mined path when the tendril fell away.

As we circled the hill a face came into view on the far side of the melonlike plant, a face at least eight feet tall. My father's face. The tendrils began just above his molded eye-brows. His eyes were closed.

"Father," I yelled, but he gave no sign he was aware of me.

"What do we do now?" I asked Dara.

"I don't think we're in any danger from him. Let's climb the hill."

The red moat made our skin tingle slightly as we waded through it. The grass was slick and the hillside steeper than I'd realized; we made slow progress. The face took no notice of us.

We had to step over some of the flaccid tendrils, thread our way between others. Each ended in a red-lipped mouth above which was sketched the same simplified caricature of a Bathory face. None of the tendrils tried to attach themselves to us, even when I stumbled over one.

We reached Father's huge green face, but though we were standing directly in front of him, he remained unaware of us. Around us tendrils continued to leap into the sky, drain their victims, fall back again.

"Father!" I yelled again. His eyes remained shut. I hit him on the chin, the only part of his face I could reach. The flesh was as soft as an overripe tomato; it split and began leaking the red fluid, but still he refused to respond.

"What do we do now?" I asked Dara. "He doesn't seem to be conscious at all."

"Maybe he isn't usually conscious, not on this level." And then, whispering: "I can try to call him to us."

I gave her control of our body. She stared up at the face without moving our lips or doing anything else I could feel with our shared vocal apparatus, yet soon I began to feel a presence pouring into me, a sort of awakening, almost like a hit of coke just after you've gotten up in the morning, not enough to wake you up completely but enough to clear away some of the confusion.

"Hello, Father," I said when Dara returned control to me. "What do I have to do to defeat you this time?"

The great vegetable lips moved sluggishly. "Nothing."

"Then why are we here?"

"To gain power from me."

"How?"

"By drinking the life that I take for yourselves."

"The red streams?"

"Yes."

I couldn't sense any resistance, anything to indicate he was trying to trick us, but I didn't trust him.

"How do we get back from here?"

"I will send you back."

"What if Dara hadn't been able to make you hear her?"

"You would have found a way. Do you wish to return now?"

"Wait," Dara said. "What is this place?"

"A subjective reality."

"Explain it."

"This plant is our undead family; it wore my father's face before mine. The streams flowing from beneath my roots are the lives of those we love. The plain from which this hill rises is the body of Satan and this hill is you, my children, all three of you."

"Michael is here too?" I demanded.

"Yes."

"Can we communicate with him?" Dara asked.

"You are all three this hill and within the hill. There is an entrance beneath my roots, by the spring from which the streams flow."

A sloping tunnel led into the hill. It was tight and twisting, slimy-walled; we had to wriggle through it on our belly.

Inside the hill three faceless obsidian figures, two male and one female, sat around a fire fed by drops of the sweet red liquid that fell from the roof. Within the flames a tiny red figure lay in an open coffin: my father.

One figure must have been Michael, the other two us. None of them gave any indication of life or awareness. I couldn't even tell which was me.

"Michael," I said. "Dara." And then: "David."

The figures remained immobile, lifeless stone.

"Can you make them hear you like with Father?" I asked Dara.

"I'll try," she said.

"Michael," the flames whispered with my voice, "we need your help." The words were those I would have spoken but I had not willed them.

"We're all in this together," the flames insisted in Dara's voice. "The three of us. Stephen is as much your enemy as he is ours."

"What do you want me to do for you? And what can you offer me in exchange?" Michael's voice asked.

"We offer you our combined strengths and the chance to awaken your Naga powers. We offer you sanctuary in Patala, our ancestral home, if you will join us."

"What do you want?" Michael's voice repeated.

"We need to know more about Stephen. About SUSTU-GRIEL and his familiars, our own dhampire's powers and weaknesses. We need the Naga bracelet David hid near the house," Dara's voice whispered.

"Can you free me from Bathomar?"

"Not yet. But maybe, with the bracelet—"

"The bracelet has been destroyed," the flames whispered back, "and what knowledge I have I will keep for myself. There is no point in further bargaining."

The flames were silent once more. The stone figures had never moved.

"So much for Patala," I said. "Can he still hear us?"

"I don't know. I don't even know if he was ever really conscious of being here with us."

We crawled out the tunnel.

"Send us back," I told Father.

And in the cave, Monteleur was waiting. I spasmed uncontrollably in an agony that went on and on as the worm drained me, bloated itself on the power our lovemaking had generated.

Chapter Thirty-two

We waited until the last light was fading from the sky over the canyon before leaving Indian Gardens: we wanted to make sure no one saw us when we left the path and climbed the loose rock to the cave.

The cave was as I remembered it, elfin and beautiful, shimmering with soft silver powerlight. We unrolled our sleeping bags and spread them out.

There was a last moment of utter agony as I finished undressing and then I was free. Free until we returned to our bodies and Monteleur drained our force from us again.

We tried to hold back as long as we could, keep to our separate selves, but all too soon the walls separating us went down and we met and merged, melted into the living energies surrounding us. Only to be wrenched from our joy, find our androgynous body once again standing knee deep in the salmon-gray mud.

Dara gave me control. We started for the hill.

"Is Monteleur here, Dara? Or Stephen?"

"I don't think so." Her sibilant whisper. "And Father's not conscious of our presence here yet."

"What about Michael?"

"I don't know. He's under the hill, just like we are, and he's half Naga. But I still don't know if he can hear us."

"What about our grandparents, or the cobra Queen, the one who saved me? Is there any way to get through to them, get them to help us?"

"I don't remember anything about a queen but— They don't care. No, they care, they care more than anyone, but it's not like— They don't try to stop anything. That first time, when they gave me to Father, they just stood there all beautiful and peaceful and shining while he made me watch one of the vampires—his father, I think it was—kill a girl the same age I was, and then he gave me to the other vampires to play with, not hurt, he stayed there and made sure they didn't hurt me, but they were all around me, staring at me and touching my face and all over my body and telling me how much they loved me and wanted me and wanted me to be like them—And *they* just stood there watching, they didn't do anything to save the girl. It didn't make any difference to them how horrible it was for me, how frightened I was, or— But before they left me alone, grandfather took one of the— serpents—from his . . . aura and gave it to me to wear on my arm—"

"And Stephen found it where I hid it and destroyed it."

"It was part of Grandfather. It couldn't be destroyed. It must have gone back to him."

"Or Michael's lying."

"Maybe."

"But you don't have any other way to find them or—I don't know. Let them know you need their help."

"No. I tried. All those years, even with the . . . bracelet, I tried to get them to come back for me and take me away but they never did."

I would have held her, tried to reassure her if we'd been in our own bodies. Here, there was nothing I could do. We waded the moat, climbed the hill. Just before we reached the crest Dara had me kneel and drink from one of the streams. The sky was suddenly filled with floating figures again.

"More, David. We may need the strength. Let's take it now, before Father's aware we're here."

I swallowed more and had started to straighten when an idea struck me. Scooping some of the liquid up in our cupped hands, I scrambled the rest of the way up to the top and splashed it on his green face. The face opened its eyes, stared down at me.

The awareness that washed over me this time when he awakened was sharper. I could feel his strength and his rage, the way he was constantly testing his bonds, hoping for a weakness that would allow him to turn on us and sate his hunger.

"How do we get to the next level?" I asked.

"There are no more levels," he said. "From here there is only return. Return to your own bodies or to the bodies of those joined in me."

"Michael and Stephen?"

"Your ancestors. Those already joined in the communion."

"How would I return to one of their bodies—to my grandfather's, say? What would it involve?"

"I would merge you with him. You would be a passenger only, experiencing what he experiences without awareness of yourself."

"How would I get back?"

"I would bring you back."

"And what would happen to this body while I was gone?"

"It would remain here."

"I don't trust him," Dara whispered. "Not even here. But one of us could go while the other stayed."

I tried to find the passage whose walls were doors leading to my ancestors' souls, as I'd done when I first defeated him, but I was unable to recognize it. Perhaps it didn't exist on this level.

Yet I still had dominion. "Put me in Grandfather," I said. "Dara will stay here to command you until I return. Bring me back at dawn."

And I was Mihnea Bathory, beating wings of furred membrane high above the deserted streets of a small town. It was sometime after midnight. I had no awareness of myself as David Bathory. I was Mihnea.

My thirst burned within me, made me shiver with rage even as I flew, though I had drunk the blood of two young girls tonight. But I had not drunk deeply enough to satisfy my need, drunk them to death and beyond, till they were emptied and I could fill their emptiness with my love, make of them my other selves and share their love for those they cherished among the living. They had been only strangers, my love for them only brief and trivial.

Suddenly, there below me, at the edge of town, walking across the bridge to the tiny island in the artificial lake that was the only break in this town's monotonous checkerboard of housing developments, I saw a girl crying softly to herself. She was thin and without beauty, but her tears made her infinitely desirable.

I swooped down at her from behind, coming so close that she felt the wind of my passage stir her long hair. She looked up, startled, saw me climbing, black skeletal wings clearly visible as I wheeled in front of the moon, dived at her again and halted, hovering just above her in a flurry of hairy wings, so close she could see the red fire in my eyes, smell my rank odor. She screamed, began to run. I climbed back into the sky, let her go a hundred yards, halfway across the island, then swooped down in front of her again, letting one of my wing tips brush her shoulder. She tried to turn back, stumbled, then picked herself up and ran for the bridge, but I was already there, hovering, red eyes gleaming.

I ran her until she collapsed, hysterical and sobbing, then came to ground on the other side of the bridge and resumed my human form. I was dressed, as I preferred, in clerical black.

She heard my footsteps on the bridge, heaved herself up off the ground, prepared for a last desperate attempt at flight, but the moonlight gleamed on my clerical collar and when she recognized me as a priest she collapsed once more, still sobbing but this time with relief.

"What's wrong, child?" I asked, helping her to her feet.

"Thank God you're here, Father. I'm a—a Lutheran but— Thank God you're here!"

"What's wrong?" I asked. "Is it something that I can help you with?"

"There's a giant bat—" She broke off, realizing for the first time how impossible her story was, then went on defiantly.

"—a giant bat chasing me. It wouldn't let me back across the bridge . . ."

"A vampire?" I asked. She looked eleven, perhaps twelve. She'd scratched her face in her flight; the scratch had already scabbed over but I could feel her warmth, see the delicate pink tracery of the capillaries just beneath the surface of her skin, the throbbing in her throat.

"Yes!"

"Surely you're joking," I said. "If there's something you don't want to—"

"You're a Catholic priest!" she accused. "You're supposed to believe me!"

"I believe in evil, yes, but vampires? Perhaps you did see a bat, or a big bird, maybe an owl, but—"

"It chased me. And it wasn't just a bird or something. It was too big and it knew what it was doing. I could smell it."

"Where is it now, then?" I asked reasonably.

"I don't know—it flew away. You must have scared it off."

"In that case it doesn't really matter whether or not I believe in it, does it?" I asked. "Do you think you can make it home safely?"

"Please come with me, Father," she pleaded. "I don't—want to be alone right now. If you could just, take me home—"

"I can't, child. Not now. One of my parishioners left a note saying she was going to drown herself here tonight. I've got to find her before it's too late."

"Could I, could I borrow your cross?" the girl asked, chastened. "I'll mail it back to you or something—"

"My crucifix?" I asked, delighted with her. "All right. You can bring it by the church tomorrow."

"Thank you, Father." She smiled hesitantly as I took the crucifix from around my neck and handed it to her. She started to put it around her own neck, then stopped, stared at it, seeing it clearly for the first time in the semidarkness.

"B-but—" she stammered. "But Christ is upside down!"

"That's right," I said, smiling gently, letting my eyes glow red as I held her with my gaze forcing her to lift her head, bend it back to expose her neck as I caught her in my arms, bent to her bared throat.

But I had no fangs, I could not bite into her, feel the thick rich blood spurting forth, I had to suck it painstakingly through the unbroken skin, and it was never enough, a pitiful trickle that only fed my rage, my need, and for the third time this night I hated my children for what they'd done to me, what they had reduced me to.

When I sensed dawn approaching I left her unconscious but still living, to recover with a story she would never dare tell, and flew back to the estate.

I lay down in my coffin, closed the lid over me, felt my consciousness begin to fade . . .

I was myself again, back atop the green hill, facing my father's great vegetal face. But I couldn't feel Dara's presence in the body we shared.

"Dara?" I asked, but there was no whispered response and the muscles of my mouth and throat remained lax when I tried to relinquish control of them.

"Where's Dara?"

"She ordered me to put her into Father's mind as soon as you quit him." My father's speech was slurred; his tendrils hung limp and flaccid. The blind fliers passed unmolested overhead.

I could detect no falsehood, no attempt at hiding anything from me. I decided I had no choice but to believe him and sat down on a root to wait for her return.

"Son," he said presently, "you know that I love you." His voice was still slurred but for the first time it felt as though he was the one speaking with me, the father I remembered and not just something using his voice.

"And?" I twisted around to stare up into the green darkness of his eyes.

"Merge with me. Submit to me. Let me fill my veins with

your blood so that I can submit to you as even now my own father submits to me."

"I already command you."

"It is not the same. Our souls are divided."

"No thanks," I said, remembering the unassuageable isolation that was so much of Mihnea's thirst. "You made the same offer to Dara?"

"Yes. She refused."

"Has any member of the family ever accepted?"

"Many. My own great-grandfather—"

"And how does he feel about it now?"

"He never tried to declare the Compact void."

"The compact you make with Satan to become a vampire?" I asked, remembering the letter he'd written me just before his death.

"Yes."

"Tell me about it."

"After you die the wind claims you. But if you are to become a vampire Satan offers you a chance to escape."

"And the terms?"

"Satan offers you new life as a vampire, with immortality and freedom from Hell—"

"I thought death was just the falling and the wind."

"That is death. There is also Hell. But Satan offers you escape from both death and Hell and will grant you the powers you need to satisfy the hungers of your new existence. In return He asks only that you worship no other god than Him and that you spend your days in adoration of Him."

Which must be what Dara was experiencing now, unless she was just lying trapped in Mihnea's body while his soul was elsewhere.

"You told Dara this?"

"Yes."

"What is it like, the adoration?"

"My transformation is not yet complete, so I have not yet

spent a day in adoration. But I know from my other selves what it is like. They sleep."

"That's all? They just sleep?"

"They dream of dancing."

"Has anyone ever withdrawn from the Compact? Declared it void?"

His face wrinkled, as though he was trying to frown. "I don't remember," he said at last.

"What about your wife?" I asked. "Saraparajni? When you sealed her into her coffin for seven years?"

He seemed confused. "Saraparajni . . . underwent the transformation but she— No. I don't remember."

I brought him some liquid from one of the streams, splashed it over his mouth. "Does that help?"

"Before she had ever tasted blood she let me . . . I sealed her into her coffin and—"

"Tell me about that. About the seven years."

"It is part of being a vampire, part of our natures." He sounded more sure of himself. "If we are sealed into our coffins for seven years without being released or tasting blood and we emerge from our coffins onto the soil of a foreign country where a different language is spoken, we become mortal again, though we only live for five years as human beings."

"And after the five years?"

"We either become vampires again or we—die. Forever."

"So you sealed Mother in her coffin and took her—where?"

"Mexico. It seemed safer than trying to take her overseas."

"Did you have friends in Mexico, people helping you?"

"No. There was no one we could trust."

"What happened after that? After she had Dara and her five years were over?"

"She returned to Patala."

"Did she die there?"

He seemed confused again. "If she'd been human . . . That

was one of the limitations, but she was never truly mortal. She was a Naga. The Queen of the Nagas.''

The cobra-headed Queen on the ivory throne? I splashed more liquid on his face. "Did she die there?"

Because if she was still alive Dara might be safe there, might not have to become a vampire when she died.

"I don't know."

"Where is Patala? Did you go to Patala and then bring her back with you, or what?"

"No, it was a temple. A temple of Shiva. In India. We were underwriting a mission there. One of the missionaries wrote us about a beautiful woman the people said was a Naga, a snake goddess. She called herself Manasa then, or that's what the people called her, I don't remember exactly, but— She was so beautiful. So graceful. I'd never seen anyone so beautiful.''

"But she looked human?"

"Of course she looked human." He sounded irritated. "When I learned she was really a Naga I wanted to marry her, so we could gain her powers for the family. I thought that with the Naga intelligence my sons and daughters might be able to become vampires who wouldn't need dhampires to control them. . . ."

"Why did she marry you?"

"I don't know. I never really knew."

"She converted you to her god, didn't she? To Shiva?"

"No. She tried but— No. I worship Satan. Only Satan."

I continued questioning him, splashing his face whenever he grew sluggish or confused, but learned nothing he hadn't already told me.

I was sitting on his roots when I felt the subtle alterations in the rhythms of our shared body that signaled Dara's presence. My father's tendrils began darting up into the sky again, seeking out victims. It must have been dusk in Illinois.

"Dara?"

"Give me time, David. Give me time. I've spent the day in

Hell." She was using our mouth and throat to speak, too tired for her special way of whispering. I drank more fluid from the stream, sat down by its edge and waited.

At last she said, "I was in Hell, David. That's what they do when their bodies are asleep, they're in Hell, dancing the dance of torment. Satan feeds on their agony and despair, He taunts them with the knowledge of how He's cheated them and how He's going to do the same thing to them forever. There's no way they can ever escape. He makes a Compact with them—"

"I know about the Compact," I said, then gave her back the use of our mouth.

"But Satan cheats. He has never honored His Compact. His vampires, all His slaves and servants, spend their days in unending torture, but when night comes He makes them forget what happened so they don't know He's broken the Compact—"

"Why don't they renounce it during the day?"

"I thought I told you— During the day they're all merged with Him, part of Him. His will is their will and He tortures them by torturing Himself. Their pain is His pain. . . . He has created a Heaven so the damned will suffer from their knowledge of its existence, but He Himself is all the damned, they're part of him the same way I was. I was part of Him, I was Satan—"

She broke off. We were shaking. I stood up, walked around a little, cupped us some more of the red liquid and drank it.

"Some of the damned are there eternally, but the vampires are only there during the day. They could renounce the Compact and free themselves at night, when they're themselves again, but they've forgotten what they knew during the day."

"You remembered."

"Because I have two souls. The human soul endured Hell, was swallowed up by Satan, while the Naga soul looked on. When Satan released the human soul and made it forget, the Naga soul remembered."

"Does that mean Satan knows everything you know? Everything about us?"

"It isn't like that. Satan isn't interested in what you thought when you were separate from Him. He just wants to force you to share his agonies."

"What about Christ?"

"What Stephen said: Satan's finest creation. The bait for His hook."

"Father," I said, "did you hear what she said?"

"It makes no sense."

"But you told me the same thing in a letter before you died. And you haven't signed the Compact yet."

"He can't believe it, David, not even if he knew most of it when he was alive. That's what happens in the forty days—the other vampires make him over in their image, strip him of everything that would keep him from being exactly like them. He's part of them already, even if he isn't completely a vampire yet. And none of them will ever believe the truth.

"It's part of Satan's game, the way he tortures them and Himself: they actually have the ability to renounce the Compact and free themselves from him at night, but they can't believe the truth about themselves, even when someone tells it to them."

"But if we could find some way to give them their daytime knowledge at night?" I asked. "Or seal them all in their coffins for the seven years and make sure none of them escaped and that Michael and Stephen didn't free them— No. They've already tasted blood."

"It would be useless anyway, unless you could reawaken their memories of Hell. Remember who they were when they were alive, who they'd be again. Elizabeth Báthory, Vlad the Impaler, David Mathewson, the one who had all those women hanged as witches in Scotland. All the rest of them. Even if we could bring a few of them to believe us and accept a death from which there'd be no returning, the rest would be only too glad to become vampires once again."

She was silent an instant. "I always hated Alexandra,

David. She and Michael used to torment me when I was growing up. And when Father forced me to use the bushmaster to kill her—I wouldn't have done it if I could have resisted him. But part of me was glad that he was making me do it. Enjoyed watching her agony as she died. But that was before I spent a day with her in Hell. It all got burned away. I can't hate any of them anymore."

"You could . . . feel Alexandra there?"

"No. Her forty days aren't over yet. But I could feel Satan's anticipation, how He was waiting for both her and Father. Nobody deserves that. Nobody."

"So what do we do? Try to escape and hope I live long enough to put you in your coffin and keep you sealed there for seven years and finally let you out again? And that you can do the same thing for me?"

"I don't know, David. Try to get free and stay alive long enough to find a solution if there is one."

Unless we could get to Patala. If it really existed and there really was a way there. And if I could free myself of Monteleur first.

Monteleur, who was waiting for me back in my body. Waiting for me to recover consciousness so it could hurt me the way it had hurt me when I'd returned to my body in Carlsbad. And the longer I waited, the worse Monteleur would make the pain.

"Send us back," I told Father.

Chapter Thirty-three

John was sitting bare-chested in the sun on the front porch, his eyes closed. He'd lost weight. A great purple butterfly with pale-blue eyespots on its wings and tails like a black swallowtail's, only much longer, was resting on his right shoulder, slowly opening and closing its wings.

He opened his eyes, stared up at us without moving. "Hello, David. Welcome home." There was no warmth in his voice or face.

"Hello, John. What are you doing here?"

"Waiting for you. Stephen said you'd be here today or tomorrow. This is Dara, I take it?"

Yet another betrayal, one more person I'd trusted who must've been working against me all along. But he'd always been Alexandra's acolyte: it would have been too much to hope for that she wouldn't have recruited him.

"You said Stephen told you I was coming? Is he here now?"

"He's back in the cave. You're supposed to wait for him here."

"Is my brother with him? Michael?"

"Michael won't be arriving for another month or so."

"For the Lammas Day Sabbat?"

"Right."

"John, just how well do you know my uncle?"

"Meaning what, David? Are you trying to find our just how much he's told me? Whether I'm a friend and associate or just an innocent dupe?"

"All of that, I guess."

"A friend and associate, then. Alexandra introduced me to him about four years ago, but I didn't join his coven until you and your sister tried to kill her."

"John, Dara and I had nothing to do with that. That was Father, not us. But what do you mean, *tried* to kill her? She's dead."

"No she isn't. Stephen rescued her for me."

He twisted his head cautiously to the right, gazed at the butterfly fanning its wings on his shoulder. It was bigger than any North American butterfly—it must have had an eight-inch wingspread—and though it was abroad in daylight, it had the feathery antennae of a night-flying moth.

"That's her, David. Alexandra. She's a butterfly now. And she's mine, like she always wanted to be. You can't have her back."

The butterfly shifted position on his shoulder. Alexandra. But I'd touched her cooling skin, watched the coroner's deputy probe her wound with his thick red fingers, close her eyes. I'd seen her uncorrupted flesh in the coffin next to my father's on the cavern floor.

Alexandra. And the dead rise up never, unless they're vampires, and then they're still dead, and then they'll always be dead. And she couldn't be a vampire, not before her forty days were up, not there on his shoulder in the hot sun when a vampire would be dancing the dance of torment in Hell.

But maybe there was some way to use the spirit during its forty-day transformation, pluck it from the freezing void and give it a temporary body.

"That's really her? You're sure?"

"Of course I'm sure."

"How did it happen?" Dara asked.

"She'll tell you about it herself, if you'd like her to. But we'll have to go inside. Her voice is too tiny to hear over the wind."

We went inside, sat down at the table. The wall where the bookcase holding my aunt's grimoires had been was a lighter color than the rest of the room. John sat down across from us.

"Don't get too close. Don't even breathe on her hard. She's very delicate now."

"We won't do anything to hurt her," Dara said.

"Just don't. And speak softly. You're talking too loud already. Loud noises hurt her.

"Alexandra?" I asked, leaning close and whispering.

"Yes, David?" The words were so faint I could barely hear them, but it sounded like Alexandra's voice.

"Tell me about it. What happened, how Stephen saved you."

"After you and John left to go swimming, your father made me open the bushmaster's cage," the thin voice—Alexandra's voice?—said. "Then he kept me from doing anything to save myself when Michael and Dara—"

"Just Michael," I said. "Not Dara."

"—while they used the snake to try to kill me, and then to keep you from getting to me with the antivenin."

"You were still . . . alive?" I asked. "You knew I was there in the cave with you, trying to save you?"

"It's lying," Dara whispered with that whisper that only I could hear. "I was there. It wasn't just Michael, Father made me do it, and I felt her die."

"They weren't expecting you back so soon," the butterfly said. "Not while I was still alive. But I'd been in Stephen's coven for a long time—I always knew that Michael was just planning on using me and then getting rid of me, that he never meant to give me any of what he promised—and so even though you weren't able to get past the bushmaster, Stephen was there waiting to snare my escaping soul. He gave me this butterfly to use until Lammas Day, when the constellations will be right to give me a new human body."

"Whose body?" Dara demanded.

"Perhaps yours, perhaps somebody else's. He hasn't told me yet," the butterfly said with a tiny tinkling laugh.

But it wasn't Alexandra's laugh, could never have been her laugh, no matter how physically altered she was. Unless she'd become a vampire, and even so it was too soon after her death. I knew Alexandra, knew her for all her lies, for all the ways she'd tried to use me: whatever she'd done would have been to satisfy her hungers, her greed. I'd fallen through the void with my father, felt his insatiable need, shared Mihnea's hunger as he hunted: distorted perversions of the needs they had felt in life, nothing like the cold passionless delight that rang through the butterfly's laughter.

And if Stephen, if any Bathory, could snare escaping souls and give them new bodies, the family could have had the immortality it sought in the flesh, without having to die and become vampires. Another lie.

The butterfly shifted on its six legs again, uncurled its thread-thin black proboscis and jabbed it into the base of John's neck. John held himself very still, careful not to dislodge it. He looked proud, a bit shy. I could see that his neck and shoulders were covered with tiny red-brown welts, almost invisible against the tan. Not a vampire, but some other form of parasite.

"What is it?" I asked Dara.

"It's not her, David," she whispered. "Not exactly. But there's something of her in it."

"I keep her alive," John said. He was pitching his voice low, avoiding looking directly at the thing while he spoke. Protecting it. "She'd prefer to live outside where she could drink nectar from flowers like a real butterfly, but it's too dangerous. There are too many things out there that would like to eat her. Birds, spiders, lizards. Frogs and toads and bats. Even other insects, real ones. Blood's better, a sacrament we can share between us."

He was looking at me as if to say, a sacrament that only the two of us will ever share, that unites us in a way you'll never know. Another victim. Like Uncle Peter, Aunt Judith. Like Alexandra herself, deluded into thinking she was part of some inner cabal when she was only a tool.

The butterfly withdrew its proboscis, delicately recurled it. A new body on Lammas Day. Was it some other kind of familiar being prepared to take possession of Dara where Bathomar had failed?

The door opened and Stephen and the teenage girl who looked like Alexandra, Lydia, came through it, followed by three men in blue suits who looked like Jehovah's Witnesses.

John was staring at Lydia the same way he used to watch Alexandra, but she ignored him.

"Don't bother to get up," Stephen said, playing perfect host, and as he smiled Monteleur jabbed knitting needles through my knees. "How was your trip, David?"

"Why not just ask Monteleur?" I demanded, unable to put up with any more of his unending cat-and-mouse. "Since you're going to anyway."

"Because I have no need to ever ask Monteleur anything. Ever. I keep in constant communication with him through my own familiar."

"That?" I jerked my head in the butterfly's direction. John scowled, hunched his shoulder protectively.

"Not at all. That's Alexandra, whether you want to admit it or not, David. I already showed you my familiar. I carry it around inside me like you do yours. That way it can keep me young and healthy, protect me from heart attacks and sudden catastrophic kidney failures, that sort of thing."

I ignored the implied threat, said, "Then you don't need me to tell you what happened."

"True. I know all about your attempt with the cobra and I intend to punish you for it. Both of you.

"Your own punishment, David, is unfortunately going to be more of a demonstration of our respective positions than an attempt to actually hurt you. I have few illusions about my ability to outdo Monteleur in inflicting physical pain.

"But in Dara's case, as I think you can see, things are a bit different. If for no other reason than because any pain I cause her will provide you with a further demonstration of your own helplessness. So—

"Here." He picked up one of the cotton sacks I used for my snakes, handed it to her. "Go back to David's truck and get the cobra. Put it in the sack and bring it here. David, you stay with me."

Dara returned a few minutes later with the bagged snake.

"Take it out of the bag and hold it where we can all see it.

Good. Now kill it. Twist its neck until it's dead. Do it *now*, Dara, or I'll see that Monteleur hurts David while I kill the snake myself."

She held the cobra a little longer in her cupped hands, staring into its eyes. The cobra stared back at her, absolutely motionless, making no attempt to escape.

She killed it.

"Very good. For the rest—the two of you come along with me. I've got some things to show you.

"John, you stay here. Give me Alexandra. I'll keep her safe until we return."

John reluctantly took the butterfly in his cupped hands, gave it to Stephen.

"John isn't quite ready to be permitted inside yet," Stephen explained, "but all that will change on Lammas Day."

One of Stephen's assistants preceded him through the door, waited outside. Lydia clung to Stephen's arm, like a junior-high-school cheerleader who wants to make sure nobody misses the fact that she's with her football-hero boyfriend. The other two Jehovah's Witnesses followed us.

"I told it what I was going to do but it wasn't afraid," Dara whispered. "It didn't feel any pain."

There was a small stand of stunted live oaks just outside the entrance to the herpetarium. The bushmaster was nailed to the trunk of the biggest tree, hanging from a thick nail through its head, its tail dragging in the dust. Dozens of other dead snakes—garter snakes, king snakes, all the local varieties—were heaped in a rotting pile beneath the tree.

There was a new door blocking the entrance to the cave, thick brass-studded wood, perhaps seven feet tall. It took three keys to unlock it.

While the first Jehovah's Witness was unlocking the door, Stephen turned back to us, nodded to indicate the crucified bushmaster and the dead snakes. "All that training you gave John in the care and collection of snakes turned out to be useful after all. As you can see."

He smiled and Lydia smirked on cue. She was just the right

age for the Khmer Rouge, Pol Pot's genocidal child soldiers, too young for her fanaticism to be tempered by anything else. The perfect disciple.

I tried to keep my face expressionless but Stephen just kept on smiling, as though that had been exactly the reaction he'd been hoping for, and gestured us inside. The Jehovah's Witness with the keys locked the door behind us.

The cages and tanks were gone, replaced by racks of swords and lancets, quills and wands, cloth-covered altars, jars full of teeth and bones; other, larger jars in which homunculi floated in varicolored fluids; pentacles drawn on floors and walls, hanging sheets of parchment: all the apparatus and equipment of a magician's laboratory.

One table was stacked with rotting limbs, mainly severed hands and arms, a few feet, some still in their shoes. Most of them were too small to be anything but children's, though there was one heavily muscled arm that looked as if it must have belonged to a weight lifter.

In the back of the cave, where the fissure through which the bushmaster had escaped had been, a broad keyhole-shaped doorway had been cut through the purplish-red stone. On either side of the opening a hand of glory was mounted on a slim black marble pillar. Through the arch I could see a huge cavern, high ceilinged and very deep, the granite floor covered with shallow depressions in which wood fires smoldered. Men in dark shirts and tunics were feeding the fires, kneeling before altars, chanting prayers; others were constructing something massive in the center of the open space. The rock glowed faintly silver.

A straight-backed old man in black was sitting at a high table just our side of the archway, copying an ancient manuscript onto fresh parchment. Nicolae. He didn't bother to look up as we passed.

We threaded our way between the fire pits, came to another brass-studded door set into the silver-glowing rock. Another, smaller cavern, coffins arranged in concentric circles. And in the center of the circles, Alexandra's and my father's coffins, sealed with lids of thick clear glass. Stephen opened Alexandra's coffin, carefully deposited the butterfly on her still face. It uncurled its proboscis, gently thrust it between her waxy lips. We continued on past the other coffins to yet another door in the rock.

Even before the assistant with the keys had unlocked the door and drawn back the bolt I could smell the stench of the room beyond: blood, rust and urine, woodsmoke and charred meat.

The room was twice the size of the cabin, full of antiques that Stephen said had been in the family since the Inquisition. Thumbscrews, Spanish boots, the ladder. Instruments for ripping and cutting, burning, breaking and crushing.

The worm shifted in anticipation within me as the Jehovah's Witness locked the door behind us.

I was blindfolded and gagged, manacled to a post, and whipped. My lesson in humility. Stephen wielded the whip himself—a nine-lashed scourge, like the cat-o'-nine-tails with which British sailors had once been flogged, only supple braided black leather instead of rope, knotted with tiny iron barbs twisted into the knots. Another heirloom.

And each time the whip struck Monteleur hurt me somewhere else, hurt me worse than Stephen could have ever hurt me, kept me jerking and twisting and trying to cry out in no doubt exquisite counterpoint to Stephen's blows.

When it was over he had Lydia remove my blindfold. One of his assistants held my head to keep me from looking away or closing my eyes while the other two assistants stretched Dara on a horizontal ladder—the rack, as it was sometimes called—and fastened her legs to one end, her bound arms to a kind of tourniquet attached to the other.

Stephen began tightening the tourniquet, methodically increasing the force that would soon yank her bones from their sockets, leaving her crippled and disjointed. Dara gave a sudden, involuntary cry, then clamped her jaws shut, denying him the pleasure of hearing her cry out again.

I was still manacled to the post, still gagged; I could do

nothing but watch, listen to the whispered screams that I alone could hear.

Stephen continued to tighten the tourniquet. Dara's bones made dry popping sounds as one by one they were pulled from their sockets.

When it was over we were carried back to the cabin. Dara had remained silent, had only allowed her control to slip as she was taken from the rack, and then only to the extent of a single short moan as she lost consciousness.

They put her on the bed, left us alone. She was quiet now, not even moaning any more, her breathing ragged and shallow. What Stephen had done to her would have crippled a normal person for life. I didn't know if her dhampire's ability to draw on outside forces or her Naga ancestry would give her the strength to heal herself.

I lay down beside her on the bed, afraid to touch her, afraid that anything I could do would only hurt her more. I tried to stay awake, watch over her and be ready to protect or help her if she needed me, but too many days of fighting my own fear and pain had drained me, and I no longer had even the strength to keep myself conscious.

Chapter Thirty-four

When I came to the next morning my back was already beginning to heal, but I was loaded and confused, stupefied, as though Monteleur had pumped me full of barbiturates while I slept. It was weeks before I was permitted to regain complete consciousness again.

Most of what happened to me during that time is gone, forgotten or lost, perhaps never comprehended in the first place. Only a few images, a few incidents, remain.

A cavern somewhere at the end of a branching corridor deep under the hills, where I awakened to find myself looking up at thousands of dirty-white bats hanging from the roof, more entering through a natural chimney off to my right.

Another cavern. Warm, silver-dark, half flooded, filled with the hopping gray-brown toads and scuttling eight-inch reddish salamanders that John had caught and on which Stephen and Nicolae were operating, setting pentangular plugs of iridescent fire opal into the amphibians' skulls so that the jewels glistened from their foreheads like third eyes. This, I remember Stephen telling me, so that the minor covens' members, who had neither the right to attend the Sabbat in their proper persons nor that of using the body of a vampire whose forty days had not yet been completed, could attend by possessing the body of a toad or salamander.

And in the main cavern, one hundred and forty-four coffins slowly filling with the bodies of the men, women and children killed by the vampires Stephen had brought with him. The bodies that the twelve lesser covens—whose Black Men were themselves members of the coven whose Black Man was Stephen—would animate for the Sabbat.

There was the small cavern where Alexandra's and my father's bodies were now laid out in their coffins with the heavy leaded-glass lids. I remember Lydia squinting with the effort of her concentration as the butterfly gorged with John's blood she had carefully carried into the chamber took flight, landed on Alexandra's face, delicately inserted its needle-thin black proboscis between Alexandra's unnaturally flushed lips to transfer the blood it carried to her, then returned to Lydia so the process could begin over again. And though Alexandra's transformation was not yet quite complete, her eyes were open and her mouth was stretched wide in a frozen grimace of lust.

I remember John returning from the Monterey airport with Larry, who'd been lured to California with a telegram signed in my name and fitted with a familiar while still being driven down the coast. He spent what might have been a week, might have been two or three with us before Stephen sent him back to Provincetown. I remember watching him hold a spoon for Dara, trying to help her walk what must have been days or weeks later. I remember how ashamed I was, listening to him crying late at night when he thought we were asleep, at how thankful I was that at least one of my friends had remained faithful to me, remember the sounds he made when his familiar hurt him.

I remember times I was manacled to a post or iron rings set in the wall and whipped while Dara was forced to watch. I remember the time I realized she could finally walk again and use her hands despite the pain, the anger I felt that I couldn't let her know how relieved I was she was going to recover.

My other memories are more fragmentary and confused. The day Alexandra's transformation was complete and she took her place among the vampires whose coffins Stephen had brought by truck from Illinois. The summonings in the main cavern, when Stephen obtained the familiars for the members of the minor covens who were to be made Black Men at the Sabbat. Alexandra bending over Dara and drinking from her neck while Lydia held Stephen's hand and looked on in glee.

I have a vague memory of Dara trying to convince Father his days were spent in Hell, John's eyes squeezed shut in rapture as Alexandra drained his emaciated body, leaving him on the verge of death but pleading with her to take more of his blood, he didn't need it, it was all for her. . . . Fragments of conversations I had with Stephen and Nicolae in which I seem to have been asking them questions like a trusting child demanding the truth from his parents, another fragment in which Stephen was telling me that he used drugs even though his familiar could easily duplicate their effect on him because he preferred to feel himself the object of external forces rather than the prime mover.

In July Stephen had the road to the cabin graded and paved. As soon as it was ready, trucks began arriving with the equipment needed to further enlarge and furnish the caverns, with food and drink for the Sabbat and with the coffins containing almost all of the remaining vampires from beneath the house in Illinois.

An altar had been constructed among the live oaks, where it was invisible from the road and air: a flat black stone, roughly oval, perhaps two feet thick, three yards wide and a yard deep, supported by four pillars of red-painted stone carved to resemble the legs of some crouching beast. Every day at dawn and again at dusk a small animal was killed on the altar and left there. The bodies were always gone before the next sacrifice.

Behind the altar three crosses had been erected, intricately carved and painted, each large enough to crucify a man. Black goats were tethered to them, their horns painted with gilt.

There was no way to keep so much activity completely hidden from my Big Sur neighbors and Stephen knew better than to try. John had been telling people that I'd arranged to sell my land to some obscure Eastern Orthodox monastic order that wanted to build a hermitage and retreat on it, but which was going to allow me to retain lifetime tenancy of my cabin. Now, with trucks arriving daily and construction well under way, I was awakened from my delirium to accompany John to the bars and restaurants, the baths at Esalen and private parties, where I could support and confirm his story. Even with Monteleur inside me to ensure my obedience, I was never allowed off the property except in John's company. And while I was gone Dara stayed in the caverns, chained to the wall in the room where Alexandra's coffin was kept, with Alexandra scrabbling at the sealed glass lid, trying to break free and get to her.

Chapter Thirty-five

I t was July twenty-eighth, sometime around midnight. John and I were sitting at a table on the terrace at Nepenthe with a girl named Candy. She was blonde, stupid, vaguely pretty, maybe twenty-one or twenty-two; she worked in a massage parlor in Seaside. I'd met her once or twice the year before, at parties Alexandra had taken me to. The night was cool, the nearly full moon invisible in the fog. The last few days rain had kept the tourists away, and most of the people were local. Everyone was either inside drinking at the bar or over on the other side of the terrace, by the fireplace.

"Do you want another drink?" John asked Candy. He'd already managed to tell her all about the dreary monastic order. "We've got a good two hours before the baths open."

"All right," Candy said. "A Mexican coffee. With extra brandy in it, to help me stay awake."

"You, David?"

I shook my head. All I wanted to do was get back to Dara as soon as I could. "No thanks."

"You can drive, then. I'll be back in a moment."

He pushed his chair away, started to get up.

And Monteleur exploded inside me, ripped its way up through my heart and lungs, out through my stomach wall to flap wetly against the inside of my T-shirt as I collapsed. The last thing I was aware of was Candy staring at me and screaming.

I was back in the cave under the hill and I could see my headless body, Michael's body, lying dead in the heart of the flames. And standing over it a woman with Dara's face and body and youth, but four-armed, terrible, her skin a blue so dark it was almost black, her eyes dead clay, wet and shining. Around her neck she wore a garland of severed heads, around her slender waist a sort of skirt made of dangling hands, boneless forearms. A slender golden cobra was coiled around each of her arms, a final snake looped twice around her neck, staring at me from over her left shoulder.

With two of her delicate hands she was caressing her cobras' golden heads. Her third hand held a bloody sword. With the fourth she was holding my severed head to her face so she could lap the blood still streaming from it with her long black tongue.

She stared out at me, watching me, her image writhing and flickering with the flames, unbearably desirable, infinitely terrifying. Her black hair that was Dara's hair fell thick and shining down her back; the hands with which she'd been caressing her serpents were opening to me now in invitation, beckoning me to her, and I was falling, jerking closer to her with every dancing movement of the flames, closer to the midnight darkness of her skin, to the severed heads whispering eternal love from toothless mouths, to the cold shining clay of her eyes and the sharp teeth behind her blood-smeared lips.

"Not yet, Mother," I heard myself say. "Not yet."

And then I was myself again, David again, and I was lying bandaged and bloody on the jolting floor of the truck. Candy was sprawled unconscious on the floor next to me. I could see John up front driving and a small man in a black suit—one of Stephen's coven—sitting on the floor behind Candy. He had a doctor's black bag on his lap. That must have been how he'd gotten us out of Nepenthe, posing as a doctor. Unless he really was a doctor. My whole body hurt but the pain was far away, a dull throbbing that merged in and out of the sound of the truck's engine, the vibration coming to me through the floor.

Monteleur had started to kill me and then stopped. I opened my mouth to ask the doctor what had happened, why, closed it again.

My mother. That had been my mother, Saraparajni, there beneath my father's roots. And she had been more terrifying in her beauty and her hunger than any vampire.

No. That had been Michael's terror, not my own. I'd seen her through his eyes. Or maybe the terror had been Father's. It was his inner landscape. Maybe she hadn't been real, or no more real than the landscape itself.

But real or not, she was there for Michael. Michael had to have been behind whatever had made Monteleur try to kill me.

I could reach out to him there, in the cave. Monteleur was keeping me alive while it helped me repair the damage it had done to my heart and lungs, to the other organs in my abdominal cavity, but the strength to heal myself was coming from my father. I closed my eyes again, climbed the shadow tide to him.

I was in the dark corridor, but Stephen could find me there. I abolished the corridor, fell through the cold and the wind.

I abolished the void, stood knee deep in the salmon-pink mud, in what seemed to be my own body. I was closer to the hill than I'd ever been before. Perhaps because this time I was there without Dara.

I crossed the red moat, climbed the hill, crawled in through the entrance beneath the roots.

Michael was sitting cross-legged in front of the fire. The faceless stone images were in the heart of the flames, just as they'd been when I was there with Dara. There was no sign of the figure Michael had addressed as our mother.

"Michael." He looked up, noticed me for the first time. "What happened? Monteleur almost killed me—"

"I tried to kill Stephen."

"Tried?" I sat down next to him. "You mean you failed?"

"Yes."

"Why?"

"He's going to kill all three of us on Lammas Day. As part of the Sabbat. That altar, the three crosses behind it—those are for us. He's going to sacrifice us and end the family. Replace us all with members of his coven.

"I've been spying on you through Father's eyes every night. Watching and listening, making sure I saw everything Stephen did, heard every order he gave, knew everything he had you or his followers do. While Monteleur kept you drugged and Dara didn't do anything.

"He had our ancestors kill the parents and grandparents of all the members of his coven the same night and he timed it so they're all finishing their transformations now. They'll be ready for the Sabbat. And then he won't need us or the family any more. His followers will be able to do everything he needs done by vampires controlled by the living. The rest of us—you, me, Dara, our ancestors—we'll be vampires, yes, but we'll be out of control, without a dhampire to protect us from the living and keep us from destroying ourselves."

"What about Lydia?"

"She's Alexandra's daughter."

"Not yours?"

"No. Nobody inside the family."

"How sure are you of that? She could even be Stephen's daughter."

"She isn't. I've known about her for over a year. Stephen doesn't have as many secrets as he thinks he does."

"But what makes you so sure she's not a Bathory?"

He gave a sort of strangled laugh. "Blood. The family speciality. I had a sample taken from her while she was sleeping, sent it to a laboratory for tests. She's the wrong blood type."

"Are you still in Illinois?"

"Yes."

"How did you try to kill him?"

"I used Father. Stephen isn't here with the rest of us"—he indicated the stone figures—"and I knew I could use Father as long as I didn't do anything to arouse his suspicions. I waited until you were off the property and he had Dara chained up, so he wouldn't be worrying about either of you. Then I had

Father get a steel strut from the construction out in the caverns and station himself outside the door to the cabin, where he could surprise Stephen coming out.

"And that much worked perfectly. When Stephen stepped out of the cabin, Father was right behind him, ready to smash his head in with the strut before he knew what was happening."

"But he managed to duck anyway?"

"No. Father hit him. It should have killed him. It would have killed you or me or even Father himself back when he was alive, but it didn't kill Stephen. I don't know why. Father hit him with all his strength, but the strut just glanced off his head. It didn't even knock him unconscious. Before I could get Father to hit him again, Bathomar hurt me so bad I couldn't keep control of Father.

"I've got to go back to my body, David. If they realize I can come here to escape the pain, they'll stop me. But you've got to stop Stephen. You and Dara. It's too late for me to do anything."

"Michael, wait. If you'd succeeded, what were you going to do about Bathomar? How were you going to keep it from killing you?"

"I was going to deal with it from here before it killed me. Offer to do more for it than Stephen would have done."

"You think that would have worked?"

"I don't know. But even if it didn't, there'd still be you and Dara. Or at least Dara, if your familiar killed you. And Uncle Peter. Some chance that at least one of you would do what was needed to keep the family going."

"Somehow I find it hard to believe that you've been risking your life out of family feeling for me and Dara."

"Don't be a fool, David. The family has always used vampirism, used Satan, even, for our own ends. Stephen would destroy everything."

"Michael, wait. Another thing. Right after—what must have been right after you tried to kill him, when Monteleur attacked me, I came here. The pain drove me out of my body and I—I was sitting here with you. Only it wasn't me, David, I was just you. Michael. I didn't even know that I was both of us.''

"And?''

"And I saw—a woman. There, in the flames, where the stone figures of us are now. She was gesturing to you, trying to get you to join her in the flames . . . and you said, 'Not yet, Mother. Not yet—' ''

"You want to know if that was really our mother?''

"Was it?''

"Yes.''

"But how— Why was she there? Here? And what did you mean, not yet?''

"Because I was dying, David. And maybe because you were dying too, I don't know.''

"To rescue you?''

"No. To consume me. Swallow me up body and soul, David, not just drink my blood while granting me immortality in return. That's why we can't let Stephen win. If we don't become vampires, she'll devour all three of us.'' And he was gone.

Chapter Thirty-six

The pain was worse. Much worse. A band of burning metal tight around my chest, a hot gnawing in my belly, something jagged stabbing me in the lungs every time I took a breath.

I opened my eyes. The moon was out and the truck was bright with its light, with the backwash from the headlights, the green glow of the dashboard instruments, the silver phosphorescence spiderwebbing everything in shadow. We were on our way down the far side of the hill to the cabin and every time we hit another bump it tore something new apart inside of me.

Monteleur shifted, sliding through the pain. The pain was real, in a way that nothing had ever been before. The other agonies had been imposed on me from outside, something to face and defy and try to defeat, but this was me, my intimate self, telling me that I was too badly wounded to heal myself.

"Monteleur," I whispered. Even the whisper hurt, hurt bad. "Make it stop hurting. Help me. Stephen didn't tell you not to. Make it stop!"

Monteleur shifted inside me, remained silent. I lay motionless, gasping for breath, then levered myself up into a sitting position. For some reason it was very important to sit up. But I couldn't hold myself there, it hurt too much to bend like that in the middle, and I had to lie down again.

The man with the black bag on his lap was watching me. "Are you a doctor?" I asked.

"Yes."

"Make it stop hurting. So I can breathe. I've got a punctured lung."

He shook his head. "Monteleur's already done everything your uncle wants. You'll have to do the rest yourself."

He was lying. A real doctor would have given me something for the pain.

"Why?" I asked. "Why did Monteleur . . . ?"

He shook his head, told me to wait until we got back to the cabin.

I closed my eyes again, thankfully climbed the tides of my father's stolen strength up out of the pain to the shadow corridor, trying to reach through to Dara. But Stephen was there, a watchful spider, and there was no way I could get past him to her.

I returned to my body, and to the pain.

They took me to the caverns, chained me to the wall near Dara. My chains had enough slack so I could slump a bit, but not enough to let me sit or kneel, even with my arms over my head, not nearly enough to reach out to Dara and touch her.

She waited until they left us alone in the stench and the silver-glowing darkness to ask me what had happened. They hadn't hurt her, hadn't told her why she was being kept chained. But Stephen stood guard in the shadow corridor, cutting me off not only from Dara but from the deeper landscapes where we might have met in safety, and Monteleur was still wriggling through my agony, listening, ready to punish me again: I couldn't tell her about Michael or the four-armed woman who'd looked so like the statue of Kali dancing on Shiva's dead body in my father's Oriental room. My body would have given me away if I'd tried to answer her whispered questions. All I could do was tell her what Monteleur had done to me at Nepenthe and how I'd awakened in the truck.

The pain got worse and worse all the next day—I knew it was day because my father had returned to his coffin and I could no longer find my way up out of the pain to him—but when at last dusk came and he reawakened, I was able to draw on him once more for the strength my body needed to heal itself, that I needed to endure its agony.

It was enough, barely enough: if they did nothing more to me I would survive.

I finally heard footsteps outside the door, keys turning in the multiple locks. The door opened and the man who claimed to be a doctor entered carrying a lantern. He hung it on an iron hook jutting from the wall, made sure we were still securely fastened in place, then took two gags from his pocket.

"Open your mouths." He sounded bored, like a school doctor giving a kindergarten class a routine examination for ringworm. Monteleur twisted in my belly, sending a fresh wave of agony through me. I opened my mouth. He fitted me first, then moved on to Dara.

He was laying a fire in the open furnace at the far end of the chamber when Stephen entered with Michael and Lydia. Michael was blindfolded, hands tied behind his back, barely able to walk. His face was etched deep with pain and fatigue, marbled purplish red with broken veins and capillaries like some sixty-year-old alcoholic; his body and hands trembled and he kept shifting from one foot to the other, licking teeth and lips, swallowing.

Lydia was so glad to be there, so impressed with the gravity of her role and eager to prove herself worthy, that she could have been a groupie who'd finally received an invitation to visit her idol in his backstage dressing room.

Stephen removed Michael's blindfold, pushed him down into a cane chair Lydia brought forward. Michael sat awkwardly slumped, blinking up at Stephen but unable to meet his gaze. He kept glancing over at the two of us chained to the wall, at the iron maiden standing half open next to the horizontal ladder where he could just glimpse the spikes inside, at the benches along the wall where the various flaying and cutting and crushing instruments were laid out and gleaming, at the fire roaring to life in the open furnace.

Stephen took a half step back, turned to Dara and me. Smiled. Behind Michael's back the doctor was attaching a heavy rope to a massive pulley on the ceiling. There was a hook at the end of the rope. "Michael tried to kill me," Stephen said. "Tried stupidly—it's been thirty years since my familiar would've let something like that hurt me. And for the wrong reasons, if I believe him when he says he thought I was planning to crucify the three of you."

He stared at Michael, challenging him to contradict him. Michael looked away, jaws working, finally found the strength to meet his gaze and demand, "Then what are the crosses for?"

"Goats for Lucifer and his two assistants, Satanichia and Sataniciae." Stephen turned his back on Michael, ignoring him while he explained everything to us. "So that when they took possession of the goats' crucified bodies they could descend from their crosses to their worshippers in proper traditional fashion. The three of you were to have had no part in that—I was just going to use you for some ritual magic later in the ceremonies."

"You're lying," Michael said.

Stephen seemed delighted with his response. "You'll never know if I was or not," he said. "Because I've changed my plans. Three days from now I'm going to personally nail you to the center cross in place of the goat. And after Lucifer abandons your body I'm going to tear your heart out and eat it, then burn what's left. Not as a sacrifice, but just to make sure you can never become a vampire. Because I want you dead and in Hell with no way you can ever escape."

He paused a moment, pensive, then added, "Though I intend to use your three remaining days to find out the truth behind that oh-so-pretty story you told me about how you decided to risk your precious immortal life for the good of the family."

"For all of us," Michael said. "Even you."

"You'll forgive me if I don't believe you."

Stephen gestured at something on a low bench that looked like a rusty fisherman's gaff. "Lydia, would you bring that over here?" When she handed it to him, he said, "I've always thought the art of interrogation reached its finest point with the Inquisition. The first step was always to familiarize the . . . *accused* . . . with the instruments that were to be em-

ployed on him later, so he could better imagine and anticipate what was to come.

"So . . . This, Michael, is an eyeball gouger. Though you
probably won't have to worry about it until tomorrow, or
even the day after, since I want you to be able to see what I'm
doing to you."

He handed the gouger back to Lydia. "And this"—a spiked
cylinder—"is a spine roller, while *this* is a forehead tourniquet. We have Spanish boots, of course, thumb and toe
screws, throat pears, burning irons and pincers . . . everything
you were so anxious to have me teach you to use."

His smile was frozen, terrifying. "But I think we'll start
with squassation. Do you know what that is? We hang you by
your arms while we drop weights attached to your legs. Very
heavy weights. You'll dislocate your feet, hands, elbows,
knees, shoulders, hips. . . . Then, perhaps, while you're still
hanging there we can begin with the toe screws, go from
there—"

Michael slumped forward, unconscious, and would have
fallen from the chair if Stephen hadn't caught him.

"It won't help you, nephew. Not now, not ever." And,
turning to Lydia and the doctor: "Finish preparing him. I'll
awaken him when it's time."

They brought high wooden stools, put heavy metal balls
with chains attached to them—like the ball and chain con-
victs wear in comic strips—on the stools, locked the manacles
at the ends of the chains tight around Michael's ankles. They
undid his wrists, manacled them together behind his back;
attached them to the hook at the end of the rope, hoisted him
free of the ground.

I could hear his shoulders scraping out of their sockets.

Uncle Stephen picked up the eyeball gouger again, delicately prodded Michael's dangling body with it, then closed
his own eyes for an instant. Michael jerked back to life, whim-
pering.

"It won't work, Michael. You can't hide from me there."
With his left hand he was caressing one of the cannon balls.

"And this is just strappado so far, no worse, really, than the ladder, especially for someone like you, with your dhampire's resistance to pain—"

He pushed the ball from the stool. It fell, jerked to a halt just above the ground, swung gently back and forth. Michael began to scream.

Stephen said, "Now!" and Lydia darted forward, jabbed the eyeball gouger at his face.

When it touched him Michael burst into flame.

Chapter Thirty-seven

Michael hung twisting and blackening in his cocoon of ever-brightening flame, his fading screams almost lost in the greater violence of Bathomar's frenzied bellowing. Stephen and the assistants had retreated to the far corner of the room, stood huddled together with their arms up to protect their faces. The heat beat against my face and hands, crisped the unprotected skin, was beginning to sear through my clothing as the flames climbed the spectrum through ever-brighter, ever-fiercer oranges to a yellow-white blazing like the sun.

I held my breath, tried to keep the rich fatty smell of my brother's burning out of my nostrils, but it was hopeless, I could smell him anyway; and when I couldn't keep myself from breathing any longer and opened my mouth, tried to gasp air around the wadded mass of rags with which I'd been gagged, my mouth was full of the roasting-pork taste of him. My stomach contracted, heaved; I could feel myself starting to vomit but forced it back down again, swallowed it before it could block my nose and throat and choke me to death.

A tongue of green appeared where Michael's chest had been, spread. Bathomar's bellowing rose to a bleating scream and was cut off. The charred flesh was crumbling, flaking from the bone, consumed even as it fell away.

The flames drew in on themselves, shrank to a single point of intolerable blue-green, winked out. What remained of Michael's skeleton slipped from the manacles. The blackened skull hit the floor and split open to reveal the seven staring heads of a black Naga with eyes like bubbles of bright glistening clay, wet and empty, like the eyes of the four-armed woman Michael said was our mother.

The woman he'd said was only waiting for him to die so she could devour him, consume him, destroy him utterly.

What remained of Michael's spinal column cracked and splintered as the Naga pulled itself free of it, coiled in and around the charred fragments of bone, raised seven blunt Chinese dog–like heads and tasted the air with its many tongues. Michael or the thing that had devoured him? There was a watchful malevolence to it, a sliding grace, but no intelligence, no humanity, nothing of my brother. It was at least ten feet long, the thick base from which its many necks spread tapering to a body no bigger around than Dara's wrist—but though it was slender for a serpent, it was too big to have ever been contained by my brother's spinal canal, in any human spine, just as the slowly weaving heads with which it was regarding the torture chamber could never have been contained by a human skull. And yet I'd seen it emerge from Michael's shattered skull, seen it pull itself free of what was left of his spine.

Nothing Dara had told me about our Naga souls had prepared me for the thing's physical presence, the fact that I had something waiting inside me that could crack my skull open like an eggshell from within.

Lydia was cowering back in a corner, all her youthful malice gone, leaving her only a frightened child.

"Michael?" I tried to make myself heard around the vomit-sodden rags, choked on them without succeeding. But the Naga understood me.

It hissed sibilantly at me, a cold inhuman sound from its many mouths, nothing like my brother's voice. I was too tired, too confused, to try to make sense of the sounds emerging from the different mouths, orchestrate them into something meaningful.

"No, David," Dara interpreted for me. "That's Vasuki. Michael's Naga soul. Michael chose to die and forget. His soul has gone on to rebirth in another body."

"Not"—I choked on the rags, managed to continue—"destroyed?"

"No." But the Naga's hissing seemed to have shocked Stephen awake. Lydia was still huddled in the corner, useless. He glanced at her once, dismissing her, then grabbed a hooked pole like an eyeball gouger, only longer, and a long-handled knife from the furnace where they'd been heating. He gave the knife to the doctor and they began to advance, spreading out to come at the Naga from opposite sides.

The Naga had all seven heads trained on them now. Dara was whispering something to it through her gag, but I couldn't make out what she was saying. The heads were weaving back and forth on their short necks, hoods spread, and the raised body was beginning to sway.

Stephen halted just out of the Naga's striking range—and Monteleur struck. But even as it started to rip through me again, before I could so much as open my mouth to scream, the Naga had somehow come uncoiled and crossed the distance separating us with a motion fluid and effortless as an incoming wave, had flung a smooth cool coil around my left wrist and flowed up onto my arm.

The room flickered, imploded, lost all silver. There was a confused shouting from the other side of the locked door, a scream. Another scream.

But Monteleur curled in on itself and was still, smooth and heavy and cold like a porcelain egg within me. The Naga had stopped it before it could kill me.

The Naga touched two red-tipped tongues to my manacles and they fell away with a smell of hot metal. I stumbled, half fell, felt something new rip free inside of me, and then the pain was too much and my legs gave way and I fell. Lying there I instinctively reached out for my father, tried to climb the shadow tides to his strength, but I couldn't find the way back to him.

I made it to my feet, lurched the rest of the way to Dara. Steadied myself against the wall as the Naga freed her. She plucked the gag from her mouth, freed me of mine, held me up to keep me from falling again.

"David." A whisper in my ear. "They're going to rush us.

You've got to bring your arm up, hold it out so Vasuki can strike at them. . . . Now, David! Now!"

I lifted my arm. The Naga anchored itself with a few tight coils around my wrist, lashed out in warning at Stephen and the doctor before they realized what was happening. They fell back.

"I can't. . . ." The Naga weighed almost nothing, but even so, I was too weak to keep my arm out straight in front of me. Dara took hold of my arm, helped me support its weight.

"You can't hurt us now," she told Stephen. "If you try Vasuki will annihilate you as it annihilated Michael. But if you unlock the door and protect us until we're safely away, we'll let you live."

"I may not be able to stop you," Stephen said, lowering his hooked pole, "but I can't protect you either. With Michael gone and that Naga cutting David off from Gregory, I've lost control of the vampires. They're waiting for us on the other side of the door."

"Then get Monteleur out of me."

"I can't. Not with that Naga paralyzing him."

"Is that true?" I asked the Naga.

"Yes." A sibilant hiss.

There was a long, drawn-out scream from beyond the door.

"Can they get in here?" I asked Stephen. "Force the door or come sliding under it as mist or something?"

"Not until they break through it. There's a veneer of wild rose wood on the outer surface and around the frame they can't penetrate."

"But they'll break in eventually?"

"Of course." A patronizing smile. "They're not stupid. Just limited in what they can turn their minds to."

"He's telling the truth," Dara said. Then, whispering again: "Vasuki can't stay here. Now that Michael's gone he has to return to Patala. We have to go with him. Monteleur will kill you if we don't."

"I can't. I'm not strong enough. Not without Father's help. . . ."

"You have to be. If Vasuki frees you to draw on Father, Monteleur will kill you."

"Why can't he kill Monteleur? Or get my Naga soul to do it?"

"He can't. It would kill you like it killed Michael. Not even in Patala, but Monteleur can't hurt you there, there's no death in Patala. Vasuki can take us back to Patala with him."

Something heavy crashed into the door. The wood cracked but held.

"You see?" Stephen asked, like a proud parent. "Not stupid at all."

Another crash and the door burst open. Four vampires were wielding a steel beam as a battering ram, and behind them I could see a confused struggle filling the main cavern. A few of Stephen's followers were still fighting but most were down, dead or dying, Bathorys lapping blood from wounds torn with blunt teeth and nails in their victims' necks.

The vampires with the beam tossed it aside. Behind them Father was crouched over John's twitching body, his cheeks working as he sucked at the gaping wound in John's chest.

I tried to force Father away, make him make them all stop, but I couldn't reach him. And the depths of the cavern were dark, shadow filled, without trace of silver.

Father looked up, staring straight at me but not seeing me. His mouth and face were smeared with congealing blood, flecked with shredded skin and flesh. Like an infected wound with the scab torn off. John tried to hold on to him, but Father pushed him away effortlessly as he got to his feet, started inexorably toward us. As Father entered the torture chamber, one of the vampires that had battered the door open bent over John, put his mouth to the wound in his chest. The others came gliding silently after Father.

Father made straight for Stephen, stood there before him waiting until at last Stephen closed his eyes, offered him his throat, moaned with what could have been pleasure or pain as Father took him gently by the shoulders, closed his blunt teeth on his uplifted throat and then ripped it open with a single convulsive movement.

Alexandra came darting in through the door, moving with inhuman grace and speed as she made for Lydia, whose attention was still riveted on Father and Stephen. She had almost reached Lydia before Lydia saw her.

Alexandra leaped for her, but Lydia brought her hand up in front of her as if to push her mother away and Alexandra stopped dead, everything about her still seeming to strain forward even as she was slowly driven back. Her hands were clenched, the nails thick yellowish talons, her mouth was open wide, snarling in frustration, showing long wet fangs, yet the most horrifying thing about her was how much of the old Alexandra remained in the slavering thing she had become.

Lydia was grinning, all kittenish adolescent malice and triumph now she was over her fright. Stephen's star pupil.

Two gray-haired men had the doctor down, were ripping him open with teeth and nails while a crowd was clustering in a circle around us, just out of Vasuki's striking range. They were spattered with blood and flesh and they stank of the grave. They all looked like lighter-skinned versions of me. My ancestors.

One younger-looking man in clerical dress came fractionally too close and Vasuki lashed out, seven heads striking as one, and the vampire he'd bitten screamed, a high hoarse shout of rage that died to a gurgle as the man collapsed into a twitching pile. Yet even when the flesh began to smoke and run and the bare skull beneath the vampire's handsome face had begun to show through, it continued to struggle, scrabbling at the hard rock beneath it with its fleshless hands.

The others watched it, impassive, silent.

A woman who looked like my grandmother in the old sepia photos on the dining room wall was creeping like a spider up and across the wall by the door to come at Lydia from behind. Totally absorbed in her contest of wills with her mother,

Lydia didn't see the woman until she came scuttling down the wall and leaped, grabbed her by the neck, and broke it with an audible snap.

Alexandra came rushing forward, but the woman tossed Lydia behind her and stood guard over her body, keeping Alexandra away.

"She's mine!" Alexandra hissed, her face working helplessly. "Stephen promised her to me!"

"Stephen's dead." Another vampire with a Bathory face moved between them, blocking Alexandra as the other woman knelt by Lydia's body, plunged her hands into her chest and tore her ribs apart, burying her face in the open abdominal cavity.

Father was still feeding on Stephen. A woman had joined the two other vampires bent over the doctor. Alexandra's body was taut with rage as she watched the Bathory woman feed, but somehow, for an instant, despite the grotesque violence all around me all I could think of was how, in spite of all her betrayals, the years she had lied and spied on me, and even though what was enraging her was being prevented from ripping her daughter's still-living body open and devouring her herself, in the end she had still been the one betrayed, a Bathory victim even after her death and resurrection.

Then she finally looked away from Lydia and saw Dara and me. Her face went smooth, her body took on a deceptively languorous grace as she came gliding toward us.

The family moved aside, let her reach the front of the tight circle around us, closed in behind her again. More and more of them were crowding into the chamber, rising to cover the walls like clinging insects, held back only by Vasuki.

"David." Alexandra's voice was soft and low, rich with a throaty enticement it had never had in life. And yet somehow it was still her voice.

"Alexandra," I said.

"David, I love you. I always loved you. That's why they killed me, because I wouldn't betray you."

"She's lying," Dara said, but I didn't need her warning: Vasuki was shielding me and I felt none of the hypnotic fascination, the flood of love and trust that Aunt Judith had used to snare me when she fed on me in the woods, only Alexandra's dead, raging, insatiable hunger.

"I know," I said.

"It's not a lie," Alexandra said. "I love you."

"David," Dara said, "Vasuki can take us to Patala and free you of Monteleur there. But only if we swear to return equal value for what we are granted."

I was feverish, only half conscious. I couldn't breathe. The hot gnawing in my belly and chest was getting worse. I no longer had the strength to fight it. "Meaning what? What do we have to do?"

"Repay it with something of equal worth."

"Who determines what it's worth?" I demanded of Vasuki.

"You decide." Its multiple voices were totally inhuman, more alien to me than the vampires could ever have been.

"Is that what you want?" I asked Dara.

"Yes." And suddenly Alexandra launched herself, not at me but at Dara, trying to use Dara's body to shield her from Vasuki. The other vampires used the diversion to rush me as Vasuki lashed out over Dara's shoulder at Alexandra and struck her in the face. Alexandra convulsed as though she'd been hit with an electric cattle prod, but her momentum took her into Dara and sent all three of us skidding into a confused heap against the wall, Vasuki's smooth coils sliding between and over us as he took up a position on top of us, protecting us. Alexandra's body was still spasming as she clawed at Dara with strengthless hands. Dara pushed her away and got unsteadily to her feet, her face bleeding. I no longer had the strength to move. Alexandra lay on the floor, her face inches from mine. Her mouth was open, her body shuddering with weaker and weaker convulsions.

And I felt sorry for her, for all her lies and malice. I *pitied* her for what she'd become, how she'd ended.

"Can we take Alexandra with us?" I asked Vasuki. There was no death in Patala; she could be no danger to us. Perhaps there would even be some surcease for her there.

"Yes."

"Then I swear."

And the caverns were gone.

Chapter Thirty-eight

There was nothing but the void. Infinite darkness, limitless emptiness, without even the absence of color, shape and form to give it definition, yet alive with a thousand gliding serpent shapes bleeding in and out of existence, in and out of emptiness, like color bleeding from new clothing into hot wash water and then somehow back again. The thousand serpents were one sole serpent, thousand-headed, its ivory scales and crimson eyes burning like a swarm of suns, and Dara, Alexandra and I were only three of its myriad heads. But even that solitary serpent that was all there ever was or could be was only a coiling in upon itself of empty nothingness, a curdling in the void.

Yet four grass-green elephants stood upon its ivory coils, and on their backs they supported the world-mountain.

The earth was a tiny protuberance, a minuscule bump high on one of the mountain's four faces, but we were within it, hurtling through a network of caverns forming a world vaster than a thousand earths, looking out and down and through the living stone into the void. The caverns were filled with fires the color of burning blood, with rivers of flowing gold and silver and platinum, incandescent white oceans through which winged serpents of turquoise flame flew and coupled. Vasuki was a river of liquid jade carrying us up and out through the world-mountain's iron crust to its surface, where he became a fountain falling as sweet-scented green rain into the infinite sea surrounding the world-mountain, in which it floated on the back of four great turtles of blood-red copper.

And seeing them I remembered them, remembered that I was David Bathory and had read a description of all this in a book in my father's library, and then my memory of the book seemed to expand and I was falling, falling into the memory that was the book that was the ocean, and around us the waters were cool and golden, sweet-tasting and delicate.

Indolent dragons with shimmering amethyst scales and long emerald barbels swam in the luminous waters, laired in drifting undersea palaces. Great ropes of shining pearls were looped around their necks, around their long fishlike bodies and short reptilian legs. I clung to the ropes of pearls wrapped around Vasuki's broad scaly back as he took us deeper, ever deeper, until at last we came to Patala, to the land beneath the sea, all jeweled palaces, groves, streams and gardens, through whose golden skies the great dragons drifted and swam like luminous clouds.

And yet behind it, or around it somehow, like shifting constellations of half-glimpsed afterimages, were the fiery caves beneath the world-mountain's roots, the golden ocean that was at the same time both all around us and overhead, Patala's sky. The ropes of pearls to which I clung became the edges of huge iridescent scales, then soft turquoise and crimson feathers longer than my body, warm velvety golden fur and naked skin, and yet there was no moment I could grasp in which something could have been said to have changed, no rupture, only the realization that what I had thought was something was something else, had always been that something else . . . and that that too was actually something else, had always been something else. In the silver-shimmering darkness of Stephen's torture chamber, the vampires were still clustered in a motionless circle around us; Alexandra frozen in midspasm as she died for a second and final time, and yet she was here beside me, hanging desperately onto Vasuki's back.

And within and beneath it all, bleeding in and out of the multiplicity of worlds as it bled in and out of the void, the thousand-headed serpent coiling endlessly and alone in the dark.

I could feel myself dissipating, losing myself in the transformations. I squeezed my eyes shut, concentrated on Monteleur, the agony in my ripped and torn tissues, but even the pain fled me, lost itself in the fires, the golden sea, the beauty of the world through whose skies we were gliding, so intense it burned its way through my shut eyelids.

I opened my eyes and stared at Dara, trying to anchor myself to her. But she too was lost in a welter of half-glimpsed visions. Other Daras, a toddler running and laughing in a luxuriant tropical garden, an ancient four-armed hag draped in hissing serpents, the terrified young woman huddled by the desiccated bodies of the dead rangers at Carlsbad, all the other Daras that had ever been or could ever be, beautiful and hideous, human and reptilian and other things I could not name but somehow recognized. Yet they were all Dara, and she was looking around her with such wonder and burning joy that I was suddenly terrified I had lost her to the landscape, to her Naga soul, that the woman I knew and loved, who knew and loved me, was wakening to something so strange and inhuman and beyond me that she would drown in its vastness and be lost to me forever.

Beside me Alexandra was slowly regaining consciousness. She was easier to focus on, shifting between the vampire she had become and versions of the woman I had known as she clung tightly to Vasuki's ridged scales that became soft feathers, warm flesh, ropes of pearls that coiled tight around her and held her whenever the vampire struggled to break free. Yet when she was human the awe and terror with which she stared around her seemed closer to what I was feeling than the transhuman rapture transfiguring Dara as the world altered and melted and redefined itself around us, threatening to shift into something completely incomprehensible.

We were flying low over an immense landscaped park, all flowing curves and broad arcs, sinuous meanders, approaching an open pavilion, its delicate, intricate lacework carved from a single block of lapis lazuli. Vasuki furled his great scaly wings as we neared but instead of landing he faded into a winged mist, a soft shimmering blue-green cloud, and then we were slipping gently down through the spice-scented coolness to find ourselves in the pavilion, Vasuki a slender-bodied golden serpent at least forty feet long twined around and around us, holding us gently but inexorably imprisoned in his warm, smooth-scaled coils as he regarded us steadily from the lidless green eyes in his seven heads with their shiny, elaborately curved lips and protruding doglike teeth.

I was wearing jeans and a T-shirt, sandals. Dara sometimes seemed to be wearing a short black velvet dress, sometimes jeans and a top, while Alexandra's outfits all seemed to be more or less tight-fitting and flamboyant, emphasizing her body, but different every time I looked at her. A faint greenish mist still veiled the landscape, but Patala itself seemed relatively substantial, though I could still glimpse hints of other scenes, other worlds, embedded somehow within it. Yet the breezes brought the fresh rich scents of real flowers and lawns and trees, the soft babble of crystalline streams. Footbridges arched the streams at intervals and in the distance I could see further gardens, more pavilions. The air was warm and though there was no sun, only the liquid gold of the sky, it felt as though it were just before noon in a late spring ripening into summer.

It was the kind of fairy-tale paradise you dream of as a child. Even Vasuki had an alien, hypnotic beauty about him that was in its own way nearly as disturbing as the malevolence that had emanated from him when he emerged from Michael's charred remains.

I felt within me for Monteleur, caught a glimpse of it curled in on itself like a sleeping fetus, but in some other world, tied to this one but not in it. My body was my own.

Alexandra suddenly cried out, struggling to free herself. The shape of her jaw changed, fangs pushing out from beneath her lips as her human panic merged into a vampire's cold rage, only to shrink back to human teeth and disappear beneath her lips again as the rage faded back into merely human fear, but Vasuki kept her immobilized in his coils until she quieted.

"Tell it to let me go," she said finally. She sounded almost human again—frightened, but defiant, using the Dragon Lady voice she'd always employed to bluff her way past customs and cops—but the tone was still too flat, somehow empty. Still *dead*, and when she added, "I won't hurt you," the implied threat was the vampire's. Her face was cycling back and forth again between the vampire dying its final death, fanged mouth open in a silent scream, features convulsed with cold hatred and impotent rage, and the Alexandra I remembered, calculating but anxious, fighting her fear by denying it.

The woman who had spent our years together spying on me for Michael, who had used John's hopeless passion for her, the rage he had tried to keep bottled up and harmless within him, to destroy him.

Vasuki abruptly rearranged himself, a swift sliding and shifting that left him somehow outside the pavilion, wrapping it in his coils as he had previously wrapped the three of us. Though his body was no thicker than before, he was now far longer and he had more heads, sixteen or seventeen, though with the way they wove back and forth in the air it was hard to count them.

"Nothing will harm you here," Vasuki said. The voice issuing from his multiple throats was less sibilant and more melodious than it had been in the caves, almost like a chorus of woodwinds yet with a strange underlying hint of Michael's midwestern accent.

Alexandra looked slowly around at the landscape beyond the pavilion, her face empty. "Where is this?" she asked.

"Patala," Dara said. "Where the Nagas live." Like the Takshakas, the two Nagas in human form who had been supposed to be my maternal grandparents, she was surrounded by a faint aura of turquoise-green flame that shifted when I tried to focus on it, sometimes suggesting the head of a single giant cobra, sometimes a multitude of smaller cobras.

As I looked back at Alexandra I caught what seemed to be a suggestion of sinuous movement in the blue-green mist, only to realize when I tried to make it out more clearly that there wasn't any mist, that I too was veiled by an aura like Dara's, though mine seemed to contain every kind of snake I had ever known. Their heads faded out of existence whenever I tried to focus on them, always replaced by others.

Our Naga souls, as Vasuki had been Michael's Naga soul.

"Patala? I don't understand." The bewilderment in Alexandra's face and voice was purely human.

"We brought you with us when we escaped from the caves—do you remember the caves behind the herpetarium?" I asked.

"Yes, but—" She broke off, stared me wide-eyed in the face, looking lost and vulnerable. "David, I'm alive again, aren't I? Not a vampire, but really alive again, the way I used to be."

"Yes."

"I was"—she looked at Dara and her face suddenly hardened—"I remember, I was a vampire and Lydia, the Bathorys had taken Lydia away from me even though she was *mine*, Stephen had promised her to me, and I was trying to get to you and then that *thing*"—she nodded at Vasuki—"bit me and it was like a fire inside me, I was burning up and I knew that you had destroyed me and all I wanted to do was tear you apart, take you with me but I couldn't move. . . . Only I wasn't destroyed. I'm not even a vampire anymore."

"Patala is outside time. There is no death here," Vasuki said.

"And so I'm alive again? Just because I'm here?"

"Yes," Vasuki said.

"Why?"

"David asked that you be granted sanctuary," Vasuki said.

"Why, David?"

"I felt sorry for you. Whatever Michael and Stephen and my father told you, they lied. And despite everything you did, you didn't deserve what happened to you."

"Nobody does," Dara said.

Alexandra looked back and forth between Dara and me. "Michael was half Naga too. Where is he?"

"Dead," Dara said. "Vasuki was his Naga soul."

She stared at Vasuki. "You're *Michael?*"

"No. Michael has gone on to find rebirth in a new human body."

"We have twin souls," I said. "Human *and* Naga."

"You let Michael die but you saved me?"

"Michael's death was his own choice," Dara said, her voice harder than I'd ever heard it. "But that's not what you're really asking. What you really want to know is whether we saved you because there was something in it for us. Because we had a use for you. We don't."

"Then why did you do it?"

"Because I felt sorry for you, Alexandra," I said. "That's the only reason. If we'd left you there you wouldn't be just a vampire, you'd be finally and irrevocably dead."

"And the idea bothered you so much you arranged for my miraculous resurrection. Despite the fact that I was always Michael's, never yours, and that your oh-so-innocent and infinitely forgiving sister, who you're now fucking of course, like any other Bathory, was the one who killed me with the bushmaster in the first place."

I recognized the self-righteous edge in her voice, the shrillness that said Nothing you can do will ever convince me I'm wrong, this is all your fault and you're going to pay for it, yet there was still something tentative about it, as if she were trying on her anger, testing out her humanity to see if any of it was real.

"We weren't the ones who had you killed. Dara did what she did because Father made her do it."

"You'll forgive me if I resent it somewhat nonetheless."

She sounded completely herself again. My wife of nine years. And it was both strange and pitiful to think that after having died and been resurrected a vampire, then been reborn to her lost humanity in a place that seemed like a paradise, she was still trying to score points.

"You are free to return to your world whenever you want," Vasuki said.

Alexandra showed no surprise. "Return how? Go back to being a dying vampire?"

"Not necessarily. Patala is outside time. You may return to any moment in your existence that you choose. But if you return to an earlier moment, you will forget everything that happened to you subsequently."

"Including being here?"

"Unless you choose to return to the same instant you left."

"You can really do that, send me back to any time in my life and I could live it all over again?"

"Yes."

"But if I did return to sometime earlier everything would just continue on like before. So either way I end up getting killed by that bushmaster and then turning into a vampire until you poison me and I die for good?"

"Either way you go back to the life you have chosen for yourself."

"What happens if I don't want to go back?"

"When you have determined the true value of your existence here, you will have to choose to either pay the price to remain or return to your world."

"Like us," I said.

"Yes," Vasuki said.

"What kind of price are you talking about?" Alexandra asked. "Pay you with what?"

"You must choose an action or set of actions that you will carry out, either in Patala or in time."

"Like doing penance or flagellating myself or doing public service?"

"Whatever you choose."

"Who decides whether or not what I choose is acceptable?" Alexandra asked.

"You do."

"Anything I want?"

"Whatever you determine that your existence is worth."

"So I can decide that in return for spitting in Dara's face right now I get to stay?"

"If that is what your existence is truly worth to you."

"How long do I get to make up my mind?"

"That is up to you. No matter how long the time you spend here is for you, no time will have passed in the world you came from."

"If I want, I can stay here forever before making up my mind?"

"Yes."

"Eternal life?"

"There is no other kind. Say, rather, the possibility of maintaining unbroken continuity of consciousness and memory until time ends, though should you return to the world you left, you would become mortal once again."

"Right. So what's the catch? I assume there *is* a catch?"

"Of course." There was a trill of contrapuntal amusement in Vasuki's voice. "The catch is that until then, you remain tied to your self in the world you left."

"Tied how?"

"Close your eyes." Alexandra hesitated, then closed them. "Let your mind go blank. You will find you are still aware of your original self." All expression and color suddenly drained from her face and she opened her eyes again suddenly, looking shaken. "Until you pay the price you have decided upon, you will always remain tied to your world. And not just to the instant you left your world, but to your entire lifeline. You will always be simultaneously both what you are here and everything you have ever been there."

"What if I stay here? My body there just disappears?"

"No. All that happens is that your connection with it is severed."

A tiny orange bird with a long scarlet bill, green throat and extravagant yellow crest landed fearlessly on one of Vasuki's looped coils, cocked its head as it regarded the three humans in turn. Just before it flew off again I realized it had three eyes.

"That's it? The entire catch?" Alexandra demanded.

"Over eternity, you may find that the fact that you cannot

escape from anything you have ever done or experienced is sufficient.''

"Wait," I said. "These actions we have to perform. Are they the same for us as they are for Alexandra?''

"In essence.''

"You said they could be in Patala or in time. What did you mean, in time?''

"Any part of your lifeline prior to the moment I brought you here. Though Patala opens on all eternity, your future will remain closed to you until you have chosen to act.''

"But you said that if you returned us to before you brought us here, we wouldn't remember anything that happened afterward. So how can we act?''

"From Patala your past is open to you. You exist in both worlds simultaneously: your past selves are part of you. When you become aware of them, you will find you can influence them.''

"Because they're half Naga?" Alexandra demanded.

"No. You too can influence your past selves.''

"How?''

"They are you. You can act through them.''

"When I was bitten by the coral snake I saw a cobra-headed Queen on an ivory throne,'' I said. "She saved my life. And then before Michael died I saw a four-armed woman draped in snakes—''

"Saraparajni. Your mother. You will meet her when you are ready to make your decision.''

"Is she really a queen?" Alexandra asked. "The Queen of the Nagas?''

"Yes.''

"Michael said—he said that she wanted to devour him. His soul. That we had to become vampires or she would destroy us.''

"Michael was afraid to risk losing what he already had. Of losing control. He chose to die and be reborn rather than become anything more than what he already was.''

"How do I find her?'' I asked.

"She will be there for all three of you when you're ready to choose."

Alexandra laughed sharply. "No more favoritism?"

"None."

"What about our Naga souls?" I asked.

"They will help you. But so long as you remain tied to your world you will be human, and you will have to choose as humans."

"Does that mean that if we choose to stay in Patala we *won't* be human anymore?"

"If you wish, you can remain human."

"*Are* there any other humans here?" Alexandra asked.

"No."

"Then if this is supposed to be the land of the Nagas, where are all the rest of you?"

And suddenly we were on a broad avenue of gleaming white marble winding through groves of flowering trees and over bridges spanning rushing streams. Small, dark-skinned people in bright clothing thronged the avenue, aware of us but passing us by in utter silence, their faces alive with unvoiced laughter. In the trees clouds of tiny multicolored birds were flitting from bough to bough chattering to themselves, and in the distance I could see great palaces of gold and silver and precious stones, their domes and spires shining in the light from the burning gold of the sky.

"Here. All around you," said a tiny mahogany-skinned man in a scarlet robe worked with gold thread who looked almost like my brother, and then the avenue was gone and we were back in the pavilion, surrounded again by Vasuki's sheltering coils. But Vasuki was elongating, expanding, his seventeen heads now hundreds, thousands, uncountable, filling the sky as his innumerable coils slid over and into and through the world, permeating it as he melted into the green land and golden sky and was gone, leaving the three of us alone in the exquisitely carved lapis pavilion.

Chapter Thirty-nine

I looked around at the empty landscape.

"Do you remember this again now?" I asked Dara. "What it was like to live here, before they took your memories away?"

"No, I—I recognize it, David. I mean, I remember it, living here, but—" There was a pain in her voice, a longing, that seemed to confirm my fears even as it reassured me that I hadn't lost her. "But that's all. I'm not part of it anymore."

"That's just great," Alexandra said. "Your mother's some sort of queen here but you still don't really belong here. So where does that leave me?"

"Alive," Dara snapped.

"Look, you lived here before, right? You know how to find things to eat, things like that. I don't know any of that stuff."

"There are always fruit and berries and you can drink from the pools and streams," Dara said. "Nothing here can harm you."

"It still doesn't sound like much of a life. Those people we saw—they weren't really people at all, they were Nagas just looking like people, right? There aren't any real human beings here."

"Us," I said.

"You're half Naga."

"It doesn't mean what you think it means."

"You're going to get to choose whether or not you even want to stay human. That sounds pretty different to me."

"You heard Vasuki," Dara said. "You can always go back."

"That's bullshit. All I have to do is close my eyes and I *am* back there, burning up from your vanishing friend's poison."

She paused, took a deep breath. "Look, I don't expect you to think that I honestly and sincerely want to be your friend or anything. We all know better than that. Right now all I have to do is close my eyes and let my mind drift a little and I'm a vampire again. All I want to do is tear you open and drink you dry, only I can't because Vasuki's poison is destroying me. And even when I try not to think about it the hunger's still there, I can still feel it and it's horrible."

"What are you saying?" I asked.

"I guess that I don't want to be forced to just wander around here alone with myself and I don't have a lot of choice about who to be with."

I looked at Dara.

"You can stay with us," Dara said.

Alexandra got to her feet. "Then let's go somewhere else. Not just sit here." All her normal nervous energy was back. "Unless there's something special keeping you here?"

"No."

Three broad steps led down from the pavilion to the lawn. The grass felt springy underfoot.

"Where do you want to go?" I asked Alexandra.

"Is it all like this?"

"Not exactly, but the same kind of thing," Dara said. "Gardens and pavilions."

"What about that street with all the Nagas and the palaces?"

"That's here too," Dara said. "Coexisting with us. If you try, maybe you can sense it. We should be able to get there if you want to."

"No." Alexandra actually shuddered. She pointed at a jade pavilion half hidden in a grove of distant trees. "Let's go that way."

We walked together for a while, the grass always as springy underfoot, the breezes bringing us a constantly changing tapestry of floral perfumes, the fresh scents of growing things.

On the other side of a stand of small acacialike trees with

red and purple flowers we came to some bushes laden with gleaming multicolored fruit about the size of plums, though no two were exactly the same shape or color.

"You said we could eat anything that grows here?" I asked Dara.

"Yes."

I plucked a canary-yellow fruit, took a cautious bite. The flavor was delicious, something between an apple and a peach, with a custardy texture and hint of ginger or perhaps nutmeg that seemed to change slightly with every bite. There was no pit or seed at the center.

Alexandra watched me finish it, plucked a soft pink fruit from the bush, bit into it. A look of intense pleasure crossed her face and then suddenly she was spitting the pulp out, hurling the remains away and wiping the red juice frantically from her mouth.

"What's wrong?" I asked.

"It tastes like blood."

"You're sure?" She just looked at me. I took a similar pinkish fruit from the bush, tried it for myself. It tasted like some kind of rare but still cooked red meat, a little like beef but with a curious hint of lamb.

"Well?"

I shrugged. "It just tastes like meat to me." I looked at Dara.

"They taste like whatever you want them to taste like," she said. "But you don't have to eat them if you don't want. You don't have to eat anything here. Your body won't get any weaker."

Alexandra picked a mottled blue and yellow fruit, took a bite, spat it out.

"Let's go," she said and started off without waiting to see if we were coming. We followed a yard or two behind her.

"Dara," I asked, "can you talk directly with your Naga soul now that we're here? Ask it questions and get answers?"

"Not exactly, but if I . . . open myself to it I know things. As if I'd always known them but just hadn't been thinking about them. Try it, David.''

I tried to focus on the aura surrounding me, the serpents fading in and out of existence, open myself to them. I felt an intense flash of burning heat, then nothing. But when I tried concentrating on the individual serpents as they faded, I suddenly saw how I could follow them deeper into the turquoise flame, through a tunnel of twisting blue-green fires back into my past.

I followed a Mexican rattlesnake to the beach a little north of Acapulco where I had been taking scuba lessons the day I met Alexandra. The beach was lit with the same sourceless, colorless radiance that had illuminated everything when the Naga at my father's house had pulled me out of my body.

Though it was a scene out of my own past, I was not part of it but a detached observer, seeing everything with an inhuman neutral precision, from a multitude of angles and points of view. Seeing it though my Naga soul's eyes. And that meant, I realized, that the Naga that had pulled me out of my body to show me Dara in the caverns beneath the house must have been my own Naga soul.

My younger self, skin glimmering with pale-blue fire, was standing in the front row facing the diving instructor, a muscular man running to fat, and Alexandra was behind me in a skimpy string bikini that I remembered as fluorescent yellow, though it was without color now. My earlier self had not yet noticed her but she was watching him closely.

But as I stared at my earlier self, I—the I I had once been—felt someone watching and turned around, caught Alexandra staring and smiled at her. She smiled back. And that, I suddenly remembered, had been how we had met.

But it hadn't been Alexandra's eyes I had felt on me, it had been my own. By observing my past I had intervened in it, had myself brought about my earlier self's meeting with Alexandra.

I watched the scene playing itself out, me clumsily trying to strike up a conversation with her, the much more skillful maneuvering on her part that had led to our meeting again that night to go dancing at a club she knew. Everything was exactly the way I remembered it now—but had it been that way before?

I remembered something I'd once read about quantum physics, how there was no way to observe anything on the subatomic level without disturbing the thing you observed, so there was no possibility of knowing what things would have been like if you hadn't intervened.

I retraced my way through the blue-burning tunnel to Patala, looked at Alexandra. No time at all seemed to have passed, yet the vampire in her seemed to have maybe receded a little further, leaving her even more like the woman I had known, while I myself felt solider, more myself again, as if by returning to our shared past I had rooted us both more solidly in our human reality.

Was this what Vasuki had meant?

I selected another serpent from my aura at random, followed a milk snake like the ones I had collected in the crater forest back to the cavern beneath the house, where a barely adolescent Alexandra stood arm in arm with Michael, a picture-perfect young couple disfigured only by the ugly self-satisfaction on their faces as they watched five-year-old Dara's bewildered terror at the vampires crowded around her, reaching out to stroke her cheeks with long-nailed hands kept gentle by my father's will alone.

I was suddenly afraid to keep on watching, that I would be making myself part of the ugly scene, rendering it even more real than it had been.

I pulled myself back to Patala. And still no time seemed to have passed.

I concentrated on Dara's aura, trying to isolate the cobra that would lead me back to our meeting on the highway, abruptly recognized the baby cobra I had kept in my glove-compartment cage and followed it back to a moment when

Dara was sitting with my earlier self in the truck driving east. Again, my earlier self felt me watching him—but so did Dara. Something of the love I felt for her, my need and tenderness, passed between the three of us, and I remembered that sense I'd had that my destiny was somehow linked with hers, that we had been meant to meet, abruptly realized that I was *creating* it now, that my knowledge of what we were going to mean to each other had passed from me to the person I had been then.

And then I felt Dara enter the past with me, completing that rapport that had united us so immediately and inexplicably.

Alexandra's voice wrenched me back.

"So what do *your Naga souls*"—twisting the words to make it sound like something below contempt—"say we're supposed to do now?" she asked.

"Learn more about Patala," Dara said after a brief pause. "Get to know our lives they way they really were, not just the way we remember them."

A little farther on a bed of brilliant crimson flowers bordering a tiny meandering brook caught my eye and I bent down to examine them more closely. A tongue of blue-white flame burned fiercely in the heart of each flower and within the flames tiny green and yellow fish swam.

The route Alexandra had chosen took us across a stream spanned by a gently arched bridge constructed of narrow hardwood strips joined in a complex interlocking pattern of mahogany reds and paler brown and blond woods. Alexandra started over the bridge, glanced down at the water and suddenly froze.

"What is it?" Dara asked, joining her.

"When you look into the water—what do you see?"

"Colored rocks and pebbles. A few fish. The way the water eddies around the rocks," Dara said.

"What about our reflections?"

"What about them?" I asked.

"When I look I can see all three of us but—I can also see myself back in the caves, only it's like I'm looking at myself from outside and . . . I can see other things."

"What kind of things?" Dara asked softly.

"Things that happened to me before. I can see . . . see myself with my parents, when I was little and my father, he— You can't see them?" she demanded, suddenly suspicious.

"No," Dara said. "Not in the water. But here in Patala all of us are connected with our former lives. Everything that ever happened to you is still happening, right now."

"I don't know what Dara can see," I said, "but I can . . . go back and see things that happened to me. I went back to Acapulco, the time we met. And to the caverns, where you and Michael were getting off on watching the vampires play with Dara."

"Michael's dead. You said he was dead." Her voice was that of a little girl. "But I can see him, he's there with me and he's alive."

Alexandra suddenly wrenched her gaze away from the water, fled the rest of the way across the bridge, threw herself down on the grass, crying.

I looked at Dara.

"She was always with Michael." Her voice was neutral. "From the time my grandparents left me with Father."

"What I said about going back—" I explained. "I followed one of the snakes in my aura back and saw you beneath the house. You were just a kid and Alexandra and Michael were watching you. They thought it was funny, the way the vampires scared you."

"I used to hate her, David. Both of them. But that all got burned away. I can't hate anyone anymore."

We walked the rest of the way across the bridge, joined Alexandra. She sat up, wiped her eyes.

"What do you remember about being a vampire?" Dara asked.

"I don't have to remember." She sounded angry. "All I have to do is close my eyes."

"What about the daytimes? When you slept in your coffin?"

"Why are you asking me that?"

"It's important. Try to remember."

Alexandra closed her eyes. All the life drained from her
features and I could see her closed mouth bulging as the teeth
behind her lips lengthened momentarily into fangs. When she
opened her eyes again her voice was cold, flat, somehow ab-
sent.

"We dream. We dream of dancing."

"Those are lies. False memories, to keep you from guessing
the truth. When vampires sleep they merge with Satan and
share his torments. Because Satan's entire existence is
agony."

She got to her feet, stood with her fists clenched glaring at
Dara. "I don't believe you. You're lying."

"Alexandra, the memories you have when you wake up at
dusk are the real lies. Satan takes away your memories. But
here in Patala the daytimes you can't remember are open to
you. You can go back, see what really happened."

"And you're telling me this for my own good. Out of your
innate generosity and because of the way you've been concerned for my welfare all these years."

"I'm telling you because I know the truth. Because I spent
a day in Hell and don't think anyone deserves to suffer like
that."

"Spreading the truth. That's just like you, isn't it? Sweetness and light. So sickly sweet it turns your stomach."

"Whereas you and Michael got off on tormenting her," I
said.

"What if we did? Who are you to judge me? You could be
all nice and generous and kind because you didn't have any
idea what the world was really like. Everybody you knew always lied to you, they kept you safe and protected in a little
cocoon so you'd never learn enough to be a threat to them,
but the world's not really like that. Not even the world outside your sacrosanct family. I protected you from that, let you

play the outlaw coke dealer without ever having to deal with just how really crazy and dangerous those people are. But you'll never have to learn what any of that's like now that you're here where it's all flower gardens and butterflies and your mother is the Queen of the Nagas and you can live happily together forever after."

"What was it like for you, Alexandra?" Dara asked. "Why was it so bad?"

"It's none of your business. I don't want your pity."

"What Vasuki said, about how we can influence the past," I said. "I tried it and if you go back, you're not just an observer, you can change things."

"Great. So I get my big chance to go back and do something to prove myself worthy to stay here sniffing exquisite flowers like a three-year-old in your select company forever after, or until the two of you turn into snakes on me, whichever happens first."

"No. You don't understand. Maybe you can change some of the things that were so bad for you. Make them so they happened differently."

Alexandra stared at me in silence for a long moment. "You really mean that?"

"Yes. I don't know how much you can really do, but you can change things. I already have."

Alexandra nodded slowly and turned away, walked back to the bridge and sat down on it, hands clenched tight as she stared deliberately down at her reflection in the water.

"I think it would be better if we left her alone for a while," Dara suggested. We walked on a little farther, past a stand of slim, smooth-barked trees with leaves like pink-veined maples to a meadow filled with waist-high russet and orange lilies that gave off a thick, heady feverish perfume like nothing I'd ever smelled before.

I took Dara's face in my hands and kissed her. As we embraced the serpents in our auras twined around one another, merging and separating, merging again. Naga memories swirled and spun through me like velvet-textured translucent leaves on a wind: the day I arrived back home for the summer after my first year at Saint George's Academy and the sensation of something heavy pressing down on me, crushing me, I felt as soon as I entered the house . . . watching David and Michael arguing in the living room from a hiding place between the walls, my wrist gripped tight in Aunt Judith's hand before something alarmed her and she dragged me back below . . . Father talking, talking, endlessly talking with my grandparents about something and though they smiled at me and whispered that they loved me I knew they were leaving me with him again, that they'd never ever take me back to Patala with them. . . .

And then I was in Hell, dancing the endless dance of torment as my flesh burned in eternal agony that brought no relief, that could never bring any relief from the torment that would go on forever, world without end . . . until suddenly I awakened and I was Dara in our shared body and David's presence was a healing balm that brought my sanity rushing back, that obliterated the eternal lie and freed me again. . . .

I felt an overwhelming rush of desire for Dara. Yet as we sank down together onto the soft mossy ground, kissed and caressed each other, our clothes gone, the branching corridors leading back through my father to my ancestors took on shape around me; as I entered Dara I was also plunging down a long twisting corridor of blue-burning flame and malachite green shadows to Wallachia, where I knew myself to be Vlad Tepes. I was sitting dining alone at a table in the midst of what had recently been a battlefield, terrified servitors hovering around me. The table was laid with spotless linen and I was eating a joint of lamb with my hands from a heavy gleaming metal plate that must have been made of gold, though my Naga vision leeched all color from the scene. Around me— stretching as far as the me sitting at the table could see in every direction—the bodies of my enemies hung skewered on long stakes, and though most of them were dead a few still had the strength to moan, struggle feebly.

As Dara and I moved together in our mutual need the

scene grew ever clearer, closer, until when at last we climaxed I could smell the stench of the blood and carnage, the excrement voided from the bowels of the dying, taste the delicately spiced lamb.

And when Vlad Tepes good-naturedly threw the remains of his joint at a carrion crow that had settled on an impaled Turkish officer's head a few yards away and was picking at his eyes, I felt the motion of his arm as if it were my own. The crow let out a squawk and took flight, only to settle on the body of a Boyar a little farther away who had not displayed the proper enthusiasm in battle.

As I withdrew from Dara the scene slowly faded. Yet though it finally disappeared I knew it was still there, latent within me, waiting to be called up at any time.

"Dara—" I began, then broke off. I had no need to ask her what had happened: the knowledge was already there in my mind, available from my Naga soul as soon as I knew I wanted it. Dara and I were both Bathorys, both dhampires: where Alexandra was only tied to the events that she had experienced in the few years since her birth, our lifelines stretched back to encompass the entire history of the family we carried within us, all the undead ancestors whose stolen life force had fed our dhampire's vitality. But that knowledge branched outward, led to a fiery network of other memories, a vast unlimited sea of knowledge and experience encompassing more time and space than any human could comprehend and remain human, that stretched back beyond the beginning of the human race to the creation of the universe to the void in which the thousand-headed serpent Shesha knotted himself in and out of a darkness that was not absence but paradoxical fullness, that contained all meanings, all possibilities, even as it encompassed, was their negation—

Panicking, I pulled back, reestablished limits, refused to encompass any more before I stretched myself so thin I was lost completely, and then I was only myself again, only David Bathory, Shesha just a fading memory of something beyond all human comprehension. But I was left with the knowledge that I carried in myself all my undead ancestors: they had not only helped form me, passed on to me the energy they had stolen from the living, they were within me, inseparable from me.

By remaining in Patala, I would be granting them eternal sanctuary, life without end. I had no existence apart from them; I would never be free of them, never free of Hell and Satan's everlasting torments.

Chapter Forty

Alexandra was still sitting on the bridge, staring down into her reflection. Her clothes had changed again and she was wearing a short-skirted floral print dress that made her look not much older than Lydia. She looked up as I approached and I realized that she had changed physically as well: the Alexandra I had been married to had been three years older than me, but this Alexandra was a much younger woman, scarcely out of her teens. And she looked frightened.

"What did you see?" I asked her.

"I was back in school, at first. At a dance, with Michael." She shook her head. "I met him at a high school dance, that's how it all got started. Then I was with you, we were in Venezuela collecting coral snakes for the Seattle Zoo, and then other places. So many places I don't remember them all. But no matter where I go, what I do, I always end up dying. First the bushmaster kills me, and then Vasuki."

"What about Hell? Did you go back and see how you really spent your daytimes as a vampire?"

She didn't answer and I knew she had not, that she never would.

"Did you change anything?"

"I tried. I tried to change lots of things. At the dance with Michael, another dance, near the end, he asked me if I'd do anything he asked, no matter what, and I was about to tell him yes, but I—I thought about everything that happened to me afterward and I—the me watching—didn't want to tell him yes even though the me dancing with him did and somehow that changed things, I could feel it change things, and I said I'd think about it. Only that's what I said then too, that's the way I remember it, how I wanted to say yes but said I'd think about it instead. So it must have always been that way. . . ."

"No, it wasn't, or you wouldn't have tried to change it. Why you can't remember anything else is because you *did* change it. You made it happen that way and so that's the way it always was. You can't remember something that you kept from ever existing."

"So if I change something I can—make it so it never happened? So none of the pain ever happened?"

"I guess so."

"Ask your Naga soul. Find out for sure."

I focused on my aura, the serpents fading in and out of existence, tried to blank everything out of my mind but Alexandra's question, concentrate on it alone, but the answer was embedded in a vast fiery network of greater implications and significations that radiated throughout all time and space, that encompassed everything, and everything was part of Shesha, Shesha was the universe and all it contained.

It was as if He breathed. When He exhaled, His breath, which was no different from His self, became the universe; when He inhaled, the universe was drawn back into Him. And yet though the universe had been created and destroyed, it had always been Shesha and He had neither been created nor destroyed. . . .

It was easier to pull back this time, let everything but the answer to Alexandra's question fade from living reality back into abstract concepts.

"Well?"

"Yes. You can keep things from ever having happened. But it's not that simple. Almost everything depends on a whole lot of other things, and changing one or even two or three of them won't make enough difference. Events just are, in and of themselves, they resist change."

"You're saying I can't go back and keep things from happening?"

"No. What it is, you have to go back and find the initial causes out of which all the other causes radiate and change them, or events will just . . . sort of stretch themselves around changes and back into their original form."

"OK. Thank you, David."

"You want to continue on to that jade pavilion you wanted to see?"

"All right. In a little while." She turned away from me, dismissing me, looked back at her reflection in the water.

"I'll get Dara."

"You do that."

I saw Dara coming around the stand of trees from the field where we had made love, went to meet her.

I caught her in my arms, held her tight, kissed her, feeling that resonance between us, the way in which the boundaries separating us blurred and went down whenever we touched.

I don't know how long we held each other, gloried in each other. But when we turned back to Alexandra she was melting away, her clothes a flickering, constantly changing blur as the woman inside them grew younger, smaller. For an instant everything stabilized and a ragged little girl who couldn't have been more than six or seven years old sat frozen with her white-knuckled hands clutching the sides of the bridge, glaring with furious concentration at her image in the water, and then she was gone.

The bridge was empty and as I tried to grasp what had happened, how the bridge had come to be empty, all my memories of Alexandra suddenly swirled, overwhelmingly powerful yet drained of all color, through my mind.

Only they weren't my memories anymore, they were my Naga soul's memories. My own memories were gone, vanished to the same place where Alexandra had gone when she uncreated herself. Maybe some other Alexandra had branched off as a child to live another life, was alive as someone else I had never met somewhere, but the Alexandra I had known had nullified her life, erased her existence.

When I focused my attention back on the cavern where Dara and I still stood surrounded by the vampires trying to get past Vasuki to us, the vampire lying caught in midspasm as she died from Vasuki's venom was not Alexandra but Liz, and I remembered meeting her in a club on Ibiza nine years ago, then living with her, though we never married, until she was killed by the bushmaster while John and I were smoking psilocybin spores and swimming. And from then on everything was the same or nearly the same, my new memories meshing almost seamlessly with those my Naga soul had preserved from uncreation for me.

Yet Liz had come much closer than Alexandra to killing Dara before Vasuki had stopped her, had slashed her face and neck and chest open and so much blood had come gushing forth that I had been terrified that Dara would die before we could reach Patala. It had never occurred to me to ask Vasuki to bring Liz with us, so her lifeline ended there, dying on the cold stone floor, and by the time I saw Dara completely healed and restored in Vasuki's sheltering coils Liz had been forgotten, written off, though she had been as much of a Bathory victim as Alexandra had been.

And the Bathorys crowded around me in Stephen's torture chamber where Liz spasmed and died forgotten were as much part of me now as they had been before Liz had taken Alexandra's place.

I held Dara close, trying to think of an alternative, a way to evade the price I sensed we would have to pay for sanctuary in Patala. But there was none, and I was unsurprised when the world shifted around us and became a cave in the world-mountain's fiery heart that was at the same time a milk-white chamber in an undersea ice palace that was itself only an eddy in a boundless ocean of living blue-white fires through which winged serpent shapes of azure flame flew.

Saraparajni's palace shimmered into existence in front of us, colossal beyond all imagining, and its domes and spires and balconies were all of gems, rubies and emeralds, diamonds and topazes, amethysts and sapphires and glorious stones I had never before imagined, and some of the individual gems were hundreds of yards across. A pair of great golden doors set with purple stones carved in the likeness of dragons drew aside and we passed within, flickering through gardens and courtyards, corridors of dark wood and semiprecious stones, crystal inlays, until we found ourselves in a delicate pavilion carved of sea-green jade in a garden at the palace's heart where Saraparajni awaited us on a canopied throne fashioned from a single great ruby.

Chapter Forty-one

Saraparajni. My mother. The cobra-headed Queen, the four-armed woman I'd seen lapping Michael's congealing blood with her long black cat's tongue.

But there was nothing inhuman or frightening about her now. She was small, with eyes of liquid gold, lustrous brown skin, long dark flowing hair and a face that could almost have been Dara's but which was younger-looking and somehow more sharply defined. She wore a long, half-transparent sari-like garment of emerald-green silk sewn with myriads of tiny pearls, and there was only the depth to her eyes, a sort of infinite still resonance to her every feature to indicate she was anything more than an exquisitely beautiful girl just ripening into adolescence.

She gestured us to cushions, and her movement was like the opening of a window on memories I'd never known, understanding that no human had ever possessed.

Shesha writhed thousand-headed and alone, bleeding in and out of the void, creating and uncreating the universe, and Shesha was Patala and all within it, as He was all there ever was or ever could be.

Yet though Shesha was One, He manifested Himself as Duality, as Shesha and Devi. Where Shesha was pure, limitless, changeless consciousness, without form or qualities, Devi was that power by which Shesha veiled Himself to Himself and negated and limited Himself in order to experience Himself as form. Devi was the Veiler, the Creatrix, the Womb of all things.

Devi had created the universe from Shesha's limitless substance; Devi would destroy it. Yet it was Shesha and Shesha alone who had created and would destroy it, for Devi was none other than Shesha.

Their union in opposition was the basis of all creation: the universe was made up of paired opposites reflecting that primordial duality—male and female, life and death, good and evil. Yet these oppositions were only apparent, each polar opposite real only in relation to the other, and none had any existence beyond that granted by their union in opposition.

Man was a microcosm: Whatever existed in the universe existed in him; that which was not to be found in him was nowhere else. But where man was a microcosm, the Nagas were Devi and Devi alone. First created, the Veiler, the Demiurge, the Power by which the One hid Its identity from Itself to become the many, they would be the last to be drawn back into Shesha when the universe ended. In a sense they *were* the universe. . . .

The reality was too vast to be grasped, yet for that timeless instant I experienced it directly, without need for comprehension. But then Saraparajni gestured again, drew us back to ourselves, the transcendent reality fading into concepts the human mind could encompass until even the memory was gone, I had only the memory of having remembered, the certainty that for an instant I had *known*.

My mother, the barely adolescent girl smiling serenely at us from her canopied throne, was Devi, the Demiurge, had created the universe. Even here in Patala it was beyond anything my human self could understand. But I saw now how my father and his plans for us had gone so wrong. He'd had only himself, his life as a Bathory dhampire, with which to comprehend what Saraparajni had shown him . . . and the knowledge that was even now fading ever further and further from my comprehension and taking on the abstract factuality of something learned secondhand, like the theory of evolution or special relativity, could never have been truly understood by the person my father had been, retained its meaning in the life he had led.

I moved closer to Dara, took her hand, felt the same fading memory resonating in her.

"Have you decided what value you place on your existence here?" Saraparajni asked gently.

I remembered my father crouched over Stephen's body, Larry leaving for Provincetown with the familiar squirming through him. Remembering my father's face smeared with blood and torn flesh, I knew it for my face, the Bathory face I'd always kept carefully concealed, even from myself, behind my outer masks. It was there, too, behind Dara's face, and as we stared into each other's faces, we knew that we couldn't bear to see that face looking out at us from each other's eyes, from every mirroring surface, for all eternity.

Alexandra had been unable to face an existence in which her past would be eternally alive, eternally present. But we carried within ourselves not only our own pasts, but those of all the Bathory vampires, all the suffering they caused others, every night they spent in Hell.

We had to do what we could to keep the Bathorys from hurting and enslaving more people, from turning more innocent victims into what they themselves had become. Because we were both Bathorys, both alive only through the use we'd been able to make of our ancestors' stolen strength: the vampires we had left behind to spend their nights in insatiable hunger, their days in Hell, were not only our responsibility but ourselves.

We had to return to the world, risk not only death and forgetfulness, a new life in a new body, but an eternity of torture and degradation in Hell.

"We can't stay here," I said. "Not as what we are now."

But even as that decision took on final form within us, the Queen allowed new memories, new knowledge to surface within us. I was submerged by my past, our past, all our Bathory pasts: the unending round of days spent with Satan in Hell, merged with Him, suffering the infinite agony of His self-inflicted torments.

Was submerged by the horror, the despair of that eternally repeated realization that there was no satisfaction, no escape, no hope, that we were Satan's now and forever, that He would never let any of those whom He'd assimilated ever find an instant's peace or freedom again.

Yet Satan was a god. A totally conscious being, self-created, self-creating, capable of becoming anything His consciousness-of-self could encompass. And—gods were mortal. Totally conscious, they had only their consciousness-of-self to sustain their existence. Deprive them of that consciousness and they ceased to exist.

Satan was a god, and gods could be destroyed.

We could destroy Him.

Not for vengeance or to punish Him, but for the same reason the vampires and His other victims had to be liberated. Out of compassion for His suffering.

Because the balance of the universe had shifted. In the eons of Shesha's Exhalation the Nagas had been ruled by the joy of creation, and though they had destroyed as well as created so that the old could make way for the new, yet it had been the will of the One to become many that had filled them. But Saraparajni's marriage to my father had marked the midpoint of the cycle, and with our births Shesha's Exhalation had ended and His Inhalation had begun.

Again that transcendent knowledge faded back into factuality and I was left with the knowledge that it was for this that Saraparajni had entered the world, for this that Dara and I had been conceived: so we could attempt to destroy Satan.

Attempt to destroy Him only, because the Nagas no longer knew the outcome of the train of events they'd set into motion. They were not omniscient; they too were capable of forgetting; in pouring themselves into the universe they had taken on the limitations of created beings, so that now, at the midpoint between the cycles of creation and compassion, they had forgotten the future and knew only the role they'd chosen to play, the broad path of their destiny.

We could fail, be swallowed up and consumed by Satan as our ancestors had been, our sacrifice only the beginning of the process, serving some larger purpose the Nagas no longer remembered.

"How can we destroy Satan?" Dara asked.

Saraparajni opened us again to Satan's eternal present, in which He suffered His entire existence, His every torment, simultaneously, world without end . . . in which Aunt Judith's suicide, the agonies of those hundreds of thousands of men Vlad Tepes had had impaled, the way Michael had used me and Dara, Christ's tragic farce on the cross—the revelation granted him in the moment of his dying that he was not the Son of God but only Satan's creature, that he had bought with his sacrifice only another means of reinforcing the deception and despair of those who would come to believe in him—all this was part of the process by which Satan had wrenched Himself into existence. . . .

Satan was at the same time the product of men's fears and the self-created cause of those fears. He had been created afraid—afraid of losing His individual identity and dissolving back into Shesha's undifferentiated Self. Every god creates itself in its own image, and Satan had created Himself through pain and fear. Hell, where He was tormented, He had spun from his own substance, both His refuge and His prison.

For Satan had created Himself out of His pain. Pain is the interface of the self and the not-self; pain delineates boundaries and limitations, defining its victim to himself while providing ultimate proof of that experienced self's own separate and unique reality. Satan, who as a god had no existence independent of His consciousness-of-self, had been led by His fear of dissolution to adopt the sharpest possible definition of Himself.

The opposite of pain is joy. Joy threatens the fortress integrity of the barricaded self, breaks down the barriers separating consciousness from what it experiences: Satan dared neither feel nor share another's joy, for that shared pleasure would erase the very boundaries that determined His existence. But no entity can define itself solely through its own suffering and survive. Pain is a drawing-in, a contraction, and without expansion to balance that contraction a being will define itself smaller and smaller until it defines itself out of existence. Yet when Satan caused another pain, He imposed His proper reality upon that of His victim and thus avoided dissolution. So Satan found the pleasure necessary to His survival in inflicting pain, then merging his victims with Himself. Sharing the vampires' insatiable hunger, Alexandra's death agonies, even Uncle Peter's struggles to free himself of the werewolf he had never really been, Satan was able to preserve His existence.

But His need to make those He tortured part of Himself rendered Him vulnerable. If He could be tricked into expanding His self-boundaries to encompass a human experiencing the most intense of all possible joys, union with Shesha, then Satan, experiencing it, would be freed of His self-inflicted, self-creating torments . . . and would cease to exist.

And that was the price we would have to pay: we would have to liberate Satan from his agony and so destroy him.

"What do we have to do?" Dara asked.

Transcendent understanding exploded within us once again, faded to factuality. I saw the Ritual we would have to perform. I opened my mouth to protest, said, "No—" Fell silent again. Because I *knew* and there was no way I could deny that certainty, pretend it was other than what it was.

Dara would have to die and become a vampire; I would have to remain alive so I could reawaken her to the memory of her humanity, then bring her to share with me the ultimate ecstasy of union with Shesha. There was no way I could take her place: I was too much of a Bathory and a dhampire, too shut-off from my Naga soul to ever reawaken to my lost humanity once I became a vampire. Our roles were set, immutable, and had been ever since Saraparajni had allowed Herself to die and become a vampire so that the daughter She bore during Her five years of renewed human life would be marked by Satan for His own, destined from birth to become a vampire.

Saraparajni could never have contaminated Satan through union with Shesha and so destroyed Him Herself, because She was a Naga and the Nagas, first created, would know that ultimate union again only at the end of time, when Shesha's Inhalation was complete and the universe ended. But Dara and I were human, microcosms where the Nagas were Devi alone, and Dara had already spent a day in Hell: Satan would accept her, would consume her to bloat Himself on her agony, could be destroyed by her. . . .

If I was strong enough to reawaken her lost humanity without succumbing to her first. If I could conquer my own fears of dissolution, open us both to that ultimate union with Shesha that even the Nagas were denied.

I knew what to do, how to perform the Ritual. Not whether I could fight back the Bathory and the dhampire in me long enough to succeed in doing it.

Yet though Dara would have to die, true death was neither extinction nor loss, but only change. And even that necessity could be transcended with the aid of our Naga souls, so that we could shed our mortality like snakes shedding their worn-out skins. Our Naga souls could reanimate our bodies so that we could be reborn as ourselves, with our memories intact, wander the world for ages if we wanted before returning to Patala. As Michael could have survived the death of his body and been reborn renewed, had he not fled in horror to a new body and forgetfulness of that moment of intimacy with his Naga soul, from the knowledge of who and what he truly was.

"What happens afterward?" I asked. "If we succeed in destroying Satan?"

But that too was forgotten, lost here at the midpoint between the cycles. Perhaps Satan's destruction would release his victims to go on to new rebirths—and then Dara's Naga soul would reanimate her dead body for her, so that she would be reborn as herself. Perhaps Dara and all Satan's other victims would dissolve back with Him into Shesha's limitless formlessness, sharing His liberation and annihilation, never to return.

The task had been set for all time, but the choice was still ours. Whatever we decided, Satan would eventually be destroyed—if not now, then years or millennia or eons later—while other, equally evil gods would survive His passing and still others come into being after He was gone. There was no one to force us, no one to reproach us if we decided to remain safely sheltered in Patala until time itself came to an end, or returned to the world and let our Naga souls grant us eternal rebirth as ourselves in our own bodies.

I remembered the first time Michael had taken control of me in the forest at my father's funeral, the way he'd used me to violate Dara, had used our shared pain and degradation to provide him with the power he craved. As Satan needed not only His victims' pain, but even His own, to maintain His continued existence.

No one to force us. Only Satan's agony, our Bathory faces staring out at us through the masking flesh for all eternity.

"Send us back," Dara said.

Chapter Forty-two

Saraparajni gestured and I felt Monteleur within me again, retrieved from whatever alternate aspect of Patala he had been banished to, curled in on himself and inert like a heavy cool porcelain egg, and then a sudden emptiness within me where he had been . . . saw Dara start as the familiar passed from me to her.

Taking upon herself the death that should have been mine, that we had taken sanctuary in Patala to escape.

The space around us was filling with clotted red-black shadows, drifting darknesses. I took Dara's hand, held tight to it. Around us I could still see the jade pavilion in its gardens, the undersea ice palace and the sea of living fire, but superposed on them was Stephen's torture chamber, my father frozen motionless in the act of gulping down the last of the blood spurting from the severed jugular and carotid veins in Stephen's neck.

I took Dara in my arms, pressed her to me, held her.

At last we let go of each other, stepped forward together into shadow.

Dara screamed—and within her Monteleur too screamed, a terrifying frenzied bellowing as the familiar awakened to find itself in her alien, Naga-contaminated flesh. There was a sudden burning explosion in my belly, a horrible sickening internal slithering as my own torn and damaged tissues imploded to fill the void where Monteleur had been . . . a frenzied thrashing visible beneath the taut skin of Dara's belly as she collapsed to the floor of the torture chamber, Monteleur still bellowing within her as she arched her back in a single, final bone-breaking convulsion and died.

Monteleur was silent. Gone. Had deserted her body as soon as she was dead.

The pain from what the familiar had done to me before Vasuki paralyzed it, from the wounds that would have killed any normal human, came rushing back, but I held it off, refused it: I was the sole surviving Bathory dhampire now; all the life the vampires had stolen from those they'd killed, those they were even now feeding upon, came flooding into me, a black burning tide . . . and I drank it, used it to keep on my feet, wall off the pain, heal myself even as I held Father and all the others back—their skin dull white, smooth and dry as polished bone, all of them reeking with their victims' blood, their own rotting graveyard sweetness—used the strength I drank from them to resist the insane hunger in their eyes like dead glittering sapphires and emeralds, dilated black opals.

Dara lay dead and crumpled at my feet. Falling through the cold and the wind, the empty darkness, already beginning to forget me, forget everything but the hunger blossoming within her.

Perhaps Monteleur was there with her in the freezing void where I dared not follow, taunting and tormenting her.

Around me the cavern blazed like burning metal. Liz's daughter Lydia's ripped-open body lay discarded in a corner. The family was bloating itself on the last remaining members of Stephen's coven, his other followers. I made no attempt to stop them, contented myself with forcing the vampires outside the cavern and back in Illinois to leave their innocent victims alive and healthy enough to recover as I drained the Bathory vampires of all the life and strength they stole.

When at last I was strong enough, I carried Dara back out of the caverns to the cabin, laid her on the bed I'd once shared with Alexandra, with Liz. Dara felt light, empty, a hollow wax sculpture. I lay down beside her, climbed the shadow tides back to my father, forced from him the knowledge that had enabled him to prolong the forty days of Aunt Judith's transformation for so many years.

Stephen had a stock of everything I needed. I waited until dawn came and I could relax the hold I was keeping on Father and the others, then treated the hundred and forty-four half-transformed victims in their coffins—all those who were to have been possessed by members of the secondary covens for the Lammas Day Sabbat—with garlic and holy water, shoved thorns from the wild roses that grew in such profusion on the family estate back in Illinois in under the loose clammy skin, directly above their unbeating hearts, suspending their transformations as my father had suspended Aunt Judith's for so many years.

I was interrupted by a delivery truck full of food and drink for the Sabbat, twice more by disciples arriving early to take care of tasks Stephen had assigned them. I used my power to focus the deliveryman's attention to pass myself off as Stephen . . . used the same power to deal with all but one of the others the same way I'd dealt with the two Provincetown cops so long ago, turning them away from all possibility of disbelief when I told them the Sabbat had been rescheduled for All Hallows' Eve and that Stephen wanted them to remain in seclusion without trying to contact him or any of the other coven members until then.

The final man was the only member of Stephen's prime coven who hadn't been in the caverns when the vampires killed the others. An undertaker from Salinas. Stephen had told him to keep the locations of his parents' and grandparents' bodies secret, telling no one—not even him—where they were, but I kept the man from noticing I wasn't Stephen and that what I was telling him to do was in contradiction to Stephen's orders, sent him back to Salinas to treat the bodies he was keeping hidden in his funeral home with garlic and holy water and wild rose thorns.

There was no way to find out where all the bodies of the dead coven members' parents were hidden, no way I could control the vampires they would become on Lammas Night when they'd emerge from their coffins for the first time, to converge on the cavern, reclaim their children's bodies . . .

And kill me if they could, rip me open and drain me of all the life and force the Bathory vampires had stolen for me, the force so strong within me now that my skin blazed brighter than the caverns, the vampires, as though I had become a silver sun.

When the undertaker was gone, I dragged all the bodies to a chamber deeper in the caverns that my father's memories had told me Stephen kept as a refuge, its reinforced-steel door covered inside with rosewood veneer, its stone walls protected by spells.

I built a bier for Dara from the stacked corpses, laid her naked body out on it.

Kissed her chill lips one last time before returning to the outer caverns to clean up the remaining signs of the slaughter, make sure all the familiars Stephen had summoned for his Sabbat were secure and harmless in their pentacles.

When night came I stationed a vampire to keep watch over the familiars while I used the rest of my ancestors to search for the coven members' murdered parents. A few I found—two backpackers in a ravine behind Chews Ridge where their daughter had buried them after killing them; another man in a fresh grave in the Monterey Cemetery, just across from the college; an old couple in their family crypt in a cemetery just south of San Francisco—but the rest were too well concealed.

Would be emerging from their graves on Lammas Night.

Coming after me.

Chapter Forty-three

The undertaker returned the next morning with everything I'd ordered him to get for me: a chunk of flesh from the fresh corpse of a man who'd died a natural death, silver bowls and platters, bone china and food coloring, pastes . . . everything I'd need for the night when Dara emerged from her transformation. I put the flesh in the freezer in the cabin, veiled the undertaker's memory of ever having known Stephen or been a member of his coven, sent him away. Spent the rest of the day reinforcing the chamber in which Dara lay on her bier of unrotting corpses, beginning my preparations for the Ritual.

Peter arrived the following day, Lammas Eve, as did the Black Men from the lesser covens who were to have been fitted with familiars before the Sabbat. I turned the Black Men away from their memories of Stephen and their covens and sent them away, but it was harder to decide what to do with Uncle Peter. I finally turned him away from all his memories and fears, left him a child with only enough self-awareness to feed and clean himself. There'd be time to restore his memories if Dara and I succeeded; if we failed he'd be doomed anyway. This way he'd at least escape his fear and guilt for a while.

I had been half expecting Larry to appear. When he didn't I tried phoning him in Provincetown, only to be told his number was disconnected.

Lammas Day I dealt with the few new arrivals as I'd dealt with the others. That night I locked myself in my secure chamber, stationed my ancestors outside the door to deal with any non-Bathory vampires or other intruders who might try to force their way in.

Three vampires tried. I let them continue until I was sure that they couldn't make it past the door and protective spells, then had my ancestors capture and hold them till dawn.

I used my Naga soul's mastery of fire to burn their bodies to ash, then returned to the chamber. I spent the next thirty-eight days in the clotted shadows beside Dara's bier of stacked corpses, watching over her as I opened myself to my Naga soul, immersing myself in Devi's infinite multiplicity and creative force, leaving Dara's side only when I had to do something for Peter. Thirty-eight days watching the beauty drain from Dara's face and body only to be replaced by something else, a cold aggressive parody of the woman she'd been, an obscene exaggeration of her natural sensuality and sexuality. Watching her lengthening canine teeth push their way like slow-crawling ivory worms out from beneath her ever-redder lips.

Every night I stationed Bathory vampires outside the door, kept the other Bathorys from doing their victims any lasting harm. I caught two more non-Bathory vampires trying to force their way in to me; a third escaped.

One of the vampires we caught was Larry. There was no way to save him, return him to what he had been, and I burned his body with the others. That night Mihnea surprised a female vampire killing a teenage boy just off my property, and I burned her too.

But though I could force the Bathorys to leave their victims alive, I had no control over the new vampires, and every night brought a dozen or more killings in Monterey, Carmel, or Seaside.

It was almost impossible to keep myself from climbing the shadow tides to Dara, prevent myself from using them to enter her consciousness as once we'd entered Father's together, but she was of the same generation as I was: had I joined her, I would have been lost, swallowed up in her transformation. Yet though I dared not open myself to her, I could still feel her transformation reflected in the vampires I ruled, sense their growing elation as the moment approached when her transformation would be complete and they would be free of all dominion.

Even barricaded from her as I was, I felt the change when her transformation reached its end and Satan took her from her body for her first day of torment in Hell. On that last day of my dominion I sealed all the other Bathory vampires in their coffins while they slept to keep them from taking any physical part in what happened between us.

Then I knelt naked beside her bier and concentrated until I could see Saraparajni in Dara, see the All-Mother, the Creatrix, simultaneously mother, mate and daughter to all created beings. She held the body of an infant to her mouth with one hand, lapping its blood with her thick black cat's tongue, while with the other she held a second infant to her breast, suckling it. Her hair and skin were glossy black and around her waist she wore a skirt of dangling hands, boneless forearms, while cobras coiled and twined around her neck and shoulders.

She was utterly horrible, utterly beautiful. Kneeling there beside her, I worshipped her until at last she shuddered on her bier of waxy corpses, a convulsive trembling that twisted and contorted her body and face without touching the dead stillness within.

Her face was a mask of rage and pain and hatred, the Bathory face that lay hidden as well beneath my own features, yet it was still only a mask and beneath it I could sense the hungering emptiness, the need to gouge me hollow, empty and consume me and make of me only another vessel for the hunger that had already eaten her.

She opened her eyes and stared at me, making a low inhuman glottal sound deep in her throat. Conflicting emotions, none of them truly hers, chased themselves across the smooth perfection of her face, never touching the hungry deadness beneath, and then she smiled.

Her teeth were shiny white behind too-red lips, her breath was foul, and yet the very foulness, the deadness of her drew me, awakened all my need for her. I let her draw me down beside her on the bier, lay trembling with pleasure as she trapped me in the shimmering depths of her golden eyes, while she ripped open my throat and warmed herself with my living blood.

Through the door I heard muffled screams from Uncle Peter. They went on and on while she drank from me, suddenly stopped.

When she'd drunk enough to warm herself, feel my life flowing in her veins, I wrenched myself free of her eyes, used the strength I'd taken from my ancestors against this day to hold her will and my need away from me just long enough to open myself once more to that total memory I'd learned to summon, just long enough to use the last of my stolen strength to send that memory flooding into her on the dark tide of life she was draining from me, shock her into awareness, into readiness to receive her own lost memories, there where they awaited her in the keeping of her Naga soul.

She remembered Hell.

She choked, tried to scream. Her hands fell away from me and her eyes lost their fascination, grew dull and confused as she fought her body and its hungers, her vampire's inability to believe the truth her Naga soul was showing her. She began to shake, suddenly vomited up all the precious blood she'd drunk.

The blood that would lend her the life she'd need for the Ritual.

"David, I'm—I'm not strong enough." Her voice was ragged with need, and yet still a cold, angry monotone. Dead. "I'm afraid and I . . . need more blood, I have to have it to go on but please, David, don't let me take too much—"

I helped her sit up, held her steady as she drank from my torn throat until I was too weak to let her continue, then pushed her gently away from me, over to the far side of the chamber where I'd set up everything we'd need for the Ritual, all the objects and symbols that would reinforce and imprint the meaning of what we were doing on our consciousness.

"David, *hurry*, they've got Peter, he's letting them out—"

We cleansed ourselves, rubbed each other with the scented oils and pastes for the first part of the Ritual, dressed each other with clumsy haste in robes of coarse red silk. The air around us was heady with flower smells, fragrant oils and spices, the green richness of tree saps and grasses, everything that was freshness and life.

We faced each other across a low silver table set with platters of human and animal flesh, fish and dry hard bread, goblets of bittersweet nectars. Trays held the objects to be contemplated during the Ritual feast: heaped wildflowers and blades of freshly cut green grass, the skull of a weasel, grains of rice, water containers of different sizes and shapes, a lump of kneaded clay with five aromatic eucalyptus leaves across its top, a chunk of yellow sulfur.

The moment of total memory I'd summoned was beginning to fade back into empty factuality; I could see Dara trembling with her need, feel my own need to sacrifice myself to her hunger twisting inside me.

Through the steel door I could hear a confused din: Peter and my ancestors beginning to try to force their way in.

I thrust the Bathorys from consciousness, dipped the fingers of my left hand into the shallow silver bowl of vermilion paste in front of me, drew an equilateral triangle on the silver surface between us, its apex pointing to Dara, then touched my paste-covered index finger to Dara's forehead, just above the space between her eyes. As I washed the paste from my hand in a second bowl, Dara dipped her right hand in a different bowl and drew a second triangle over mine, but with its apex pointing to me, so that the two superposed triangles formed a six-pointed star. Then she touched my forehead as I had touched hers.

It was as though an eye opened, but not an eye in my forehead where she'd touched me, not an eye that was in me or any part of me at all. But it opened and I saw:

In the center of the six-pointed star Saraparajni sat on a throne of burning diamonds, and everything about Her was golden. She had rich lustrous golden-brown skin, long flowing tawny hair, golden eyes, the slim graceful body of a girl just barely adolescent, yet from the waist down She was serpent and She rested on Her golden coils.

Her coils that were Shesha's coils as She was Shesha, thousand-headed, bleeding in and out of the void, in and out of existence; and on Shesha's coils stood the four grass-green elephants that supported the weight of the mountain that was the universe on their backs. And within that mountain, in the caverns beneath its roots, She was a winged serpent whose feathers and plumes were bright-burning blue flame, a winged serpent burning Her way up and out of the ocean of white fire, up through the rocky core of the world-mountain to emerge as a flowering tree, the Tree of All Life that was the serpent twined around the tree and around the Cretan priestess who took the serpent and held it to her bared breast, fed it with her own milk and then let it slip from her into the pool where the sacrifices' bodies were thrown, which led to the golden ocean in which Dara and I drifted and swam, indolent and purple-scaled, our garlands of pearls streaming as we made our way up and out of the ocean into the waiting channels of our spines, began to ascend—

We sat facing each other across the six-pointed star of drying vermilion paste. Dara raised her left hand, moved her hands in a remembered gesture, awakening my response. I bent myself to the appropriate position, made the corresponding gesture with my right hand, feeling the eons come alive in me as I began following the fiery red solar breath in through my right nostril, throughout my body, my many bodies bleeding in and out of the golden ocean in which we swam, followed the breath out through the same nostril . . .

The Ritual had begun.

But the description of the contemplations and visualizations and symbolic gestures, the taste of human meat or the feel of Dara's chill flaccid flesh against and around me when at last I entered her, the ways in which we bent and moved our bodies as we made love . . . none of this would tell you anything. There is no way to describe what happened except to say that for a time we were allowed to pass from the imprisoning darkness of our limited selves through the infinite multiplicity of Devi's creation and beyond, to the unbounded radiance of Shesha's infinite Self, from the joy of our lovemaking to the infinitely greater bliss of which it was a reflection.

There are no words. I will not even try.

And yet what memory of that Oneness I still retain calms me as I sit here in the cabin watching over Dara's vacant body there on the bed where I put her when the stench of the decomposing bodies on which we lay drove me from the caverns.

I know that we succeeded, that Satan has been liberated and destroyed, because when I returned to consciousness of my limited self and surroundings I saw that Dara's teeth were human again and that the parody of life with which Satan had animated her had departed.

As I staggered with her body out of the caverns, blind in the darkness beyond the lamp-lit chamber in which we'd lain, now that I no longer had my dhampire's powersight to show me the way, I stumbled over stiffening corpses, dry brittle bones already crumbling to dust, slipped in stinking pools of putrescent corruption: all that remained of my ancestors and their victims now that the normal processes of dissolution had resumed their course.

Just inside the entrance to the cavern I found Uncle Peter's twisted body, as though he'd been trying to crawl out of the inner darknesses back to the sky when he'd died.

The Bathorys are silent within me, drawn back with Satan into Shesha or freed to be reborn in new bodies, take on new identities, perhaps even fall victim to the new evil gods that will rise to take Satan's place or to the others that have survived His destruction. Yet the dark tide no longer links me to them; both their strength and their hunger are gone.

She is so still. I press my hand to her chill breast, touch her neck, but I can feel no heartbeat, no pulse. Dead. Yet I know that life will soon be returning to this, her body, that even if in liberating Satan and His victims she has been drawn with Him back into Shesha, uncreated, never to be reborn, the Naga soul with which she shared her mortal body will reanimate it for a time.

Liberation.

Annihilation.

There is a faint hiss of indrawing breath and her chest begins to rise and fall in a ragged rhythm that gradually becomes smoother. Once again I press my hand to her breast. Her flesh is warm now, heated by returning life—and I feel the gentle flutter of her beating heart.

Who is she?

"Dara," I say, but she does not respond. Perhaps she doesn't hear me, perhaps she is not yet strong enough to reply.

Perhaps she is gone, never to return for so long as the universe endures.

Her eyes are shut but I think I can see her eyelids beginning to quiver. When she opens her eyes I will know who she is.

When she opens her eyes.